by Mary Lee Settle

CELEBRATION

BLOOD TIE

THE LOVE EATERS

THE KISS OF KIN

The Beulah Quintet

I. PRISONS

II. O BEULAH LAND

III. KNOW NOTHING

IV. THE SCAPEGOAT

V. THE KILLING GROUND

Non-fiction

ALL THE BRAVE PROMISES

THE SCOPES TRIAL

WATER WORLD

CELEBRATION

Mary Lee Settle

CELEBRATION

Farrar, Straus & Giroux

NEW YORK

Copyright © 1986 by Mary Lee Settle
ALL RIGHTS RESERVED
Printed in the United States of America
Published simultaneously in Canada by Collins Publishers, Toronto
Designed by Tere LoPrete

Library of Congress Cataloging-in-Publication Data
Settle, Mary Lee.
Celebration.
I. Title.
PS3569.E84C45   1986   813'.54   86-12100

A signed first edition of this book has
been privately printed by The Franklin Library

CONTENTS

The real knowledge of death is sudden and certain. It takes different people different ways. After that crossing to the less naïve side of the river Styx, stripped of the useless armor of blindness, nothing is taken for granted. Objects are more defined. Colors are brighter. People know this who have been in wars.

I

KURDISTAN

On April Fools' Day, 1969, a
woman woke at daybreak from a pitch of familiar dreams
released by her first night without pain or drugs. She stumbled,
yawning, into one of those kitchen mornings when the sun was
just touching a supermarket tomato that she had put on the
windowsill to be warmed into some taste. A cucumber and an
eggplant lay beside it. On the butcher-block table, the apples
in the ceramic bowl from Malakastan were still dim in dawn
shadow.

She kissed the place on the tomato where the sun touched
it. But it didn't smell like a tomato. It didn't smell like anything.
There was only the scent in the kitchen of Lemon Fresh Joy
and, when she started it, Mr. Coffee.

Beyond the bars of her windows the snow still lay in patches.
The crocuses and the early daffodils glittered in the dew. At the
end of her garden she could see in the distance the fragment of
the river that she had been told enhanced the value of her
mortgaged property. The sky was pale blue, celebrating the end

of March, gone out like a lamb. When she opened the door, wind from the water lifted the nearest curtain and her hair and the pink frill of the peignoir her mother had sent by air from Paris. She had waked up to a burst of joy and anger that was still shaking her heart, her weak invaded body, and the ruffles she clutched in her fist to keep the peignoir closed against the cold she had let in.

Her name was Teresa Cerrutti. She breathed the cold air slowly, then closed the door and poured coffee, conscious of ritual. It made her smile. She sat down at the table, huddled in the froth of nylon, and warmed her hands around the mug. She stared at the bowl that she had nursed all the way from Malakastan, nearly nine thousand miles. Her tears had fallen on it, then dried, then fallen again in her flight.

The black stick figures processed around it, streaked with age and tears. Their formal procession had something to do with the night. She tried to capture it. The dream had not left her mind; it had only receded so that it was hard to see and hear again. As dreams do, it flirted with her in glimpses. She knew she had been debating or arguing or something like that, and it was, as always, with the black monk. He seemed to be the center of the joy and the anger. She caught at a shard of recall. He wouldn't turn around so she could see his face and she remembered being grateful for that.

She had had the same, not dream, but landscape of the dream so many times that it was almost a place she lived in at night, sometimes remembering, sometimes only knowing she had been there when she waked; there were the people, always Michael, and her black monk, and the Derebey, and the Sheika, and the dancers.

At first she had had it often. Part of her still lived there in the months after she "lost her husband," as people said. The phrase made her grin. It sounded like losing money, or something rolled down a drain, not her dear old Michael. Everyone said what a shame it was when she was so young, and she had wondered, So young for what? She had been twenty-six, and now was thirty, and none of that seemed to matter, not in the bright new morning.

With some shame she remembered that when she had left Michael in the high valley she had let herself drift into doing what she was told. She had thrown herself, and even that was someone else's way of saying it, into her doctoral dissertation on Malakastan, and, of course, in the United States and at that time in the century, she had submitted to three obligatory years of therapy on the advice of everyone who hadn't grieved. They were like bachelors advising on marriage, meaning well. There was no way to tell Dr. Dangle, her therapist, that he mustn't worry especially about the black monk; he had tried to get rid of him, and had almost succeeded.

He said that the black monk was her animus, made up of all the people she had loved and trusted, as if that were what love was—ingredients, like making a cake. But she didn't want to be too hard on Dr. Dangle. He specialized in grief. She had felt guilty at letting him down from time to time. Sometimes she had wanted to yell, For Christ sake, let me cry, but she didn't. She felt that tears were none of anyone's business, and she could see all her tears lined up one by one across a table to be filed and understood. He said that grief lasted three years, and hers had only lasted two, so she had thought, Well, at least I can analyze the black monk for him if it will make him feel better. He had such sad eyes.

So she had constructed an intellectual carapace for her dear black monk, who'd been with her ever since she was a child, although Dr. Dangle doubted that. He said time changes were a protection.

She had put on file cards, eight by six, the Praetorian Guard who walked backwards in front of the Emperor of Rome and whispered, Remember you are mortal (blue card, ancient), and the black monk who did the same thing in the *processio solemnis* of the Popes, see "Blackfriars" (yellow card, medieval to mod).

On the pink card, mod, she had put the dominie from the Church of Scotland, who had given the Queen of England the Good Book at her coronation.

When Dr. Dangle saw "Black Monk, the"—"Chekhov, Anton," on lavender for literary, he was very disturbed. He called it displacement and said she must have read it and forgotten about it. He almost begged her to admit it, but she couldn't. It wasn't true. Yes, she was a deep disappointment to Dr. Dangle.

She was a little ashamed that her black monk wasn't evanescent and poetic and fearsome like Chekhov's, flying through the sky. But he just wasn't. He was just a plain old black monk, but her own at least. It was like those conversations about archetypal dreams with the mother goddess and all that, when she told him about her dream of forgetting to buy milk at the supermarket.

"Ah, milk!" Dr. Dangle said, pleased for once.

Now, after the night, she knew, surprised after all that money, and relieved after all that trying, that none of it had worked. There he was again at the edge of her waking in the bright morning, a glimpse, a shadow, winging it at her eye's corner if she didn't turn and try to see him. He was jigging a little to the music and watching the lines of men and women, not the black stick figures on the bowl, but alive and real in their *shalvar* and sashes and vests of shot silk, red and yellow but never blue, that was taboo, an insult to Lucifer, the Melek Taus.

The silver necklaces and the coins sewn on their caps shimmered as they danced the *debka* across the sun-soaked dancing ground. They trampled the poppies and the anemones with their bare feet while the fife wailed and the *zebek* twanged and the drums beat; the colors could have been painted by Courbet. She stood again beside her black monk and watched Michael dancing with the men in a kind of solemn joy. He was so awkward that she felt a wave of tenderness go toward him as he tried to follow the intricate pattern of the dance, intent on his feet. He glanced at her forever with smile so tender, in a moment of childlike trust, that reseeing it made her eyes swim, and she had one of those flashes of love that can't come very often. She couldn't have lived that way every minute.

Sometimes her black monk was as small as the Derebey; sometimes he was tall and gangly, like Michael. Always, though, he had the voice of Noel, her first childhood friend, a lovely lilting English voice, even though he instructed sometimes in the Derebey's formal funny words, and sometimes in her father's elegant unreachable wise words high in the frosty air. But she had never seen his face, dear to her as he was. She knew, in the logic of the dream, that if he looked at her she would die.

Now, for the first time, she was determined to conjure him when she was awake. The thought crossed her mind that she ought to report such a desire to Dr. Dangle, and then she thought, No way, it was none of his business. She was conscious of trying too hard at first, so she let herself fall into the half sleep where she had glimpsed him last, her head down beside the coffee mug.

The movement made her belly muscles hurt, and forced her to think of being cut open and sewn up again when she didn't want to. She had more important things to do than remember her brave and boring self, all alone and so damned Anglo-Saxon and silently suffering, lying politely about why she was going to the hospital. She saw herself sliding along the river road, not even able to downshift fast on the curves, just slithering around and wondering if she would wreck and thinking it didn't really matter, not anymore. The snow was banked on both sides of the road, reflecting the early streetlights in the gray afternoon twilight of the last of February. She was facing the whole thing, she told herself, with icy practicality. She had refused all thoughts of mortality and loss, as she thought a soldier might reject the prospect of dying when he has made up his mind to go into battle.

She would have preferred speed and Keats on death but she

couldn't think of anything. Instead, she got slipping and sliding and Dr. Johnson: "Depend upon it, sir, when a man knows he is to be hanged in a fortnight, it concentrates his mind wonderfully." She resented the intrusion. She didn't like Dr. Johnson much. Looking back, she knew that both the ice and the irony were nothing but substitutes for fear.

There had been no use bothering her parents. They were still in Paris. Besides, her father was retiring at the end of April and she would not have dreamed of interfering with any crisis of her own in her mother's meticulously planned panic. She never had.

So she had waked in the pale green hospital room with no one there, feeling like she had been kicked in the stomach by a mule. Somebody had sent flowers. She wondered who it was and went to sleep again. But later, in a far corner of the night, she thought or dreamed or said, "Shit, I'm going to die. Me. Now I know it, not with my brains, we all know that, but with my whole sore self. That's going to be the difference between me and most people, except maybe those who have been to war. They know." She remembered vaguely that her doctor had come in in the afternoon and told her she was completely cured.

He had pulled up a chair beside the bed. He looked relieved. She remembered that, and a phrase, in something, in sutu? situ? suttee, like an Indian woman? He was trying to tell her something important and she wished she hadn't had drugs. She wanted to remember, something about, oh, for a long time you will be aware of every cough; every bellyache is the cancer again. "Don't put yourself through that any more than you must." She could hear his voice: "I'll tell you something, though"; oh, that was important, his voice again in the night. "You will never be afraid again of the word the way people are who have never been to the well. We'll say it together, one, two, three." Could he have said that? "Cancer."

In the night she found herself giggling, whispering, Shit, fuck, cunt, prick, money, Nixon, cancer, malignancy, carcinoma—a night game, all alone. One of those was a devil's word, another like an Italian opera, and the third the goddamn President of the United States.

Gutless, that's what she had been. She thought of how she had pondered long and seriously, Christ, seriously, about whether she should wear toilet paper around the sleeve of her academic gown at the convocation to show she was against the Vietnam War, and was back with her head on the morning table, hot with a flash of shame, and told her new self, "Oh, you were a one," Noel's favorite phrase from so long ago. "With infinite courage and much thought, discussion and deep commitment, you wrapped a piece of toilet paper around your arm and thought you were staunching the blood of the world."

The wind had grown stronger and the sun cast shadows of bars across the table, bars she had put there to keep her safe from rape, seduction, robbery, and life, liberty, and the pursuit of happiness. She laughed aloud at the self who had opted for such mean safety and such small gestures that had been quietly killing her, politeness and grief and obedience and bars and toilet paper. The sound drifted into the bright morning.

There she was in the same old place, trapped behind shadows of sun bars in the ruffledom menopausal pink peignoir, a cancerous color that fell in alcoholic folds. She took it off, rummaged for the kitchen scissors, and cut it into small pieces. She piled the pieces on the table, found a plastic garbage bag, and put the whole pink pile into the trash, not knowing or questioning why, for once in her life. She thought, That gesture would keep Dr. Dangle happy for weeks.

She stood there naked, thirty years old, with an angry red line from her navel to where her pubic hair had been. "You must face bravely the physical loss of your sex; but remember, there are compensations for not having children," Dr. Dangle had said, the bastard, and she answered aloud, naked in the morning, "You're goddamn right there are, mister."

He had confused the organs with the chords, seeing God

through a gland, love through a hole. Now, divested of all that, including her clothes, she was ready to get on with whatever it was. She took her old gardening shirt from the hook behind the back door and put it on, poured out the nearly cold coffee, got more, sat down again to decide what to do. All she knew was that she had better act at once before she lost her newfound nerve. It was time, now that things had changed, to be newly vested, but she had no idea what the vestments were to be. She only knew they wouldn't be pink peignoirs or academic gowns, or all those trappings of intellectual and emotional orthodoxies, or all that caring about things she was supposed to care about and didn't. She stretched out a leg and watched the fine hair on it, gold in a sun shaft, and decided that, for a start, her legs were assets. They were long and elegant, and the fact of that had been neglected for far too long.

She wanted to forgive herself for all her wise decisions. She wanted back her sense of the uncanny, which she had nearly analyzed away, the sense that conjured gods and men out of the raw substance of shadows and memory; she wanted again to listen to the wind whispering words and music. She remembered that once she had been able to hear the shape and color of things. It was as if she had let a room in her brain fill with dust and darkness from lack of use, and now that it was too late—it could be too late for another thirty years, too late for the rest of her life—she wanted it all back. The loss brought heavier tears to her eyes than the loss of some organs and the scar on her stomach.

"You haven't lost anything, darling. You've just misplaced it somewhere in your past. It's all there. Pick it up wherever you dropped it. There's nothing like a spot of cancer to throw things into perspective, is there, now?" There, at last, some honest tears had brought the black monk with Noel's voice out of the night into the cold light of day.

She said she knew that, and he said, "Then why are you sniveling, you look awful." Then, carefully, she told the air or the black monk or Noel, "I am not. I am just not going to miss anything ever again because there is no time to lose, or throw away, no drift, no blank, no dead-leaf time."

"There never has been, you silly woman," he said with that old arrogance.

She was suddenly blushing hot with fury at him and at herself. She had turned her back for all the four years since Michael's death on hints of joy and sorrow, and had accepted instead an existence without mistakes or tears.

"Oh, come on, dearie, stop feeling sorry for yourself and start planning how to get us out of here. I know you. NOW. You have to do it now. How much money have we saved?" She could see beyond the voice her beautiful Noel, lolling on a bed, and herself at fourteen in the robes of a queen. "You mustn't droop, darling, you must stand as if you had those robes on all the time," he was saying, her first friend, her first love. She could see him, in her mind's eye, touch his lank aristocratic hair. "After all, darling," he was saying then or now, it didn't matter, "it's all so awful. One might as well."

She stood up and stretched her arms high, wanting the pull of slight pain. Then she called out to the mortgaged glimpse of the river, "Ten thousand four hundred and seventy-three dollars my grandmother left me. I was saving it for a rainy day."

And the joy and the anger flowed full of light through her empty body, a real taste of the time when high summer was a sparkle through her skin, and she felt translucent and could see the edges of things. It was completely familiar, like going home when she was already there.

"It has to be or I wouldn't recognize it," she told the black monk and the tomato and the cucumber and the eggplant, the red and green and royal purple now all glowing in the sunlight, brighter than she had ever seen them. It was an oil, a scent, a nonsense, a sweetness, that was part of it, and litheness. She had known such moments walking down a street with Michael; they both felt it then, turning a corner and walking into joy and out again as if it were a place. She had known it when she first walked into the Derebey's courtyard, and once just sitting on a 74 bus in London with her hands folded in her lap, touched by joy like the flick of an angel wing. She thought, I've crossed the river Styx, and on the other side, not death, but maybe only London.

She looked at the sky through the trees as if it were the first time she had seen it and was, for a second, Madame Du Barry, looking at the sky from the scaffold and saying politely, having been trained to please a king, "*Un autre moment, s'il vous plaît.*"

She was being granted *un autre moment.* No matter how long it lasted, months or years, it was to be a respite, and the respite was a landscape of the past and the present that she would wander in without having to try anymore. A bird sang high in one of the trees, fussed a little, stopped, leaving stillness in the air.

She felt the wind or the black monk fingering her hair and could hear Noel, "You don't want to miss anything, even the essence of things that have already happened. God knows you've done that. Now sit down. I want to talk to you." She went back to the table and sat in what her grandmother called her shimmy shirt. "First, your dissertation. The whole thing was a statistical lie. All those impersonal statistics, all that language! So solemn. So American. So academic *faux distingué!*"

"Well, you're dropping French."

A hurt voice above her head. "I have the right. I'm bilingual."

She didn't dare look up.

"Darling Teresa, you told all the facts about Malakastan and left everything out. Where was the water and the green and the blood? After all, it was there you knew more joy and more sorrow than anyplace else in your life."

"There is all that to do over again, isn't there? All those wasted words and all that wasted time." She was aware of her black monk standing across the table between her and the sun-light, leaning over it to toss her hair, her pretty hair. She had forgotten that, too, for so long. "Now, isn't that a shame," she said, about her hair and not the waste of time.

"Look up, darling. Why not? After all, you've seen me before, and as Mr. Blake answered when he was asked where he really saw the angels, In my mind's eye, you fool."

She let herself turn him around, or let him turn. Noel's voice said, "April fool, darling!" But he had the face she had seen of St. Francis at Assisi, and for the first time in weeks or maybe months or years, she laughed so that she heard the birds fly out of the trees. She was nine and looking at him, not the un-earthly nobleman in the Giotto murals, but the man that Cimabue knew. He had strayed into a corner of a painting of the Virgin and angels, as if he had blundered into the wrong house. He was just standing around in the painting; she never had seen anyone standing around in a painting before. She looked at him for a long time, while way up over her head, her father instructed her. That's how she knew it was Cimabue. In the vast church she and the small man with the big ears and the weepy eyes looked at each other and they both understood that they were in a place that was much too grand for them. There he was, poor little fool of God, kicked upstairs into sainthood. But even that, in the kitchen, in the morning, was only a glimpse, and when she tried to hold him, she could see only the sun and the garden, the bars and the back door.

"You see," she heard Noel say in his what-am-I-to-do-with-you voice. "At least now that you've done that, we can get on with it." She heard him sit down opposite her, the black monk, or the chair creaking, or the kitchen door in the wind.

"Close your eyes. What do you see?"

"I see blackness and the afterimage of the kitchen door."

"Try again. What do you see?"

"Words. I see words. I see 'brachycephalic' and 'marriage customs' . . ."

"For God's sake, try, darling. Do you want to sit here for the rest of your dull life, a beaten body in a safe kitchen and you not touched fondly for too long? Need I remind you that the life you've been leading has nearly killed you? You've let your soul get dusty. I like that word 'fond.' It means foolish. Now what do you see? Remember, you can't fool a fool."

"Wow! Pictures."

The chair creaked. "What?"

"Dr. Grod. Dear Dr. Grod. Poor man, he was our advisor. He hadn't been on a field trip in years. His face is lined with tenure and a sickly wife and two children in college. There is a slide, the first picture I have ever seen of the Derebey. He looks very dignified, and his clothes are threadbare. Dr. Grod is explaining that he is a Yezidi 'lord of the valley,' very poor, very hospitable. The Yezidi are considered to be devil worshippers by their enemies."

"Now you are there, darling, make me see. That's what you have to do that you didn't do before."

"Well, there we sat across from him, Michael and I. It was early December, but there was already snow, a dusting of it on the ground. Dr. Grod called me by name, a little impatiently, I remember. I must have been staring at the snow. He said there was strong evidence for me as a historical anthropologist to trace the contemporary female mourning ceremonies for Ali, and for Hussein, all the way back to the mourning for Tammuz. He said he had proof that the rites reliving the death of gods or their fall spread down from the mountains, not up the rivers from the coast. He told us to look for sacred fire, water, trees, and sun worship. He had only seen the valley of Malakastan for one night and morning, but he told Michael that he was certain that the foundations of the sacred tomb were pre-Hittite. Their deity, the Melek Taus, the peacock angel, could be a shortening of the word Tammuz, but there again, *tavuz* does mean peacock in Turkish. Adonis, Adonai, was connected with them through the taboo against eating lettuce. It was sacred to him because Aphrodite was supposed to have made love to him on a bed of lettuce. The Melek Taus is also supposed to represent Lucifer, Son of the Morning."

"All very interesting, dearie," the black monk told her with a rude sigh, "but you are slipping into the safety of words again. Go back to seeing."

She giggled. "Oh, this is lovely. Michael and I are in bed and we have made love, and we're all warm and totally happy, lying there trashing Lévi-Strauss and Mellaart and Mallowan. We have our research grants, we've pooled our savings, gotten married, and applied for our passports, and we are in New York both working in the Frederick Lewis Allen room on background."

"Now at last, thank God, a story, a true story. You've fooled everybody else but you can't fool your April fool."

She laughed. She had forgotten so much and there it all was again, glowing with unimportance, and she was going to see it right there and right then in her old shimmy shirt, as new and as alone as Adam, but she had to tell the black monk, "Of course, Adam didn't have a black monk like you. At least you listen. He only had that anthropomorphic vision he named God who did all the talking and wouldn't let Adam get a word in edgeways."

It was Dr. Grod who said we should take the foam-rubber mattresses and the kerosene stove. He hadn't been to Kurdistan since 1952, but he said he would never forget the cold nights. I longed for an L. L. Bean sleeping bag, he said; he sounded like he was confessing a weakness. He told us to be sure not to forget pitons and a rope ladder, because the mountains were riddled with caves and every town had a well.

Michael prepared so carefully. He always did. He was the kind of man who prepared the bathroom when he was going to shave and shower, everything in place ahead of time. He said it was more efficient. It took him hours. Dr. Dangle had expected me to face the loss of Michael's body, the sexual loss, and the intelligence he said we had in common; he said that was the reason for the abyss of loneliness.

But what I remember and long for most are things like how long he took in the bathroom, his heavy feet on the stairs, his constant child's wonder, the way his voice tilted on the telephone, the way he would touch me as if he wanted to convince himself I was there. God, I even miss the terrible arguments we had because he actually admired the cruel, cold-blooded arrogance of my Anglo-Saxon family, which I hated so much. He said it was cool, and I would yell, It's not cool, it's dead, and all the time all I wanted was his noisy volatile Italian Catholic family he was so embarrassed about. We never could see eye to eye about all that, not until we left it behind.

I remember how we made lists that winter and changed them and made more, a game of lists. I insisted on a garlic press, an iron skillet, a salad bowl, and a copy of Elizabeth David's Mediterranean cookbook. He fastened on the garlic press for serious argument. How do you know there is garlic in Kurdistan, let alone one small valley in it? I can hear him now. There's always garlic, I told him. Most primitive people use it to cure madness and avert the evil eye. He couldn't argue with that. I was, after all, the historical anthropologist.

Dr. Grod showed us more slides, life-size women on the academic wall, beating clothes and rugs on the rocks in the river, caught in mid-gesture, their arms thrust into the water with its film-frozen veils of white foam. Behind them in the distance we could see the glittering white cone like a witch's hat, and the gold dome of the sacred tomb, half hidden in Kodachrome-green trees. Rags of bright cloth, caught fluttering, smudged their branches, so that even the morning wind was frozen by the camera. I remember that morning, and I remember coincidences, or what we took to be little bits of good luck that seemed to bless us.

Michael found a Turk. He was a resident at New York Hospital, where we went to get our shots. Kemal was the first Turkish person to welcome us into his life as he would have into his house had he been at his family door instead of sitting in a bar on Seventy-third Street, one lonely Turk with two near-strangers. I think that bar was where the physical journey to Malakastan really began.

We stayed there half the night, while somebody played "Sea Cruise" over and over on the jukebox. We tried out the Turkish we had been studying on Kemal. Kemal said that silences and gestures were more important in Turkey than they were in America. He taught us carefully to pass our fingers over our fists and then slap our wrists, and when we had finally got it right he said, "Never never do that to a Turk. He will kill you. It means not only fuck your mother but also your sister, your donkey, and a chicken, which is the worst insult of all." We laughed a lot that night, and slapped our wrists with our fingers.

Kemal was from Izmir, and he advised us to start from there, since we had to go by sea anyway. He ignored the map of Turkey that Michael spread out over the table. He set his drink down somewhere around Gaziantep, and leaned his elbow on Lake Van. We were sitting on the Black Sea side of the table.

"I have not been to eastern Turkey," he told us, and then he said the magic words. "I will send you to the friend of my father who is Fazih Bey. Fazih Malacoglu. He is in Izmir in the spring. He is from Malakastan. His name means Eloquence. The first part of his last name is the name of his father. Malak. It means buffalo calf. The last syllable shows that Fazih Bey is the son of his father."

So it was because of the friend of the father of Kemal in a bar in New York on a raw February night that we landed at the round harbor of Izmir in mid-May in 1965, when the rains were newly over and all the hills around the city were covered with wildflowers.

It was the two rubber mattresses and the Aladdin stove that seemed to defy the customs man. He stood in the customs shed and stared at them for a long time. "*Allah din?*" He examined the stove. "*Nichin?*" I knew that meant why. Then he clicked his tongue, tossed his head back, and said "*Yok.*" It was our first experience of the full gesture, click, and word that make up the Turkish "no." It is the most final no in any language.

We finally called Kemal's father in the early evening, having waited at the customs shed nearly all day. I had taken the Berlitz course, so I was supposed to deal with things like immigration and customs and manners. Michael had gone deeply into Turkish and knew twenty-six Turkish tenses, including the rumor tense, but couldn't yet speak three words, so I had to try to use the telephone.

But night was coming on and my Turkish was getting fainter and fainter. All I could do was stare at the closet wall of our room at the Büyük Efez Hotel. It was covered with a huge black-and-white grainy blow-up of an eighteenth-century etching of a Turkish harem scene, as if the hotel was committed to giving the tourists at least a glimpse of what they expected before they went out onto the street and faced facts.

When I heard, "*Effendim?*" I was struck dumb. "*Allo,*" the man's voice said in French, and then in English, "Hello. Are you there?"

I was finally able to tell him who I was, but he already knew. "Kemal told us which boat you were taking. We have been waiting for you. We want to hear all about Kemal. Do not eat. You must take a taxi at once. He will know our house. Now where are you?"

I told him we were at the Büyük Efez.

"But you must stay with us. You are Kemal's friends." I looked at the life-size etched sultan on the closet door.

"Here is the address. You will write it down?" I thought he laughed. "Tell the man at the front desk where you are going."

We had learned the words for friend, the layers of subtlety.

Arkadash means comrade, has whiffs of influence. *Dost* is more intimate—pal, even lover. Going down in the elevator we decided to use the word *arkadash*. Michael pointed to the address in his hand and said, "*Arkadash*," his first word of the language spoken on Turkish soil.

The desk clerk answered in English, "Timur Bey. Your friend," and then the universal, "No problem." We didn't even have to pay for the room.

The taxi climbed up and up through narrow winding lanes of rough cobbled stones. It stopped in what seemed to be a dark tunnel between stone walls so close that it was hard for us to open the taxi door. The silence was total.

It was so dark that we could look up and see the stars. A square door opened and light spilled out of it on us and the car. We were pinned in it, and I was being kissed on both cheeks by Kemal's father. He said, "*Hosh geldiniz*. Welcome." In the shaft of light I could see how much Kemal looked like him, tall, mustached, surprising blue eyes.

We were in a large walled garden with white plastered walls and a white floor. It was honey-scented with flowers and vines. One wall was only waist-high, opened to the sky and the sea below us. An arbor covered the center of the floor, hanging lamps filtered light through the leaves. Kemal's mother got up from a large table under the arbor. She took my hands and said, "*Hosh geldiniz*." I was only vaguely aware of being introduced to the man standing beside her.

"Do you know who that is?" Michael whispered. "That's Fazih Malacoglu!" It was already happening. In one day on Turkish soil, we were being passed from *arkadash* to *arkadash*.

We sat that night on the terrace, looking down at the dimly glowing crescent of the ancient harbor of Smyrna in the distance, the riding lights of ships like fallen stars in the black water. The spring vine leaves caught the sea breeze and made shadows flutter along the table over the *meze* of plates of white cheese, humus, dolmas, tomatoes, and tiny triangles of pastry and meat, the smell and vision of a way of eating as ancient as the harbor. Here and there, touched by lantern light, there were geraniums the size of small trees.

Fazih Bey was delighted that we were going to visit his father. "He has just returned from Europe," he said, "and he is always lonely at first. Alas, I cannot go for several weeks, or I would take you there."

We were no longer an anthropologist and an archaeologist going to study a subtribe of the Yezidi. We were the friends of Timur Bey's son, Kemal, and we were going to visit the father of Timur Bey's friend Fazih Bey.

I wondered if all the Yezidi were as handsome as Fazih Bey, but decided that this man certainly could have no part of the little lost tribe that we were being sent to study. He was obviously rich. His clothes were beautifully tailored. He was tall and clean-shaven. It was a clue. I had read that Yezidi men consider it a sin to shave their faces. The book had been written in 1912. He also spoke an elegant, somewhat old-fashioned English, and when he told us that he had just returned from Belgium and West Germany, where his export business took him for most of the winter, I realized that he must speak at least four languages.

But I couldn't think too much. I was conscious of being at last in Asia Minor, suspended on a night terrace above a five-thousand-year-old city. Beyond the discreet lamps the stars were not only piercing bright but dense, layer behind layer into a depth of night.

Vaguely, I heard Michael explaining that we had decided to go by bus to Malakastan instead of flying to Diyarbakir, as Fazih Bey suggested. "It is the best way to get a sense of the country," he explained. I knew that he was embarrassed to admit to such an elegant man that we were going by bus because we had to carry a footlocker, two foam-rubber mattresses, and an Aladdin stove.

Timur Bey laughed. "*Aman Allah*, you will certainly see it.

It is a thousand miles and it takes at least twenty-six hours by bus."

The next morning Timur Bey called the customs. He came back into the garden, laughing. "What infernal asses." He leaned over the table where we were having breakfast under the green arbor. "They say you have insulted the poverty of the Turks by bringing an Allah din stove. I will go with you there." He called through the door for coffee. Then he turned and smiled at me benignly. "You, my child, will be very quiet and you will not cross your legs in front of the customs inspector, and you"—he turned to Michael—"will call him *effendim* every chance you get. Now you must both think of me as your *dayi*, your uncle. In Turkey anyone who can open a door for you is your *dayi*. It is very Byzantine."

Our new *dayi* drove us to the customs in his Mercedes, got us through in fifteen minutes, sent the luggage to the bus station on a handcart, and took us to catch the one o'clock bus. When we had found seats he came to the window. "Fazih said you were to ask for Cüchük Mehmet at the bus station in Diyarbakir. He will take you in his *dolmush* to the village. Fazih has sent him a message last night."

Then he spoke to the bus driver. I could hear the words "Fazih Bey," and "*arkadash*." We were being passed from hand to hand a thousand miles across Turkey.

Michael was so elated. He looked like he had already discovered something wondrous. He was studying the map, then checking the window at the crowded outdoor terminal through the window. "The agora; this space must have been the agora, don't you see? Big spaces like this stay pretty constant . . ." he was whispering, more to himself than to me. I suddenly realized that he hadn't been out of the States before, and I, who had been such a diplomatic nomad, was taking too much for granted. I caught his excitement, and looked around as if it were the first bus in the world, there, for just a minute, all awe-struck in the Izmir bus station, clinging to Michael's arm.

There were lace curtains at the windows; a blue bead hung from the driving mirror to avert the evil eye. Fresh flowers were in a wall sconce beside the driver's seat. Across the front of the bus, over the windshield, MASHALLAH—"What wonders God has willed!"—was printed in large Roman letters, and I thought, in that minute of elation caught from Michael, how right it was.

The driver slipped into his seat and blew the horn. A young boy in a white jacket jumped aboard, closed the door behind him, and stood in the well made by the step. The bus groaned, the air brakes sighed, and we were on our way up toward the western hills.

Hours don't pass on long-distance bus rides. Places loom up and disappear. We were in the mountains, and then in the high plains covered with wildflowers. It was the time of *chichek*, the flowers. The sun lowered behind the bus; the passengers wrapped themselves in cocoons of silence. There was only the purr and grumble of the bus, and from time to time—no, not time, there was no sense of that—the attendant poured lemon cologne in my hands. I put it on my forehead and my wrists as I saw people around me doing. The bus smelled of food and lemon cologne.

I watched the blue bead swaying with the movement of the bus; it hypnotized me. My head lolled back and I was so nearly asleep that I remember snatches of scenes, as in a dream. The bus stopped in a town square. Shadows stretched across market stalls. A small boy called, "*Ayran. Ayran.*" He carried a brass tray on chains. Later, three men were at a table in the window of a *kahve*. They were playing *tavla*, the Turkish backgammon. It reminded me of Van Gogh's *Potato Eaters*, so it must have been night.

I don't think Michael stopped looking out the window or consulting the map for several hundred miles. He leaned across me to point at mounds, boulders, cliffs, fragments of temples, ruins of time and old forgotten wars, seeing a world five thousand years gone. He was sweeping the Hittites, the Greeks, the Romans, the Seljuk Turks out of the way of his vision. All day and into the night I could hear his voice, murmuring to himself, and the rustle of paper as he turned the pages of his notebook, and then I fell asleep.

And you and I, Noel, were on the sand dunes at the end of Long Island. It was 1945. We stood deep in sea grass and you said, "Oh, God, darling, landscape," in that way you had. I was six and you were fourteen and you were going to Eton, but first you had promised to teach me to fly, so you took my hand and we flew up right over the ocean, and the little houses down below us looked like a Monopoly game, and you told me to mind the power lines. I've had this dream ever since I was little, and what Dr. Dangle wanted to know first when I told him was if I were scared, and I told him, no, not ever, not with you. You were the most sophisticated boy I had ever seen in my life. I was deeply in love with you when I was six, and for so long afterward, oh, not like you are now, a black monk in my mind, but lithe and blond and, what is the word?

"Insouciant will do for now," the black monk told her. "Get on with the story and, for God's sake, leave Dingle Dangle out of it. You can't know how much all that has bored me."

"Well, there was a light in my face. It threw prisms on the window glass. The shadow of the lace curtains lay in my lap. I was awake. I was not at the end of Long Island with you and I was not six years old. I was twenty-six, and outside the bus window stretched a valley of the moon, and my dear old Michael was shaking me gently and saying, "Look, oh, Jesus, look!"

We were in Cappadocia, purple in the distance, but near us, lion-colored in the early sun. It is the central font of Anatolia, this wild volcanic upthrust. It was there that the desert saints carved churches and monasteries in the tawny conic tufa. In the far distance we could see one of the volcanoes that had made this a land of desolation, but now, in spring, after eons of sediment and rainwater filling the hollows and carving the cones into fantastic shapes, it was no longer desolate, not in spring.

There were people moving about the yellow cliff caves and the doors carved in the cones. They were the troglodytes, the cave dwellers. I watched them as we passed, as they fed their animals, tended the vineyards, which seemed to fill every hollow and tiny valley. Every place there was root room, poppies, hyacinths, anemones, and wild tulips caught the dawn sun. I could smell the wild fennel. Was it this time or another time? I remember yellow mustard growing in the fields of wheat and camel bells when I saw a camel train plodding slowly along the side of the road, the animals ignoring the dust from the bus. I remember, too, that this valley was made of bone, as if the body of earth were interred under the yellow ash and the brutal sun. The flowers were gone and the cones stuck up like tombs of the dead. But that was later.

The road stretched on, endless and dusty, toward the sun. The sun passed over us and at last we saw the mountains of Kurdistan and Armenia like a mist on the horizon, beyond the endless fields of wheat. We passed huge stone monuments, some isolated in the fields, some so near that the road wound around them. Michael studied them to see if he could glimpse any carving. "Glacial erratics," he said, disappointed.

By two o'clock we were rolling through one of the gates in the huge black basalt walls of Diyarbakir. Mountains that stretched all the way into Russia loomed beyond the Tigris. We could see the snow. "Here." Michael told me what I already knew. We had studied every report on the area we could find, all through the winter. "An eastern outpost of the Roman Empire, fortified against the Parthians." He looked up and up to the top of the high wall. "Look at that construction. Basalt. Hard as iron. A kind of Roman Maginot Line. Great Wall of China. Berlin Wall."

Two jets from the nearby NATO base carved the blue air

with thin white lines. It was too much for Michael. He said, "Holy Jesus! Will you look at that?"

We didn't have to find Cüchük Mehmet. He found us. We had expected a small man, since Cüchük means little, and he may have been Little Mehmet when he got his nickname. Michael, who was six feet tall, looked up into the sky at him. The rest of him was like the slides we had seen, a long white shirt buttoned to his neck, a striped scarf, wide *shalvar* stuck into leather boots. But instead of a Yezidi turban, he was wearing a baseball cap. He did have the Yezidi full face beard and his long hair curled like an ancient Assyrian's. He carried a long, old Enfield rifle, and a dagger was sheathed in his sash.

"You are the daughter of Matthew Bey." He stated this fact, still-faced.

My father was named Matthew Samway Leonard. He had never been called anything but Sam in his life. I had not been brought up in the diplomatic corps for nothing. Someone had looked up my background. We were certainly not two graduate students being escorted across Turkey, but the daughter of Matthew Bey, career diplomat, and her husband. I was an *arkadash*, the way to a *dayi* in a powerful position in a powerful country. What they had not found out was that my father was finishing his career as a first secretary and was soon to retire to Loudoun County, Virginia.

"*Evet*, yes," I told Cüchük Mehmet, and sighed.

"*Gel*," he said, and walked ahead of us, spreading the crowd, to the luggage that was being unloaded. He showed no surprise at our embarrassing pile of belongings, which was already dusty and drooped. It looked like luggage carried too far by people with too little money.

Cüchük Mehmet carried both mattresses over his shoulder, and the footlocker in his arms. Michael followed behind him with the Aladdin stove and the largest suitcase, looking as small as an adolescent boy.

There it sat, one of the leftovers from the Second World War that has opened the backlands and the mountain passes of the Middle East, a jeep with a canvas roof. This one, like all the others we had passed on the road, was decorated with paper lace; MASHALLAH was painted across the front.

There were already four people in it, three silent women in bright cotton *shalvar* and shawls and a young boy on whom dignity sat like sadness.

I whispered to Michael, "I cannot go on another four- or five-hour drive without going to the bathroom."

"Neither can I," he whispered back.

One of the women unfolded from the back of the jeep. "*Gel*," she said, and took my arm. Michael followed us. "*Adam!*" She pointed to the men's room.

In the *dolmush* again, with the mattresses already lashed to the roof with brown and black woven camel straps, the foot-locker and the suitcases between the back seats so that the three women and the deer-eyed boy rode with their feet tucked up and Cüchük Mehmet's rifle on top of the luggage, we started toward the mountains. In the vast open savannah, the mountains seemed to be coming toward us. No one said a word. Michael gave up trying to follow his map.

We had been driving for two hours when Cüchük Mehmet stopped. He took off the baseball cap and wound a long, multi-colored turban around his head. We drove on. Michael and I were riding together in the single front seat. I was practically on Michael's lap the whole time. He kept his arms around me and I was glad. There was a lot of shifting of gears and avoidance of ruts. We rushed the swollen spring fords and crossed high ancient bridges.

In the foothills the dirt roads climbed past small mountain pastures with fieldstone walls like I had seen in Connecticut. The upland creeks were humped and brown with spring flood. We had gone from a tawny world, even in spring, to the deep green and cool of the mountains—cool, then cold. I shivered against Michael. Cüchük Mehmet seemed never to look at us, but when I shivered, he stopped the *dolmush* and spoke to one of the women. Someone from the back draped a goat-hair shawl close about me.

The mountains rose around us; the sun had been behind us as the afternoon waned, but as we climbed the winding roads south, then east, then north, it seemed to turn around us. The streams were silver where the sun touched them and all around us there was the purl and rush of falling water. We went through ancient corridors cut so deep in rock for thousands of years by nomads and their animals that we could see only white stone walls on both sides of the jeep; then through passes where an unknown river rushed below us and loose mountain rocks seemed to hang above us. We passed a caravan of pack mules, led by a young boy. One of the mules blew and stumbled, making a tumble of rocks that we could hear hit the water far below us. Even in the desolate passes there were narrow terraces where the new grain was beginning to show green.

Wildness is watchful and silent, the final silence of mountains that is the sound of water, and wind in the trees, and evening bird calls. At a cleft in the rocks, Cüchük Mehmet stopped the *dolmush* in the middle of the road. The boy climbed out of the back and stretched. Cüchük Mehmet handed him the old gun, which was higher than his head.

The boy stood watch at the entrance to the cleft. Cüchük Mehmet disappeared. He was gone a long time. No one else moved.

When Cüchük Mehmet came back he was carrying a five-gallon can, half hidden behind him. He looked up and down the road and along the skyline of the mountains across the river. Then he filled the *dolmush* with gas and handed the can to the boy to carry.

It was early evening when he stopped again. The women, who had not seemed to move a muscle for five hours, jumped out of the back, not even stiff from the ride. Cüchük Mehmet pointed to a hollow where a blue-green creek ran through a grove of willows and walnut trees along a tiny valley between gaunt gray ridges.

"Walk," he told us, and pointed the way. He and the others stayed by the jeep.

In the sky ahead of us the mountain snow was pink in the sunset. We were totally alone after a few hundred yards. We walked slower and slower; we had caught the silence of the evening. Neither of us spoke. We sat on a rock by the water and took off our shoes and washed our feet. We had no idea where we were. I took off my sweater and washed as well as I could in the icy creek.

It was as quiet as prayer. Then, high on the mountainside beyond the creek we heard what I thought at first was a bird call. We looked up. A woman sat on a rock. Her *shalvar* made a pool of bright cotton around her. Her face in her black shawl was like a nun's. She smiled down at us. She raised her head and made the high-pitched trill again, the *helhela*. I found out later it was the sound that the women made for cheering or forewarning.

Behind us, up the road, Cüchük Mehmet carried his load. The women and the boy came behind him with the suitcases and the stove. They put their loads down and took off their shoes and washed their feet. Without knowing it, we had done the right thing, and there, not so many miles from where Noah landed and Abraham was born, I thought, Take your shoes from off your feet, for the ground you tread on is holy ground.

The *helhela* echoed ahead of us as we walked up the faint rise of the valley. It was getting wider. We stepped out of the dark woods into the evening sun and long shadows of the village.

All of the houses were white. Their walls gleamed with gypsum. They climbed both sides of the valley, so steep that the roof of one house was the terrace of the house behind it. On the highest terrace, a line of them had been carved within the mountain, some with only a door to the cave rooms, some with one room jutting out from the cliff.

In the distance beyond the treetops we could see the gold ball of the sacred tomb gleaming in the last sun. Everywhere along the stream and up the mountainsides there were small terraced fields and orchards. We crossed the stone bridge over the stream where the women had washed their clothes in the photograph, and then the first sacred tree, with its rag prayers moving in the mountain breeze that came down the narrow pass behind the valley. In the central square there was a large cistern with an undulating snake carved in bas-relief on its stone front.

On one side of the square there was a *kahve* covered with spring branches where two men sat so deep in a game of chess that they didn't look up. All the other villagers were watching us. Every man was armed with a dagger and a long pistol in his sash. On the other side of the square a man stood at the door of the *bakal*, the only shop in the village. Strings of tin and copper pots and camel straps hung in the door around him.

Then, up ahead of us, to the left, we saw the Derebey, standing in front of the white wall of his house beside the high arch of its entrance, waiting. I recognized him from his picture. He was older. His beard was white. But that was not the only difference. There was nothing threadbare about him. He was dressed in a fine, snow-white, long cotton shirt with a white wool toga, and his six-inch-wide belt was heavily jeweled. His dagger was gold, and his wide turban was colored silk. He didn't move or say a word. All the awesome dignity of age and station was held in his small body. As we came nearer I saw that he was no taller than I. There is something about small, lithe men that never grows old. Even with his white hair and neatly trimmed beard, the Derebey always seemed young to me, especially when he smiled. His cheeks crinkled then around eyes as clear as a virgin boy's.

He said, "Welcome, my dears. Jolly good. You must be exhausted," and shook hands.

The Derebey led us through the carved arch and into the large courtyard of his house.

I remember the courtyard not as a place seen first by two strangers but as familiar as one of those places we arrive at and recognize, not knowing why, but knowing as in no other place that we are home. There is the Sheika, his wife, all in white, with a headscarf like the white wimple of a nun. She stands, then or another time, by a huge urn. Red flowers flow down its sides, and her hand rests there and I think her hand is bleeding, but it is the flowers. Wild thyme is growing among the paving stones, and there are flowers in niches in the walls. White and red and evening shadows and the smell of thyme as our feet crush it; white and red and terrible morning, and the cocks crow over and over.

But that evening the Derebey and his wife took us to their upstairs room in the white house at the back of the compound and left us to wash. Cüchük Mehmet brought our luggage in and with some ceremony took off the embroidered cover of the bed and the linen sheets, leaving for a minute the mattress that had been prepared for us, to go to the door and snap his fingers. I saw the mattress was labeled *Army and Navy Store, Victoria, London.* He laid our foam mattresses over it, and a young girl came in, too shy to look at us, and remade the bed. I was told later that the villagers thought we had a taboo against the cotton cover of the Army and Navy Store mattress. They had so many taboos themselves that they were not surprised. I first noticed it when the women stepped back if I got near enough to touch their clothes. This hurt my feelings, but as an anthropologist I told myself to study, not react, and began to keep the hair on my arms shaved, thinking that was why they wouldn't let me touch them.

The next morning the good mattress had disappeared and we had to sleep the rest of the time on foam rubber, which the

little girl with the downcast eyes examined every morning to
see if we had made love. In the corner, unused and half forgotten, sat the Aladdin stove and the footlocker. Kerosene was
taboo in the village. Except for the faint electric light provided
by the Derebey's generator, the lamps were filled with olive oil
every evening. Down in the village, up the sides of the mountains, and all night at the saint's tomb, they winked like fireflies.

In the evening we sat around wonderful rugs in the Paradise,
the walled garden behind the house under the oak trees, the fig
and mulberry and terebinth. I knew from my reading that they
were sacred, but then the Derebey explained that all the trees
in the village were sacred. He said that many of them had been
brought as shoots from the holy center of the Yezidi in Iraq by
his grand-grandfather. That was the only mistake in English
I ever heard him make.

I woke to the dawn scream of the peacocks in that cold
mountain time before the sun touched the valley. The spaces
seemed larger then, and I could smell the dew and the green of
the trees. I stood at the back window and watched the slow
oxen drinking in the stream at the end of the Derebey's garden.

From the front door of our room, beyond the balcony over
the courtyard, I could see the Sheika walk up to the tomb and
kneel and kiss the stone of the wall where the sun first touched.
She disappeared through the carved arch into the shrine. Down
below in the courtyard, as the sun found it, the household began
to stir, and as each person came out, he kissed the first place he
saw the sun touch. Far from being devil worshippers, they
seemed to honor everything that grew and moved and flowered
and lowed and bleated at the beginning of the day. They lived
in a sacred world.

After breakfast on the first morning, the Derebey took us
up to the room he called his office and unlocked the door. It
was the only lock I ever saw in the village. He called for coffee,
and when it had been brought, he ushered us in and locked the
door behind us. The room was as near a student's room at

Oxford as he could re-create. There were heavy, ugly, over-stuffed leather chairs, a large fumed-oak desk, a brass lamp, and all around the walls there were bookshelves.

"My dears," he said, and sank into one of the chairs and stretched out his legs, "this is my *sanctum sanctorum.* Go ahead, look at the books. I know you want to. I always do in other people's houses. Books tell so much they don't know they tell, don't you think?"

I passed the line of catalogues from Christie's, the eleventh edition of the *Encyclopaedia Britannica,* the *Oxford English Dictionary,* all thirteen volumes bound in leather, bound editions of anthropological and archaeological journals long since defunct, the complete works of Sir James Frazer, bound volumes of *Punch* and *The Yellow Book.* His collection of English novels stopped in 1923. One whole wall was devoted to editions of Lewis Carroll.

"That's my hobby," the Derebey said behind me. He sounded shy. "I've been trying to translate *Alice in Wonderland* into Kurdish. I have struck a snag with 'Jabberwocky,' to say the least."

I bumped into a body and almost screamed as it began to bow, and then I realized that it was a life-sized cardboard cutout of Aubrey Beardsley's Salome holding the head of John the Baptist. I caught it and straightened it, and stood staring at Salome's exhausted eyes.

Behind me the Derebey called out, delighted, "Fooled you, didn't she? Isn't she marvelous?"

Michael had forgotten us. He had found the *Archaeologist.* He squatted on the floor beside it. "Good God," he muttered, "all the way back."

"I do have a few notes in volume 3 for July 1924, on the tomb. You might find them of some interest." The Derebey watched while Michael took out the volume. He was as excited as Ben Gunn looking at a bit of cheese. "Of course, you have to realize that foundation stones like that were thought to be Assyrian then. But I do hint that they might be Hatti or even earlier. Coffee? You may borrow the book."

Michael sank into an overstuffed chair. He was cradling the book as if it kept him warm.

The days passed. I was getting nowhere in my field notes and it was the fault of the Derebey. He set up a table in the court-yard, and each morning he lined up village women and told them exactly what he thought I wanted to know. He translated as they recited their ages, the time of their first menstruation, their age at marriage, at first conception. In the ancient, time-less place, they stepped up, one after another, and recited statistics as if they were answering questions in a classroom, while the Derebey enjoyed himself.

Michael was faring no better, and for the same reason. We took to whispering in bed at night. "The foundations are certainly pre-Hatti. There are two damned many clues. Ani-mism, double axes, bull's horns, votive penises, carved moons, boy, you name it. The tomb's been salted."

As soon as my daily ration of women was over, the Derebey followed Michael up to the tomb. He took him into dark vaults where the water moaned through stone conduits below the floor. "The water is blessed as it flows through here," the Derebey told him, "so that all the water you drink and wash in is blessed. It cures all diseases, even unhappiness." When Michael asked who was buried in the square sarcophagus, he said, "I have evidence that it is Semiramis herself. She was from these mountains, you know. A much maligned woman. The ancient Jews and the Romans had truly dirty minds."

He showed him the limestone bas-reliefs of the snakes that stretched up to the lintels of the tomb door, rubbed with lamp-black so that they looked like they were carved from black marble. He told him that one of them was from the Garden of Eden, and that the Muslims, the Jews, and the Christians had perverted the story. "You will find the snake as an object of worship long before those silly little naked people, Adam and Eve, were made so important," he told him.

The one place he warned Michael about was the sacred well that stood half in a cave up beyond the tomb courtyard within a stone wall of its own. It, too, had the carved snake around its wellhead. Michael told me that it was so sacred that no one, not even the Derebey, went close to it or drew water from it. But he did show Michael what looked from the cave mouth like a carved stalagmite deep in the dimness behind the well. "That," he said, "is most old and most holy, but you must not go closer. It is not allowed."

It was the Derebey who found the obsidian mother goddess and presented it to Michael. We sat on the bed that night staring at the three-inch primitive body, only half released from its sharp dagger of stone, and Michael muttered, "I wonder where the hell he got this."

I waited for the Derebey to get to the point. I had not forgotten that I was the daughter of Matthew Bey, but the Derebey didn't mention it. Now, looking back at him as he sat on the grass, cross-legged beside the fine rugs under the trees in the evening, his white stole flung down beside him, his hands crossed in his lap, looking from son to son, none of whom said a word in front of Baba, I see that there were clues.

He reaches for the Gentleman's Relish and says, "Is it not most interesting, really almost a miracle, that we have in this one small valley a living museum of customs and artifacts all the way back to the Flood?" And again, he sips coffee and looks over the cup. "The preservation of things of value . . ." and doesn't finish, but says instead, "I fear decisions made in other places."

Most often I see him carefully offering me a Balkan Sobranie, and he says, "We are strong because we have been wiped out by the Turks, the Kurds, the Christians, the Muslims, the Jews, and the League of Nations," and he giggles that schoolboy giggle and lights my cigarette. But he does not mention the tenuous thread he is weaving toward my father.

Once, when we are standing in front of the tomb, looking down the valley, he breaks my sense of peace like an egg. He says, "Poor Teresa." We watch each other and I see him smile. "It's happened to others, you know. You are falling in love with us. You people," and he sighs, "you long for homes you never had. You are all children who yearn for different parents. American cuckoos in the nest. Some of your young ones have strayed here on the road to Afghanistan or Nepal, places they haven't seen and haven't earned, a weedy, sad, children's crusade."

I, who had gone as a child from pillar to post, country to country, with parents who were diplomatic Bedouins, was hurt by this. I wanted to tell him it wasn't my fault, but I didn't say anything.

Michael and I wandered through the early evening, holding hands, up the pass that cut through the right side of Nuh Inme, the mountain that loomed behind the village, where the Derebey said that Noah's Ark had really landed. He said it was still there, that his grand-grandfather had seen it sticking out of the snow. Away below us we could see the tiny figure of the Sheika lighting the lamps around the courtyard of the tomb.

I remember the first evening we stopped at the *kahve* where the two men played chess. One of them looked up at us and then back at the board. Between games he came over.

"Hi, kids," he said, and sank down beside Michael. "What the hell are you doing in this godforsaken dump? Teresa and Michael Cerrutti? Right? I heard you were coming." He looked a little embarrassed.

"Oh yeah"—he grinned when we told him what had been happening—"the old man tells you everything you want to know, right? He gets lonesome. I'm Fred Funkhauser from Milwaukee." Solemnly we all shook hands. "Government survey for AID, geo expert. I got sent up here three years ago when somebody found this pass on a goddamn map and decided it was a hot area. That guy is Russian. He got sent here the same way. Agro expert. Hot, hell. The only thing hot here is what that Nestorian *bakal* owner smuggles over the Iraqi border."

"We got it made here, me and Ivan," he said, but he sounded sad. "When he goes back to Russia to make his report he brings back vodka, and when I report to Diyarbakir I bring back cigarettes from the PX. We got it made," and then his eyes wandered. "I guess," he added. "Come and meet Ivan."

Fred Funkhauser and Ivan looked like brothers, both Slavic, both blond. Ivan's hair was longer. Fred's was cut like he had just left boot camp. Ivan had a wonderful grin. "You come here when you can get away from the old man. I sing you Russian songs. We get drunk."

They were both glancing longingly at the chessboard.

By the time we had walked out of the leafy, trellised porch and into the sun, they had already sunk back into their game. "Come on back," Fred called.

"We get drunk," Ivan added, but they didn't look up from the chessboard.

"You have met my Tweedle-al-dum and my Tweedle-al-dee," the Derebey said as soon as we got back to the garden. Sometimes I thought he knew things almost before they happened. "That is the CIA man and the KGB man. They have become friends. I am pleased about that. I feel sorry for them, and many times I invite them to dinner. I think they have been forgotten. You must go and get drunk with them, for they are very lonely. It is not a good life for young men, no women except the whorehouse in Diyarbakir. Play chess. Get drunk. Make reports on each other, and all of us."

So we went to the *kahve* sometimes in the evening and drank the harsh local mountain wine, while Fred and Ivan got slowly drunk on Russian vodka and sang Russian songs and "On Wisconsin" over and over. One night Fred told us about the road. "The old man is scared. Some NATO guy from the Corps of Engineers came up here and did a survey for an alternate route east. It's the only east-west pass he found on the map. He didn't look for any more. He was due for leave. Didn't have time. Nice guy. It won't come to anything. I've seen them come, I've seen them go."

Ivan grinned. "You build it. We use it. We come over the border with snow on our boots."

"The hell, Ivan."

"My name is Feodor."

"Okay, Feodor. I pointed out in Diyarbakir the pass is six feet under snow in the winter. I told the colonel." Which colonel he didn't say, and his mind veered to Diyarbakir gossip. "He's going to be recalled. His wife talks too much. Jesus, she never shuts up. Classified. Unclassified. You name it. It's all in my report."

"Mine, too." Ivan or Feodor grinned. "I write about you, you write about me. We cover the ass, *arkadashlar, tamam?*"

The road had been forgotten. Feodor was singing a Russian song, something, he told us, about longing and the steppes and love, but he said he couldn't translate it. It was very sad. He sang it with tears in his eyes.

"My name is not Feodor, either," he said after the song. "Nobody here knows my name. Don't you think that is sad?"

I was hardly listening. Fred had given me a real clue as to why the Derebey was entertaining the daughter of Matthew Bey.

As we wandered back to the Derebey's house through the village, where the firefly lamps seemed to mingle with the stars, we could hear them still singing "On Wisconsin," fainter and fainter in the darkness.

Three weeks after we got there I woke at dawn as usual to a bustle of preparation in the courtyard. Even the Sheika, who never moved without a slow, almost ponderous dignity, made her prayers quickly and almost ran across the large, flat, open space in front of the tomb wall that was the village dancing ground, where in April they sacrificed a bull to Sheikh Sham, the sun god. When she saw me standing on the balcony she called up, "*Gunaydin!* My son comes!" There were already several sons, from forty years old down to twenty, all married, all with children, around the *meze* table set out on the rugs under the trees every evening.

All day they watched the sky and the treetops, judging the wind. When it dropped toward evening and there was stillness, they began to move up toward the dancing ground. Michael and I followed them.

A helicopter appeared above the hollow, its shadow like a huge pterodactyl over the square. It lingered above the dancing ground and then set down. A man climbed out of it. He was too far away for us to see his face. He was in Yezidi robes, the jeweled belt, the turban, the dagger. He hugged the Derebey and then the Sheika.

The other person in the helicopter was a beautiful, delicate girl with the eyes of a small boy who hasn't been caught yet. Her coined cap and her wide jeweled belt glistened in the late sun. She wore a heavy silver necklace that hung in a series of strands down to her waist, and at her throat a large jasper surrounded by gold and rubies that looked as if it should have belonged to Nefertiti. Her *shalvar* were a delicate peach-colored shot silk that changed with the light.

The man was Fazih Bey. He came up to us, smiling, and shook hands. "I'm so sorry I could not save you that long trip," he told us, "but I had to wait for my sister, who is studying in Paris."

That evening there was the usual *meze* of plates of salad, humus, eggs, and yogurt, börek filled with spinach and white cheese, stuffed vine-leaf dolmas as small as little fingers, the sweet scent of lamb and tomato kebabs cooking on a charcoal brazier that cast light up into the trees. But instead of the local wine that was harsh in my throat, the wine was French and the vodka Russian. Gentleman's Relish and Major Grey's Chutney had been brought out, and there were piles of delicate white French loaves and spiced *köfte*, the small raw meatballs that taste like steak tartare. The Derebey said, "*Hoshgeldiniz, canim*," and shook my hand as if I had not shared their food for three weeks.

From the time the fine gold and red weave of the rugs faded into black and the lamps were lit and the stars came out in the black sky, the Derebey talked. More and more of the people from the village came in silently as he talked, until they surrounded us, sitting cross-legged and patient, all the way back to the stone walls of the garden. The *köfte*, made by the Derebey, was passed among them. It was his specialty, and the word of his making it was the sign to the village that they were expected to come and share it.

The Derebey began in English. "As it says in *Alice*, as you no doubt remember, 'Begin at the beginning and go on until you come to the end: then stop.' That is good literary advice. But now I will tell a story within a story within a story within a story that does not come to the end, for that is more like life." He put on his storytelling voice, and I could feel patience all around me in the twilight.

"It is naïve to assume that the political way of the world does not concern us all. My passion is for the works of Aubrey Beardsley, Lewis Carroll, and above all my close friend Sir James Frazer." There was a little stir at the name Frazer. He stopped and waited for the rustling to subside. "As I was saying, this has a most amusing connection with the dissolution of the Ottoman Empire. We must go back together to the time of the border courtship with England and France. Now, this had been going on for a long time, and we had learned not to trust such courtships. We had seen England and France arm and then desert the Armenians and leave them to a terrible fate. You can see Russia arming rebels today in countries near its eastern border, and the United States in Central America, and both of them in Africa, a sort of musical-insurgents game. Even in the last few years the CIA has been arming the Iraqi Kurds at the request of the Shah of Iran, and when there is a change of policy, they, too, will be left to their fate. Now it is oil. Then it was oil, too, and minerals. My father was especially fortunate in that, unlike many chieftains, God had not made him a fool. Persecution had sharpened his mind."

I saw Fred and Ivan shadowed in the door of the garden. They came over and sank down behind Michael and took out notebooks. The Derebey waited politely until they were ready. "Cobalt, iron, tungsten, copper, and above all—oil. It amuses me to consider how much of world politics is affected by visco-elastic creep." He grinned as he watched them scribble.

"By 1918, as you know, the Ottoman Empire had crumbled, and two things were taking place. One"—he lifted a finger— "the attempt of England, France, and Greece to carve up the dead giant. Two"—he lifted two fingers—"the birth of modern Turkey. My father watched and weighed and waited. We were then in what the British were pleased to call their mandate, near Mosul, right in the center of the oil region. They called it a mandate instead of a colony, but it was the same, except for the language. Then Lebanon and Syria were French. Egypt, Palestine, Iran, and Iraq were British. Part of the Caucasus was Russian, and everybody had his eye on Kurdistan. So short-sighted." He peered at Fred and Ivan.

"This has been going on since the time of Nebuchadnezzar, and they all find out that you cannot rule people who live at altitudes of over five thousand feet. Even Xenophon and the ten thousand had sense enough to march on through, poor things. There they were, up to their popos in snow and longing for home." The Derebey was still for a minute. We all waited. "To be in a sphere of influence is a terrible thing." He sighed, and then he remembered that he was telling a story.

"So I was given by my father to the British at the age of twenty-one, although I was already two times a father, daughters only. Also, since I was not the heir, I had been allowed to go to Robert College in Istanbul, where I had learned English. He considered, and rightly so, I think, that three of his four sons should be trained in one of the three contending languages and customs that could, at any moment, be of the greatest advantage. He also chose the British for me, for God knows what romantic reason, mostly I think because they were good shots. He chose them for himself also. He hired a teacher, a young man from the American University in Beirut, and for six months he spoke nothing but English until he had learned. The young man, whose name was Ahmet, was a city boy, and he spent the six months with a sore bottom, since he was required to follow my father on his day-long rides on horseback while my father chanted, 'My father, my mother, my sister, my brother are going for a picnic in the park,' and since he liked that word you could hear him call, 'Picnic, picnic, picnic,' at the hillsides. It pleased him to hear 'picnic' echoed back.

"The Kurdish villages were the first civilian towns ever to be bombed from airplanes. Did you know that?" He sounded proud. "Of course, we could hear the planes coming, and so we sat on the hillside and watched bits of the village where we lived in southern Kurdistan go up pop pop. The leader of the Muslim Kurds sent a message to the British: 'If you will not come out and fight like men, we will be forced to surrender.'

"My father moved us all across into this valley, where we were almost certain to be safe, at least from the planes, if not from the Muslims, since it was deep in Turkish territory and well beyond border arguments. He also drove a good hard bargain for oil leases in the valley that we left, banked the proceeds in Switzerland, invested more wisely than the Muslim sheiks, and here we are! It was easy to convince our tribe to follow him. The tomb had been a sacred pilgrimage for centuries. We had always summered here when we were still nomads since before the time of Semiramis."

He saw that I was scribbling notes, too, and spoke slowly. But later when I read them I found that I had written, "Evidence of cross-cultural influences after World War I in the extended family. Look up British Mandate 1919–1926." Only the feel of the book in my hand, not the words, brings back the shadows, the scent of oil and food and wine and the kebab cooking, the charcoal glow reflected in the trees and on the face of the Derebey, and I hear his quiet slow voice.

"He sent my younger brother to fight for Mustafa Kemal Atatürk, since no one knew which way the cat would jump. That was also an excellent decision. My brother was a stupid boy, but blindly brave, and he ended the Turkish War of Independence with the nickname Aslan, which means lion. He was a handsome boy and Atatürk liked him. One drunken night, to please him, he declared our whole valley *Gazi*, a heroic place, and we have not had a large-scale massacre since.

"The third son my father sent to Azerbaijan in the Russian Caucasus. He and his wife and family visit us every summer, but alas, only my brother and I can speak together. The children have become Russian and very healthy. We have some import business together." I think he grinned at Ivan.

"So when the borders were agreed on in 1926, we became Turks, at least in public. But to return to my own story within a story within a story. I was, in short, the one to be courted by the British by being sent to Oxford, Balliol of course, since the Middle Eastern desk at the F.O.—Foreign Office," he said to Fred, who was scribbling as fast as he could. "Where was I? Oh yes, most of them were Balliol men. I have, as you have noticed, a quick and shallow mind, and I learned many things at Oxford. It was the beginning of my quite pleasurable erudition, and so you see how my passion for Aubrey Beardsley and Lewis Carroll is connected to politics.

"I was not happy at Oxford, though. We Yezidi are used to persecution and to hatred. Hate sees your face, but I had not suffered that cross between amusement and indifference before and I found it difficult. I find indifference a great evil. One"—up went the finger—"to let no human being get in the way of a policy. Two, not to care about the human results of your decisions. My father knew about this. He called it *machumyet*, innocence, but he saw it in grown men as a kind of moral idiocy.

"I used to walk up the Thames to Binsey to the sacred well when I was very homesick and pretend I had a friend. You see, at Oxford I was just a little wog, so it was necessary to remind myself that I was a prince in my own valley to keep my spirits up. I was at Binsey, but in the landscape of my soul I was at my own sacred well. Now, here, at this minute, I am again at Binsey and it is a cold day and I dip my hands in the water and watch it turn to mist against my palms. It was after a walk to Binsey one winter day that I came back to my digs to find two things." Again he lifted a finger. "One, the telegram that made my future tremble like the mist on my hands." He caught my eye again. "A good touch. Write it down.

"My older brother had been killed in a *kahve* in Diyarbakir for no better reasons than that he wore his shirt buttoned to the neck and refused to eat the lettuce on his plate. Actually, it was to rob him, since the rumor had spread among the Muslim Kurds that we were rich. That is why, unless we have reason to trust you, we wear Western clothes outside the valley and poor clothes when a stranger comes here." He laughed. "It is pure hell, changing clothes in a helicopter, isn't it, Fazih?" He didn't wait for an answer.

"So I packed my books, left my English mistress in Walton Street, and prepared to come home. Two. There was also a letter that day from Sir James Frazer asking me to dine with him at the Café Royal in London. Now can you imagine what it was to a twenty-two-year-old wog to have such an honor? That night he gave me a great gift. He asked many things about the Yezidi, and he made notes, too. When you have been persecuted for the religion or the place you were born in, you tend to have an inner shame which makes you overproud. That night he asked me questions that gave me a certainty that there was somebody in an alien land who cared who I was.

"Then I came home, and when my father decided to die, I became the Derebey and have been ever since in my valley of Malakastan, except for a yearly visit to London. I stay at the Savoy. I go to the British Museum to see what they have stolen since my last visit. Then I always go to Primrose Hill, because that is where Blake saw the angels sitting in a tree and I hope someday to see them too.

"Then I must arrange for wine, Gentleman's Relish, Major Grey's Chutney, kippers, Stilton, and tea to be sent from Fortnum & Mason, buy Dr. Collis-Brown for my stomach, get my teeth seen to, visit my doctor in Harley Street, order a suit in Savile Row, a hat at Lockes, which I leave in our flat in Diyarbakir for my next visit to London. As always, *inchallah*, I make my pilgrimage to the Café Royal. Alas, I find London much changed. Too many Arabs."

He was quiet for so long that people deep in the shadows of the garden were beginning to whisper. "*Sus!*" he called out. The whispering stopped. Someone giggled.

"You must forgive us," he said, "but the young ones have heard me say Café Royal. It is their favorite story. I must tell it in Kurdish. They have been very patient."

He began. Someone touched my arm, and in the firelight the silver coins of her cap flickered. It was the young girl who had come with Fazih in the helicopter. "Come," she whispered, "I will translate for you. Would you prefer English or French?" It was the first thing Zephyr ever said to me. "English," I whispered.

I crawled away from the rug side after her and we found a place in the dark against the garden wall. In the distance the Derebey sitting in the pool of light looked to me like a Pre-Raphaelite painting, but I couldn't think which one, or even if there was one.

"I am Zephyr. I am at the Sorbonne, but we all come back to Baba every year, and I put on these things and behave like a proper Yezidi girl. It is nice to find you here. Now Baba is telling them about how the great bey Camus, or water buffalo, al Fazih—Sir James Frazer—invited him to his sacred palace of the Kahve Sahane, or the Café Royal."

Much of the story is gone. But I remember the rustle of Zephyr's silk clothes, the clink of her jewelry, and her warm breath as she whispered. I was too entranced to take notes, but some of the whispered phrases come back.

"This is Yezidi version of a boring dinner in London," in her voice, full of amusement, but never actually laughing, and the whisper goes on in the dark while I watch him. His arms spread in a gesture, then he claps his hands. He has told this story over and over, for when he pauses, there is a prompting word out of the darkness around him. He is telling them about the great temple of Kahve Sahane in the sacred city of London, and how Camus al Fazih sat him right in the center and how they were served their feast by fakirs dressed in black, just like their own fakirs. He tells them how everyone around them was lighting fires to the Melek Taus with matches that were called by his English name, Lucifer, son of the morning. There are shadows in the garden door as Ivan and Fred slip back to their chess game.

And now he tells about there being many priestesses with the sacred peacock feathers to fan them and how there were many princes of the City of London. I hear Zephyr giggle. He names them all, from Beerbohm Bey and Wells Bey and Bernard Shaw Bey to Aubrey Beardsley Bey. No matter that Beardsley had been dead for some years, for this is a *masal*, a myth, and everyone knows it. Now he tells them that all the way to the City of London the Yezidi are honored by Camus al Fazih and the princes, who light sacred fires to him with matches called Lucifers.

I hear him call in English, "The devil you say!"

Now he tells them how they do not have a taboo about saying the names of Lucifer and how they call to him in times of trouble as the Yezidi say, "Allah, Allah."

It was late at night and the people had gone. There were only the lamps at the sacred tomb in the distance, and a mountain rain pounded on the roof and made the courtyard glisten. Zephyr and I sat on the balcony making friends and watching the rain. She told me her eighteen-year-old troubles which were like eighteen-year-old troubles every place.

"Baba," she said in the darkness, "lets me be educated and then he expects me to come back here and marry one of my stupid cousins. He does not know what he is. He stands between the old world and the new." She sighed. "Sometimes I wish he had not allowed me to leave the valley. Then I would not know."

Somebody in the house began to snore, and we tittered like schoolgirls staying all night together and whispering sleep away. We complained about having to visit our families. Zephyr whispered that Baba lived in a dream. "Fazih," she said, "foots the bill. He is in charge of our investments and he has a good business, import, export. Not drugs, idiot!" She had sensed my question. "Figs, olive oil, rugs, but he is not above a few antiquities, I tell you, and maybe a little gold. Baba lives like we still have royalties from the Iraqi wells, but that stopped in 1960."

When the snoring stopped we were whispering about places we knew in Paris, and she told me about her French boyfriend. "He is a Communist and plays classical jazz. Django Reinhardt and Grappelli. Grappelli and Reinhardt. We find old records in the flea market. Don't breathe a word of this," she warned, and planned to the rhythm of the rain about living in Paris and having a job as an interpreter. "I speak five languages . . ." she admitted.

Sometime in the night she said, "We are Shamsanis, descendants of Cyrus the Great, but who in Paris cares about that?" Later, in the doorway to the balcony, the Derebey said gently, "Go to bed. It's time to go to bed."

Michael was not asleep. In the darkness he held me close to him. I stroked his back while he whispered his plans. "I've got it worked out. When he mentioned the sacred well, I knew what I ought to do. Now why is it the one tabooed place here? I tell you. He hasn't salted it. Don't you see?"

We made almost silent love to the sound of the rain. When I woke up the rain had stopped. It was nearly dawn. I heard a cock crow. Michael sighed and stretched. I think he had been awake all night, planning.

"Tomorrow morning I will take the rope ladder and the pitons and go down the well. The Derebey says this place has been pre-Hatti and then Hatti and then Zoroastrian and then Mithraic and then Christian and then Muslim before it was Yezidi. Always a shrine. All of these religions except the Yezidi threw out the sacred objects of the one they replaced. Right? Where better than down a well? Look at the well at Nimrod. Remember what Dr. Grod said when he told me to pack a rope ladder and pitons. Don't neglect wells."

He was still murmuring, half asleep, when I heard the Sheika get up and go down the stairs to her morning prayers. I suppose we walked and questioned and made notes and had dinner the next day, but I don't remember. We were waiting for night and then dawn.

But I remember Michael's step on the bare floor at pre-dawn, and he still leans over me. I can see the shadow of the ropes over his shoulder. He kisses me and says, "Cover for me. Okay?" and I promise and then he says, "I love you. You know that," and strokes my hair.

It was nine o'clock when I saw a man run across the dancing ground and I think that I already knew, because someone, maybe it was Zephyr, a woman, tried to stop me when I ran through the courtyard.

Michael lay on the ground in front of the cave mouth. His body was already swollen from the snake venom. His face was dirty. Some damp moss clung to his hair. He looked ridiculous.

Cüchük Mehmet had found him when he saw the end of the rope ladder tied to a rock. Michael was still alive when he hoisted him up. He hung on the rope rungs, or maybe he had tangled in them. I don't know. He had put his notebook in his pocket. The last thing he had written was "Wow! For a minute I saw it!"

But what he had seen no one can know. He must have dropped his flashlight as he put the notebook in his pocket. I could see it still shining under water at the bottom of the well before Cüchük Mehmet pulled me back.

The Derebey stands at the courtyard door with his hands out to me and I am walked toward the house from the right. He takes me in his arms.

"I tried to warn him," he says.

"He thought you meant a religious taboo." I am not crying.

"No. Adders. It is full of snakes."

We buried Michael at the sacred tomb in the courtyard under the trees, where the sunlight filtered through the leaves and fretted the stone. The Derebey read the Christian service from the Anglican prayer book he kept in his office.

After it was over, the Sheika and Zephyr walked me between them back down the valley. I was imprisoned in their kindness and their formal mourning.

The last I saw of the valley was as it sank smaller and smaller below Fazih's helicopter until the faces looking up were the size of flowers. Zephyr came with us and held me in her arms. At Diyarbakir I insisted on riding the bus back across a land already grown arid with summer. The flowers were gone, the fields burned under the ruthless sun. The dust rose around the bus, and the rocks were bone-colored. Michael and I had planned to come back that way in August, stopping along the route to trace the flow of the mourning customs down toward the sea. Besides, I had to bring back the foam-rubber mattresses and the Aladdin stove. They were entered in my passport and I would not have been allowed to leave Turkey without them.

Don't look for Malakastan. It doesn't exist. It has disappeared under asphalt. Michael's grave, the well, the cave, the shrine, the rag-laden trees fell in front of bulldozers that pushed through the valley pass as the warrior Hittites must have done. Zephyr's letters were like her father's voice. She wrote me that all that was left was half a high courtyard, a few stone rooms of the cave houses, a field wall that missed the blast. She picked up a coin dropped on the mountain. A few trees were left of an orchard where the turtles copulated in spring, its downhill edge a snaggle of broken trunks. In the winter, under six feet of snow, I think there would be a ghost of the valley's shape still.

The villagers were moved, as being in a strategic position above the NATO highway. They were shipped to abandoned barracks somewhere near Eskişehir, far enough away so they wouldn't cause trouble, since they are classed as Kurds and Kurds are troublemakers. The young found jobs in the Pazar and the restaurants, being naturally polite.

When the Derebey heard of the decision to destroy the valley he called his family together, Fazih Bey from Brussels, Zephyr from Paris, even his brother from Azerbaijan. It was late fall and the snow was already deep in the valley. They sat on rugs around the *meze* in the winter dining room.

After they had eaten, the Derebey told them in what Zephyr called his storytelling voice that he had decided to die. In late April, after the last bull sacrifice, when the snow still patched the hillsides as it does the garden this morning, he lay down and died, with everybody around him, as he wanted.

Fazih Bey took his body to Izmir and buried him where the bulldozers could not disturb him. He moved the Sheika and all his family to Izmir; he was now the Derebey without a valley.

Zephyr says the Sheika wore Western clothes, and enjoyed television, especially *I Love Lucy* dubbed into Turkish, but at dawn she still kissed the first place in Fazih's house where the sun touched and at dusk she lit an olive-oil lamp that burned all night long and made Fazih's Izmir wife nervous. In two years she was dead.

Zephyr now works in Brussels for the Common Market and her letters tell about her new friend, a Walloon who is an international monitor scuba diver. They dive together in the Red Sea. She says she is learning through her lovers. So few people admit that."

"Which brings me to the point I wish to make." Noel's voice intruded into the story from across the table. But it was faint, as if Teresa were trying to get the black monk to leave and not quite succeeding. She was too tired after all she had lived through to be criticized, and Noel tended to do that.

"Oh no, you don't, dearie." She could barely hear him, even though he seemed to be shouting. "I'm not accusing you of lying. I am only reminding you about forgetting a few things. Your story is magic, idyllic, tragic, and all that. But there was some important dailiness that you can't leave out. The difference," he said carefully, his voice stronger, "between losing your mate through divorce and through death is that in the first you remember only the bad, and in the second you remember only the good. They are both sentimental self-protection."

"Fights. I mentioned the fights," she defended herself.

"You're so right. Fights. Mention isn't reliving, dearie. So long as you remember Michael as a sort of dear bright fool you're safe. You do tend to run to bright fools, don't you? Look at me."

"Yes, we did fight," she said, suddenly furious again at Michael's ghost and the black monk, "and it's none of your business."

"Need I remind you that I had to listen to it?"

"Then you ought to know what it was about. Michael died too soon, while he still thought I was a cold-blooded Wasp and that even my manners were phony, and I thought he was second-generation paranoid academic instant gentry. But that" —she sounded pathetic even to herself—"was only when we were quarreling."

)50(

"That's better. Now you can love his memory instead of overprotecting it, at the risk of using Dingle Dangle language."

"All right!" There she was, yelling at the black monk in the empty kitchen, with the new tears running down her face at last. "I still long for the home he was trying to forget. Each of us was struggling free of the other one's dream. But nine thousand miles away we had forgotten all that. We met at last on neutral ground in Malakastan, and we were friends and lovers. Now go away." She laid her head down on the table and cried and cried, and when she had come to a stop, she called the Dean.

The sun was high in the sky. She had gone back to Malakastan at last. The black monk had been right, as usual. There was not a stone, not a color, nor a smile, a touch, a tree that was gone. Michael was where he belonged in her mind, his sweetness cleansed of fear and trouble and quarreling and all the destruction time would have worked on him. The important thing left to her was not that Michael was perfect; she knew he was far from that, but that she had loved, and knew it.

She wrote on her calendar for April 2: "Ten o'clock. Dean Withers," and noticed, shocked, that it was Michael's birthday.

Mr. O. Stuart Starr was only a deputy sheriff, but he had dreams and he had duties, official duties. One of them, at least he saw it that way, was to cleanse Prince Rupert County of all enemies, foreign and domestic, Operation Chaos, Duke Wayne stuff, hot diggity dog. He whirled his wife's black 1955 Buick into a parking space with one hand, drag-race style. He lounged back in the seat, looking downhill at a sprawl of students who were star-scattered across the grass, catching the deceptive warmth of early April. He loved Omar Khayyam. He told himself the little Jew Commie cowardly un-American bastards were all going to catch pneumonia, and good riddance.

All he had to do was to release the brake. The car rolled down at them, faster and faster. He could feel the crunch of bodies under the tires. Blood spurted on the windshield, blood and filthy long hair. He took a deep breath and made himself be calm. The vision was gone. He relaxed his body, turned off the ignition, and got out of the car.

He reached in the back window and patted Duke. He was sure Duke smiled. Dogs could. He said, as tenderly as to a child, "Stay, Duke." The Doberman was too well trained to wag his tail.

Mr. Starr got ready in his soul to do his patriotic duty. He could feel his jaw clench, and his skin was as tight as armor. He could feel the clink of chain mail as he strode across the paved yard in front of the Administration Building. He had the power; he had the means; and, boy, he had the poop at last. Inside himself he was doing a little dance.

"Shizomazoo," he sang to himself, a word that he used when he was happy. He was careful not to sing it aloud. Sometimes it did escape into sound and his wife said, "Stop that humming."

"Yessiree. Foreigners and toilet paper!" He forgot and spoke aloud as he slammed the big oak door against the wall and felt his arm muscles swell and harden against the wood.

Inside his office, Dean Withers was tired already and it was only ten o'clock. He knew why. He knew what was coming. Same time every Wednesday, same questions, same answers. He saw himself mounting a mild little barricade. He really couldn't let himself take a five-foot, four-inch paranoid with a doctorate from East Nowhere seriously, but like Socrates' gadfly, the little man wouldn't go away.

Lately, he had to admit, the gestalt of Truelove College, to say nothing of the ambience of Prince Rupert County, which he saw, when he was being polite, as the conservative navel of New York State, had produced an angst in him that he could not shake off. He saw his stance shifting as if he were standing on some existential quicksand. It seemed to reach its peak every Wednesday at ten o'clock during the visit of little Mr. Starr.

Mr. Starr strode in and came straight to the point, prepared for the airhead's "I don't knows" and his mean little "Nothing to report." Well, not this time, not this damned time. He paused before he sat down in his usual chair, looked Dean Withers straight in his weak, bespectacled, liberal eyes, and said, "Foreign connections and toilet paper."

He got out two manila folders from his briefcase and tried to slam them down on Dean Withers's disgusting modern desk, which looked like a petrified kidney, but the paper didn't slam very well. For a minute, from Dean Withers's astonished look, he thought he had caught the liberal son-of-a-bitch protecting his nest of libertines. Then he realized that for once he had no idea what he was talking about.

"Sleeves," he explained. Ever since he had gone on the crash course to the Farm, he had loved the language, and he used it whenever he could. Of course, he was still only an asset, but he had hopes in the night of becoming an agent. He read every thriller by Eric Ambler, and often when he walked down Main Street in Rupert, he was in Istanbul or Vienna. He usually got a lot of blowback from the airheads at Truelove, but now, with the evidence lying right there on the desk between them, he settled back in his chair and waited for the L.S.O.B. to stop staring at the folders as if they were snakes. He managed to wait out the Dean, who finally said, "Why do you call them sleeves?"

Mr. Starr had no intention of letting him in on the language. He picked up the first one. "Now," he said, "I took the names of all your professors who wore toilet paper armbands at your convocation." He managed to make the word sound like a mild sex orgy. "Most of them were . . ." He couldn't think of a word in the new language, so he just said, "Deadheads. But these two already had sleeves." It had been a triumph, two goodies.

It was time for the imperial "we."

"We," he began, "have decided to take you into our confidence. We will notice what action you take on this matter. You have a man here"—he settled back, reading what he already knew—"a Russian named Mischa . . ." He couldn't pronounce the Russian name, so he skipped it, "whose name was changed to Michel Ronsard, right? Right. Sorbonne. N.Y.U. Right? Right. We have evidence that while on sabbatical in Paris he took part in the Commie uprising in May of '68. We also have evidence that he has had sexual intercourse with a female student, which, as I need not point out to you, is moral turpitude." He waited.

Dean Withers sighed his Wednesday sigh. "Look—" He tried to be as patient as he would be with a student who was on the wrong track and needed guidance. "Michel's parents emigrated to France in 1914, for God's sake. They changed their name when they became French citizens. Michel is twenty-eight years old. He doesn't chase the girls here. They chase him. They like his accent and his looks. As for May '68, he told me all about that. He took croissants out to the barricades. He had a good time."

"Why," asked Mr. Starr, ready to make a note, "did his parents take a pseudonym?"

"Because they had an unpronounceable Russian Jewish name, I suppose."

"Ah!" The Cross pen bounced on Mr. Starr's notebook. "Jewish. Now. This next one is more serious. Much more serious. Teresa Cerrutti. This woman"—he leaned forward and tapped the manila folder—"is a real American. Her father is a high State Department official." The word "high" confused Dean Withers for a minute. In 1969 at Truelove it had another meaning.

"It has come to our attention that she has had close and continuing contact with known Russian agents and sympathizers since 1965." He had memorized all this so he could keep eye contact with the L.S.O.B., as an effective way to soften him up.

It was disconcerting, since Dean Withers was slightly walleyed in one eye when he was under stress and the eye continued to wander away from Mr. Starr's steely gaze. "In 1965, she and her then husband made these contacts near the Russian border through a Turkish family, one of whom"—he lost the thread for a minute, and tapped his finger on the manila folder until he found it again—"was a Russian citizen living in Azerbaijan. Also, they were friendly over the same period with a KGB agent in the same territory. All of this was filed at the time."

He leaned back again. "Since that time she has kept contact with one of the family members, who was in Paris and is known to have cohabited with an avowed Communist until she was transferred to Brussels."

"Have you been intercepting her mail?" Dean Withers asked in his sternest voice. He was a liberal who read the *New Republic*.

It gave Mr. Starr a chance to practice plausible denial, which pleased him. "Of course not. It is common knowledge. She doesn't keep things to herself." Then he waited in what he considered a meaningful way. "The rest of the information has been collated in the last year. Not only has she been in contact with this woman . . ." It had been his first practice in flaps and seals on Teresa's European mail and it had been fascinating, especially her mother's letters from Paris. They knew all sorts of interesting people, and he had been able to pass along some good gossip about the Paris Embassy. "She has taught anti-American propaganda by criticizing the decision of the Army Corps of Engineers to build a military highway of crucial importance." He had practiced all this language. "Further, and this is of great concern to you." He hesitated. He was on his own, but he didn't want to miss the chance to practice the technique of disinformation. After all, there was always plausible denial if you blew it. "It is rumored," he said, "that she has had a continuing liaison with a student of this college which has resulted in an abortion." Here he was on solid ground. "She entered the hospital on February 27. She was *secretive* about it."

Dean Withers was finally urged into speech. "First," he said, "Mrs. Cerrutti has been ill and in the hospital with what I am informed was a D & C."

"Unhunh," said Mr. Starr in a meaningful way.

"Second. We have every confidence in her relationships with her students. Third. Michel Ronsard is an American citizen who is very conscious that it is against the law to take part in foreign politics. He took the croissants to his little sister, who had been out all night in the riots, because his mother told him to." Michel had told him this as a funny story. He had translated his mother's orders: "Mischa, she should eat something."

"Ah! His sister." Mr. Starr made an elaborate note, G.B.A., his shorthand for guilt by association. "I think that's all for now. I will be back next week," he said as ominously as a small man could. He gathered the manila folders and put them in his briefcase, which had borne the initials O.S.S. ever since he had, well, not changed, but modified his name from Herman Samuel Starr to Ormand Stuart Starr. He had explained to his wife that Ormand was Irish for Herman, which she didn't believe, and that Stuart was a family name. It was when he was reading Ian Fleming that he got the idea. He loved the new initials. He called himself O. Stuart Starr to anyone who hadn't known him all his life.

His wife only said, "Which of you by taking thought can add one cubit unto his stature?" which was unfortunate, since he was only five feet four, but very muscular. He lifted weights at the police gym with his pals. He let the remark pass, since she was a strict Methodist and often quoted the Bible without thinking.

When Teresa came into the Dean's office, she said, "What was that odd little man doing here? He told me he was a health-insurance adjuster when he came to see me last week.

He asked the oddest questions. One of them was did I like to be hung up by my heels and whipped. I decided he was a sex maniac and asked him to leave."

"Well, yes . . ." Dean Withers wasn't paying any attention. As he later described it to his wife, confidentially, he made that clear, a wave of tenderness came over him for that poor lonely tempted widow that made him blush, and his eye swiveled so badly he had to close it. "Not that I *believed* she had had to go through an abortion," he confided, "but, well, you know." His wife did know. "Poor dear girl," she said, and headed for the telephone.

Teresa, who thought he was winking at her because she had mentioned sex, changed the subject quickly, took the plunge, and said, "Dean Withers, I want to resign."

"My poor child," he told her, exuding understanding, "there is no question of that. We are all adults here. This, too, will pass."

He could see a confession coming that he was truly loath to put the poor girl through, and while he didn't mind having a dialogue, he didn't want to engage in a confrontation, so he kept on talking. "I understand what you have been through and I deeply want to help. But you have to be practical. After all, you're up for tenure next year."

"I don't care." Teresa got a word in.

This iconoclasm shocked him beyond any sexual peccadillo, but he could see at once that if she was desperate enough to say such a terrible thing, it was time for practical advice.

"Why not," he said, thinking slowly, "take a leave of absence? That will be perfectly understood by your colleagues. After all, your trauma . . ."

"I am not in a trauma. I am making a decision about my life," Teresa told a newly green tree that was waving at her outside the window. "I want to sell my house and go to London." That seemed to her such a simple statement that she was surprised at any complication.

"Ah, London!" he said, forgetting himself in nostalgia. Then he pulled himself together. "I cannot allow you to take such a step without due consideration." He used the same phrase he used for bright underachievers who wanted to drop out and who had already turned on, especially those whose parents had entrusted them, and a large fee, to his care. "We," he went on, "can call it a leave of absence, unpaid of course, due to health. Take a year"—he felt expansive—"but by all means, hold on to your house. We can rent it for you. That way you will have some small income beyond your mortgage payments." He had always found that practical advice of this kind brought the most emotionally traumatized down to earth.

Since Teresa really didn't care, she agreed, to stop him talking.

Ever since the first one in the early morning in the Hudson Valley, Teresa's decisions had been very clear and unsurprising, which was a surprise in itself. She had thrown out, stored, saved, rejected, packed everything she still wanted, including the iron skillet, the salad bowl, the garlic press, and her much torn and stained Elizabeth David for the right kind of continuity, and rented her house. She had arranged with the bank for the mortgage payments, and for the extra two hundred dollars a month to be entered in an account at Barclays Bank in Piccadilly, where her father had told her always to bank when she was in London. "It's so near everything," he said. His peripheries, like most Americans', were Oxford Street, Bond Street, Green Park, and Park Lane. Then she wrote to her parents in the casual language they demanded of one another, saying that she was going to London.

She got to Durrants Hotel in George Street on the fifteenth of April, and slept and read detective novels for two days. Then she set out to find a place to live. The right place.

Her father had called from Paris when they got her letter, a transatlantic call that woke her at four o'clock in the morning. He liked to call at ten, Paris time, before he was too busy. He said, "I've alerted the Embassy. They'll help you find a place to live. Take advantage of that. London can be difficult," and then he used a phrase he had acquired from having spent five years in Grosvenor Square in the fifties: "Oh, before I ring off, your mother and I are delighted with your decision. We have always felt that your teaching was a dead end." By that he meant that there was no one they approved of to marry. They were both natural yentas. They had simply ignored Michael's existence, which had been one of the lies the marriage was based on, successful so long as she could keep him off the same continent.

"We're off to Cairo for a few days, and your mother is frantically packing for the great retirement at the end of the month, but we do want you to run over to Paris if there's time." She thought of Road Runner running across the English Channel and giggled in the darkness, and her father said, "There must be something wrong with this line. I can hear someone laughing," and she wanted to say, "Never mind, Dada, there's nobody in bed with me," but didn't. When she hung up there was a wave of disappointment, unnamed, that she told herself was her own fault. She hadn't told them about being near to death, and it was not to spare them. It was to keep from wasting precious time. She went back to sleep with the faint wish that they all liked one another more.

She tried for three days on her own before she succumbed to asking for help. The places she had seen were hopeless. There was not in any of them the sense of *déjà vu*, of already having lived there, that she knew she would find. The commercial secretary her father had told her to ask for was named Frank Proctor. She could hear her mother's mind buzzing from Paris, wondering who he was.

Yale. A parody of Yale. Upwardly mobile, downwardly sliding—whether Anglo-Saxon, Jew, Hispanic, or Arabic—there was a Yale mold they were fitted into like an iron maiden, and they came out Yale; the tie a little out of line but not too much, trousers a little too short, a rigorous casualness. Their faces all looked square, even Frank Proctor's, until she looked more closely, and it began to change. Tentatively, the smile faded; a boy peeked out behind Yale. Not, she thought, a very nice boy. He had been teased a lot and resented it still.

He wore a mustache like Stephen Crane's. His hands shook. She saw fatigue in his eyes that reminded her of the last photograph of Hemingway. They were sunken, without light, hopeless. He seemed to be fighting through whatever it was to pay attention to what she was saying, and she thought, He's been there, too, across the Styx, but I wonder if he knows it. Then, as he talked, she knew he didn't.

The grief, if that was it, was too personal, too childish, as if it had happened only to him and it was somehow unfair that he be chosen for it. That, the black monk told her, was why despair is a sin. There is in it no commonweal or commonwoe.

Frank Proctor was saying, "Regent's Park. Well, just north of it. Leased to a colleague. Um. Transferred so quickly he didn't have time." He stopped. "Sublet—cheap—to the right person." He sighed, then smiled, and she liked him. "Goddammit," he said, "it's a bargain." But he wouldn't look at her, just kept turning a ruler over and over and glancing at the clock. ". . . heard from your father. Glad to help." He put the ruler down carefully, foursquare on an open manila binder with her father's letter. She could see the handwriting and the seal that all through school and holidays and even Malakastan meant a letter from her father, from the mild, safe, green leather world she had always known, under the Great Seal, an American smell no matter what jungle you came out of. It made you hope for strength. She remembered it was the same in Izmir, the too quiet faces of the career boys. She could see in them her father, grown dim with discretion.

"That was thoughtful of you." She fell into the language.

"You don't have to take it." He got up and buttoned one button of his Brooks Brothers jacket, so new it didn't yet sit to his body.

He was leading her out into the glass lobby of the Embassy; the walk was easy, casual, and he was ready to take cover behind any one of the desks. "As a matter of fact," he was saying, "I live up there myself across the hall." He sounded shy, or ill at ease, or both. Something was out of place with the easy voice, the easy suit, the easy driving along Baker Street and into Regent's Park.

He seemed to go into a different gear, not only with the small English car up the Primrose Hill Road, but in himself as well, as if he had put off persuasion as long as he could. He pointed out the pubs—the Queen's, the Duchess of Athlone, the Prince Albert, the good greengrocer, the good cheese shop, the best Indian restaurant absolutely, he had tried them all. She knew what it meant.

London had caught him, that pride of neighborhood, an ease she remembered and had thought was part of adolescence, of the days being longer, time for coffee, time for the pub, time for tea, time to mosey along pushing a shopping cart, just time, even time for gray despair in February. She had longed for it. The chestnut trees were already lush and green, and the yellow daffodils, the shrubs, the weeping willows were still pale and clean along Prince Arthur Road. It seemed to be one great garden, tolerating the houses. Between them she could see Primrose Hill, and she let herself catch a glimpse of the Derebey, walking in his Savile Row suit, looking for angels.

For two days after she moved in, she walked the new peripheries to find out where she was. She went to the zoo, and to the top of Primrose Hill to look at St. Paul's in the dim distance, and then all the way through Regent's Park to the Nash terraces.

She stopped for a long time and stared at Stanhope Terrace and wondered which of the pinnacled houses behind the dirty white columns had been Noel's. The whole terrace had been deserted since the war, and only a Ministry of Work sign was there to show that anyone still considered it. It was raining the first day she saw it, and she stood there across the street in a raincoat and wondered why she thought she had done it before, a *déjà vu*, a strong one. She told herself it was because she had done too much in the three weeks since her new morning, and that she was still weak.

Dr. Dangle had told her that total recall—a stumbling into "I have been here before and done this and made this gesture"— was a sign of fatigue, and then that it was displacement due to something or other. In the rain she had forgotten. She had even forgotten what Noel had told her about the house. There was only faint sense of gold and champagne color and warmth, nothing else. The whole of Stanhope Terrace looked as if it had been rained on for too long.

She had looked for Noel, not the friend within her, but real Noel, every time she was in London, just lying on whatever hotel bed it was, studying the telephone directory; no Noel, no mother, the only Atherton it could have been, a doctor in Bayswater, N. David, nothing else. She even began to think of N. David as a friend, she had looked him up so often.

Something had happened to real Noel. She knew that, because when she asked her family they said he had dropped out of sight, and changed the subject and looked at each other, like they did when her father's brother who had been to prison for fraud was mentioned. The only thing she ever heard her father say about that was "Well, at least my damned brother hasn't done anything to louse up my security clearance."

She had long since learned not to ask. Finally, standing in front of what might or might not have been Noel's house, she came to a full stop. She saw herself as coming there to her first friend like a homing pigeon to a deserted cote. She stood there in the rain, sick with loneliness, and began to be afraid.

So she did the other thing she had always done in London: she retreated into the British Museum to think. She made the excuse to herself that she ought to do some useful research, but she knew all the time that she had gone there to wait. She had no idea what she was waiting for; she was harsh with herself. At least, she told herself, or the black monk told her, that was it, in a dream, that she might be waiting for a lover, and she looked around in the dream at the scholars and the scarecrows and said, "Here?" and laughed so hard in the dream that a thousand people looked up and said, Shhhhhh. They all had Michael's face, or at least when she woke up she remembered that some of them had; they looked interrupted. She told herself not to be a fool, that the last place in the world she would go for love was the British Museum.

She stood in the door of the Reading Room, lost, as she always was at first, under the great gilt dome. It was so quiet it could have been empty. Then she was conscious of the sound that was like no other she had ever heard in her life.

It was a carrier wave of the concentration of a thousand people in the isolated cells of their minds. She walked around the rim of the huge rotunda, past the encyclopedias, and began to hear separate sounds—a controlled cough, a page turning, a paper dropped, a chair moved, a pen scratched. Someone whispered hello to a friend in F.

She found B8 empty at the end of B under Folklore, and sank into the seat as if she had come home, and wondered where to start. She sat for three days, staring at the blue leather of the long desk, at the row of people sitting in B, too. She yawned at books she had read before. She was conscious of the smell of wood polish and damp clothes and books and book dust and people blowing their noses. She got used to the people around her, and on the way in, in the morning, she began to nod, but not speak. That, she knew, was taboo in the Reading Room.

She thought it was the most unchanging place she had ever known; she was sure it had been the same when Karl Marx and

Thackeray and Lenin and all the others worked there. There was the woman in the tallowed shorts who was reading Sanskrit; there were genealogists in lavender scarves; a Finnish scholar with a slightly pointed head sat beside her, translating Oscar Wilde; there was a thin man sitting in D8, his head always down over a jumble of books. She noticed him first because he looked like he had been ill, and then she noticed his totally still excitement. It reminded her of Michael. She noticed that when she paused at Natural History on her way to Folklore. He kept on passing by her seat on the way to Judaism, and she found him looking at her and then looking away when she caught him. It was nothing more. She could have sworn later that was all, but she knew it wasn't. It was part of the inevitability that had brought her to Natural History on the way to Folklore.

The basement canteen of the British Museum wasn't the right place for it to happen, and she told herself it wasn't the right time, but she couldn't help being more conscious of herself than she had been for so long. She sat, feeling ordained, at a dirty table, pleased with herself, aware of her hair, which she had taken to washing every night so it would gleam, and of looking neat and American, warming her hands around a cup of steeped tea and hoping that the long skirt she had chosen and her boots made the girls around her in their miniskirts look sexless and skimpy.

They shared a table accidentally, only she knew it wasn't, because she had seen him get up from D8 as she passed by. He followed her down the winding stair. They were elaborately casual, happening to meet. They moved carefully toward each other.

She confessed that she had noticed him, and once, when he was at the catalogues, had looked at his name, Ewen McLeod, a neat, square signature that she liked, and the pile of books he had left at D8. She thought he was working on a study of the Bible, since he kept consulting Judaism right over her head,

but he admitted, much later, that it was because he could watch
her there. At the time he said, no, vaguely, it was geology. He
didn't yet know her well enough to say any more. He wound
his long hands together and looked at the wall where the
Ministry of Health told him to eat more vegetables.

She thought at first that he looked tall as a bean pole and
way too thin—she used her grandmother's words—or like one
of those scarecrow scholars who haunted the Reading Room in
their dirty raincoats, only his clothes were so new, and she suddenly thought, but didn't say, Oh, God, he's gotten out of
jail. It was because of the clothes and because he looked so
pale. She made a joke of it; she said the ones in the dirty raincoats reminded her of flashers, and she had to explain that. It
wasn't his language.

He said no, it was because he had just come home from five
years in the Middle East, where he had been working for an oil
company, and he had taken a year off and saved his money to
travel the length of the Great Rift from the Taurus Mountains
to the Zambezi, only he hadn't gone all the way.

He said he would go back someday and then was so quiet she
sensed that she ought not to speak, that he might not even hear
her. After the blank wordlessness, deeper than stillness, when
he hardly seemed to know she was sitting there, he told her he
had caught malaria in Africa and lost two stone in weight.
He had bought his clothes two sizes too big because he planned
to gain his weight back and he saw no reason to buy twice. He
said he supposed it was because he was a Scot and had learned
to waste not, want not, and she said her grandmother said that,
too.

He confessed that he had looked at her books at B8 by Folklore, and had been afraid she was studying necromancy, since it
wouldn't be surprising in the BM with all those oddities, but
she said no, it was anthropology, an unfinished study she
thought was finished, and then added, "They never are, I
suppose."

They laughed at his clothes and because they were happy. They laughed at the mistakes they had made about each other.

Then, on the third day, over the empty cups, he began to tell her about sand, as if he were trusting her with a secret.

He started in the middle of a memory, and she found she had to get used to that, because when she asked questions it made him go quiet again, as if he didn't trust himself to say any more. "It wasn't until I ran aground in Mombasa with nothing to do, stuck there just waiting to get to the Olduvai Gorge and the Ngorongoro crater that I began to think about coming back, you know, coming back and seeing what it was like here. I think it was something like a turning point. People say they have them, don't they? It's a way of saying something, that's all. I only knew that with every muscle and in my soul, if I have one, I was sick and tired of seeing the world.

"God, I'd seen a lot of it, Saudi and the countries all the way from Syria to Mombasa, and I was homesick, only I wouldn't admit that, because there wasn't really any home to come back to." Then, with one of his abrupt changes of subject, he said, "Sand! All that bloody sand. That's when I knew I was going to write about sand someday. It's not a thing, an entity, it's a quality, a size. The stuff that gets in your teeth on picnics and in your drinks in Saudi can come from the ends of the earth, wind borne, water borne." He stopped, and apologized. "It's what my Fama, my grandmother, called a hobbyhorse with me. I had one, a hobbyhorse, I mean, an old one, hand-carved, that belonged to my father."

She knew that he had almost trusted her with the sand, and that there was love in trusting another person with your hobbyhorse, and that if she didn't speak he wouldn't trust anymore, so she said, "Tell me, about the sand."

When he told her, he was full of joy and anger somehow. He told her about its colors, its shapes, and its sizes. He described its kinds, hard and soft and round and jagged, red, black, pink, pale flesh, white, how long it took the water and the world and the wind and the fish to make it, how to read the colors, the sands of Saudi, sands of the Great Rift into Africa, reef sand, coral sand, sandstone from old oceans long since gone. He spoke of millions of years, of fish excreta, sand deep under the earth, the sands of time, the silica sand that was the graveyard of trillions of skeletons of radiolarians.

He repeated that word to be sure she understood, and when she smiled, he said, "I have a passion for it. That's what it is, a passion, a fast, strong current in the mind. I've seen all this, you see, miles of it and fragments of it. I can read the age of the world in sand." For a long time he said nothing, and then he said, "But even so, I have always envied the ease of people who live in morasses, the insouciance of it, the not giving a damn." The word made her think of Noel. She had been going to tell him about Noel, her first friend in England, when he said, as passionately as if he were talking about sand, "We've got to find a better place to have tea. This stuff is bloody awful."

They had both gone to the Reading Room to find a structure for their days in London in April of 1969, still wondering at low moments why they had come. So in the basement canteen they chose each other as if they were children to whom nothing had ever happened until that shock of being chosen when they least expected it. But they were careful.

Teresa was, and she knew he was, too, from the way he stepped back from abysses she didn't see. She had abysses of her own. They had already told each other so much, as people newly in love and not yet quite knowing it do, as if they must tell where they have come from to reach that miraculous place. But she knew in her soul that because they had let it happen that way, in that innocence of the canteen, it is the child who dies when love is betrayed. Infanticide is the nature of that sin. She had to protect herself and the child within her, the only one, she realized, that there would ever be, and thought, I have no right at all to offer this.

But still, from the magic point of the basement table—they

always chose the same one, with the dull plastic surface and the teacups and the dried dead buns—they closed in slowly toward each other; at least it seemed slow, from their separate, still unknown ways. They had been talking for four days.

They then, together, moved out, first around the museum. They stood in front of a predynastic skeleton called Mike in the Egyptian Room and told each other where they had been born, Teresa in Virginia when her mother had been sent back to stay with her grandmother so she would be born in America, and he in Ross and Cromarty. She wanted to ask which one. He was hearing things unsaid, too, by then, and answered, "It's a county in the vairy north of Scotland. I'll show you it sometime," not hearing himself speaking of a future.

In the room of the Elgin Marbles she told him about Michael and the high valley and the Derebey and Zephyr, and in the room where the Nimrod ivories were, she traced her finger along the glass above the tiny gold wire curls of the Negro ravished by the tiger among the lotus flowers of precious stones, and the tears ran down her face. He waited, and then touched her hand, and lifted it carefully and led her away without saying a word. At the wall of the Assyrian lion hunt he ran his hands along the flanks of the dying lioness as if he were blind.

Then beyond the museum they went to all the things they had wanted to see and put off because there wasn't anybody to see them with. And all the time they talked, and went into their separate silences, and talked again. They talked in the pubs. They talked in the National Gallery. They sat and watched the ravens on the grass at the Tower of London and made miraculous confessions. She told him about her cancer on a bench by the Serpentine, and he told her about his malaria in Kensington Gardens.

Teresa never remembered the towers of the Battersea Power Station across the Thames without being in Scotland as well.

"You see," he explained carefully as they walked along Mill-bank, "when you are born a Scot, a boy, and not the first-born, there is a thing you know right from the start. You see it in the hard granite, and in the braes, where only the heather grows. There is no room for you in Scotland. There is a place for you in the world, but you have to find it for yourself, and you have one ticket, your brains."

His voice was drowned by the rumble of an army lorry. "That's a Bedford lorry," he said, and then nothing more until they were walking up the steps of the Tate. In front of the Edvard Munch of the haunted girl, he told her about Fada, his grandfather.

"The only way out, laddie, is wi your God-given brains, he told me, and he had a great voice, trained by the pulpit; he said, You have brains and that's all in God's world. It's a fine inheritance. You get the scholarships and you go to the university. There's no a thing for you here but the kirk, and you don't have the calling. I think it's because your mother was Irish. Was, he said always, as if she were dead. You know, even at seventeen I still saw God calling to Fada from behind a tree, crooking his mighty finger. Fada said, Alas, God has not called ye. Ye must dree your ain weird.

"He let himself speak that way when Fama wasn't listening. She was firm about the language. When I would say no instead of not, she would say not, not, not. She would tell me it was all right about the vowels but not the dropped endings. She said aindings herself. She had been a teacher in Galspie up there among all that plutonic granite. I loved her face, och, I thought it was the most beautiful face, pink and white and brushed by the northern wind, and her eyes were blue as ice but never cold," he said, looking at the Munch but not seeing it. "She was soft, and she had a white halo of hair. You see, until I was, oh, three or four, I thought she was my mother."

They strolled through the first and second galleries, holding hands while Ewen talked.

"She and Fada had lost three sons in the war and one of them was my father, who was killed in the desert. It was just before I was born, and so I was a posthumous child. It was the first long word I ever learned. 'Posthumous' and 'transgression.' Transgraission," he said in the long gallery, imitating Fada.

They let the paintings pass them, intent on each other. "I can still feel the touch of her hand on my hair," he said. "We were sitting on the rug before the fire, my Uncle Gordie and me, and we were leaning against her chair, staring at the fire we allowed ourselves even in wartime for the warmth of it. Two feet away from the fire it was as cold as charity, for it was the December of 1945, the tenth of December, and it was my birthday. I was six years old that day. My Uncle Gordie was twelve and he rubbed it in. He said, Whatever else you are, you will never be as old as me, so I am always the leader, do you hear that?

"Fama had something on her mind. I always knew, for she let us stay up long past our bedtime, and her mind was on Gordie, her last wee one, she called him. I've known so many like my wee Gordie, she said that night. You can tell, you know. They have a way with them, right from the beginning. It is what was once called glamour, which meant magic, not what it means now. Charm maybe is a better word. Yes, I would say it's a better word. That night she told us about Ouida, who had been her favorite author before she married into the kirk. I remember every word, how her voice went all lilting, like it did when she wanted things to sound beautiful; he had a face like a girl but he could light his cigar without a traimor of the wrist while his adversairy lay dying among the rank red grasses, and then she added, as she did when she let herself say something like that, Oh, draidful nonsense. But she patted Gordie's head and called him her Deadly Dash. I remember I wanted to be Deadly Dash, too, and not have the only way opened to me to travel with my brains.

"We sat there that night of my birthday until it was one o'clock, and for once we didn't dare ask what the trouble was. When the telephone rang its three double burrs that were for us, she tumbled us both away from her legs and went to answer it and stop the noise. It's odd what you remember, isn't it? I hear her running along the stone floor of the hall.

"When she came back she seemed to have forgotten that we didn't already know. She was annoyed. One o'clock in the morning. No consideration that she had waked six households. That was your mother, she said to me. She said she would come on your birthday. She missed the bus in Inverness. Now to bed with you. She will come tomorrow.

"So I was sent to bed cold and wondering. I had only seen the pretty girl who was my mother three or maybe four times, and never away from the watchful eyes of Fada and Fama; they let fall remarks in front of me that made me afraid of her. She was nineteen when I was born and then she left me with Fada and Fama and went off and joined the WAAF. When she came back in uniform on leave she was always a stranger. I had a feeling even then that she was unwelcome, and her clothes itched my face.

"But that time when she came back she stayed longer and she wore pretty clothes, prettier than I had ever seen on a lady, a fine, light blue sweater and a real silk scarf all different colors she said she had been brought from Alexandria, and she told me where that was, in Africa. I could feel the softness when she hugged me. She kissed me on the forehead and left lipstick, and Gordie told me I had the mark of Cain. She seemed to like me, though, in spite of what they said. I could hear them arguing in the night all the way to my cold room.

"Every day she was there Gordie and I were sent out to play with a lunch packed by Fama. She was trying to act as if it was a holiday, but her mind was someplace else.

"We ran wild. I had always followed Gordie like a wee dog, and when he paid attention to me I wagged my wee tail. One day we sneaked down to where an Englishman had left his MG, the one who thought he owned the burn where we poached salmon. Gordie put the sugar in his petrol tank that Fama had given us for tea out of the ration. Gordie knew all sorts of things like that to do.

"We hid in the heather while the Englishman tried to start the motor, and lifted the bonnet and got red in the face and kicked the tires, and we held our breath to keep from laughing and only let ourselves roll around giggling and catching the giggles from each other when he had almost disappeared, walking the five miles to where his Sassenach house was.

"Gordie stopped laughing and his eyes went vacant and cold. He called the man a word we weren't supposed to know, and then yelled in the wind to the tiny figure down in the valley beyond the brae, I am the direct descendant of Donalbain, the King of Scotland, and Roderik Dhu and Bonnie Prince Charlie and the black Campbells of Argyll. God, there he was, the wee furious boy, and nobody but me to hear. Then he turned to me and said, And he is a low Sassenach, and you are half Irish. Fada and Fama will never let you go with her; it has to do with being a Christian. He called my mother the Irish bitch and said she had inveigled my father and now she wanted to get shut of us all. He said she was straining at the lead and wanted to take me with her into what Fada called a life of sin, which Gordie said only meant that she wanted to live in Glasgow.

"Then one afternoon we came back and my mother had gone, Fama said it was better that way. I tried to find her again when I went to Glasgow, but there was no way. So my mother is still a young girl in a blue sweater. Maybe she has long since died. I have no way of knowing. All I remember is the silk and the soft sweater. Did I tell you my mother was Irish?"

Teresa nodded, and even her nod sent him into silence. They were in the last Turner room, the one full of northern light, and they walked slowly around in the white glow from the paintings.

"When I got the scholarship and went to Glasgow to be a geologist," Ewen told her in front of *Norham Castle, Sunrise,* "Fada said I could go anywhere in the world on that training even if I did have to get it in Glasgow, that Babylon of a city full of Irish Catholics. God, people do dreadful things to each other when they are sure they are right. That poor young girl, only floating around in a war, and running aground in that cold Eden that Gordie and I came out of, all unprepared, into the twentieth century."

It was in a pub a way up the Thames, when on a day that felt like summer they walked for miles along the towpath and watched the swans and crossed the river on the little ferries that were only dinghies, that she finally told him about her black monk, trusting him even with that and shocked at herself for doing it.

He said he had a real, living black monk for her. She thought he was making fun of her and then knew he wasn't. He had folded himself along a seat by the window like a praying mantis. His face was thin and dried by the sun and his eyes were brown, and he had let his hair grow into a Prince Valiant cap like everybody else in the King's Road. She knew he wouldn't reject or try to explain a vision that was such a secret, a thing like that, even though there was an edge of amusement, a little irony that brightened what he said as if he were hiding something too serious to speak about. She liked that, and she liked his long silences, and she couldn't believe she could be so happy and question so little. Back there where the Styx was, the black monk had taught her to accept gifts. She even told Ewen about crossing the Styx and how different her days were, and he said he had crossed, too, but didn't explain.

He didn't ask, and didn't invite, just said they were going to dinner in Dean Street, and she dressed up and got there a little late, playing the game of having a date. She even bought a rinse at the chemist that would lighten her hair.

He was sitting at a table in the Fleur d'Alsace with the most elegant black man she had ever seen, a priest with a white collar that shone against the blue-black of his face and the good cut of his black clothes, and when he stood to be introduced, he kept on going up and up. He was nearly seven feet tall; his face, high in the air above her in the candlelight, looked gentle and small, deceptively delicate. He was so slim he seemed to be waiting to move with the long, muscled grace of a distance runner, a messenger, she thought, ancient and tireless. He could have been one of those elongated carvings blackened by time that represent the prophets or the hours. It wasn't until he sat down again that the candlelight caught the tribal scars across his forehead, like lines of beads that imitated the creases of age and wisdom.

He was what Ewen had promised, a black monk, a real one, Father Pius Deng, S.J.

They ate pâté and roast beef, and Ewen ordered a bottle of Haut-Brion because it was expensive. It was, he said, a celebration. "I have two friends in London." He looked at them both, pleased.

He and Pius talked about Africa as if they had been on a holiday together. There were lacunae in their stories, as if she already knew, or they took most of it for granted somehow, or left shy spaces. It was almost as though they had made a resolution to skip over Africa lightly. They made a story to entertain her about an Indian tailor in Khartoum. "I knew," Pius said, "that I had better have a suit made there. The Indian tailor called it my holy clothes. I knew I would never find trousers off the rack that were long enough in London, and besides, I had come out of the jungle from the mission in rags, and I knew better than to arrive at Heathrow looking like that, even if my passport had said I was the Pope." His voice was like a drum, deep and resonant; it was full of amusement. What jungle and what mission he didn't say.

But he told her all about being born a Dinka in the south of the Sudan, and how his birth name was Majok Deng, from the color of his pet bullock. He said, "You are an anthropologist, Ewen tells me, so this might interest you. But, you know, it was changed so long ago that I seldom think about it anymore. For thirty years I have been Pius Deng. It was chosen for me when I was thirteen and I received the water of God at the mission school. Now the names are the same. Deng is the Dinka word for deity and Pius means holy. What a burden for a boy! I think I always knew I would become a priest, but I did not really know, all the way through my head, until I had graduated from Catholic University in Washington, D.C. You see, it was there I realized that with all my training in the mission schools I was still damned ignorant, and so I decided to become a Jesuit and train to go back to the Sudan and start a school. That," he said, "was always my plan. Only I had forgotten it for a while.

"But first"—his smile glittered in the candlelight—"I had to run the gauntlet of Catholic University. I was a little piece of the Marshall Plan or the student exchange, I think they divided me between them. Now, you see, I was picked to be sent there because I am a natural linguist. Some people are. We can't help it. There I was, a big black boy, speaking ten languages"—he held up a finger for each language—"Dinka, Swahili, Bantu, Balese, Lingala, Arabic, English, French, Italian, Greek, and Latin. Oh, eleven. That's eleven, and after all that schooling I was as dumb as a rock.

"When I went to Catholic University, it was the first time I had ever seen the ocean, or a ship, or a city, or a bus, or streetlights at night, or a woman with clothes on." This made him roar with laughter, so that the somnolent restaurant quickened around them.

"The first essay I was asked to write was an analysis of Moby Dick. So I wrote about how he was either a god who dived to great depths in his own sphere and destroyed people who came to him, or he was the ghost of Ahab's enemy, who had put a curse on him. I told about how my grandfather had had a curse put on him by a woman he betrayed and she became a hyena. Then I compared him to the lion who travels in his own sphere and eats a man if he is the ghost of someone who has put a curse on him. I thought it was very learned, and then my Jesuit teacher and I had a long talk and he sighed a lot."

When Pius laughed, a couple at the next table looked at him with special we-accept-black-men smiles. He whispered this to Ewen, and smiled back.

When they parted at the tube station, Pius said to her, "Look after my dear Ewen, Teresa. He has had a hard time." He leaned down and kissed her cheek, and then he was gone without saying any more. All evening he had treated her as if he had known her for a long time. When she said that to Ewen, he said it was a gift that Pius had.

They walked through Soho Square.

"I have two friends in London," Ewen said again out of one of his silences.

II

LONDON

Ewen and Pius had come such a long way together, sun to shade, red world to green, latitudes of space, longitudes of time. The British Airways plane had left Khartoum at noon where the sun beat the desert, had flown down a Nile as thin as a pencil line, across the Mediterranean, Europe lost under fog, and had arrived in the cold rain on the first Monday in April in 1969 ten hours later, eight o'clock at Heathrow.

For six years in the sun Ewen had remembered London as a green city, upthrusts of whitened towers of oolitic limestone, Jurassic, calcerous from skeletons, and he remembered colors as in an underwater city flashing red, buses, uniforms, bright signs, women remembered as wearing red, after the brown Cambrian shield of Scotland. It had been for him, with his first job, and a sense of his future assured, a free fall into the first week of his life when nobody knew his name except the Indian clerk at the Imperial Hotel in Earls Court.

While he was waiting to be sent to Saudi, only a word, an adventure in his mind, he walked all over London with his hands in his pockets, didn't know anybody, and didn't want to for once. He saw himself a marvel of a lad, handsome and lucky that week, and felt like a man singing. Then, as he strolled through streets whose names he knew, past red clay lines of houses of aged brick, into Westminster Cathedral, papist and rainbow-colored, around Trafalgar Square, along the Thames, the Strand, Fleet Street, to Ludgate Circus, St. Paul's, Tower Hill, the East India Dock, it was all his. That had been the nostalgia, something to dream about in the endless sand.

Now, after six years of heat and money saved, waiting for him at Barclay's Bank, after the sun at noon and Africa rolled out of sight below him, stripped of dignity and hope and two stone in weight, he stood with his only friend in London, at nine-thirty, when it was still twilight so far north on the globe, at the entrance of Victoria Air Terminal and watched the mild rain stain the high Victorian buildings across the road, and there was nothing left to say, nothing at all. The damp seeped through his light jacket and permeated his thin chest, and curled his hair. His canvas shoulder bag was heavy, even though it contained so little. He was concentrated on trying to keep from shivering, not wanting Pius to notice.

It was time to face the matter, after he had thought the unthinkable and found it so mundane; it was time to halt on his road to damnation, as Fada would have called it; it was time, at that pivot point in Buckingham Palace Road, late in the bitter, selfish, murderous century he had helped to make what it was, it was literally time to stop, stop cold and cleanse himself if he ever could. It was time to be still, strip down and listen. He prayed to shed, a watershed, what had gone before.

He was six feet tall, thirty years old, and sick as a dog. It made him, he was aware when he saw himself in the mirror of the men's room at Heathrow, a bit poetic-looking, and was ashamed of that too, being a puritan.

Pius, who stood beside him, at his own pivot point, was loath to commit himself to the street, much less the city, nignog city, the city of rain and cold in his bones and his soul, that had been his exile once and would be again, a city he had gone to from Washington nearly twenty years earlier in the naïve hope that in London there would be a place a black man could live, a promise fulfilled that he had heard all his life in the language, a heart of empire after the cold pink faces of people who looked through him in Washington as if he were his own ghost. He was the youngest of his father's children, a prince in his own tribe, a nigger in Washington, D.C., *ageeb* in Khartoum, nignog in London, and priest everywhere. He clung to that, as he clung to that old rugged cross till its burden at last he could lay down. That had been the first song he had learned in Washington, D.C., the first time he had been invited anywhere.

Pius stood there, poised and elegant, an *adheng*, a gentleman, and looked out at the rainy battlement of London and thought it *frigidus, lapideus, albus*, the white of death, shook the thought away as he would have shaken raindrops from his shoulders, and prepared himself, in a pause he hoped was prayer, to step out into the rain, a new duty and, above all, a friend to work with. When he thought of Paddy Ryan, his only real "mate" (as Paddy called it) in England, he felt a sense of warmth in the dim rain.

There was a glimpse of the long valley, the snow light at first dawn, the Gothic aerie of St. Beuno's in Wales, of a dark corridor of stone. It was after Mass. The wafer still clung to his dry mouth, and the greasy smell of bacon from the distant kitchen made him feel slightly sick. The cold wind and the snow light blew through him and he had to lean against the stone wall. He wondered, not for the first time, if he were really the ghost his father said he would be if he went off to a strange world and did not have children to keep his life. It was his ebb tide, his dark night of the soul, right there in the stone corridor in Wales, with the smell of bacon and snow.

The hand of an angel touched his shoulder and Paddy Ryan said, "You come along with me." The light was his grin and his accent had a tinge of the Isle of Dogs, where Pius had spent three years teaching in the dockyards, looking, when he was lonely, at the spaces of Greenwich Palace across the Thames, but that was London, its contrasts. He knew, as if he had gone along right beside Paddy Ryan, that his road from the East End of London had been as long in its way as his own road from the Sudan.

They walked along the corridor to breakfast together, and into a friendship where each led the other. Paddy took him to the dentist to get his bottom teeth replaced—they had been knocked out when he was initiated—and he led Paddy to Africa.

That had been the beginning of the long journey that ended for a while when Paddy had been sent back from the mission on the Congo at the death of Father Shannon, to take charge of Ogilvie House for African students, because he was a Londoner who knew Swahili. Now the journey was beginning again; Pius had been sent back to join him to help with the students, so that they would not be as lonely and lost as he had been when he first came to London.

A friendship that had started over ten years ago, but still the moment of its beginning was as new as standing in the entrance of the Victoria Air Terminal.

Aware again of Ewen beside him, he smiled and said, "It will be okay, all right?" But when he looked at Ewen he said, "I wish you would come with me and let Paddy put you up for the night."

"No," Ewen told him again. "No, I can't."

There wasn't really anything left to say. They had been so far and talked so much. They had seen, too, so much together, had been brothers that loved each other then, and now they were withdrawing from the terrible intimacy of circumstances, sad and relieved, reminding Pius of the death of old people. Pius held out his hand formally. His language, out of sadness, retreating into his priesthood. "You know where I am if you need me. You have the address and the telephone number," and he added, not knowing he was going to, "My son, oh, good grief!" and they both began to laugh, laughed hard, it was so crazy, and Pius said the last word, "You know where I will be," said again to be sure that Ewen had heard him. As close as if they held hands to jump into the water, dodging blind umbrellas, they moved into the street. Pius said, "Goodbye," but Ewen had already turned away. Pius watched him go toward the tube station through the still, pale, swimming streetlights.

The light on the water made Ewen's back chill with fear like an ague and he knew he was going to have to get into someplace where he could see all the walls in light, because it had been coming a long time and he was going to have to go through it as through a door and he had to hurry, hurry, oh, God, hurry, before it caught him in the street. He couldn't do it with Pius there, because Pius insisted on guiding him. He couldn't help that, he said, it was his job.

The chilling had begun again. He tried to stop a taxi but there was none empty in the rain. He just stood there wet and full of terror, and then turned quickly and walked down into the tube station at Victoria, trying to remember how to get to Earls Court without asking; he was afraid of his voice, what it would do. He remembered the place where he had stayed before and he trod through the thick terror into the dry light of the tube, even stopping to buy an *Evening Standard* to hide his face behind, ashamed of what was happening to him, and knowing Gordie would laugh, going toward the first place he had stayed in London just because he knew it was there, no other reason. He found a wall map that told him where to change, and it was coming fast, and he prayed he wouldn't pass out.

He sat in the tube and read the ads above the heads of two

girls who watched him blank-eyed and talked to each other in those brittle voices of the southern English, saying darling too often because they were quarreling. They both cradled violin cases like babies.

He was in the dark street again in the drabness of Earls Court and somehow he knew where to go. The canvas bag was leaden on his shoulder. He passed through and around all the voices and robes and drifts of languages getting smaller, farther away, like looking through a telescope backwards. It was the sign that it was coming, roaring toward him, he could hear the roaring. He managed to find the neon sign, IMPERIAL HOTEL, in front of the tall Victorian house. Its plaster was peeling and stained by rain. One step was still broken. The tiny figure at the desk recognized him in his singing voice: "Ah yes, you have been here. I never forget. A Scottish gentleman. We have now two Irish gentlemen," and Ewen was pleased to be remembered.

At last in Room 7, the narrow hall room above the sign that said a dim blue IMPERIAL HOTEL off and on, haloed by rain, growing brighter as the darkness came, at last he could pull the blind down, put his bag on a chair, and fall onto the thin mattress in his wet clothes. He knew he had to get up. Get up. He made himself move. It was so cold. He managed to hang his wet jacket in the cupboard, find a dry sweater, a dry shirt, dry underwear, everything else he had, and he stood before the mirror, where his image was gashed by silver streaks and, by habit, combed his wet hair. Carefully he held his foot up into the sink, washed it, and then the other, as he had learned to do in the Tropic of Cancer, the Crab. He made himself get into the bed and register the room as he would have a new terrain, because he knew he wouldn't be there for long and he wanted to recognize it when he came back.

The naked bulb over the bed with its long cord, the cheap chest with the mirror over it where a thousand imperial faces had watched themselves, the poor thin upholstery of the one chair placed carefully catty-cornered near the window, a failed coziness under an old floor lamp with a little scarred table beside it, the rug; he had to be sure about them all. He didn't know whether it was age or his own eyes that made it seem so faded, such poor, familiar poverty. But he had been in the room before. He remembered that. He had asked for it, No. 7, because it was familiar, and he needed that. But the first time it had been an excitement because he had never been in London before, never across the border.

Now full circle, he had come back to it carrying a burden and ready to go through it as he had seen Fama do, as she would an old trunk, throwing out what she didn't need anymore, but provident, always provident for what would come in handy later, and explaining every time that she was a Scot, after all.

He set up the perimeters of the room as they had set up camp, placed the guards of his mind around it, judged ten feet wide, fifteen feet long from the door to the window, where even through the blind he could see half of the blue signal flash off and on, IMPERIAL, IMPERIAL. He had inspected the cupboard and left the door open so he could see inside, and all he saw were the wet jacket he had bought in Khartoum and the wet shirt, and his trousers, thin pickings, just a coat upon a rack, that phrase from someplace. He made himself look under the bed for insects, crocodiles, hippos, mambas, and there were none there, not in Earls Court.

He lay down at last. His feet were very far away. He didn't dare reach up and turn out the light. He simply lay there, too long for the bed. He could feel his toes grip the thin brass columns as if the bed were going to toss him out like a boat turning over, and if it did he would fall, fall deep into the primordial slime of the floor.

At first he told himself, or tried to, that it was the noise of the street, only a floor below, the chitter-chatter, maybe Indians passing. But the chittering was stronger than a roar and screamed, filling the room, and God, he felt the cold sinking in all the way to the bone, and he reached out a worn arm to pull himself up a little off the flat pillow, pulled himself half sitting against the bed head, or the tree trunk, and his last thought before his soul sank into where he knew he would go was "I've lost two stone in weight in two months. I must begin to take care . . ." and then, "If I have to go back there I will be in control and it is not real and there is nothing to fear anymore. I am not dreaming. I am awake and reading this as it comes."

Read it. That was the way Derek used the word "read," all mixed up with his hippie slang. Do you read me, man, driving Helmut crazy when he talked like that. Someone was speaking in the room and he knew it was himself. "I have money for a year in Barclays Bank. I will go to the hospital tomorrow and then I will go to the British Museum and get a reader's ticket and I will begin." He said all this as if he were checking documents before a journey, which, God knows, he had done often enough. He told all of this to the naked bulb. The bulb was getting bigger, weighing him down like the fierce heat of the enemy at noon.

Then he was nearly asleep and he thought he had beaten it, taken the pills in time, even felt a little warmer, though he was lying in a bath of his own cold sweat when it hit, a rush, and he thought, I am going to hallucinate, and Derek said to Helmut, "Remember, it is not real," and the sound of laughter came through the wall, laughter trying to get into the room, that and the Beatles on someone's radio, but the heat was real, even though the sun was going down, and Pius said, "Promise me you will go to the hospital tomorrow," and he promised he would, to get rid of him, but then his Fada said, "Dree your ain weird, Ewen. Be a man." So there he was in Room 7 of the Imperial Hotel to do that first and he wanted no man alive and no nurse to see him do the terrible thing he had to do to wash himself clean.

The laughing was some animal out in the dark. "You'll dree the bugs," Gordie said, and he laughed, too. Ewen knew not to look toward Gordie's laughter. He knew who was sitting in the chair in the corner of Room 7 in the Imperial Hotel in Earls Court. It was Gordie, wee Uncle Gordie, not dead for a little while, as the Africans said of a man who was sick or asleep, but dead forever, as Pius's father and mother were. He could see Gordie, though, even with his eyes closed, stronger then, growing darker, heavier, water-logged, rolling over and over downstream under the brown water, over the cataracts, all the way to the sea. If he opened his eyes, there would be Gordie, smiling at him, not with him, with what was left of his red lips, his face half eaten by fish that left their blue scales where his cheeks had been, and dripping with weeds and muddy water on the thin rug.

Pelting rain on the canvas, and the *hee hee hee* of live things.

He said to himself, and to whatever was there, spoke clearly, it was necessary to speak clearly, his own voice like a lighted road, "Be specific, one fact after another," like steps, one foot in front of the other. Helmut had told him that, something like that anyway.

Pius sat by the narrow bed and waited for Ewen to wake up, not wanting to disturb him, because his sleep was peaceful and his face like a child's who has gone through dreams into the sweet sleep that comes before morning. He had thrown off the thin blanket and lay, his body open and spacious, his arms flung out. He sighed and turned again, opened his eyes to the sun that lay across the floor and gilded the brass bed.

"Where the bleeding hell?" He pulled himself up on his elbows. "Pius?"

"You have had a noisy night. The boys in the room behind you came in to see if they could help, and they found my address at Ogilvie House and my telephone number. They are good Irish Catholic boys. They called the priest instead of a doctor."

"Do you know where the bathroom is?" Ewen was as polite as if Pius were a stranger.

When he came back, shaved and awake, Pius had almost finished packing for him. "I am going to take you to the Hospital for Infectious Diseases. Paddy is with me. You see, we thought it would be a little difficult for the boys if I turned up alone." He laughed. "When we went to their room, there they were, two nice brothers from University College, Dublin, with their room all neat for the priest's visit, with their mother's antimacassars on the chairs and their clean shirts and their Sunday suits, as mild a couple of IRA boys with a mission as you could find. They said they thought you were being attacked, but when they came they saw that you were ill, and that whatever was attacking you was in a fever dream. I shouldn't have let you come here alone."

He sank back in the chair, holding Ewen's trousers. "There on the wall, if you please, was a small Cézanne. Paddy said, Now then, boys, what have you been up to, and he didn't wait for an answer, just grabbed a large plan of the National Gallery they had spread out on the table and shook it at them. Shame on you! That's what he said. Shame on you. You are to take this back at once."

"I don't like to go to hospital without a change of clothes." Ewen found himself sitting at the end of the bed.

"Afraid the Sisters will see you in your dirty knickers? To use your favorite word, don't be daft." He threw Ewen's trousers to him.

"Liam, I think he is the older, said, Oh, Father, we were only doing our duty. And Paddy said again, You are to take this back at once. Duty! What kind of duty is it to be a thief? Oh, my God, however will you get it back without being caught? You two are a trouble. Yes, Father, was all one of them said, and the other one looked at his feet. And what do you do when you're not robbing the National Gallery? Paddy asked them. We work in the Midland Bank, Father, Liam told him. Paddy said, I see, nice boys Monday to Friday, send money to your old mother, thieves on Saturday. We were on a mission, Liam told his feet."

The room was full of sun and people: two neat small brothers, Liam and Desmond, as chastened as only Jesuit-trained boys can be, their choirboy haircuts catching the sun shafts, and Pius's friend Paddy Ryan, coatless in an old black shirt and a frayed clerical collar. Both of the boys carried suitcases.

"Well, that's done." Paddy grinned. He had a large, flat parcel wrapped in newspaper under his arm. "Na then," he said. "You are all coming with us to Heaton Street, where we can keep an eye on you. Come away now. Who has money for a taxi?"

He waited until he had shut the glass between them and the taxi driver, and then said, "The brothers O'Neill here saw their Christian Irish duty as nicking a bit of the Lane Bequest from the English thieves and returning it to Ireland. An admirable sentiment, but a stupid way to do it. Do you know, they simply walked into the National Gallery, nicked the painting off the wall, and walked out with it. It's an impossible thing to do." He was riding on a jump seat, facing Pius and Ewen and one of the brothers. He leaned forward and banged him on the knee with his fists. "You could have been in quad for years."

They rode toward Victoria in that rare London sunlight after rain, not the brute light of only nineteen hours before, where the airfield floated in a heat mirage like a lake, but as gentle as if the sun blessed the stones.

They stopped in Heaton Street in front of one of the narrow white hotels, so like the others in the spacious street that only their names, and here and there window boxes and vines, broke their regimental lines. There was the Ritz Heaton next to the Victory; the Claridge had a blue door, the Cavanaugh a green one; the Plaza had a tree growing up from the areaway, the Earl of Warwick blue railings, blue steps, a blue door, and the spaces between the plaster Doric columns that supported the six-foot-wide portico had been filled with lattice, covered already with a veil of green leaves.

Paddy Ryan yelled through the narrow white hall of the Earl of Warwick and banged the bell. "Thomas! Thomas Green, where the devil are you!"

"Belt up, Father." A man, gnarled, bowlegged, flapping a dust rag, ran down the stairs. "Shut your mouth now, Father, you'll wake me guests."

"We want two rooms. A single and a double."

"Well, I'll see." Thomas Green went behind the desk and found his dignity by slowly, slowly turning the register around.

"Come on, Thomas, they can have Peter and Simon's rooms." Paddy drummed his fingers on the counter. "We put our overflow here," he explained to Pius, and to the two boys, their faces clear of guile before him, which he read as deeper guile.

"Oh, now, you don't. Na which will it be? Mass every morning or jail? We say Mass at six o'clock in the morning so all our boys can get to work on time. Thomas will show you where."

No answer.

"Mass or jail?"

"Mass." Desmond spoke for the first time.

It was for that morning the London of Ewen's nostalgia, the city set to catch the oblique and seldom sun that arches always south of it, where the white stones, the vistas, the statues, the gilt, the green parks, the red buses, and flowers wait below the sky-veiled reaches of every day, to be touched, caught, and remembered. On such days, the people lift their heads and look at one another, say good morning to strangers, and make love in the parks, sharing a light as bright as under water. He and Pius passed Buckingham Palace, drove down the Mall past the white Horse Guards, through the Admiralty Arch, by the National Gallery, and it was all turned toward the light, and even the Euston Road seemed to be brighter, as if the people going to work along it might know one another.

Neither of them spoke. They had waited for such mornings, when the sun would be a blessing and not a curse. They were enjoying what they had hoped for in the noon mirage in Khartoum. The silence was sweet and Ewen was enjoying watching the girls with their shiny long hair, and their long legs, their miniskirts like the tunics of principal boys in the pantomime.

St. Pancras floated, red and gilded, against the blue sky, more a fairy castle than any other place in London, a carved and pinnacled roofscape in the sun, which hid its trains, its smoke, and its dirt, so evident in rain.

"I wonder," Pius said, "how many people know that St. Pancras was a fourteen-year-old Roman martyr?"

It was finally midnight. Pius had seen Ewen into the Hospital for Infectious Diseases. Paddy had captured Liam and Desmond and housed them where he could keep an eye on them. They had comforted Mr. Mubatu, who had found out that his village wife, the one not recognized by the Church, was pregnant by another man. He had threatened several times to throw himself under a No. 11 bus. He had even picked the number. They had heard eight confessions from young postgraduate students who had long since run out of anything to say, but who thought confession was required of them, since they were living at Ogilvie House free.

They had settled Pius into his room, which had taken time, since there was not a bed in the house that was long enough. So they had gone to the ironmonger's and walked back along Heaton Street with a thick piece of 4 by 8 plywood slung between them, and had stuck two pillows at the end beyond the mattress.

They had gone to the Duke of Wellington for a pub lunch,

run a seminar on Christianity and African Symbolism, said Compline when the same seven young men had hurried home. Besides Mr. Mubatu, there was one from the post office; one from a No. 19 bus, who was planning to be Prime Minister when he finished his studies; one on a No. 16, who was a revolutionary from Uganda who kept a picture of Patrice Lumumba beside his crucifix; one on a No. 74, who was articled at the Inns of Court; a lamplighter who was a painter in the daytime; and one lucky one who had a job at the Victoria and Albert Museum. He was an art historian. They all were graduates of universities around the dead empire.

They had had a late dinner, so bad that Paddy had torn a strip off the cook, an ex-drunk convert he had rescued and now carried like the old man of the sea. They had made several decisions about the Cézanne, which was still propped in the corner behind a Virgin made of matchsticks by a Catholic convict who was serving a long term at Wormwood Scrubs. But after every decision Paddy had said, "It's not as simple as that," so Pius had finally given up.

Paddy kicked off his shoes and let his toes wiggle through the torn ends of his socks and thought of the good old days when nuns had done that sort of thing and then was ashamed of his thought.

Pius wore his old khaki shorts and a cardigan of Paddy's so small that the sleeves reached halfway down his forearms. He was bare-footed. He sat in an old overstuffed chair sprung to the bum of many a comforted suppliant. He was just beyond the soft light from a floor lamp made of chunks of faintly gilded plaster, which looked like it came from the tourist-class bar of the *Queen Mary*, which he remembered from when he had crossed the Atlantic in 1948. He hadn't said anything for a while. He was too contented. He was watching the patterns of the wallpaper, which volunteers had hung in 1951. It had once had pink-and-white Regency stripes, but now looked as if someone had whimpered down it. After some thought he stated very slowly, "I think that I am drunk."

"We are very hardworking and therefore I find it imperative that once in a while we relax," Father Ryan said as carefully.

Pius was completely happy for just that midnight time, with his best friend in England, safe for a little while, so at home he could almost feel his genes relax. They were keeping a ritual that they had kept together for, he was trying to count, six times. No, five. The last time Paddy had landed at Kinshasa the customs man had confiscated the brandy.

Between their two dirty slipcovered chairs sat an insanely carved table made by the same man who had made the Virgin. He had killed a white man who had called him a nignog, and when the judge asked him why he had become so violent after a good record, he said he had had enough.

On the table sat an old Sheffield tray someone had given Ogilvie House when the copper began to show, a fine silver coffee jug, two Crown Derby coffee cups, what Paddy called snob sugar from Fortnum & Mason, and an Imperial Quart of Rémy Martin Cognac V.S.O.P. Maison fondée 1724, or at least part of an Imperial Quart.

It was time for Paddy to apologize. He had done that before, both times in England. It was part of the ritual. Pius let the brandy snifter down gently on the table and leaned back out of the light pool to listen again, still wondering at a new ease he had found in Paddy, that, and a basking in the Cockney voice of his childhood and his old mum, as if he had thrown away the neutral sounds of his years of training like old clothes, but not the words.

"It's like this, mate." Paddy watched the brandy slide down his snifter slowly, speaking slowly, so as not to get to wherever he and the lovely amber drop were sliding to. "I am aware that it is faintly reprehensible, as me old mum would not say, but there it is, all me worldly goods on one tatty little tray, and I like it. I"—here he was careful—"inherit a propensity for nice things. All me mum ever wanted, she always said, was a little posh bit of the old Crown Derby. One day she come home from a trip up west to the Portobello Road Market and there it was for a shilling, a cup and saucer. It sat, now you've seen it, right beside the Virgin on the mantel, and on holidays she'd take it down, the cup of course, and drink from it. She said the bones in the china kept the tea hot. It was a scientific fact."

The drop had reached the bottom and Paddy took the snifter again. He'd waited a long time for Pius to come, so he could put his feet up and let down his hair, and have a natter with Pius, as he could with no one else, not even his director; that was too serious.

"I think," that deep rumble came out of the shadows, "that *stultus* is more correct. I know that Father Kolve prefers *insipiens*, but I have thought about this for a long time."

Pius was for a minute alone in the jungle clearing he had found beside a delicate creek, a place to meditate, and how many times there he had thought, I'll talk with Paddy about that. "It seems to me that the greater weight and danger is from the stultified mind and not so much the flighty, uncomprehending, insipid ..."

"You know, I did discuss it with my director once, liking the bone china and the crystal and all, and he said that I was indulging in coffee-cup sins. Coffee-cup sins. I like that. You know, all these are gifts from me bruvver. It's odd about me bruvver. Gifts to Mum and me and the Church and all. 'E feels left out of fings. Oh, it's a lovely time just now in London. You'll find it changed. Cast off the garments of shame at last, nobody ashamed of their accents or their"—here he had some problem with his tongue—"pro-cliv-ities. As for me, I found me raising invaluable and simply cast off the garment of posh. Me poor bruvver couldn't do it. 'E's older than I am. Been too long on the razzle. There 'e is, all successful, films and all, all that lovely lolly, out in the cold. 'E spent five thousand quid getting rid of 'is accent and now, poor bugger, 'e can't get it back. It's too late."

"In translation it says fool. The fool has said in his heart there is no God. But then they are corrupt . . . abominable works . . . I don't think that *insipiens*, simply *unknowing*, is strong enough." Pius sat, feeling as if he were holding the words in his two hands, weighing them, feeling their texture, one harsh, one soft and smooth. He had waited so long to talk to his friend about things that mattered to him. He had had four years of work without anyone to talk to from the inner core of his heart, no, not that. Core and heart were the same. He put down the words and picked up his glass again, and leaned forward into the light.

Paddy grinned. "You will find it changed. None of the old nasty. The men here notice it. You won't feel so exiled."

"Not to put too fine a point on it"—Pius used one of his favorite English phrases, one he could see, its shape, its honing—"in the country of the mind we are all exiles." That was when he realized that he was being portentous—portentous, unnatural, full of monsters, monsters in the dark at the periphery of light, breathing, whining, he knew then that he was as drunk as he knew Paddy was, and could be insulting him, who was exiled from the Isle of Dogs and trying to find his way back to the music of childhood's vowel sounds. He watched his friend, not wanting to disturb his new naïveté with the dark shadows in the corners that would rush to fill the room when they turned the light out. "The leopard," he said after all that thought, "does not change his spots."

Paddy digested this and thought about it. "There can," he finally came up with an answer, "be fewer leopards." That pleased them both. They promised each other one last small drink.

At one o'clock, having drunk together a quarter of a bottle of brandy and two glasses of milk with sugar, since they had to celebrate Mass together in five hours, they went slowly up the stairs, satisfied with their conversation, Pius certain that they had settled all the problems of the translation of the Fourteenth Psalm by St. Jerome and Paddy happy that his friend understood weaknesses that seemed too silly to be called sins.

Pius said his last prayer of the night. He prayed for the intercession of St. Joseph the Workman, spouse of the Holy Mother. He knew St. Joseph would understand that he prayed not to be too unhappy in London, where he had, when he was twenty-two, been so black. He asked that he be neither *stultus* nor *insipiens*, not a fool, not *fatuus*, not *insulsus*, above all, not *ineptus*, tasteless, silly, pedantic, absurd, tactless . . . well, un-English.

He ran down all the words toward sleep, his second night in London, knowing that when he got to sleep his father would come to remind him that he was a lord in his own country, to give him strength for the day.

In the abandoned office in the dark, the small Cézanne was left between the desk and the wall, still wrapped in newspaper, one of several things that Father Ryan had filed there to do something about when he knew what to do.

When Ewen remembered his week in the hospital later, he couldn't quite separate the memory from other hospitals. He had once been in the infirmary in Glasgow, twice in Saudi in the compound, and something of all of them in his mind crossed as lines cross, taking a fix on a map—it was a kind of peace, not a good one, but a sense of being caught, of giving in to what? White starch, a pain in his gut from medication, finding himself —that was in London—trying to please a very young intern, who looked at the wall as he told him what he had, ahem, trying, Ewen thought watching him, to be old.

"You have," he told the wall, "both falciparum and quartan malaria. The pyrexial we," the imperial we, "are giving you will cause some discomfort, abdominal pain, not to worry.

Shotgun treatment. You will be debilitated for several months. The falciparum is cyclical, twenty-four hours on, twenty-four hours off. Then the quartan attacks every four days . . . spores in your liver . . . several months . . . drink a lot . . . but no alcohol—none—you'll be put on chloroquine . . . feel terrible for a while, then pretty bloody for a long time. Not to worry. Give it time. There may be some retinal atrophy from the chloroquine. Not to worry. Temporary. Nasty stuff." He was turning toward the Indian with bilharzia in the next bed when he remembered to tell Ewen that he would have a problem with, ahem, performance for a while, not to worry. It would pass. Having warned Ewen in words he seemed to have just learned that he might well be temporarily impotent and slightly blind, he attacked bilharzia with more pleasure. "Fascinating disease," he told the Indian.

In the luxury of white sheets, and a discipline of days after what he had been through, Ewen found himself almost enjoying it. He could hear the dogs bark in the Veterinary College, and was afraid the sound would bring dreams. He was aware of trying to please nursie, be a good boy, caught, Please, sister, please, ma'am, please, mum, please. Half asleep, all asleep, half asleep. "It's the medication," the strong female fingers said, gripping his little skinny weak wrist.

There was an unspoken demand for cheerfulness. Anything else annoyed. Depression was caught and exposed. "It's the disease," the iron grip said. He never was able to remember a face, sweeping aside past sorrows that returned too easily to his weakened self. Once the Indian with bilharzia whispered, "She requires the medication of sexual intercourse to improve her temper and her figure."

Awake, finally, after some days—five, he thought—he planned with his eyes closed so he wouldn't be accused of being uncooperative, just asleep. He read, as if the words were already written, all about the sand of the Great Rift, its colors, its ages, its bones, its size, and all its dead, in a blue book of his mind with his name, he could see it, *Ewen Stuart McLeod*, in gold. No more hallucinations. Gordie stayed safely lodged in his day memory.

When Pius came to get him, he insisted on stopping at Aquascutum, where he bought a wool-lined mackintosh, two pairs of gray flannel trousers, a good Harris tweed jacket, all of which he got two sizes too large. He explained to the salesman and Pius that there was no use wasting money. He bought underwear and socks at Marks & Spencer, and then he piled the parcels on his bed at the Duke of Warwick and felt it was a new day.

He spent a week wandering around the wide white streets near Victoria Station, feeling silly in the mackintosh in 70-degree weather when the English around him were down to their shirt sleeves. He was cold, but less cold every day. So he walked around looking in windows, drinking ginger ale in the pubs, or lay on his bed behind the green vines of the Duke of Warwick, reading science fiction and waiting for strength. Every day he walked a little farther along Heaton Street into Warwick Way, then Buckingham Palace Road and, as the fear of passing out in the street receded, along Buckingham Gate to the palace, where he watched the Changing of the Guard, a scarecrow of a man searching for his health through the same streets he had owned six years before.

He took a No. 11 bus on a sunny morning and went to his mailing address, Barclays Bank in Piccadilly, which he had chosen because he liked its looks. It had reminded him of an Egypt he had yet to see, with its terra-cotta columns and its tessellated marble floor.

The young man at Inquiries lived with his mum and dad in Crouch End, but went to the King's Road every Friday and Saturday night in proper gear—red velvet and a ruffled shirt he had made himself. He looked at Ewen with some disdain. He prided himself that his collar and cuffs shone, his black bank suit fitted, and he could recognize any important customer

by the same signs. Ewen held on to the counter and hoped he
hadn't tried to come too far.

"I have an account here." He controlled his voice.

The young man thought he had been drinking.

"Ewen Stuart McLeod. A year ago I wrote and asked that
my mail be held here for my return."

With a sigh, the young man disappeared.

Ewen waited to find out if a year's work was safe while a
woman in butt-sprung tweeds behind him tapped her foot on
the marble floor.

"You should have warned us, Mr. McLeod!" The young man
came back. Respect and annoyance fought. He had looked up
Ewen's bank balance. "There are twenty-one cartons."

Ewen was so relieved that his head swam. Relief or chloroquine, what did it matter? A year's work was safe.

"They are very heavy." The young man's curiosity won over
his West-Endness. "What is in them?"

"Rocks." Ewen smiled. "I will call for them when I have a
place to live."

"We would require some notice . . . sir." The young man,
whose name was Bert, was called young man at the bank,
OurBert at home, and Toddles in the King's Road, because he
used the old West-Endy word "toddle" as in "toddle along."
The birds loved it. He had finally decided that six thousand
quid had earned the word "sir."

Ewen stood in the sun at noon in the rich street. Behind him
the woman said, "I am waiting."

The twenty-first of April was a date he could not forget,
because he woke up alive, really alive. He went to the British
Museum Reading Room for the first time to find the book on
sand and the book on the Great African Rift that he had not yet
written. He thought of his Reading Room ticket as a passport
to the blue leather with the gold words down the spine.

But on the way to the blue books, there was the angelic surprise. He needed to put it all into what he called perspective. What he was really doing was putting into words what he couldn't get out of his mind. After the first time they had tea together, he had to tell Pius about her. They met in Pius's neighborhood pub, and when Ewen began to talk about Teresa Cerrutti, very casually staring at his pint, the way he said the name made Pius smile.

When he said that of course he had faced the fact that nothing could ever come of it, because with what he had done he didn't deserve it, Pius said, "You puritan men. You wear your sins like medals."

That was before Pius met Teresa. Afterward he said, "Don't be a fool, Ewen. If God gives you hope, don't be arrogant about it."

But Ewen knew, for reasons that he couldn't tell even Pius, that it would have to be hope deferred for a long time.

Teresa and Ewen stepped slowly over the lace shadows of the laburnum that lined the long brick wall along Adelaide Road. It was in bud, a yellow mist in the last week of April. She glanced at him. He was looking at the line of trees. She needed to consider what she was doing. There was no guile. She was sure of that. She simply wanted him to see, the first time she showed him where she lived, how easy, how inevitable, that word again, inevitable, was the road from home to B8 and D8.

They had come out of the British Museum, past the record shops and the sleazy clothes, to Tottenham Court Road tube station, then through the tiled corridors of Chalk Farm station, like some unending passage in a public convenience, and out of its Byzantine arches into a neighborhood, a real place to live.

"You know," she told him, "when I saw it I thought, Here is a house I could die in. I have lived so many places. To live in for a while is easy. You put your fingerprints on whatever little oasis in the world is allotted you for a while, a dog rucking a rug into its bed. But a place to die in. Oh, how different. A sense that there will be time enough to do it well."

"That's a definition of luxury," he told himself, and let her hear. He hadn't said a word since they left the tube station. Below them as they crossed the great trestle over the railroad the reach of the sunken line was vast. Down to it, even there, they had made their gardens. "Look. All the trees. You know, window boxes and even gardens are for travelers. But trees. You mean to stay. It's a sign you mean to stay."

She touched his hand. "Do you like it?"

He spoke to the great space of the tracks. "What do I like? The way you dress. I like your hair and your wit and your legs. Your big sloppy bottomless shoulder bag with everything in it. I like the fact that the sun feels benign and that the greengrocer has Jaffa oranges and Smyrna figs. I must also get inside and take a pill, because I am beginning to shiver."

They walked on faster through Tuckertell Mews, a shortcut, she told him. She went on talking so he would concentrate on her voice and hold the attack at bay until he got inside. She had seen the urgency before, the fear of falling in public, once in Kew Gardens, once at the Victoria and Albert Museum.

"Mr. Evans-Thomas says it's called Tuckertell Mews after an eighteenth-century town crier in Primrose Hill who was known as a great gossip, an unsung Pepys, an eighteenth-century yenta. You can see rows of eighteenth-century houses here that were the village before what he calls the Prince Albert connections. Mr. Evans-Thomas knows things like that."

They passed the dead-red church of St. Dunstan. "Mr. Evans-Thomas calls him St. Dunstan the Twit. Are you all right? He says it's just the right saint for a section of London full of civil servants." They walked on faster.

"Is it far?" They were in an avenue of trees already heavy with green, along Prince Albert Road, where behind the gardens of the high brick houses to their left there was a presence of Primrose Hill. "No. Look . . ."

A semicircle of pavement off the main street was marked Battestin Crescent. The carriage entry was only a few feet from Prince Albert Road, a gesture of privacy. Once there had been a chain across it, but only the stone lions were left. Small and pert, they sat as upright as dogs begging, with iron rings in their mouths, their bodies stained with grime from the prevailing wind. Behind the semicircle, three monumental houses faced south. They were dark red brick, marbled, mullioned, thrusting out glass oriels where the leaves of indoor plants were like flat green hands plastered on glass to catch the light. Their high gables cut the sky. Someone had put a bright Japanese fan on a window. At the roof of the central house a circular room beside the right-hand, Blenheim-style gable was topped with a blue tin Eastern bubble with a high red tin hat, an Arabian Nights' amusement. There were two gabled and windowed façades in the central house. The flanking houses had only one, as if the center had split and spawned.

Ewen stood stock-still, shiver and all. He was for a minute in Inverness, the city he had yearned for when he was a child and where he was taken so seldom. It was the way a city was supposed to be, the Jacobean façades with their high sky thrusts of gables, the river, the castle where Fada picked out where Ewen's four clans stood at Culloden, and white linen napkins in the hotel dining room.

A pink Italian marble portal with a double scroll over it that held a coat of arms framed the heavy oak door, nailed with brass. Along the only flat surface above the door there was a banner of terra-cotta tiles with leaves, flowers, the date of 1896, and shy among the foliage a series of initials shaped like vines. It was all in the pink and brown that was the color of evening sunlight.

He had only a glimpse of a lush garden along a paved path

between the houses and a gray flannel behind upended among the roses. Teresa pushed open the heavy door with her shoulder.

In the entry, on a marble-topped table that had been too big to move when the house was made into flats, there were six neat piles of mail and a huge vase of narcissi, daffodils, and early tulips that scented the hall. Teresa took one of the piles of mail without stopping. He followed her to the stairs in the paneled main hall. All the way up, three floors beyond them, rose a stained-glass window. The sun to the west cast prisms of blue and red and yellow over the heavy oak stairway from the glass names of Bach, Beethoven, and Brahms, three great B's in primary colors in a glass riot of nymphs, lyres, and blossoms. On the newel post a large bronze virgin held a lamp.

Teresa was talking over her shoulder as she climbed the stairs, leading him: ". . . a Lancelot hallway. That's what she used to call it. The only real home. I guess that's why it seems so safe. My grandmother's. Daddy called it Banker's Gothic. He said it was an excrescence. I thought it was wonderful. All the fairy tales and the longings for things . . ."

Two doors on the first floor faced each other. "That's Frank Proctor's . . ." She was almost running the last few steps to the right-hand door, where she had pinned her name over the bell, and she unlocked the door, and he knew that sometime he would stay there, too, but not for a long time.

Two weeks later on the twelfth of May, Ewen moved in with twenty-one boxes of stones, all labeled. They hired a moving van with a taciturn driver who sat in the cab in Piccadilly ignoring the traffic. They lifted the boxes themselves from the bank trolley, boxes from Turkey, Lebanon, Syria, Israel, Jordan, and one from Mombasa.

Ewen had insisted on a sensible discussion about who would pay what. He said they had to be practical. She persuaded him that there was no use waiting any longer, even though they couldn't make love because she wasn't well enough yet and neither was he. In the long evenings they strolled past the couplings on Primrose Hill in the sensual summer light and were amused, they had to be, at their own celibacy. They shopped together, picking out vegetables and fruit by their colors and Stilton and Cheshire and Wensleydale cheese. They went to the Queen and the Duke of Clarence and the Prince Albert, the Prince Arthur, and the red velvet Duchess of Athlone, which had slipped for some reason in among Victoria's royal family pubs.

It still made him smile, after all his worry, how little it mattered about sex, and how much. In a world where trust was sexual, he saw theirs as the opposite, a mutual sensuous understanding that sometimes made him tremble with surprise at trusting any other human being enough to cry or sleep or even consider glimpses of being committed enough to die or escort dying, its disintegration.

On a Sunday afternoon, the twenty-fifth of May, he lay on their bed with the Sunday papers around him and watched her dark profile against the light of the window. She had turned her head a little so the rainy light made her hair silver and she was staring between the opposite roofs at Primrose Hill.

She sat on the wide windowsill, her knees up to cradle the phone. She had been trying for an hour to reach Brussels through what the operator had told her was an "extremely delicate system." She told the phone, "Sorry," covered it, and said to him, "Why do the English always sound so annoyed?" and gazed out the window again. Finally, "Zephyr! It's Teresa," and she said nothing for a long time. "No, I'm living in London. Primrose Hill. Where Blake saw the angels. Remember Baba telling us about coming here to find the angels? No. It's raining." The London soft rain caressed the window, making a twilight in the middle of the day. Ewen could feel it in his bones. "But I did see a little girl under a Morton's Salt umbrella, looking for something with the concentration that adults lose and I am finding again. Morton's Salt, I said." A fly buzz of an answer, a long one. Ewen liked to hear her talk that way, slipping in and out of information, listening, gazing, first at the roofs across the road, and then at him, and then at nothing, seeing someplace else in what Fama called the "mind's eye."

"It's a house, late-Victorian, early transitional tradesman's ducal, a hint of Blenheim with William Morris touches. It's huge. It's been turned into flats. Fifties mod cons. It's got those fireplaces made of marble that looks like potted meat and old purple and blue wallpaper, and high ceilings and heavy dark wooden pilasters and woodwork. I think we have the old parlor and half of the library and the ladies' withdrawing room. Twenty quid a week. I couldn't believe it. No. The Embassy found it for me. No, furnished." A pause. "I know you do. You are? I'll find out." A bee buzz for a long time. "I don't think so. It's full just now. There's Mr. Pizz on the top left, who is having an affair, all furtive and English. Across from him there is Abdul Selim, who is an Indian doctor and very handsome and an Urdu poet and doesn't trust Europeans." Long silence. "Of course. You know the type. If you invite them to dinner they think you are trying to take over Afghanistan. Then there's us and somebody from the Embassy across the hall. Mr. Beverly Evans-Thomas on the right ground floor, and across from him, maybe that's a possibility, there is a couple who are unhappily married and go around with their shoulders hunched telling everybody about it. They might move out and split up, but they can't afford it yet. So that's it." Another long silence.

"It's near enough the zoo so that at night, when the wind is to the southeast and strong enough to nerve-rack the animals, you can hear the lions roar and the elephants grumble. The wind reminds them, I think . . ."

Nerve-rack, rack and ruin. He suffered that. He felt it as exposed wire, stripped of insulation; tangled, singing messages he did not want to hear.

She caught the sound of it, and smiled over the telephone, and then went on watching him while she listened. Then she laughed and said, "I'll tell you when you come. *Gulé gulé.*" She put the phone down and came over to stand near him.

"She's coming to London. She's been through her Paris lover and her Brussels lover, poor Zephyr." She moved the Sunday papers aside and lay down beside him. I'm gathering a family, she thought. She lay very still, with her feet straight out.

They were late the next morning going to the British Museum. They rushed together down the wide stairs just as Frank Proctor came out of his door with his garbage.

Frank Proctor felt like a shit when he saw them—well, her. He didn't give a damn about the fellow she had picked up in the British Museum, of all places, and her a diplomat's daughter, whatever her political naïveté. There she was, flying down the stairs like a Pepsi ad, with her lovely yellow hair streaming, yes, streaming behind her against the stained-glass window that was alive with the morning sun. Oh, God, all those dreams about American girls like that, and there he was, for Christ sake, standing there with his weekend garbage.

Not that she would look at him anyway, except with that annoying friendliness. He'd had his chance and hadn't been able to do anything about it, not with things the way they were. In view of the circumstances, how the hell could he?

He started to scuttle back inside his door, but his bottles clanked, and that was when she looked up and called, "Good morning." She had a wonderful voice. That fellow Ewen was behind her, and he nodded, the son-of-a-bitch, he could kill him, and there he was, standing in the door with his damned garbage, knowing what he knew.

He felt like a shit a lot, the things he had to do that he hadn't bargained for and the people he had to please. He just had to hang on, he told himself, until he was a GS12 and then he wouldn't have to do any dirty work, just sit in an office and pretend half the time to be somebody else. What he did as a GS10 was about like the IRS when he thought about it. It was a far cry from being in the front line of the war against Communism like he'd thought it would be, and had told his mother, although he hadn't, of course, told her what department he was in. She had guessed anyway.

Here he was, only eight years later, his nerves so fucked-up the garbage bag shook, conducting some stupid intermittent surveillance on two people he wanted to get away from, just because his fucking fancy-ass boss was a paranoid drunk who thought everybody who could read and write was a goddamn Commie.

He had to do it. He had to add insult to injury by falling for Teresa, and he couldn't get her out of his mind long enough to empty the garbage. There he stood, acting like he was a junior in high school, when he had been trained to be so goddamn gung-ho controlled, objective, and cool, and he thought, in words, out loud, "There's something wrong. What am I reaching for?" He heard his own voice and looked around to be sure no one had caught him acting like such a jackass.

A rest, for God's sake; he had been sent to London for a rest. He found out after he got there it was where they sent the loonies. One week after he got there in '68, the Communist-inspired students had tried to rush the Embassy. He couldn't believe it, Grosvenor Square obscured by dark smoke from the smoke bombs, and the sound of rocks and dirt hitting the glass walls. God, he hadn't seen anything like that in Saigon, all the noise and Viet Cong flags in the trees, and the chanting.

It had been a dirty March day and when it was over the red paint flowed down the glass walls like blood, and the wind came in where the windows had been broken. It was all happening again like a nightmare. Yank, go home. Christ. Yank, go home, and he stood with his boss, not too near all that glass, and watched thousands, waves of thousands of faces that rose out of the smoke and noise and heard that crashing that meant things were out of control, windows breaking and horses neighing, and thought, Did I come all this way to meet them? It was like that John O'Hara book his mother had found no matter how well he hid it, *Appointment in Samarra.*

His boss kept saying, "I don't believe this. I don't believe this, after all we've done for them." Then the mounted police came, and the bastards, that was when they lost him, they had thrown marbles in the street, the poor horses. Why? Why were they so hated?

All that color, all the flags and the signs and the girls in their long stockings and their miniskirts and their flying hair, he had a thing about hair, and the boys with what his mother would have called page-boy bobs and she would have said they ought to be ashamed, and for a minute, he, Frank, was the one who was ashamed, because he wanted to be right out there with them. They were having a ball. He could hear the laughter. He wanted to go out and play with them, like he was still a little boy and his mother wouldn't let him because they weren't their kind of people and you had to be careful.

He wanted to call out to the world at large, well, at least to Primrose Hill, "Look, I'm just another guy. There are plenty of other guys in shitty jobs," but he didn't. He checked the dead bolt, and wanted to kick himself for having to do it again to be sure it was locked. He felt for the keys in his pocket, and trundled the garbage bag on down to the street to be sure not to miss the trash man, who might or might not come. You never could be sure in London. It was falling apart.

God, you couldn't be sure about anything. He had argued that the surveillance was a waste of time, and look what had happened. He'd only made himself do it to please his boss, well, not please, but shut him up. He was a damned national disgrace.

He'd let a man like that turn him into a government-sponsored, paid-by-the-taxpayers, fucking voyeur, and Christ, he had to admit, right there under the trees in Prince Albert

Road, relieved that he hadn't missed the trash man, that he had enjoyed it so far, the pain of it. Like last night. He had dropped off into sleep and was awakened by their laughter. He had turned on the machine, right by his bed, how symbolic can you get, but he couldn't get back to sleep. He just lay there, glad that at least they didn't make love to each other. After all, he wasn't some degenerate masochist. When he told his boss they didn't, well, you know, aware that he was defending Teresa's what his mother called rep, the asshole said, "See! I told you it was a cover. I mean, come on, Frank, what more do you need?"

It was the same thing every time he tried to point out how ridiculous the whole thing was, right from the beginning. Now, Jesus, what could he say?

It hadn't even been an eyes-only, just an urgent, and that was nothing. He'd thought it was funny, some cockamamie asset trying to make points by reporting some woman for wearing toilet paper on the sleeve of her academic gown, for God's sake. Of course, the abortion was bad characterwise, but that wasn't political. It just showed she might have proclivities toward the left. He would have said that putting it in the report was an invasion of privacy, but he reminded himself that he was better trained than that and that everything but everything was significant.

When he took the urgent to the boss he was in the middle of one of those cover phone calls that bored the shit out of him. He was saying, "My advice is to check it through the American customs." He always said that, or the World Bank, or the London branch of Chase Manhattan. He kept their phone numbers on his desk.

When he put down the phone he held his fingers across his mouth like he was going to spit something into his hand and just stared like he didn't for a minute know who Frank was. But he woke up when Frank showed him the telegram and he didn't laugh. He said, "You see, I told you. Watch the professors, especially the ones who have lived and worked abroad. A bunch of pinko intellectuals." He was always trying to educate Frank, as if he hadn't had plenty of experience of his own.

Even before he had seen her and her yellow hair, Frank defended her. He pointed out that, after all, she was the daughter of a career diplomat.

"Hah!" his boss said, he really did. H-A-H. "Traitors to their class." Frank remembered his mother saying that about Roosevelt, even after he was dead.

So when the letter came from Teresa's father it all fitted in, and he was put onto a job he didn't believe in for a minute and said so, but he had done it anyway.

They owned the flat already, but they had had to stop using it for anything important because Mr. Evans-Thomas was always knocking on the door and demanding two and six for expenses to keep the damned lawn in order from people who couldn't speak English. His mother would have called Mr. Evans-Thomas a Meddlesome Addie.

God, something in him must have known already. He believed in precognition but he never told anybody. The way he had tried to make the flat ideal for her, and fooled himself that he was using a lesson from Psych 2 at Yale, depending on the familiar for effect. He had been thorough. He'd gotten a run-down on her house in Prince Rupert County. He had kind of enjoyed it, finding a brass bed as nearly like hers as he could and putting it against the new wall that divided the old gallery that had run across the front of the second floor into two rooms, his bedroom and hers. If it hadn't been for the wall, their beds would have touched, head to head. They could have whispered in the night.

He told himself that it was something to do. He was bored and lonesome in London, and he still woke up from unsatisfactory sleep feeling slightly sick.

So he had hung the brass chandelier, and had carried the color television in at night and had one of their boys connect it so that Mr. Evans-Thomas wouldn't come around asking questions. They put the aerial where he wouldn't ever see it, not even Mr. Evans-Thomas, that old woman. A great touch, he thought, was the Rothko poster on the kitchen wall, not the living-room. That, he decided, would be too much. It did look nice in the kitchen, though. It kind of reflected the flowers outside in Mr. Evans-Thomas's garden.

He had done it all within a week after the letter arrived. They knew she would turn up sooner or later. His boss said they always did. Who the hell was they that time?

He made himself resist putting anything Turkish into the flat, though he was very tempted, knowing her Turkish connection. He had spent a two-week holiday in the little town of Ceramos on the Aegean coast in early May, and had brought back some beautiful stuff. He thought he ought to wait, though, until she came to his place, just casually; seeing the Turkish stuff would give him an easy handle.

He had gone to Turkey on the advice of one of the old overseas hands, who had told him, "If you want to get ahead in this racket, pick a Third World country where you really have some scope. Jesus, if it wasn't for the Third World we'd all be out in the street working for a living. Learn the language. Be ready when they need somebody."

So Frank had spent his first vacation outside of London casing the Middle East. Greece was no good. The big boys had tied that up. He would have liked Lebanon so he could improve his French and maybe rate the Embassy in Paris sometime. After all, he had read Proust in French; well, some of it, anyway.

Israel would have been great. All those biblical ruins on your time off. They were tied up, too, though. The Israelis knew everything, anyway. He thought of Iran, but there had already been so much agency activity there that the Iranian section in Washington was so full that guys who could speak Farsi were sitting at their desks in the hall.

So there was Turkey, and he fell in love with it. It was a revelation; friendly people just accepting you and calling you by your first name.

He waited to use all that with Teresa.

Teresa, Teresa, Teresa. He was a damned fool. He was glad he had let his mustache grow, and cut it so he would look kind of sad and slim-faced, like a picture he had seen of Stephen Crane. It looked really good for a mustache that was only a few months old. He didn't look so out of place in London, even if he couldn't let his hair grow. His boss said, "I don't want any of my boys looking like pinkos or faggots." He sounded like he was in command of a regiment and not just Frank.

He found himself bringing the thing up all the time, because it was on his mind when he told himself sensibly that if he could keep off the subject his boss would forget it. He had kept on trying to prove something.

Upstairs again and safe in his flat, he leaned against the door, and he could feel the sweat and the shame like heat. He told himself that there was nothing to be afraid of. It seemed funny, how the fear came later. Standing out there under the trees with the garbage he hadn't felt a thing.

He tried not to let anybody see that he was, well, not scared exactly, but wary, damned wary of garbage piled up, or bushes, Jesus, bushes were the worst, and trees, especially in May, all covered with leaves. The crazy thing was he had only heard about ambushes. He hadn't actually experienced them. Not that it wasn't possible. You heard things, and it was bad at night even after they cut down the trees in Saigon. You could hear your own footsteps following you in the empty streets, especially if you were stoned, and everybody was.

He had put himself through a cognitive process like any sensible man. He told himself he hadn't seen anything, hadn't done anything. My God, he hadn't been out of Saigon. He was nothing but a damned clerk. He just paid off the mercenaries and the Montagnards and made lists. Names on lists. He never saw a dead body. Just all those names.

The fear didn't come until he was safe in London. At the demonstration that day he had nearly freaked out in front of everybody. What the hell would a shrink call the fear of bushes and leaves and garbage and children?

He couldn't forgive Teresa and Ewen for helping to bring it all back. Even if he had hated what he had to do, he had felt them near all the time, almost intimate. After all, there was only that thin new wall between their bedrooms, and he could hear them talk and laugh and turn over and play music, and flush the toilet.

Once he dreamed that the wall had disappeared and he was standing right in there with them, but when he tried to go nearer there was glass between them. He couldn't see it. He could feel it. They were smiling at him. They didn't know the glass was there. In the dream they didn't know. They were innocent of the glass.

At least they had seemed that way. He had been so sure that he had persuaded his boss that intermittent surveillance was plenty and most of that was a waste of time, if not all of it, and his boss said, in that patient you-jackass way he had, "Most of our job is a waste of time, Frank, until it all comes together. Then and only then you see the pattern, the payoff."

He used Frank's name in a sentence only when he was fed up, then and the other times when he had that frightening change of personality that was the sure sign. Then he launched into one of those stories and Frank knew he was on it again. There were stories he told when he was on it and those he told when he was off it. He had orders to get him to Kensington and stay with him when he started, the security risk. Except for the stories starting, nobody would have dreamed. He was a genteel drunk, one of those who never lost his manners; they went all the way to the bone the son-of-a-bitch; he would say vicious things in that polite voice when he was on one, though. He called it cutting you down to size.

So Frank drove him out to his flat and stayed there with him all night and listened to the stories yet again, not touching a drop himself. He had had to do it about once a month since he had been posted to London. He was only a GS10 and his boss was a GS14, so what the hell could he do?

When he was on a bender everything that had happened to anybody had happened to him, only more so. He was the one who had driven Patrice Lumumba's body around in the trunk of his car after he had been terminated in Katanga, and he was the one who would have succeeded at the Bay of Pigs and he had gotten within that much of terminating Castro. He told about that in several different ways.

Frank couldn't understand why men like that stayed in sensitive jobs, and he could at the same time. After eight years he knew that permanent government organizations, especially his, were like those clubs at Yale he hadn't been asked to join because he went to high school in Antonia instead of one of those snob schools. He learned that you took care of your own, and his boss had been in the magic place for that, the OSS. He was forty-five years old and he had gone to fat like ex-athletes do. He just had to live every life he had ever touched. It was kind of pathetic. His wife had left him too.

He was burned out and he had lousy habits, but he had been to one of those goddamn schools and he'd been in the OSS and that was enough. When Frank was young he thought it was what college you went to but, boy, he sure had learned. College wasn't enough. It was what goddamn prep school, and he supposed that if he'd been at one of those he would have found out that it was some goddamn private grade school or some fancy-assed kindergarten, and there would always be that glass wall, all the way back to the womb.

He couldn't bring himself to go back into the living room the way he usually did, to drink his coffee while he rechecked the tape. It was a habit he had gotten into. It wasn't as if they could hear. He could see them already, waiting for the tube at Chalk Farm. Once he had gone with them, and ever since, he had followed them in his, well, not his mind, more his habit, or somewhere in his soul, way at the back of thought. He just knew where they were. He hated it.

He took the tape deck into the back dining room. He sat down at his dinner table and girded up his loins to listen.

He had started it as he usually did, just a quick check to satisfy himself that his boss was a fool, which was a good way to start the morning. He had hardly paid any attention at first, just let the tape run while he was making his breakfast. At places where they were just talking, it was all so familiar that he pushed the tape to Fast Forward as he passed the table. Teresa and Ewen's mid-Sunday degenerated into Chip 'n' Dale. Then there were long pauses. When he picked up speech again there it was, oh, there it was, no mistake. He reversed it while he poured his ritual second cup of coffee, and he sat with it and watched out the window where, down below, Mr. Evans-Thomas was cutting the grass with one of those hand lawn mowers that sounded like summers in Antonia when he was little. He hadn't been mistaken. Shit, there it was.

She was making the contact where his boss had told him she would, one of those Turkish Commie friends of hers from near the Russian border. It was the one who lived with the French Maoist in Paris. They were still trying to figure out her real political affiliation. His boss said she affiliated in bed. He seldom made jokes like that, not about Commies.

Frank felt a little shiver of something less than despair, but as empty, a kind of shit, I might have known this was the way it was, this is the way it is. He turned off the tape, finished his coffee, took his vitamins, brushed his teeth, used his floss, made a note to get flowers, soda, lemons, and cheese, because he always liked to be ready in case he invited somebody up to Primrose Hill for drinks, and emptied his garbage.

Finally he couldn't think of anything else to do. He sat back down at the table, very carefully pushed his half-finished jig-saw puzzle aside, wished he hadn't quit smoking, got his notebook ready, and, to the *brrr* of Mr. Evans-Thomas's lawn mower, turned the tape back on, low, so that he could hardly hear it himself. He didn't know why he did that and he usually liked to know why he did things.

He knew he would have to get a sleeve on her new friends, and thought, At least there are only two I have to check. Hell, I hate this. But you know, don't you, he told Mr. Evans-Thomas's back, that when there is one there are almost always more. It was like an ad for mouse exterminators. "Oh shit," he said then, aloud, and wrote down Ewen McLeod and Pius Deng, S.J.

He looked out the window. Mr. Evans-Thomas had missed a little bit, like a belt left in the grass, or a green snake. He tried to will him to go back, go ahead, look back. He did, and turned the lawn mower. Well, that was satisfying, anyway.

For some reason he put on his best sports jacket, the one he had bought at Burberry's on sale, to take the report to the Embassy and face his boss. All those things that he had said to the boss, all those defenses, crowded into his head all the way down the Prince Albert Road and past Lord's. In Baker Street he got caught in traffic, and just had to sit there and listen to himself say, "Look, if they were a couple of pinkos they wouldn't be so childish. I mean, well, I've been recording pillow fights. I mean, wouldn't they, you know, be colder and better organized?" He had, after all, read his Camus and his Sartre (in French).

"That is not"—his boss had paused significantly—"the way nice American women behave. Look, Frank"—here an elaborate sigh, as if he were having to say it again and again when it was the first time he had, well, that anyway—"I don't know how they do it in Antonia, but my wife and I played a lot of tennis together and got engaged at a country-club dance. We married in St. James's Episcopal Church, with six ushers and six bridesmaids we had known all our lives." He would bring up Antonia. Nothing wrong with that, but he made it sound, well . . . Frank didn't want to say. All the poor bastard had left was his snobbery.

"I remember," his boss told him once again, "when I told my wife we were posted to Caracas. She didn't even ask where it was. Can you beat that? She just said, When do we leave? Absolutely wonderful sport. We certainly never threw pillows. Oh, we argued sometimes about things. Any couple does. No. What more proof of pinko tendencies do you need? Living together without—you know—living together. Pillow fights! I mean . . ."

The traffic began to move him slowly and inexorably toward Grosvenor Square.

He remembered that after he told him about the pillows, when his boss was making him walk in Hyde Park with him; that was after he found out about the bushes, he went on worrying at it: "I want you to remember this, Frank. If you feel, well, deeply frustrated, there's nothing like a huge, thick, colored"— his voice was slow—"jigsaw puzzle. I tell you it has kept me from domestic disaster more than once. Oh, I fell from grace once when I was on my own the way we are now. It's not worth it. It made me feel uncomfortable and sort of, well, you know, furtive, so I stopped. Don't do it, Frank. Keep yourself pure. Anything else is a security risk."

He still couldn't admit to himself that his wife had left him. He explained too many times that she hadn't been able to come with him because her mother was ill and she was afraid her brother would grab everything. "She has some really valuable family things," he said, and then, a quarter of a mile later, ". . . so does my family."

Later—it felt like days but was only afternoon—after the "I told yous" and the patience, after they had a sleeve on McLeod and one on Pius Deng, the boss used that special slow, precise voice he saved for making you feel like a horse's ass.

"Well, Frank" was all he said. He had his hand spread across the cables and Teresa's dossier, like Teresa and Zephyr and the others were going to escape out of the glass wall into Grosvenor Square. "Well, Frank."

"Look." Frank was trying to be fair still. "Ewen seems to just have wandered around for a year without a job. A lot of guys are doing that these days, and he was studying. I mean, not a hippie, not like that." The boss smiled one of his how-dumb-can-you-be smiles. "And after all, Pius Deng is a Jesuit priest."

Then the boss blew up. "Look, you fucking asshole, the *Berrigans* are Jesuit priests!"

The evidence had piled up, oh, God, and up and up. Ogilvie House was a hotbed of African lefty politics. Father Ryan had been in the Grosvenor Square demonstration. By the time it was four o'clock, and he was spent by one shock of recognition after another (he'd always wondered what that meant), he wouldn't have been surprised at finding out that the whole of Battestin Crescent was one big cell, even Mr. Evans-Thomas.

It certainly looked like it when he got home and glanced out his kitchen window. They were all sitting in the garden below having drinks. Teresa must have felt him watching her. People did. She glanced up and saw him and waved, and went on talking to that fat, sexy woman in Number 2. It meant either that she sensed a pull between them or a connection, or that she suspected something.

The evening sun was touching her hair. She had bought one of those miniskirts. He started to open his mail to gain time, but he knew he was going to brave the terrible roses and the lilacs and laburnum to go and sit beside her in the garden.

Except for Mr. Pizz, who left his pound note in an envelope, everyone who lived at Battestin Crescent met in Mr. Evans-Thomas's groomed garden on the last evening of every month from April (on good days) to October (on good days). He insisted on it. After all, as he pointed out, the bit of ceremony made them feel as if they were a part of the garden, even though they didn't do anything but contribute their share of the expenses. They owed a pound each in the spring and the fall, but in winter, as Mr. Evans-Thomas pointed out to Teresa, it went down to two and six. "Autumn," he said, "is wildly dear these days, but I am careful."

But on the twentieth of May, as he pointed out in a series of neat notes left on the marble table in the hall, there was a special meeting if anyone cared to come.

"It is a lovely evening for the garden, and I want you to enjoy it." Then he added, "The motor of the lawn mower is broken—£1 each. Sorry it's so dear."

The garden was on a slight slope, down to a little level dell, so that the back of the house was a story higher than the front. Teresa lay in a newly painted lawn chair in flashes of light from the late sun, which made the great window blinding, as if she were looking into a too bright fire. It fell across the laburnum, which was beginning to shed its yellow blossoms on the lawn. It turned the red roses slightly orange. Ewen had explained to her how the evening spectrum of light changed colors, but she hadn't paid much attention. She preferred the mystery. With a hint of foreboding, which she thrust aside, she saw that that was a difference between them.

More than thinking, and less, she was existing in the fact that she didn't need to be solemn anymore, now that there was someone else, and how it was to love someone again at last, not a progression, but a state. She didn't have to do this or do that. She simply was, in the garden, in the afternoon. She went on watching as the light played on the flowers and the stained glass and Mr. Evans-Thomas's glasses as he leaned into it to make a point to Ewen while St. Dunstan's Anglo-Catholic bells sent the Angelus through the evening air.

She was listening and not listening while Mr. Evans-Thomas, in full spate, went on explaining something to Ewen. Men, she thought, would explain.

Penelope Stroud passed biscuits and Wensleydale cheese on a dark green Wedgwood plate with a design of leaves that she had picked up in the Portobello Road.

Mr. Evans-Thomas was saying, as he had to her on the last day of April, almost the same words: "Well, you see, I was jolly well on the doorstep in 1959, when the last Mr. Battestin died." She thought he must be the last person in England to say jolly well. "I should jolly well hope so, or not," depending on the stimulus, was his most habitual expression.

"Actually, he was Colonel Battestin, you see, red face, tight skin, you know the type. I had had my eye on it for some time. Provincial Regiment. Leicester? Leeds? I don't know. He was only seventy-one when he died." Mr. Evans-Thomas said this with deep disapproval. "I'm seventy, though you wouldn't know it. I keep fit. But he had been gassed in the First World War, at least that's what I was always told. He was frail and mean and never married.

"His sister Angelina was sheer delight. She was ecstatic when he finally popped off. They didn't get on at all. She was the youngest of eight children and became the only survivor. She lived in the next house, but of course she inherited from her brother, since he disliked his nieces and nephews even more than he did her. He had long since bought the freehold shares from the others."

Ewen looked beyond him, sensing that Teresa was watching, and smiled with her. Through the voice of Mr. Evans-Thomas, he was calculating how many pages he had to write a day to get one of the books done before his money ran low and he had to go off to another ungodly place. Looking at Teresa, resting like a lovely lizard in the seldom sun, he knew that love was, to him, a base where he could take off and return from the mind of his book, knowing it would be there. He prayed not to have to leave her too soon. He wished, faintly, that she would "find a new subject"; she seemed to have forgotten what she was working on. Then he felt disloyal.

Penelope Stroud, in her klaxon-Roedean voice, ignoring all, said, "Darling, I adore your dress. Aren't the clothes marvy?"

Her husband, Robin, who had just come out of their garden door to join the others, heard her and said, "Not on you, darling, you're far too pudgy." In anyone but an Englishman who was loudly about to divorce his wife, or let her divorce him, which was the done thing still, as he pointed out to whoever would listen, no matter how much else had changed, this would have been gratuitous cruelty. Penelope had a body the shape of a St. Trinian's pony and breasts that thin young actresses who played Doll Tearsheet at RADA had to make by stuffing their bodices with foam rubber. She ignored him until he said, "Darling, may I get you another drink?"

"Yes, darling, very small, I'm dining out. Oh, God," she said as he loped across the lawn. She threw herself into the lawn chair. The noise of her landing made Mr. Evans-Thomas look over with some annoyance.

"Darling, do be careful. I've just done those," he called out.

The Angelus had finished at the hour of our death, leaving with Teresa an afterglow of bells and prayer. She smiled, reminded, to think that it had been such a short time since the black monk had returned. Now that there was Pius, her black monk had his wonderful new voice. Noel had faded out of it almost completely. It wasn't that she didn't love the memory of him in her mind, it was just that she was too happy with the real people around her. When she thought of Noel, she heard his voice again, faintly. She could sense time shift, and shift back again, into the garden.

Penelope watched her husband walk across the grass again, balancing two glasses, with a pound note in his teeth. She muttered, "How can I bear it?" and began to eat the rest of the biscuits and cheese, one slow morose bite after another.

Dr. Abdul Selim came out of the French door onto the terrace a floor above them. He leaned his arms on the balustrade and called down, "Ah, a nest of Anglo-Saxon gentlefolk."

"Oh, hello, Abdul." Robin had managed to hand Penelope her drink and take the pound note out of his mouth. The exertion seemed to exhaust him. He leaned against the back of her chair as if he were too long to sustain himself upright without help. Having rested a second or two, he strolled back to Abdul, and called up to him. "You know better than that. One Scot, one Welshman, Penny's half Irish. I'm a quarter German, and God knows what the two Americans are. Polyglot, I would say. Look at the CIA fellow."

"Isn't he marvy?" Penelope sighed.

Abdul Selim was so beautiful that it was hard to look at him for fear of being caught staring. He was not posing; something in him that Teresa could recognize would have disdained to do that. He was, instead, poised at the balustrade, looking as elegant as Teresa sometimes felt. He wore a white shirt. His skin was like some very light expensive leather. His eyes reminded her of the Song of Solomon. He had slim hands, a perfect nose, a masculine delicacy, and a smile which she was sure he meant to be ironic but which she found sweet.

Robin leaned his six feet four against the garden door and gazed up. "You know, Abdul, I'm not a bugger, but if I were I should choose an Indian boy. You are the most marvelous-looking people. You make me realize what a large pink oaf I am."

Abdul walked down the stone stairs, but he talked, too, and the smile became a laugh. "All you upper-class Englishmen are buggers at heart, or whatever part of the anatomy you like to name." He trailed across the grass, with his pound note in one hand and his drink in the other, the ice tinkling so that he seemed to be his own acolyte leading him.

"Oh, Abdul, come and sit by me." Penelope's voice ripped the evening.

He seemed not to hear her. He gave his pound note to Mr. Evans-Thomas, who didn't stop the story he had gone on telling Ewen, just held out his hand.

Abdul Selim moved like a dancer into the lawn chair on the other side of Teresa. Penelope leaned across her and tried again. "I've been wanting to talk to you about the *Kamasutra*, Abdul." She seemed pleased at finding something to say.

"Mrs. Stroud, I am a Muslim." He put his drink down. "You are too ignorant to know that that is an insult to my religion, about which I care little. But I do know insult, and having been offended in my sex by your boob of a husband and in what is left of my religion—only, I assure you, a kind of pride—by you, I will go back up to my flat."

"No." Teresa caught his hand. "Please. I am determined to be friends." She was trying not to laugh at the spate of Empire insults.

"Why?" He was surprised. "Determined is an ugly word from a lovely woman. What do you want from me?"

"Nothing." She did not move her hand and she did not look at him. She was seeing someone else. "I just want to be friends. I think we have something in common." She looked at him, studied him. "You know how people become each other in your mind? You pass someone in the street and for a second they become your cousin or the President of the United States. Something like that happens when I see you. There is a young man and he is a stranger in London, and he walks on Primrose Hill every year, getting older and older, looking for something he never finds, and then he dies. I knew him when he was an old man, a prince in his own country, but when I look at you, I see him young."

"Who was he?" Abdul Selim asked the first question that was not self-protective.

"A Kurd. A Yezidi." Silence in the garden. A breeze shifted the laburnum blossoms.

The voice of Beverly Evans-Thomas, who had picked up

Robin Stroud's remark, rang through the evening. "I don't know why Englishmen always have to explain that they are not homosexual. But we do it, all the time. Take me. I do it. I do it because I have never married. I am what used to be called an inveterate bachelor. I don't like marriage." He sounded petulant. "People who are married always have to discuss things. All those voices, a chorus of marital discussion. I saw it in my parents. I quite liked my parents on the whole, but they would discuss things, and if they didn't, one of them pouted and ruined dinner. Silence. The wrong kind. They discussed everything from the existence of God to driving a nail. Now, when I want to drive a nail or hang a picture or go off to France, I want to *do* it, not discuss it. Then there is all that hair in the basin, gobs of it. I grew up in a Fabian household in Hampstead with tan walls and venous red woodwork. Picked out. Heel's Mod, sensible shoes, Alexander technique, and discussion. I've had three splendid mistresses who felt the same way I did. Well, they would, wouldn't they, or they wouldn't have been right. Then there's all that marketing and washing up and who will do it. My life is simple. *I* do it."

"Now, what would we have in common?" Abdul Selim was laughing at Teresa. "You are a white Anglo-Saxon. You own the world. Have you been ill-treated? Have you nearly died? Was this Yezidi of yours a persecuted man?" He was rude as some men are who stay too much alone and pride themselves on lurching straight at the heart of the matter. It was like academic manners.

"One question to answer yours." She was enjoying herself. "Why do you let us get by with it if you despise us so? Anglo-Saxons, I mean. Yes, I have nearly died, although it didn't seem like that. I had an operation for uterine cancer three months ago. So I know the black monk," she said, not caring if he misunderstood.

"Yes, I know him, too."

She thought it was because Abdul Selim was a doctor. "I have not been ill-treated that I know of, but I suspect that that is only luck. We are dancing this year, but sometimes I glimpse darkness ahead."

"So do I. Oh, my God, so do I." He leaned back in his chair. "Like this lovely evening in this garden, knowing night will come. Nobody believes us, you know. Most of us are refugees the English tolerate because they don't see us. God help us when they do."

Teresa called to Mr. Evans-Thomas, reminded, "Does anyone want to sublet a flat? I have a friend coming from Brussels."

Everybody looked at Penelope, but she said nothing.

"Let's see." Mr. Evans-Thomas set his face to thinking. "There is Mr. Pizz in Number 5. I have a feeling"—he lowered his voice—"that the affair is nearly over. He walks her downstairs in that sort of comforting way, you know, hand on her shoulder —'it's sad, my dear, but you must be brave' sort of gesture. She's all sunk in her coat collar."

Penelope interrupted him. "I don't know why you keep on calling him Mr. Pizz. I've told you it's Geoffrey Twigg. I went to dancing school with him and to Miss Pitpuck's nursery school."

"We're protecting his privacy. After all, he is in the government."

"Did he tell you that?" Her laugh was sharp. "He always was a bloody liar. He's one of those younger-son PRs for a fake film company in Mayfair. We used to send them to New York," she explained to Teresa, not dreaming she was being rude. "Now they're all in Mayfair as PRs. Youamericans like them."

Teresa had forgotten that for some years in England "Youamericans" had been one word.

"He probably thought he would be safe here," Mr. Evans-Thomas went on, paying no attention. "Like St. John's Wood used to be for mistresses. The sort of Tories who think that if you go north of Regent's Park you fall off."

"Don't you?" Penelope asked. When no one answered she

pulled herself up out of the low chair and went stumping across the lawn with her empty green plate in her hand, on her way to her evening quarrel with Robin. Teresa watched her sad, broad back. She looked small and vulnerable below the lacy French doors with their deceptively delicate-looking wrought-iron balconies all the way up to the top floor, where Mr. Pizz's and Abdul Selim's flats looked out over the treetops and the railway cut to Adelaide Road. The house, which was so dependable and noble in the front, was, on the garden side, as ephemeral as a summerhouse.

The roofscape seemed to ride the air, but that, as Mr. Evans-Thomas had gone back to explaining to Ewen, was because of the deceptive slope of the lawn. Ewen was listening still, and not minding. He found Mr. Evans-Thomas likable.

"Let me show you the garden." He willed Ewen to rise with him, and they began a slow walk around the herbaceous borders. "Now that"—he pointed up at the window of Teresa's and now Ewen's kitchen—"was Colonel Battestin's bathroom. Saved quite some money on the plumbing, don't you know, putting the kitchens there, in all the flats. It was my idea." They watched a string of garlic that hung beside a feathery green trailing plant. "I'm so glad someone is really *living* there. It's what they call a CIA safe house, you know. All sorts of odd people coming and going in the night, playing cloak and dagger, very disturbing to sleep, putting out the trash at the wrong time and owing back garden fees. *No* regard.

"That was his garden room, you know." He pointed to the French doors beside the kitchen window. "He kept watch from there so that Angelina wouldn't cross into his part of the garden. Jungle rather. They loathed each other. Angelina and I were dear friends.

"So! When he died and Angelina turned this house into flats to sell, you see, I was here, watching every move. My God, you should have seen it. Sixty-year-old wallpaper, as dark as a very elegant tomb, some of it's still in your flat. Can't think why the

CIA haven't spent the money to strip it. Their father spared, as they say, no expense. None. Marble, ten different kinds. Stained glass. Silk walls. Flock paper. Marvelous and terrible. Most of it had gone to ruin, and had to be stripped right down to the dry rot. So I got the pick of the flats, and of course I chose the right garden one, it's like living in a house, with its two floors. I detest the word 'duplex.' It's as bad as 'serviette.'

"I began work on the garden while they were still turfing trash, walls, woodwork, the lot, out of the house. I made them put it in the front. At first, will you believe it, I had to use a machete, a real one. That was, let me see, ten years ago. They come and go. They come and go."

He was silent for a little while. He bent down to pull a weed. "Angelina wouldn't come near it, she hated it so. You do it, darling, she would say, it's all yours. Do what you like. Keep or toss out.

"She had been a soubrette, quite a successful one. That was one of the reasons she didn't get on with her brother. Frankly, gin was another. He said she let the Battestin side down. She was known as the pocket Venus of London in her time. Then she put on a bit of weight and ran an avant-garde twenties theater for a while. She knew everybody. Sean O'Casey, Ezra Pound; oh, all sorts of people. The first one to do Edna St. Vincent Millay's *Aria da Capo* sort of thing. She used to lean out her window, full of gin, and shout, "Is it Tuesday, Columbine, I'll kiss you if it's Tuesday," at her brother sitting in his wheelchair in the jungle. Of course, by the time I knew her she was sixty and she looked like a lovely little winter apple. I adored her. You see to it, darling. I can still hear her.

"Of course she was a bit of history by then herself. Kept her house over there like a twenties set. I can't tell you. The peacock feathers, the French dolls, the Spanish galleons, Art Nouveau all over the place. A couple of Modiglianis.

"She used to stand in the weeds and yell up to his room every time anything offended her. She'd yell, Who's let the side down, anyway? I heard her lo*s of times. She seemed to dwell on it. It was usually when she had had several drinks of what she called mother's ruin. She had picked up some very Cockney habits in the theater. Then she'd lift up her skirts and trudge through the weeds. She wanted to dance, but they were so high and she was so small. There she would be with her knickers showing, and she'd call out a chant, BATT A STEEN EE, BATT A STEEN EE. She called herself that, you know. Angelina Battestini. I loved the way she said it, as if she was making a secret joke.

"Well, she was." Mr. Evans-Thomas paused before a perfectly round dome of lavender. "I found out why. It wasn't a stage name at all." He pointed to the lavender. "I cut it that way because that's the way they do it in Provence. More yield. Wouldn't the French find a way?" He moved past the lavender. "I found it, you see. I found the family secret. I don't think she thought she was being secretive. It wasn't her way. I think she just took it for granted that everybody knew it was her name.

"It was a trunk in the trunk room, which is now my kitchen. It had belonged to Battestini—her father. Signore Battestini, the original Italian violinist whom Victorian girls ran off with. He made his fortune in popular music for the panto and the music hall, and those pieces that young ladies played in drawing-room concerts. Marvelous. 'The Fly's Fandango.' 'The Fleas' Tea Party.' 'Flutter by, Butterfly,' and the most success-ful of all, '*Riga Ma Rola.*'

"Wildly popular in their day. But as soon as poor Signore Battestini went to his maker, his eight, count them, eight, well, not eight really, only seven children, don't ever count Angelina, those ungrateful bastards changed their names to Battestin, joined the C of E, and here we are. I see the mother's influence in it. She was a middle-class girl from Manchester who only once got carried away by anything and spent the rest of her life married to that one moment. She had long since wasted away from sheer English embarrassment, which, as you know, is the only truly killing emotion we have, like you Scots spending your lives just keeping from hitting each other, so wearing and primitive."

They had gone nearly around the garden when Mr. Evans-Thomas fell to his knees and said, "Bugger! Voles." He got up and dusted off his knees. "I fight and fight," he said. "Never mind. When Abdul there bought the top flat across from Mr. Pizz, and I found out he played the violin, I lent him the music, and when he is in a good mood, which alas isn't all that often, and not being Muslim and angry, he plays them for me, and I swear to you that I can hear them echoed in another part of the house. It's haunted by Signore Battestini, of course. I used to see him in what's now the CIA man's parlor, but since he came, the ghost has moved out into the hall. You can see his shadow against the stained-glass window when the sun is right." Mr. Evans-Thomas hesitated, which was so unlike him that Ewen was not surprised when he asked, rather diffidently, "Tell me, how did Teresa persuade them to let her have the other flat? It's been a CIA safe house for a long time. I don't know why they call them that. It's very odd. They seem to think nobody has neighbors. Is she in the CIA?"

Ewen's laughter rang across the garden, and Teresa heard it and smiled beyond Abdul Selim's head toward the sound. She had been waiting patiently for him to begin speaking. She was confident that, like many shy men, he was going to pour forth secrets to her once he had decided he could trust her.

Abdul Selim watched the moon-pale lady's face, alight with love as she looked toward the long, red-haired, quite graceful Scot she lived with and thought, They do not wear their hearts on their sleeves but on their naked, incurably innocent faces. That nakedness was something that in the fifteen years since he had been transferred from Doon to Bryanston, through no fault or decision of his own, he would never get used to.

She put her hand on his arm again, that curious touching that seemed so vulnerable, as if she were reassuring herself that he was still there.

He hated that. He felt blackmailed by her trust. He wanted to say, as he often had before, How dare you demand my trustworthiness as if it were a right and not a privilege of plenty? He didn't believe her about death. It was her little drama, a woman like that to whom nothing had happened. If it had, something, some heart's intelligence, would have been written on her face. She was not young. She would already be a grandmother in India.

But when she turned back to him, he looked into her eyes, examining them. He had been wrong again. She was not arrogant with innocence but, like a wise child, unsurprised. He had been fooled by the similarity of looks in Anglo-Saxons that still, after so long, confused him. After all, and he had admitted it many times to himself, who could know what was behind his own beautiful, calm face, silly, to him, with secrets.

What was it that she wanted him to tell her? His life? What he liked to eat? Money? Abdul Selim wondered what she would say if he told her. I owe my life to a first-class non-smoking carriage. Everybody in third class was dead when we left the station.

Now let me tell you that if you are going to live or die depends on the fact that at the age of eight, when you are looking at the snow on the mountains and trying not to show your fear, your Muslim parents shove you into the arms of a Brahmin woman, and she hides your face while you listen to your parents being dragged from the carriage at Chandipur, and you hear the Brahmin woman who will become your mother scream, No, no, he's mine, and she holds her hand over your mouth, even though you are trying to bite it away in your panic, and she holds your head down like that against her until the train is long out of the station, and when she lets you go, there is still snow on the mountains, then, my dear, you tend to be wary of carelessness in your heart and in your soul, and always ride in first-class carriages.

Now I will tell you how a new life began for me, he told

Teresa without saying a word. She seemed to be waiting still. I lived with the Brahmin family and they were as loving to me as anyone would wish or hope for under the circumstances. I am rich because I am the only one left alive in a whole rich Muslim family in Jaipur, like the Jews who are left. We spoke English together at home in Delhi, but I know Urdu, too, and I was cared for as their own until they found out that I wanted to marry their daughter, who is Hindu and Brahmin, so I was sent to Bryanston in England.

Because I have money, I can go wherever I like, except the one place I want to go, where my home is. So I went to Oxford and then St. Thomas's Hospital, and I ended up living alone, and playing the violin and writing Urdu poetry, and sitting beside a moon-faced lady in an English garden, where blood and truth are out of place, even rude. It is a life which is the fond hope of many, but not, thank you, myself.

So he said instead, "I am a doctor, but when I am at home I write Urdu poetry, and I play the violin. You see, there is a soundproof room in my flat, you may have noticed it, a little bit of Haroun-al-Raschid up in the sky. Signore Battestini built it to work in."

Penelope had wandered back and was waiting to interrupt. "At least you must do yoga. You have such a beautiful body." She leaned forward and touched his arm, too, but her touch was not blind like the other. It was judicious, as if he were an animal she was thinking of buying.

"I would like it if you would play Signore Battestini's pieces for me," Teresa said.

Abdul Selim laughed. "They are quite dreadful. Diddle diddle wheedle diddle dum dum dum. But I will play them for you if you care to hear them," he added, liking her.

Penelope wandered off again. "I have to dress for dinner," she told the empty air. Then, at her door, she screamed, "What the bloody hell have you been doing, Robin? I've waited a fucking hour for another fucking drink."

"Oh, don't get your knickers in a twist. I was taking a pee" came from somewhere beyond the French doors, which Penelope slammed behind her.

"Oh dear, they are a rowdy pair, aren't they? All that upper-class childish aggression." Mr. Evans-Thomas and Ewen had just arrived back at the circle of chairs from their tour of the herbaceous borders. "All imitation, of course. Her grandfather made a packet as a wholesale grocer and bought a great pile in the Cotswolds. Her father had to sell it at auction for death duties after he died. You would have thought they were selling Knole after sixteen generations. I went to the auction. All knife-voiced, jumped-up daughters talking about champers, and what a luhvely taime they had had there and wasn't it all gharstly."

"Social malice is a form of English revenge," Abdul Selim explained to Teresa. "What did she do to you? Refuse your advances?"

"She never refused an advance in her life." Mr. Evans-Thomas pulled carefully at his trouser creases and sat down.

"*Aggro.* Nice word. A bit of *aggro* for aggression," Abdul Selim went on, explaining things to Teresa.

"I think that means aggravation," Mr. Evans-Thomas said in the patient voice the English use when foreigners get it all wrong.

"What kind of doctor are you?" Teresa had finally found something to ask. She had been confused by his confession, which didn't seem to be one.

"We don't come like lickerish-all-sorts, as you do in America," Abdul Selim told her. "I am a GP."

"General practitioner," Mr. Evans-Thomas said, still patient with them. "Oh, here comes the CIA man with his pound note."

It was just then that Frank Proctor, bourbon in hand, ran the gamut of roses and lilacs to sit beside Teresa. There was a silence that hovered over the garden, and an evening breeze moved Teresa's hair. He heard her say, "You will let me know if Mr. Pizz moves out? For my friend from Brussels?"

Frank Proctor could see the cell forming around him, but he put the thought away and allowed himself a time of drifting instead, trying to enjoy the precious moment before it was jarred and broken.

III

HONG KONG

She watched Ewen move deeper into the flat and it frightened her a little for both of them. She, too, was making a home as quickly as a Bedouin setting up camp for the night. It reminded her that she had done this when she was a child, in Cyprus, in London, in Rome, always praying that this time, just once, they would stay or, as her grandmother said, stay put. After all, she told herself, she had been trained for change.

It was nearly noon on Saturday morning, and she was waiting for Ewen and Frank Proctor to finish hanging maps. She had gone into the kitchen to make coffee and avoid discussion, while they both stood with their hands on their hips and examined the walls of the front living room as if they had just discovered them. She sat in the sunny kitchen contented, well, almost, waiting for the coffee to brew. She felt as if she had been there forever instead of two months. She ran her hands along the figures of the Malakastan bowl, where she still kept fruit so that the seldom sun would touch it, and she checked that the iron skillet was hanging in its place, where she could see it and feel somehow blessed by small permanences, habits, colors, the scents of herbs, the garlic hanging in the window, the garlic press, even the butcher-block table and the Rothko poster she had found in the kitchen and had thought, This is some trick, and then put that thought away, telling herself that she had learned to accept gratuitous things.

When she explained to Ewen about the strangeness of finding so much she thought she had left behind, the brass chandelier, the brass bed, she was afraid he would destroy her suspicion, it was only that, of the miraculous by pointing out how little in anyone's life was truly individual, how much was a fashion. She had thought that herself, and didn't yet trust him not to say it, but he had a kindness about him, either too delicate or too preoccupied, she didn't know which yet.

He said nothing, thank God, but he had a curious way of touching or caressing the objects she had brought with her, depending on his tactile sense as if he were blind. He would examine the Malakastan bowl that way, or pick up an apple and turn and turn it in his hand. It was that gesture that made her know, each time she saw it, that he, too, was afraid of disappearance; it was his own childhood and his training, the recognition of a growing, splitting, heaving world, no terra firma, no illusion that even the apple in his hand would pause for him in its death, its rot, its planting, its waiting, its growth.

She was learning to live with these moments of awareness, listening, recognition, which she no longer mistook for anxiety but accepted as its opposite, a poise for whatever came. She was aware, then, of polishing a pretty glass she had found, and gazing, preoccupied and happy, out the window and across the green grove interrupted by rooftops. Below her Mr. Evans-Thomas puttered among the daisies, the bright fuchsia, the lush roses in the June garden.

The hints she had of what was happening to Ewen had made her want to explain all this, put it into words for him and for Pius, who she knew had been in the same undefined place.

But when she tried to explain to Pius, he thought for a little while and then said that the sameness of change was *exemplum extensionis secundum Aristotelen*, and Ewen said, "Pius, you really get to the heart of the matter."

They had sat around the kitchen table after dinner, drinking wine. She remembered laughter and the stains of wine-cooked meat in the black casserole, bits of salad left in the bowl, bread crumbs, and the scents of herbs and wine and coffee, the color of the light pool on the table, and their shadows and their voices.

She was beginning to piece together hints of Africa, not what Ewen called B-movie Africa, mercenaries, safaris, politics, and elephants, but a real place where they had been, where the lions were and life was grass and space and rain, and death a dry expected thing waiting always.

That night, or another night, Pius had said, "Teresa, I think that you are a center, a hearth. Some people are, you know. You will gather people around you now, a harvest around this table and this house." Then he said a strange thing, "Ewen, you will have to get used to this and not resent it. It is a gift. Has it always been like this?"

She had to say, "No. Not in America, not at the college, anyway, not before things happened to me."

They went on talking that night until the wine was gone and it was nearly time for the last 74 bus. They walked with Pius in the moonlight across Primrose Hill to the Prince Albert Road and the bus, and she told him about the Derebey and the angels, aware and not caring that she had told him before. She remembered that the moon was full that night in May and now it was full again.

It was Ewen's depth of trust in the place that allowed him to concentrate so deeply, that frightened her for him. She glanced beyond the kitchen door into what Mr. Evans-Thomas still called Colonel Battestin's garden room, where the morning sun through the French doors made a long lane across the floor. The furniture they had moved from the front still looked strange.

They had decided to make it into their living room after carefully asking permission of Frank Proctor. She thought they ought to. She did, after all, pay her rent through him to his friend, who seemed somehow ephemeral, except that he had a name, Charles Ogham. Frank Proctor, for the life of her she couldn't think of him with less than both his names, never talked about him. Teresa would have liked to know. They had, as she told Frank, so much in common, the things they both liked. He said he would tell Charles Ogham, that he certainly would be glad to know that.

Ewen said he wouldn't talk about him because they were both obviously CIA, as Mr. Evans-Thomas had said, and Teresa said, "Oh, that. That's just Mr. Evans-Thomas's gossip. They'd be a lot cleverer than Frank Proctor. If not, then God help us." She explained to Ewen that wanness and vagueness were diplomatic training, and could hear her mother's voice saying, They let in all sorts of people now, dear, you have to be careful. It's all security check and no manners, not like it was. Never, for her, like it was.

She and Ewen had gone on Wednesday to the map shop and had bought twenty feet of aerial navigation charts covering the whole of the Great Rift from the Zambezi in the south to the Taurus Mountains in the north, and across Lake Victoria to the Mountains of the Moon, which Ewen said were active, but some geologists working for the Kenya government wouldn't admit that. "Politics. Wow!" he added. "I'm glad I was on my own."

As soon as they got the maps home, they laid them on the floor and traveled across them on their knees. They crawled the length of Ewen's year and then into her time above Diyarbakir. The space was faintly beige-colored, and yellow, and the mountains were etched lines. She had to guess which pass had been the Derebey's high valley. It was all reduced—their going and Michael's ambitions and Ewen's hopes—to faint blue seas, fawn-colored piedmonts, pale orange heights, and wrinkled gray lines like old faces, all abstract but releasing within them stories, and then those fearsome hopes of Ewen's.

On his knees he pointed at the Danakil, the most hell-hot place on earth, which produced killer tribes, where the Rift came into Africa from the Red Sea, and it was, to him, still happening, still being formed. He went on looking at the map where the Danakil was, and stroking it with his hand as if it were warm to the touch.

He said, "I have to watch myself to keep from reaching conclusions that are dreadful fancies, but I do think that more belligerent people live in more active parts of the globe. I can't help it," belligerently himself. "You can almost always find old volcanism where the fighters are. Look at Scotland." Then he said, "Here, from the Danakil down to Lake Natron, and Ngorongoro to the Zambezi—that's where I will have to go and you will go with me and work on the tribes there." He sat back on Kilimanjaro, dreaming. "We will take a Land Rover. I know how to maintain one." Then he added, worried, "I can't take you to the Danakil. It's too dangerous," which made her smile.

"Yes," she said, instead of what she was thinking. "We'll do that."

The front living room and part of their bedroom floor had been the only space large enough to spread the maps across the floor, with all the furniture forced against the wall. It was after a few nights of tiptoeing across the crackling paper to get to the bathroom, somewhere, she judged in the dark, near Lake Natron, that she said, "Why don't you take this for your workroom and put the maps on the wall. We can move the living room back over the garden. Besides, here are all the library shelves for your rocks."

It was nine o'clock on Saturday morning, and he was still in bed. His eyes wanted to do it, but he said, "Maybe . . . you don't know . . ." and whatever else he said was lost when she shut the door and went across the hall to ask permission of Frank Proctor, who seemed to curl with embarrassment, she supposed, because she had caught him in his Saturday jeans and an old T-shirt that said *Hoshgeldiniz*, Welcome, in Turkish. It delighted her, and they talked about Turkey while he was helping them put the maps up. They put up the battered, marked Michelin road map of East Africa, the contour map of the Holy Land from Mount Hermon to Aqaba through the Jordan Valley and the Wilderness of Zin and the sunken desert rivers.

Frank Proctor had insisted on taking his car to get more tacks, on lending a hammer. He acted like he had been invited to a surprise party. He told them absolutely not to worry, that they had a man at the Embassy whom they always used to reconnect the television set in the back to the hidden roof aerial. He made a joke of old Charlie hiding it up there away from Mr. Evans-Thomas. He was fascinated with the Russian geological map of Africa, with its legends in Russian, English, and French. It spread bright yellow, green, red, blue, orange blots and swirls as they tacked the sheets up on the wall nearest their bedroom door. He kept glancing through into the bedroom, and Teresa was glad it was straightened, while he asked Ewen questions. Ewen, delighted that someone was paying attention, ran his blind hands as high as he could reach, saying over and over, "So much of it is new. You see how new? All that red and yellow Pliocene?" He thumped the wall. "Look here. Only thirty thousand years. I picked up volcanic rock that new." He pointed to a small red splash. "Look. That's Lengai. The Masai call it the Mountain of God. Sodium carbonate. Erupted last year." He looked up. "Thank God for Signor Battestini's fourteen-foot ceilings."

"Why Russian?" Frank asked casually.

"They're the only people who've done one." Ewen went on looking at the wall. "It isn't quite right, though."

She heard Ewen call, "'Come and see."

The wall to the bedroom was a huge Russian blot of primary colors, and the aerial navigation maps ran in a pale-yellow, robin's-egg-blue, green track up the long wall opposite the windows, over the picture railing, and partly across the ceiling, where she could look straight up and dream of where Malakastan might have been.

Ewen was already piling books on the floor and labeling the bookshelves on either side of the fireplace by eons and countries, all the way down from the Turkish border and up from the Triassic. As she came in, Frank Proctor was saying, "Hell no, Charlie won't care. He won't care a bit."

They had moved the sofa, the two soft chairs, the coffee table, all the living-room bits and pieces to the garden room. Only the brass chandelier was left, gleaming among the maps and labeled rocks, as if it, too, had history in it to be found.

It was midnight. The full moon flooded Regent's Park and made shadows under the trees like some false day. At the most exotic of the Nash terraces, the one said to have been inspired by Mrs. Fitzsimmons but named for Lady Hester Stanhope, two shadows jumped down into an empty areaway. They forced open a window that had not been opened in years into a long-disused kitchen. They lifted an 1832 shutter from its hinge and made a bridge across the space of the areaway to the window-sill. Fifty people, including four small children and a baby, crossed it silently into the house. The baby threatened to cry, and its mother put her hand over its mouth.

Up the first flight of stairs, in what had been the dining room, lit only by long strips of moonlight, dimmed by the dirty windows, they put down their burdens of bedrolls, food, primus stoves, candles, wine, marijuana, and began preparations for a siege.

The baby threatened once again to cry, and when his mother ignored him instead of putting her hand over his mouth, he set up a wail that echoed up the grand stairway, through the dead drawing room, the deserted library, the empty music room, into the twelve bedrooms, until the ghosts of maids heard a faint cry in the servants' quarters on the sixth floor, where the moonlight was faint through small dormer windows, where the rain, the war, and the city had deposited nearly thirty years of dirt.

Torches whirled through the house as they ran through the emptiness, up and down the stairs, looked at where the ceilings in the upper rooms had come down and been cleared away, leaving patches of dark concrete where the molded plaster had broken and left half a goddess, fragments of classic dentils, hints of friezes, broken rosettes, the faint smell of plaster dust, and here and there a shard on the floor where the traffic beyond the terrace had brought a patch down.

Couples laid claim to rooms. The child stopped crying. One of the toilets was already fouled by two o'clock.

It wasn't until noon the next day, when Ewen went out to buy milk, bread, some apples, and the Sunday papers, that Teresa read that Noel's house, long since condemned and then left to indecision, had been occupied by squatters.

There was nobody to tell, no way to tell it. She lay across the bed and looked at the molding on the ceiling cut off by the new wall between their room and Frank's and thought, Can Frank hear my heart beat? She saw him, too, full of love and lust and visions. She was wide awake then.

The memory of Noel had been sprung on her when she was unwary. Later, when she thought of how it began, she saw the whole episode as that, an episodic place in her brain, mind, soul which had lived for all the years quite independent of the daily movement of life. It was in a stillness containing love, all the kinds of it, all the learning, nothing in that place forgotten or past. She let the wall between herself today and that place fall, and herself be there again, oh, be there in pure sun and pure sand, pure sea and Noel's pure hair, that slightly damp hair that ever after she identified with aristocracy. That was it, the place. It really was about love. Was love. Not about.

The difference? The black monk had told her. There are pleasant memories and there is total pastless recall, as he had made her do with Malakastan. And it is always present. You are there, when you let yourself in, as into a room. It always waits for you and you can always be there, live a life there, the same, never changing, often nothing very important, except to oneself, even the bad parts, and there are bad parts there, because in love there cannot be any evasions, any lies.

A lie, she told the ceiling, makes it something else, a seduction. Manipulation. Manus—hand. That's Pius, the black monk. You be quiet because I am standing there, still standing there, and I can't be interrupted, not now, she told Pius, who would understand if anyone in the world would. It is summer. I can smell the sea and the sand and the sea grass on the broken dune that the tide has carved, and below it a shore that is as near to Europe as you can get.

Noel and I have made a body of sand on it. A man. Man-size. He lies there, ephemeral, Noel says, and when I ask what it means he won't, or can't, tell me. He just says that when the tide comes it will be washed away, and I already know that.

I have run away again, and Noel lets me play with him. Sometimes he doesn't, because he is fourteen and I know he is—not ashamed, never ashamed, not Noel—but a little embarrassed in front of the others, who don't like him, at having a best friend who is only six. They don't like him because he has an English accent and they say he is stuck up because he is a lord. He isn't stuck up at all. He is not.

He knows I have run away, because my red wagon is behind the dune and it has my best dress and some socks in it and my old-fashioned costume from Halloween, because I love to dress up and be somebody else, but we both know, although we don't ever say it, that he will take me back before my mother misses me. She is playing bridge and Noel says she can drink six gin rickeys and not lose a trick. He's seen her do it. She is a champion duplicate player with the partner who is Noel's hostess for the duration, only the duration is already over and he is watching the sea and counting the days until he gets a passage back across the ocean, and when he does I am going to die because nobody understands me in this lousy dump but Noel.

We are under a wide blue sky and the sand stretches away on both sides of us down the deserted beach as far as we can see. It is deserted because of gas coupons.

The man just lies there below us. A little wind brushes sand from his face. We watch the water creep nearer his feet. Noel says the water is inexorable. The man lying there in the sand is almost like a real man, asleep or dead. A dead sand man. Noel's face is above me in light that seems to come from his own brown skin and his own blond hair and his sad blue eyes. And that swing of damp-looking hair he won't let anybody cut American style because he says he doesn't want to go home looking like a convict. He is as beautiful as a prince in a fairy story.

So here I am, years hence, and far too late to warn myself. It's always too late when you come to think of it. Now, listen, I know about myths. It is my job, no, I didn't say discipline, but I'll tell you, oh yes, beware of the person who is nice to you first. I mean beyond your mother or whoever is instead of her. They will get into your soul like a picture on your soul's wall and you'll be forever trying to match them or find them. You'll recognize them again and always in a gesture, a movement, a fall of hair, a phrase, a set of their eyes, a way of treating you — offhand and loving at the same time in my case—and you'll know in a minute your fairy godmother/father, your prince, your principal boy is leaning over your crib and putting the mark on you. It's your blessing, your granted wish that will come true if you don't watch yourself.

Noel doesn't wait for the tide. He jumps down from the broken dune and he kneels beside the body and he destroys an arm. Then he crawls down and destroys a leg. Then he sits on the dune with his feet near the body's head and he doesn't say a word, and for the first time I am afraid to go near him after what he has done.

I go near him only when I realize that he is crying, crying in front of me, and I know it is because we are friends and he trusts me, because as far as I know he has not cried one drop during the whole duration, not even when his first boat back was canceled. There wasn't room for the Greyhounds that his mother had sent with him, and they were too valuable to travel alone later. That is the most binding thing, the worst thing to bind me to him forever he has ever done or ever will do, crying and letting me see.

I touch his hair and I can still feel it under my fingers, delicate hair that makes my heavier hair feel tacky, but he has already told me not to mind when I moan about it. All Americans are middle-class, anyway, so it isn't my fault. It's genetic, Noel says.

Then he looks at the man on the beach and says, *Le blessé.* That means the wounded. All the wounded and the dead young men in the war. All of them gone and everything over, and he too young to go; he will always be too young, all his life.

He takes me in his lap and tells me about the pilots and the soldiers and all the dead people, and then he tells me about the way he lived in England, not pigging it like it is now for everybody, that is part of the war effort, and it will never be like it was.

Then, as if he hasn't just finished saying it was all over, he tells me all about how we will have tea in the drawing room of the beautiful house in Regent's Park named for Lady Hester Stanhope. He tells me that the carpets are so thick you can't hear a footfall, and they are the color of champagne and so are the curtains. The room is huge and warm, and has caryatids holding up the marble chimneypiece—never say mantel, fireplace is all right. Up on the ceiling right over it is a plaster Aurora, flying out of a plaster cloud, leading Apollo the sun god. The firelight and the lamps make everything golden warm when you come in from Regent's Park or when you come home from school, which he hated in England before the war. But Eton, he says, will be different, and he will go there as soon as they can find a ship that will take the damn dogs.

That room, the warm gold room, has come into my dreams ever since, a room I've never seen. Sometimes I am in it and there are people with polite voices, and once right in the middle of the room there was a white horse, but only once. But when I am older there is another dream. I stand across the street in Regent's Park in the dark rain, and I am wearing a trench coat like an English B movie, looking up at the drawing room, which is golden in the rainy dusk, and they would be having tea, with me not invited. Sometimes the princesses would be there. I could see them.

But then we went to the Coronation and I was just fourteen on May 30—a Gemini, generous but capricious, my horoscope said in the *Daily Mirror*. My birthday treat was three days later. We came over to London from Paris. It was June 2, and we walked at midnight through an ecstasy of crowds along the Coronation route. They were going to bed down right there in the street and wait all night and all morning for the Queen to pass by in her golden coach. We could hear cheers following a newsboy who was yelling, "Everest conquered for the Queen!"

It kept threatening and raining and stopping, and we walked all the way, and even Mother was happy in the darkness and the laughter and all the bright banners.

We stayed at the Dorchester, but in the back. Daddy said the front was exorbitant. I sneaked out of my room at four o'clock in the morning and went into the park; they would have killed me if they'd known. Thousands of people were lying together, keeping each other warm. They didn't seem to care if the trees dripped on them. I heard a woman saying, "Whatever you do, don't get up. Once you're up, they'll shove in from behind you and you'll never get down again." They had their heads in each other's lap, and some people who had taken possession around a tree were singing quietly, singing everybody to sleep.

I would rather have stayed with them, but in the morning we threaded around through Mayfair and went to Noel's mother's flat in Park Lane, across the street from the route through the park. His mother charged my father a hundred dollars for each of us and we watched the ceremony on television and we could have been anywhere. We kept trying to find Noel, who was in the Abbey, a baron in baron's regalia from Moss Bross.

I didn't know until later about the money. We drank champagne, me too for once, and I looked down at the people in the rain below. The boy's voices sang "Vivat Regina," and the minister from the Church of Scotland handed her the Good Book.

Later the procession came up Piccadilly and into Hyde Park. You could hear it away in the distance, a pure scream of joy coming nearer, then there were the soldiers and the carriages, and the Gurkhas and the Queen of Tonga, and then, well, the golden coach seemed to float for a minute in the air at Hyde Park Corner, and there she was, for one day the fairy queen of the world.

I was still staring out the window. It was later and it had turned into a noisy cocktail party. I had been forgotten. I was just watching the crowds melt away, and someone touched my shoulder. It was Noel. I hadn't seen him for eight years, not since Long Island. He was so beautiful. He was dressed in black velvet knee breeches and he wore a scarlet robe with an ermine cape collar and he carried a coronet and his hair was still blond and damp-looking and he seemed to own the world and not to care if he gave it away, and nothing, no, nothing had changed, except that he was twenty-two and looked like a king and I was fourteen and Mother kept telling me to stand up straight.

"I knew you would be here, so I kept all this on until you could see it," he said, and smiled, and I just stared like a fool.

I was going to speak but his mother came up then, not looking at me, and said to some weedy girl with a buzz-saw voice, "May I present Lord Atherton." A lord. I knew that already. Mother said a peer, the same thing really. "Come along, Noel." His mother sounded as if she were talking to a dog, and he rolled his eyes the way he used to and turned around to be polite.

Later he came back in his ordinary clothes, and he said, "How would you like to put it on? Do you still like to dress up and be somebody else?" I had forgotten that for years, but he hadn't. He'd thought of it with all the people there and his mother lording it over people who paid. He took me to his bedroom and he let me put on the coronet and the robes, and there I was, framed in the big pier glass, and here I am, right now, on this bed, still framed in the big oblong of dark mahogany in a coronet and a robe of scarlet velvet with ermine right down over my shoulders, and Noel said, "Never mind, darling, you're prettier than any countess I saw today, even if the fur is rabbit and I rented it all from Moss Bross. Anyway, you can be my countess," but he spoke as if he were already very far away. I didn't care. I was a countess right then. He said I looked lovely, like a colt or a faun or a boy king.

That's when he threw himself on the bed and was looking up at the ceiling, not at me anymore, and he said that I was to stand as if I had the robes on all the time. He said things were so awful one might as well.

Nobody had said I was lovely before in my whole life. I was at what Mother called an awkward age, fourteen and gangly. She said I was going to be tall, not petite like the women in her family, who had been belles in the west end of Richmond.

Lovely. I remembered it in the bad times.

I wonder what happened to Noel. No one ever told me, or they did something worse, they shut up when his name was mentioned. I wondered even then why they didn't still live in the house in Stanhope Terrace, but something about Noel kept me from asking that day with the rain outside. I wonder if he is alive. I wonder if I can find a way to see the house . . .

The news of the squatters went from the front page to the back pages of the papers, and then was dropped by all but the *Daily Mirror*. It was two weeks later, and there were no longer crowds, but Teresa and Ewen walked down the canal towpath in the lush summer green of the cold jungle and past the house whenever it wasn't raining. She had told him about Noel, and that she was still drawn there. She didn't know why. It had all been so long ago. But she said, "It's still in my mind, in a corner, a might-have-been." Ewen held her hand and didn't say anything. He had the grace not to invade her kingdoms, and she wondered if he had kingdoms of his own.

She thought at last of how she might do it. There were, after all, lots of stories in the papers, or had been. They seemed to want the publicity, the notice. It was a protest, after all. She said, "Now, don't stop me," to Ewen, who hadn't tried to. She went in behind the wrought-iron fence and knelt by the area-way and called to a boy who seemed to be standing guard by the basement window. He opened the window. He was about nineteen and he really did have hair like a boy king, it lacked only a lovelock. It was right that Noel's house should have a guard like that.

When he spoke, his voice came from the World's End. He said, "You'll 'ave to wroite."

Someone came out onto the balcony above her head, out of the French window beside the great front door that had been nailed shut. He leaned over the rain-stained plaster railing. He was older, thin as a rake, bearded. "Are you from the press?" He sounded hopeful.

"American," Teresa called up. "I'm an anthropologist," hoping the word would be magic.

It was. He called down, "Come back tonight. Ten o'clock. We're letting the press into a meeting. Bring any press people you know. 'Ere"—he scribbled something on a piece of paper—"you'll need a proper pass."

By the time she had waited for the dirty bit of paper to flutter down among the weeds and had picked it up, he had gone in and slammed the window shut.

Six stories up among the pinnacles above the classic roof façade, behind the balustrade of rain-streaked gods and nymphs and satyrs, a line of dirty London *putti* stood in the rain and chanted to the sky over Regent's Park, "No. No. We won't go." The weather was too bad for anyone to listen except Teresa and Ewen. She had a shiver of *déjà vu*, standing in the rain, watching the house.

· By nine-thirty in the evening the rain had stopped. They walked down the Prince Albert Road and crossed into the park, where they could see the water of the canal dark with night, protected from city light by the heavy tree shadows. In the distance, the roofscape of Stanhope Terrace and the London Mosque made an eastern sky vista of roofs, pinnacles, and domes. Night lights and car lights made the gold dome and the rain puddles gleam.

When they got to the house, it was so dark that Teresa thought the squatters had been evicted. Then she saw a dim glow beyond the dirty windows of what had been the drawing room. Beside the areaway, in a ragged queue, a small gaggle of people waited in turn to cross the guarded shutter into the kitchen window. It was too dark in the shadow of the house to see who any of them were, and Teresa hoped she would have guts enough to cross over the black space on the shutter into the nearly dark basement room, where a kerosene lamp seemed to be the only light. She could smell it. It made the shadow of the guard who helped her down off the shutter huge and black against the ceiling. She realized that she had crossed when she felt a hand in hers.

The stairs to the first floor were wide and smelled of old dust. Dry wood creaked in the dark. They filed around the hall, too dark to see anything but the faint outline of the front door, and up what had been an elegant sweep of a double circular stairway, feeling their way along the wall. Most of the stair rails were gone. She was beginning to see spaces and shapeless objects in the dark. Up ahead there was a faint light and the voice of someone making a speech. The house was haunted. Teresa brushed past the starched uniforms of housemaids long gone. The boards that had been nailed across the balcony door in the upper hall made a dark cross on the bare floor in the city glow that filtered through the dirty beveled glass.

She remembered that it should have had a champagne-colored carpet so that no footsteps could be heard. Instead, there were echoes and creaks, and the wind blew in from somewhere on the floors above her head, and somewhere far above she heard the thin cry of a child. Should have was what haunted the house and haunted her. It was like visiting the tomb of a lover everyone had forgotten.

In the middle of the space of her dream of golden light there

was darkness and dust and the shifting of alien bodies, in-
vaders, and destruction by time, the luxury of muted sound
gone, the baffles of curtains and carpets, of velvet cushions and
polished furniture, and the discretion of money, and in their
place the sound was raw in the empty space.

She was crying for everything unimportant that was lost and
she was suddenly afraid of being touched by something she
couldn't see. She whispered to Ewen to walk close behind her.
Ahead of her, someone, tall, that was all she could tell, walked
in a djelabah. She supposed it was a man from the height, but
the hood was drawn low over the face so she couldn't see. It
was just a djelabah or a monk's robe, and a black shape, and
she felt panic rise in her chest. Then they came into the faint
glow of the meeting in the drawing room and she could see
that the robe was white not black. It was a djelabah and not
a monk's robe.

The people ahead were sitting down, and when the djelabah
sat in turn against the wall, she slid down beside him, Ewen
on her other side. She could feel the wooden paneling against
her back. Had Noel said linen fold, or had she dreamed that?
Linen fold from somewhere. No. Wrong period. Part of dream's
freedom.

The drawing room was as large as she had imagined it, huge.
Several lanterns sat on the floor in the center of a circle of
figures, who were shadowed by the light, as if they were around
a campfire. Some were leaning against the arch into the library.
The lantern light barely reached the carved ceiling, but she
could see, yes, she could see Aurora and hear Noel's voice,
"Aurora darling, or Eos, if you like. I love the ceiling."

There she was, leading Apollo's chariot out of the plaster
clouds and there, dim, was Apollo, blandly making the sun rise
in the gray waste of plaster with the broken nymphs and the
fragments of flowers floating around him as if nothing had
happened or ever would.

Below him a man, a Scot by his voice, was making a speech,

haranguing the flower children. He called them that with some
contempt. He was saying something—she dragged her mind
away from Apollo—about the squatters being a nucleus of a
general strike that would spread across the benighted bloody
land.

Ewen watched Gordie's face in the lantern light, not Gordie,
but the image and mold of Gordie, and felt a chill of darkness.
He had thought the squatters were hippies. They had thrown
flowers down from the roof, as innocent as children—the flower
children, the man was calling them—but at some time during
the two weeks of their possession there had come another kind
of possession, this time the mold of Gordie, the terrible mold.

The man was telling them that they had come down from
Glasgow to join the protest, to help them organize, and Ewen
thought of bunny rabbits sitting around a fireplace in a children's book Fama had read them: Flopsy, Mopsy, Cottontail,
and Peter, being lectured by the fox. He found, and it shocked
him, that his face, like Teresa's, was wet with tears, or maybe
it was sweat, he hoped so, at a room full of children's dreams,
his, hers, theirs, and God knows who else's, turned nightmare,
and he knew he had to get Teresa and himself away.

Two men in dark bum freezers and jeans, their heads shaved,
stood on either side of the speaker. Their faces were painted
black on one side and blue on the other. What was it Gordie
had said? Use two colors, it's harder to see? Their eyes were
dead and pale against the blue and black, monstrous minstrel
boys. They stood completely still and he thought of mutes at
old funerals.

"The guards here will see that none of our visitors leaves
until the morning," the speaker was saying, grinning. "This
applies to all visitors." He added, amused and polite, "We
have evidence that the police have filtered in with the press,
and it will do ye no harm to see how we have to live . . ."

The hooded figure whispered something. He had been
watching Teresa, not the ridiculous people sitting in his draw-

ing room. It was like a wish come true to find—he was sure of it—well, not sure, it had been so long. There in the middle of the ghastly invasion of the present, he had to find out. "Darling," he whispered. "Countess?"

She looked as wide-eyed in the half dark as she had when he told her the ex-king was alcoholic when she was six. She couldn't speak.

"Yes, darling, it's Noel," he whispered. "Not a word. They'd flay me. But I simply couldn't resist. After all, as Sheridan said when he watched Drury Lane burn, surely a man may sit by his own fireside."

Ewen felt her hand tighten in his as if she had suddenly caught the fear in the room.

"It is not what we thought," he whispered in her other ear. "These are dangerous men. Urban guerrillas. Now listen. Do what I say. We are going to crawl to the door slowly, and when we get to the stairs, you must let me speak. Do you understand?"

"Can Noel come, too?" The voice of a very young girl.

He thought she was glimpsing Noel as he had glimpsed Gordie. "Yes, now come on, follow," he said. He wanted to tell her that in a nightmare nothing is a surprise. Fortunately, they were beyond the spread of the light from the lanterns, and when she whispered to Noel, he said nothing, only nodded. He crawled after them into the dark hall, and when they got up he whispered, "Keep close to the wall of the stairs. The boards won't squeak." They crept single file down the stairs, Ewen in a nightmare, Noel delighted to find a friend and play Indians in his own house, ridiculous performance, and Teresa unsurprised. It was, for the first time in the night, the way it should be.

At the areaway window the guards had drawn in the shutter bridge for the night and were playing dominoes by the lantern.

Ewen went up to them and spoke so softly that Teresa could hardly hear him. He spoke in a silk voice, with an accent far broader than she had ever heard him use. He said, "I think now that you will put the shutter out for the lady and our friend to go." Then something else; it seemed to be as polite but too soft for her to hear. He was smiling. She saw fear dart across the eyes of one of the boys, and he got up. The other stayed, staring at the dominoes. She kept looking at them, too, black rectangles, a nine about to fall. The window creaked open behind her and she could hear the scrape of wood on wood as the shutter was pushed out into the dark.

Noel went first, his hand out to guide Teresa. Then Ewen climbed out and crossed the dark chasm, thinking of the Billy Goats Gruff and wishing to hell he could get the childishness out of his head, but in the dark, he knew it was right, that there was something childish about evil; the small boy calls, I'll kill you; grown-up, the small boy does.

Noel said it first, or something like it, in the darkness. "There was something ominous and childish for me about that. The nightmare of a child coming home to find that everyone has gone, moved away." His voice was behind them, and then muffled as he took off the djelabah. "God"—for her the shape of his head against the far streetlight, his hair blond and fine and damp still—"I won't want that again." He started to throw it into the bushes.

"No." Teresa took it from him. "I want it."

"Well, hark, missy." Teresa and Noel had caught their childhood and relief from each other, and were laughing in each other's arms. "What did you say to get us out?" Noel called over her shoulder.

"I simply said that if they didn't let us out I would carve a pairmanent smile across their fucking faces. My voice, you see. Sometimes it's a great advantage to be a Scot."

"You were so polite."

"They've a wee bit fear of the boys from Glasgow."

"A wee bit fear. I love it." Noel sounded suddenly concerned. "I'm not being condescending. I'm always accused of it. It's my voice. See how we're judged? Now, darlings, I don't know about you children, but after that I could use a drink. Come on. I know a club in Marylebone. St. Mary la Bonne. Oh dear. I suppose a taxi would be too much to hope for. Never mind. We'll walk. It isn't far. I've been walking for hours, anyway. I should have known I'd come here sooner or later. I did come to watch a bit. I saw you one day, Teresa, but you didn't know me and that cut me to the heart, so I didn't speak."

"I didn't see you." She was walking with Noel, their heads close together, their arms across each other's back like skaters. Their voices, mostly Noel's, trailed behind them.

"We'll go my favorite way past all the terraces named for the wicked uncles."

It had been raining again a little, only enough to make the pavements shine. There was faint mist from the lake in the park. Ewen could smell it, a luxury of water. It gentled the shapes of the towered terraces and blurred the street lamps as if he had lost some precision of sight. He was struggling to be where he was, in the street, in the mist, under the shadows of the Regency façades that were out of his mind's place, as if he had wandered by mistake into the wrong setting, trailing the shame of the evil he had seen, the blue and black faces in the wrong place at the wrong time, the rejects of war infecting where they wandered.

In front of him Teresa and her friend clung together and he could sense love between them. It was not the kind of love you bore, that was wrong for them, as if to bear love were a heavy thing and—what was the word?—responsible. No, the two backs, the voices, their close oblivious shadows in the night street were thrown all the way back to the kind of love you took for granted as what love was before anything had happened to you. It was the child love he had known, too, only it had been for Gordie. But the important thing to him was that, when it had begun to happen to him again, he had known what it was, and now a wiser child, at least he had not run away from her. He saw that even if it had been misplaced once, it had made him able to recognize it when it came again.

They were passing Clarence Terrace, one of the wickedest, Noel's voice drifted back. Teresa's hair hung down and in the mist had curled and Ewen wanted to touch it, touch her, go home, not listen anymore. Up behind the façade of Sussex Place a light burned in one of the houses where someone had forgotten to pull a curtain, and he was glad, suddenly so glad that he had let Teresa come into the place where he had been alone. It was the image of the trust that he had had before anything happened and when his nightmares had not yet been based on realities.

Noel and Teresa had come back for a minute to the present, remembering he was there, and they paused, without needing to speak, like dancers knowing to pause with their bodies, and waited politely for him to catch up, and fell in beside him while Noel explained.

"I had no idea, well, I did really. I knew I'd come sooner or later. I'd been to a party in Cheyne Walk, you know, all Pre-Raphaelite and everyone in costume, only some of them didn't know it. Such velvet and ruffles and ribbons you wouldn't believe and hash served on chinoiserie trays with carved ivory holders. Turn here. It's shorter." He herded them, one on each side, around the corner of York Terrace toward Marylebone Road. "Now, what was I saying?"

It was Noel's voice and it was the echo of his voice as the black monk all at the same confusing time. "Oh yes, ivory holders. Can you believe the pretentiousness? I was so stoned. It took hours of watching Putney across the river for me to make up what was left of my mind to move. I just stood at the window and waited. There was a huge Japanese umbrella, only tonight, but I remember it as if it were years ago. I was as alone in that crowded room as I have ever been in my life. I crossed the room. It took absolute hours, and there I was, out

the door and down the stairs. Two people who had left the
party long before me were still standing in front praying to
the devil for a taxi and that was too much, so I went on along
Cheyne Walk through Whistler territory and it really did look
like that, with the slight mist and the river, and I hoped the
police wouldn't notice me, and then I thought, Not to worry,
Noel, you're so Anglo-Saxon and aloof-looking you look stoned
all the time, anyway. I was trying to ignore, politely, you understand—we cross here—the fact that a huge invasion of Viking
ships was sailing up the Thames. I had just sense enough left
not to warn people; hallucinating, you know. Now let's see. I
remember being in the King's Road, then in Belgrave Square,
and past Mummy's old flat, you remember that. Now it's offices.
Let's see. Oxford Street? I don't see that. No. Wigmore Street,
of course, trusses in a window.

"It took days to get to Regent's Park, and of course I had
come down by then, and I saw your little queue and simply
followed everybody in. After all, who doesn't want to visit
the place where they've had their unhappy childhood?"

Teresa had begun to shiver in the night damp. Noel stopped
at Marylebone Road to let the traffic pass and to take the
djelabah from her and guide it over her head. He adjusted the
hood around her face and then stood back to look at her under
the day-bright streetlights.

"There, darling, you look like—oh, what?—maybe a dear
young friar." He turned to Ewen, away from her, staring. "I'm
sorry. I couldn't really see you until we got into the light. You
are Ewen? Is that right? I know Teresa's told me, but I have to
be told again. I've gone forgetful—but sweet. Not to worry.
It's *not* snobbery. You do believe me, don't you? No reason
really, in spite of what Teresa may have told you. It's only an
industrial handle, and I'm only the third one and, God knows,
the last."

He looked back at Teresa, who was staring at him under the
streetlight.

"Darling, I know you're shocked. Some of us old queens go fat. Some of us wizen. I wizened rather faster than I might have, due to the tropics. You see," he explained to Ewen, "she saw me in the shadow and I looked the same and now I look to her like someone who has been left out in the rain too long. There is a day it happens, hardly perceptible, or we would avoid it like the plague. Come on. We've got the light. Then slim turns thin and thin turns skinny. I love that word. I learned it in America." He began to whistle the "*Internationale*" as they reached the other side of Marylebone Road. "No, darling, I'm not whistling to keep my spirits up. I always do that at that corner, never mean to. I just do. I always have. I sort of slip into the space where the song is, you know. Have you ever had that happen? I see you have. Mine was a dear working-class boy called Ronald; Ron, if you like. I thought he truly wanted to better himself. Scratch any pederast and you'll find a pedant. I used to get the words mixed. Well, I soon found out he wanted me to better him, and like so many others he went where the lights were brighter and the cuff-link presents gaudier. Here we are. St. George's Place. Very late-Georgian, 1936 to be precise."

They had turned into a cul-de-sac of large houses. "A little fake club which caters to minor queer peers who've lost most of their money, to remind them of how it never quite used to be. I think you'll be amused. Oh dear, I'm prattling, please don't look like that. I'm sorry, darling, I must go on talking for sheer embarrassment." He turned to Ewen. "She's just found out that I am as gay as a wren. You see"—he pulled the bell—"I was Teresa's fairy prince; oh, darling, how were you to know I really was? I hardly knew myself, but I suspected. Good evening, Ambrose."

They moved into a velvet entry as red as the inside of a jewel box, where beyond the etched glass of the interior door the candlelight was shattered into thousands of prisms.

Teresa saw an illusion of fairy lights in an illusion of a large hallway that had been a home of someone sometime, and she wanted to tell Noel that it was all right, it was all all right. There were even family portraits on the dark red flock paper of the walls. She started to take off the djelabah.

"Oh, please don't." Noel held her arm. "Leave it on. It is so good on you, and you will be such a mystery for the boys. Come into the drawing room. Ambrose will get us a table. Please, Ambrose, one where we can loll. You aren't too disappointed, are you?" He looked worried.

"Oh, please." She was giggling and couldn't stop for a few seconds. She was laughing at herself and her dreams and at him and at Ewen, looking very awkward in the overheated, overred, overdressed place, but most of all she was laughing at the room she was seeing from the doorway. "I'm not disappointed, not a bit. It's what you promised me!"

It was. The subtle, intimate pools of light, the chimneypiece with its high-busted marble caryatids, the polished brass, its surface soft with age and care, the deep chairs, the heavy curtains with their valences of carved and gilded wood, the crystal sconces with their white candles. It was all terrible, and she hoped the tears would stay in her eyes.

But Noel had caught them, and they made his eyes glisten in the candle flames. He held her hand and led her to one of the small sofas, with two soft chairs and a coffee table. He said, "Not to mind, darling. You and the house remind me of the days before I was happy and hopeless."

They had forgotten Ewen. "Isn't the room ghastly? So right and so wrong," Noel whispered.

"It looks like an expensive abortionist's."

"The idea was to make it look as if a family has owned it for several generations. You're supposed to feel at home without Mummy telling you you can't have another drink. *Haute nostalgie.* Instant heirlooms, intimate arrangements. It reminds me of Long Island." They held hands and looked, for a minute, at the sea.

Then Noel, back in the room and the night again, sighed. "It was real. That's what I can't understand. Not the safety of one of those nightmares when you were a child and you thought you went home and there was no one there and the rooms were empty and you wandered from room to room and heard your footsteps on the bare floor and an old newspaper slid in the wind and the fireplaces were all dead. It was real. We were there. All the sounds were hollow. Did you notice that? Hollow voices. Hollow crying of a baby somewhere. I never knew how carpets and curtains and furniture muted a space. Worse than just empty. Of course it was my own fault. The house has been condemned since the war, forgotten. First they were going to tear the terraces down and then there was what they called a public outcry, which meant that a committee of people from the *Architectural Review* said no. Time passed, as it does. You can't blame those people. I read that the couple with the baby had been waiting for four years for a council flat. Living with her mum and they didn't get on.

"It was always going to be something. A school, a government office. Going to be . . ." His voice trailed off and he was frankly and quietly crying. "Oh dear." He found a handkerchief. "You don't think anyone's noticed? I can't believe you were there to rescue me, countess.

"I'm prattling again, but it's all been a shock. Not that I'm going into a lot of nonsense about where home is and how you have to go there and all life is a journey to find home. I simply can't. It was awful awful awful. Ambrose! Do bring a bottle of wine. White, I think. Gewürztraminer."

Ewen was watching the stranger, the slim friend that Teresa had been talking about for two weeks, and he could feel his jacket getting larger, his socks unclean, his tie askew, his teeth dirty, and for a minute he hated them both. They reminded him of too sweet toffee. He wanted to say, My God, you two with your doors forever opening for you, did you not see the present looming up there, threatening and weird, its awful mindlessness? But he said nothing. The thin man, with his lined and hollow face, his elegant suit, had wizened, as he called it, as if he had been through some fire of his own. Ewen wondered if he knew that in what Fada called his soul or if whatever had happened had only runneled his cheeks and sunk his eyes. He wondered if it was drugs.

He wanted to run away from them both. The chair was too soft, the lights too dim, the paneled walls too dark. He found himself, in the talk of home, longing for things that were gone, too, the stone walls of the manse, clean and cold, or the space of Africa, where it was real space, not emptiness, not deserted, and Pius lay beyond the fire, and then he was back at the lantern light and the white face of the speaker from Glasgow, the voice of Gordie haunting Lord Atherton's drawing room, with its broken plaster swags, and the two guards in the wrong place when there had never been a right place for them, with their imitation commando faces, playing at terror.

For a cold second Teresa was as strange to him as her friend. He looked down at their two hands, curled together, children wandering in a maze. He heard Noel say, "Look at the boys at the corner table, darling. They can't bear not knowing who you are. Poor dears, they—well, we really—are so insecure, so afraid of making a gaffe, when of course we see our whole lives as a gaffe sometimes, a God gaffe. We are brave, we have to be and we are, with our careful clothes and our private armor of language, and our pretty ways, knowing like black people that every time we leave the safety of our rooms we risk walking into insult or worse."

Ewen leaned over close to Teresa and made himself be as calm as he could. Gordie and the night were engulfing him for the first time in weeks, and he couldn't help blaming her. He was beginning to shiver and she was too entranced to notice. He had to get out of the hot, close room. "You both" —he was careful—"you have a whole past to catch up with. I would only be—what is it?—a third wheel or a fifth? I always get it wrong." He tried to smile, to echo Noel's flippancy. It seemed important not to jar anything or turn over the table or spill the wine. "I would like to walk through the park, and Lord Atherton can bring you home." He wanted to add, He can pray to the devil for a taxi, and suddenly recognizing a panic that had nothing to do with the color of the walls, he wanted to get out before one of the more aggressive buggers stopped him.

Teresa seemed to answer both the said and the unsaid, as she did so often. "Yes, you go home if you want to. You don't mind if I stay a little?" and then she added, "Darling," which she never said. It wasn't a part of their language together, but she wanted to make sure that Noel knew. "I'll be quite safe."

"God knows that's true," Noel murmured, pouring wine. "At least have a glass of wine before you go." He looked up at Ewen and, without prattle or irony or camp, said, "Please?" and Ewen saw then why Teresa had loved him since she was six. He saw a wise guilelessness, a boy's eyes before the dirty jokes begin.

At the etched door a large man in an opera cape with a red lining said, in an American voice that was trying to be English, "Don't go. We're just getting to know each other."

Ewen escaped into the night street. A laugh drifted after him. He didn't get angry until he was shaking with cold in the corner of a taxi. Even after taking the pills he lay shivering in bed, waiting for Teresa to come home. It was the first time he had been in the bed alone.

He tried to read Bishop's *Essays on Geomorphology*, but the words slipped past without meaning. He stared at the ceiling and thought that all fairy tales were true and that the evening, the whole thing, had been haunted by childhood—innocence and wishes and love threatened by hate and witches and darkness. All the fairy tales with the prince, the fairy prince, and, God knows, he told the ceiling, Noel is that. Children know who the witch is before they grow up and lose their wisdom, and then they forget that all fairy tales are true if you ignore the happy-ever-after bit that adults have tacked on to make themselves feel better. No. It is the darkness, the haunted woods, the whispers, the curses that the children recognize as true. He wished he didn't hate her so, and he wondered what he was going to do without her. He drifted into sleep, not meaning to, meaning to wait to tell her. It was dawn by then, without color or warmth, the time, he remembered, not sure at the threshold of sleep if he too was dreaming, when you could distinguish the black thread from the white.

Noel and Teresa had fallen into timelessness, leaning back on the sofa, letting themselves take up where they had left off, as they had when she was fourteen. The only interruption had come from the large American in the red-lined cape who had tried to speak to Noel, who had said, "Bugger off, missy, you're not wanted," and explained, "She's a bloody menace, a truly nasty creature. Her bag, as she calls it, is to buy working-class boys with acid they can't afford. Swinging London is a cesspool. You and your nice friend wouldn't know about that. One of the boys she turned on was found dead on a mountain in Morocco. But never mind about her. You first, darling. Tell."

"We were in your bedroom and I was wearing your Coronation robe, and your mother came in . . ."

They both laughed.

"Then I went back to Switzerland to school and then I grew up and then I went to Vassar and then I went to graduate school and I lived with Michael Cerrutti, who was an archaeologist, and we were married and we went to Kurdistan . . ."

"Then . . . ?"

"He was killed and I came home. I got my Ph.D. and taught and I got cancer and nearly died, so I decided to come here and do as I pleased."

"Where does your friend Ewen fit into this story that you tell in such fascinating detail?"

"I didn't want to bore you." She remembered too late how Noel, or the black monk, had taught her to tell the truth, but that had always been silent. She tried again. "I met Ewen at the British Museum. He was in D8 and I was in B8 and we fell in love with each other in the basement . . ." They were suddenly both helpless with laughter. Noel poured from the second bottle of wine.

"You're not going to get off so easily, dearie. I feel like telling all in infinite detail, and who else would I tell?"

He seemed tentative for a pause, not the old Noel, who never had been. "You don't mind, do you?" She took his hand again, cold from the glass, and said no, she didn't, to the new Noel, who had, at least, some echo of the black monk's certainty. She even patted his hand, and stopped, afraid the old Noel might not like it. "After all," she told them both without saying a word, "I ought to listen. I owe it to you. The times you've advised me. Your voice."

"You make me feel like a ghost, you do, you and tonight and that ghost moon through the dirty windows of the drawing room. What I'm going to tell you is a ghost story, too, of a kind . . .

"You see, the last day you saw me, Mum had her gimlet eye on me because she had arranged to get me an appointment out of the country and she didn't want me to get into any mischief while I was waiting to go. However many were cheering and carrying on that day about the Queen, there was many another poor queen of England quaking in his boots. 1953 was a bad year for queens, whatever you might think. *Agents provocateurs* in drag in the Underground, raids on clubs like this, friends up in the Central Criminal Court of the Old Bailey for obscene libel because they wrote about the existence of love between men without the necessary derisive terms—bugger, faggot, bum boy, poof, queer, fairy, pansy—yes, dearie, I was and am, God knows, and He does, all of those. I tried not to be. Whoever wants the door to ordinary daily life to clang behind him? I certainly didn't. I wanted to be lazy and elegant and rich and handsome and admired and stupid, but instead the good Lord made me brilliant and elegant and rich and pretty and the most popular bum boy at Eton. That, my darling Teresa, was your fairy prince.

"So poor nerve-racked Mummy was frantic to get me away. I left a week after the Coronation for Hong Kong. Oh, I forgot to say . . . I had read Mandarin at Oxford. I was, as they say sadly about boys who don't fulfill promises they never made, absolutely brilliant at Oxford. All very well. My tutor my first year went back to China after the revolution, thinking that his mind and his training and his six languages would be of service to the new world, but he was put to work as a coolie on a dam to 'reeducate' him, and he died of fatigue. From the time I heard that, I had to get to the East . . . confused a bit about why. I thought if I were already there I might be appointed to Peking, or maybe I wanted to understand the kind of forces that are being let loose all over the world, the rough beasts that would kill a man because he has a mind and a delicate spirit, not even an aristo like me, just intelligent and kind and hopeful.

"Anyway," he went on, pouring more wine. "We're going to be drunk. I hope you don't mind. You see, when I was called up for my National Service when I came down from Oxford, I was seconded to the School of Oriental Languages and learned Cantonese as well. Now, what you have to understand is that the characters are the same, but Mandarin has four tones— ding DING *ding* DING—if you say a word in low ding it means a different thing from the same word in high ding, if you see what I mean, while Cantonese has seven . . . oh, never mind . . . But it is part of the story in a way. I was quite literally the only person in the colonial administration in Hong Kong who knew the difference. There we were in a small colonial city with the same kinds of buildings that the Empire built in all the far-flung places. It was very comfortable and very attractive and oh, so cricket and racing and boring.

"Even if it was for a while only the colonial civil service when Mummy had wanted the diplomatic corps, she comforted herself that I was being got out of the country and that our only—repeat, only—truly aristocratic cousin had gone there from Peking at the beginning of the revolution. He had lived in the Far East for years. Mummy never stopped reminding my poor father of the fact that she was the niece of a proper belted earl and that James was a tenth earl when he inherited, unlike poor Father, who was quite happily growing up in Golders Green and only managed to move south to Stanhope Terrace when his father made the honors list because of some deals—nefarious, I'm sure—that he made during the First World War.

"That was when his mum, who was aye by goom North Country, insisted on Regent's Park, which was as piss-elegant as the poor dear could imagine. They spent an absolute mint creating that splendid interior, literally bought up a country house and had the late-Georgian moldings and woodwork moved to the Stanhope Terrace house. Oh, you didn't know, I'm sure, few people do, that all those terraces were no more than theatrical façades and the houses behind them were not at all grand. Grandfather bought the two in the middle and knocked them together. Oh, what you have to understand, too, is that the instinct of new aristos is to go south of Oxford Street like lemmings. That's why Mummy hated Stanhope Terrace and went to Park Lane as soon as me poor old dad succumbed to the pull from the north and the pull from the south and I became the third and last baron in a madly short line when I was ten.

"So, you see, she thought she was sending me to the safety of caste at least when she wrote my cousin James. What she did not know, or perhaps she didn't care, was that James was a vicious, raddled, agonized old queen. That's good, the raddled queen, no, it's the mobled queen. Where was I?

"James. James lived in a castellated house in the Bonham Road, the grandest address at mid-levels in Hong Kong. He dressed in Mandarin robes he had looted from Peking, and he absolutely, blatantly, kept a stable of the prettiest Chinese buggers in Hong Kong. He got by with it in the British Colony because he was the only earl they had at the time, and, believe me, among the snob ladies from Surbiton who make up colonial society, a peerage beats buggery every time.

"James's public rooms were on the ground floor and very grand, very English: heavy Thai silk curtains in what I call Mayfair yellow, English antiques, some discreet Chinese bronzes. That's where he had his snob parties.

"But the third floor was a madly expensive third-rate set for a gay Dr. Fu Manchu. You see, he was the sort of man some people think we all are, a parody, a pose. I couldn't bear him, but there was no place else to go at first. The Lord does work in mysterious ways, doesn't He just? Sometimes rather nasty . . ." Noel leaned back and put his hands behind his head and stretched his legs as long as he could and closed his eyes. He was quiet for so long that Teresa thought he had forgotten his story because of the wine and was taking a little nap. She decided to slip out and find a taxi. She was worried about Ewen. He had looked as if an attack were coming on, and she, besotted, she told herself, with Noel's flashy nonsense, had let him leave. Not that he wanted her around when he was in an attack. He skulked off, as mean, he said, as a dog shitting bones, to be left alone until it was over.

Noel said, going where she was, "That gaunt and beautiful young man you picked up in the BM. I know I've seen him before."

Oh, God, she thought, is that why he can't make love to me, not malaria at all?

"Really, darling, there you are, Miss Porridge, with your doctorate and your healthy bluish American corneas, and your cute little minidress, and you fall into love and innocence as if you had a right to it. He has been to hell. That's what I meant. I can tell, you know. I recognize my compatriots. So have you."

He opened his eyes and looked at her then. "So stop thinking what you're thinking, you nasty-minded thing."

She looked at him, but his eyes were closed again. She was aware that she knew very little about Ewen.

"I don't mean sex. Stop that. Oh, if people only knew how unimportant that is. No, I'm talking about people who've been to the well . . ."

"We call it crossing the river, the Styx." She was shy about admitting that.

"You've started speaking the same language. Yes. The Styx. Or the well or the Bethesda Fountain, William Cowper's fountain filled with blood drawn from Emmanuel's veins. It's whatever you've faced you can't retreat from. It's a stillness. Veterans have it, and old, surviving whores. After it, you're more alive, not less. You see more clearly, or you can't bear your own awareness and you take to drugs or vice or kill yourself some other way; all of that is so boring and cowardly, I think. With drugs or vice you just end up with your looks gone and your bowels in a mess. How did you get to the well? How did Ewen?"

"I don't know, only hints. All I know is that it burned him."

"I know what it is. The eyes look scorched. Saints have it in old paintings. I'm getting drunk. Are you?"

She wasn't ready to tell him any more about herself; she was superstitious. What she wanted to tell him was all future, and still too tentative to put into words. Instead, she said. "You have the eyes, too," and then she spoke the invitation that she knew was dangerous, for to unburden is to burden. "Tell me what happened."

"Darling, like the old sailor who stoppeth the wedding guest, I can't wait. I said it was a ghost story. It's that and it's a love story, too. It's a bit of a confession. I hope you don't mind. Now that we've given up priests and head shrinks are like whores and do it for money, here we are with all that's left, this wine, this awful waiting room, this friend." He took her hand again. "Oh, Lordy Lord! You mustn't stop me, you know, or I'll get self-conscious and dry up, and I must go there. I must."

"I can still see James, lording it in the Peninsula lobby all la-di-da over as frazzled a group of displaced persons as you can imagine. God knows I had that at least in common with them, trans-Atlantic and furiously embarrassed about it all through Eton and Oxford because I hadn't stayed in England, as if I could, with me only ten years old and Mummy making all the decisions.

"Anyway, there they were. Let me tell you about the Peninsula lobby, a home away from home, with all that that entails. Take teatime. Everybody who was anybody in Hong Kong turned up at the Peninsula for tea. Can you believe it? The English sat on one side of the lobby, the lesser breeds, including rajahs, rich Chinese, Australians, Americans, a lot of the *Almanach de Gotha* who'd been kicked out of Europe, and Japanese princesses on the other, while the colonial ladies from Surbiton gazed down at the rest of the world with their pale eyes under the pale brims of their pale hats, while their pale daughters waited to be noticed by subalterns who just might marry them and take them all the way to another table. The lobby is, of course, superb—huge, high columns, oceans of gilt, a gorgeous molded ceiling. I used to look up at the nymphs and be homesick for Stanhope Terrace.

"The lobby was other things, too. The most elegant whorehouse in the East. If you sat in one place you were already bespoke. If you sat in another you were available. It didn't work for boys, though. Not there, anyway.

"But there were low bars for boys, and elegant, discreet clubs like this one, all a mirror reflection of the other life, the same rules, the same snobberies, the same recognitions. We can size one another up at a glance, just as two English ladies know each other anywhere.

"James was the center of that desiccated group of rich expatriates left over from the twenties who were still in love with the East. They had lived in Soochow and Peking and Shanghai for years, and they still knew only nine words of chop-chop Mandarin—all orders to servants. They sat there afternoon after afternoon, waiting for evening and perpetual bridge games that had started during their internment and had simply kept on. One woman told about their being released from Stanley in the middle of a rubber, and weak as they were from hunger, they'd gone straight to the Repulse Bay Hotel and finished the rubber, even before they bathed. The story always ended that way. 'We didn't even bathe,' she would say, still surprised.

"So they sat drinking tea or gin and bragging about when they had been interned. There was a hierarchy, of course, even to that. Two Englishmen form a hierarchy anywhere. Sometimes I joined them. They were a lot more amusing than the Surbiton ladies, with their avid eyes on my body and my money and my handle. If they suspected that I was a bugger, they certainly didn't let on, or care, so long, as a mild little pansy in Government House told me, I was *reasonably* discreet.

"I had had sense enough not to try to live in the Bonham Road or on the Peak, where no Chinese were allowed—not in that colonial fish tank. I took a delightful house, all white with green shutters and large cool rooms with ceiling fans. It had tiled verandas on both sides, and a lovely wrought-iron balcony across the front. It was British Empire at its absolute best. It was on a hill in Kowloon, just walking distance from the Peninsula.

"I could see Hong Kong island across the harbor. Hong Kong then was a quiet, rather lazy city, a green city with parks and gardens. That was the English part, and the English had built most of the mansions and all the public buildings. Here and there, though, there were marvelous stone houses built by the Portuguese from Macao long before the English came. I used to wonder at them; Saracen arches, thick stone walls for coolness, tile and marble, and arched windows to the floor. You can trace the architecture wherever the Moors touched for a while. Lovely. There were the Chinese houses of the rich merchants, and the rich who had fled the mainland cities, some as long ago as the Sino-Japanese War in 1937. It was a city of refugees.

"That's how I saw it, including myself. There we all were, poised on the edge of the sea and another world, waiting until it was time to move again. Even the boat people, the Tanka, who had been there for centuries, were refugees from Kubla Khan. And the Hakka, the farmers who live in the New Territories, are refugees who came from the north so long ago they have forgotten who they were fleeing from. All that is left of the memory is their name—Hakka—guest.

"So, you see, the huddles of English expatriates, the buggers, the vice lords, and the Mandarins and the manufacturers and the rich from Shanghai and Canton were nothing new, just more refugees in a station on the road to somewhere . . .

"But we were all only part of the gaudy façade of Hong Kong. Thousands of refugees were arriving every day to a city we knew little of, not on that narrow road from the Peak to Government House to the Queen's Road to the Jockey Club, across the harbor to the Peninsula or around the island to Repulse Bay past the Cricket Club and the Happy Valley race track. The English lived there for years, knowing little else, while all around them a Chinese city was growing from a few hundred thousand to a million, to two million, then three, then more, in waves of refugees from hunger and the revolution.

"Christ! Hong Kong! They lived in squatter camps on the sides of the mountains under the windows of the great houses. They died of starvation in Nathan Road while their cousins served us in the Peninsula Hotel. There had been a horrible fire the year before I arrived. It had wiped out one of the huge squatter towns, and the government was beginning to do something about it. I still don't know why, but I asked to be part of a team to question new refugee families. I caught their sorrows and their diseases. No, darling, it is hardly sorrow that has blanched my cheeks, although God knows it ought to be. It is ever-recurring amoebic dysentery. *That's* where I've seen your chap. At the outpatients' ward, the Hospital for Tropical Diseases. All that's left of the Empire has fetched up there. I knew it. Never forget a face, at least not one that handsome. Don't mind me, I will be flighty. You see, I'm getting a little too near the crux of the matter. Why crux, I wonder. Cross? Cross to bear?

"The problem was so enormous that I used to find myself furious with the people for being so many, so hungry, so troubled. They, too, were a parody, a mirror of any other society, only stripped down to nothing but bones and voices, and at first, with all my fine studying, we had little language in common. I had learned to speak to people who no longer existed about things that hardly mattered in the face of that displacement. There was no Peking Embassy where people dined, and there were guests like Wellington Koo and the Soong sisters. I had to learn the language of hunger and fear, and people who had no future. Once in a while I would find a family who received me as graciously as they always had, as an honored guest from a better time, and they would let fall, subtly, that they had been landlords or teachers or intellectuals or whatever, and I would accept all this in a squatter hut where I couldn't stand upright.

"In the spring rains they washed down the mountains into the sea.

"Sometimes I went to James's. From the third-floor balcony at night you could look down on the lights of the western district and hear it, like a beehive. Chinese families had built houses on top of houses, on top of apartment buildings, on top of apartments that had once been grand houses, on one of the most famous nineteenth-century brothels in Hong Kong. If you walked down the streets so steep they were made of stone stairs, you could see old stone mansions that housed ten or fifteen Chinese families, always expanding. Every day they expected knocks at their doors and more relatives arriving on the run from the mainland, and the hunger and the fear, not Mandarins or vice lords, or the rich, or political refugees anymore, but just people swept along down the Pearl River with the tide.

"So even standing on the balcony at James's with the perpetual gay party going on behind me, I couldn't escape the stench and politeness and sorrow of my day. That night a full moon dimmed the lights of the city. It shone on the harbor, and beyond it I could see the railway station and the Peninsula and where my house was across the dark water that caught the moon and rocked it, and the boats—oh, God, this is hard to tell. I knew there was someone standing beside me, and can you believe this? I knew who it was. Please don't laugh. I had never seen him before and I already knew who it was.

"You can't know what was happening. You've had the kind of love that grows, I can tell. This was a *coup de foudre*. I knew it. I'd seen it happen. You see, all my life I had been the beloved, the one who led and who escaped and who was terribly kind to whatever poor sod I'd caught in a net I never asked to have. Now, in one minute, I began to suffer all the suffering I had ever caused. I became, as a punishment, a lover instead. There he was, that boy, Wei Li, poised, light on his feet, as if he could fly over the harbor and hover at my house.

"How can I tell you about that night? I still live it, minute by minute. It's like—I know—the night of a great event, the end of a war, the death of a king. You know, you ask a woman about the King's death and she'll say, I was standing in the fish queue, and think she is telling you about the King's death.

"I'll remember tonight like that, and that night . . . That night

I didn't listen to the usual remarks he made. I was only sorry that he felt he had to make them, not to me, who had heard them all and didn't care what was true and what wasn't—his first time at James's, how he didn't know what he was getting into, how his parents were landlords in Canton, how he needed a job, any job.

"He put his hand in mine like a child trusting a grown-up to take him across a street. So you see, whatever happened later, the lying he felt was so important, the light ways he had, I knew at that first minute. So I can't blame anyone or anything, any more than you can blame the lightning in the *coup de foudre*. It rained that night, too, one of those quick rains that come to Hong Kong, and there was lightning over the city. It lit up the narrow street and the tenements below us on the hillside. We moved back into the doorway and watched it, still holding hands.

"We didn't fly over the harbor. We didn't launch ourselves from James's balcony, although God knows I've done it often enough since in the dream life I still live with him. I am never safe from his intrusion when I sleep. No. We said good night to James, who was lying on a Chinese sofa like a great pudding in red and gold robes, smoking opium while a pretty boy held his pipe. James was so orthodox in the setting of his vices and the way he sought corruption.

"I didn't go back there to his house until his funeral a year later, and even then I wouldn't let Wei Li go with me. There was a rumor that there would be trouble—*gweilo* trouble. That means foreign devil, or foreign ghost, if you prefer. I think ghost is better, because we are never quite real to them.

"You see, James may or may not have committed suicide. There was a massive shot of heroin in him when he was found, three or four days later, a great putrid pool of flesh deserted by his servants, his boys, everyone. He had finally achieved his corruption, four days of lying in the tropics, rotting under his silk robes.

"The week before, a boy, a boy like Wei Li, had fallen, or jumped, from the balcony we had been standing on. James was a curious kind of voyeur. He didn't care much about watching sex, although he did. He liked to get the boys high on whatever was the weekly fashionable drug and then watch them. I heard that the boy ran through the room, chased by a dragon, and then I heard it was a soldier, and then a tiger, all rumor, but always I heard that James was laughing and holding his genitals, and when the boy sailed over the balcony and they heard him land in the Bonham Road, he went on laughing and holding himself.

"Nobody would buy the house after he died. People said it was haunted by both James and the boy and that there was bad *fung shui* there, which meant that the house had disturbed the flow and order of the universe, no less. It fell into a kind of neglect and then into ruin, and then one day when I passed, Chinese families had moved into it. I saw a woman airing James's Thai silk curtains on the terrace and there were three children playing near her. You see, we hardly existed, I told you, even our ghosts, when there was real survival at stake. I should have remembered that. Our insults to them, the way we used them either as objects or as people to train and save from something we never understood—none of that mattered. The woman, like so much I have brought home in my house and in my mind, always stands there, always swinging one of James's Mayfair-yellow curtains in a high arc over the stone balustrade in the sun.

"But that first time with Wei Li, the night was huge over us, with those reflections in the water of fans and streaks of clouds that always seemed to race across the sky from some source beyond the horizon. They reflected the city lights and that moment of lightning as if for once the elements were answering us instead of the usual heavenly indifference.

"It was that night that Wei Li said he took me to China. He would speak of it that way from time to time, his pleasure and his joke. I can hear him saying, 'That was the night I took you to China.'

"We still cross the night street, still holding hands, and the pavement so soon after the rain shines like black glass. The air is steaming hot and close and damp, and it holds the heavy scent of tuberoses and something else, joss perhaps, or just the steam from the rain on the trees. We cross and we start down the stairs without end in the darkness. I can't see yet, and I stumble on the broken stones. I should be afraid. We have been warned against these deep streets at night, but I am at home and more than happy accepting what is happening. Wei Li laughs and guides me and I am getting used to the dark. There are forms of people around braziers that cast light on their faces, which seem to linger there on the edge of the fire forever.

"There is no time, not this night, and never will be. It stops. Oh, the city rolls toward dawn, and the darkness of the streets is shot with wilder sound below the terraces, where I can see roof shadows of the fine houses that have become Chinese tenements, as they creep up the hillside nearer and nearer the Bonham Road.

"The air is close, and there is the smell of a man. He lies neatly in the night street against a wall, nearly naked, asleep, his belongings arranged around him as in a hotel room, the shadow of a paper shopping bag and the shadow of an English brolly.

"We enter the bright lights of a bar. There are crowds of Chinese people who respect one another's space and never seem to jostle or bump into one another or us, even in the dark, and the flashes of neon, and the splashed light as doors open and shut again. We pass open fish stalls, and the smell of new bread, and vegetable stalls arranged by colors under single, naked, hanging light bulbs. The Chinese families seem to take turns working most of the night.

"It becomes quieter only later, when the old women have

stopped their singsong talking, which sounds like arguing, and the children have crawled under the stalls to sleep. It is too hot in the close-packed tenements to sleep inside. We can look downhill at the roofs of buildings, all the way to the waterfront, with their bundles of sleepers. We pass corner altars where someone has burned a paper offering and there is still the smell of burned paper and the joss-stick prayers still smolder and I want to touch Wei Li, touch him to see if he is real. There are so many ghosts. But I dare not. It is not correct, he says. 'Not correct' is one of the few English phrases he knows, but he refuses already to speak to me in Cantonese. He says he must learn English to make money.

"Sometimes in that night he forgets that I can understand, and he tells boys he seems to know that I am a *gweilo* uncle, a dead white man whom he is guiding. He says he is a tourist guide to save face, and he is taking me to Wanchai to find a woman, always a woman, and I know I must take great care because of his fragile shame at what I am and what he is. He fools nobody, of course. They laugh behind us, and someone sings the Cantonese slang word for bugger.

"We walk now in the light along the waterfront, past the dark pile of Cook's, that building that looks as if it ought to be in St. Pancras and not displaced there facing the harbor in the South China Sea. We pass the dark dome of the courthouse. We are in the English part of the city for a little while, out of the crowded hutches of the Chinese streets, and I can see how much room we take up—the cricket grounds, the gardens, the parks, and, in the dark, the sweet scent and whisper of plants instead of the smell and rustle of a million human beings just beyond the periphery of the light.

"At the ferry a man laughs, up and down the scale, a Chinese laugh, and I sense Wei Li's terror. He is poised to run away. We stand teetering at the edge of never seeing each other again and I cannot bear this moment. I cannot bear it, no matter what happens afterward.

"Someone once told me that the difference between recall and memory is that in recall you see yourself there and in memory you know intelligently that you were there. I am standing there by the ferry and it is nearly morning. Somehow we have walked and rested and walked for five or six hours and no time has passed. We stop, and we walk again, and a girl passes in a tight Chinese dress, silk, with silk hair, and she has long legs and Wei Li looks after her and I think, Please, oh, please no. I am begging the empty air without saying a word.

"But at the ferry I do. I have to. Say the word, I mean. It has rained again. It must have. The street is wet and the moon is racing along behind clouds and it comes out and I see it glitter in his eyes as he waits, maybe for me to speak, maybe poised to make up his mind to run away and forget that I exist. All night we have not touched each other except for that first holding of hands.

"I know the word that will make him turn again and get on the ferry with me, the word that for twelve years is going to steady with a necessary illusion the permanence I hope for. I offer him a job.

" 'I am not a house boy,' he says, bargaining. 'My parents and my ancestors are landlords in Shanghai.' He has forgotten that he said Canton, and he has forgotten that he will speak only English. The bargaining is too important. He sings the bargaining Cantonese chant.

"I promise that he will be my secretary. Secretary. There I am, only four years older than Wei Li, already treating him in the way that he demands, uncle and employer of a secretary who has had four years of schooling.

"He smiles. I think he smiles. The moon has gone again and left us in the dark, that deepest dark just before the dawn begins to lift out of the horizon from the China Sea. By the time we have reached Kowloon on the ferry, fatigue and the pre-dawn sea breeze have made us both weightless and clean and damp with dew.

"We go to bed for the whole day, making love and planning.

"What we all have in common, you see, is the hope for permanence. We can't marry, as you can, with law and custom to act as ramparts in the bad times. All we have is promise and hope and that instinct for nesting. Sometimes we frighten others off with our need and that makes us querulous. I knew that. I had been a fugitive from the needs of others too many times.

"I send for dim sum and serve us both in bed, under the languid ceiling fan; just the white walls, and the white arena of the bed, and the curtains that lift and billow, showing us glimpses of the wrought-iron balcony and the harbor. The Peak across the water is covered with a dark cloud so that the government buildings and the cathedral under it look like bleached bones, tiny in the distance.

"He is a joy to me. He misses nothing. He has a wonderful ability to admire—vases, flowers, furniture he could never have been that near before. He recognizes them all, as if he had been waiting to be in the calm beauty I have constructed, waiting, too, although I had not known it, for someone like him to see it all. He pulls out clothes from my cupboard and dresses his naked bronze body in suits from Savile Row. I give him some of them. I give him everything for fear already that he will be bored and pivot in that way he has, in some direction I don't know.

"He did that later. But that was afterward. After what? Was there an event, or was it slow attrition? I was too happy to know. I have gone over it again and again to find the moment, something I can understand. I only know that before it, before the moment, if there was one, we were secure and happy and we shone, as people do, with the kind of joy that makes you notice colors and the sweet scent and touch of small things that you wouldn't have noticed otherwise.

"Surely there was a reason for the change. I guess we did become a half-hidden scandal. We certainly weren't circumspect, not at first. God forbid that I sink into circumspection. But I did, later, because of him.

"Wei Li insisted. The illusion of his employment waxed and waned, depending on how he thought the world was seeing us. We were breaking the deepest double taboo in the Crown Colony of Hong Kong, and it was not our sex, believe me. Oh, it was fine among the English to make servants and whores of the Chinese, and it was fine among the Chinese to make fools of the foreign ghosts and take their money and deny their existence. All of that was acceptable so long as you didn't make friends. Friendship, oh, what is the word?—peerage, of course, an equality of recognitions—was taboo in 1955 and for a long time afterward. In a way, what happened to us happened too early. Later the barriers melted rather than broke down. The rich Chinese were being educated in England. They were less aloof, the English less prejudiced; but not then. It was still a lazy ten-to-four colony of horse racing and cricket and snobbery, and the women sat on the terrace of the Repulse Bay Hotel, wan in the heat, and judged each other in accents they had acquired along the way.

"I remember one day—it must have been a year later, or two, I don't know. Wei Li was out and I was worried. He had been gone for two days. Yes, two years later, that disappearing had begun. I had fallen, as one does, into patience with him, and hours of relief when he was gone from my mind. There isn't any other way to tell how things change. You recall moments, small events that reflect the change, like that day, that afternoon.

"I remember that I was lonely and that the weather was bad and it was dark enough to turn on the lamps. I remember thinking he would see them in the Salisbury Road shining from the hill. I heard a knock on the door, and I answered it, knowing it would be Wei Li and he had forgotten his keys again, but it wasn't. It was Reggie Williams from Government House.

"Reggie was a bit of a joke. He started every sentence with 'Phoebe and I . . .' Phoebe was the parody and essence of all the Englishwomen there. You don't see them anymore. They have disappeared as the colonies have disappeared, and now they live in places like the Cotswolds or Devon in ex-vicarages, getting grayer and grayer, and their cardigans sag at the pockets. But then Phoebe, all the Phoebes, were the real law of the colony, never mind that their husbands kept Chinese mistresses so they could get a bit of peace. Never mind that they courted me for their pale, rapacious daughters. All they asked was that I be judicious.

"Reggie pulled his trousers up at the knees and sat down. He looked very embarrassed. He said, 'Phoebe and I . . .' I wasn't listening, really. I was listening for the door. His voice drifted along behind me while I fixed him a drink, something about my welfare, and they were so fond of me, and so deeply worried, and then I heard that word 'judicious.'

"I handed him his drink and I said, 'Judiciousness is not one of my vices, Reggie.' I was still listening for the door.

"He was in a state of painful embarrassment by then, but I knew he didn't dare go home to Phoebe until he'd said what she had told him to. 'Phoebe and I . . .' he started again. 'Well, if you would, well, sort of, you know, join us more often. You are sort of, well, one of us, you know. We know that there is nothing to the rumor, but if you would enter the life of your own set and sort of let people know, well, come on your own, sort of extra man, sort of thing, you are very popular, don't you know . . .' He ran down.

"Then I set fire to my bridges as delicately as you would light a joss stick and, in a way, burning my bridges was a kind of prayer for a permanence I no longer believed in, knowing all the time that no person was my rival, only the street.

"I said, 'I'm sorry, Reggie, you tell Phoebe that whom I sleep with I eat with. Tell Phoebe that I like to live by the only regal remark Edward VIII ever made—Discretion is not for princes.'

"I still hear him say, 'I can't tell Phoebe that!'

"Wei Li walked in then, as polished as ever. He had become very polished, very much the young Chinese gentleman, and he spoke my English, which I had taught him, almost to the manner born. I kissed him in front of Reggie and said, 'I'm glad you're back.'

"Both of them were too shocked to speak. I think I could hear the paper crackle of my bridges burning, like those paper houses and cars and record players the Chinese burn for the comfort of the dead.

"I took Reggie to his car. I saw that tears were swimming in his eyes, little bright sparks. I remember thinking, People called Reggie can't cry. They belong in comedies saying, Tennis, anyone? But he was. He said he couldn't help it. He leaned against the car and muttered. I had to get closer to hear him. 'Oh, God,' he kept saying. 'It isn't that you're a bugger, Noel. It's that he's ruining you. Sooner or later you're going to have to resign from the government. It isn't that there aren't . . . well, sort of others . . . It's . . .'

" 'I know, Reggie,' I told him. I might have been crying, too, by then. 'They're judicious.'

" 'Dammit, Noel, they don't have your money.' He stood up then and blew his nose and wiped his face. 'No, I'm sorry I said that. It denies your courage. It's that you're foolhardy,' he said, and blew his nose again, dear kind man, using an admiring *Boy's Own Paper* word. I thought of sailors with cutlasses boarding ships, not an old queen like me simply admitting that he loved another person. I was only twenty-five or so by then, but old goes with queen, it just does. I wondered for a second if Reggie, too, was, but then we always do, think everybody is, I mean, or maybe just hope, so that the gates of society cannot prevail against us. That's the Bible.

"Oh yes. I went through that, too, all the High Church boys sobbing in back pews, bringing their broken and contrite hearts to whoever would listen. I could do that broken bit, but the contrite bit just didn't ring true with me. You see, I knew that I had been, just for a little while, blessed, and the world had changed for me forever. I couldn't deny it and I couldn't go back—your river Styx, I suppose.

"I still try to fathom the change. It's hard to tell about or know. It's always already happened when you tell. I remember quiet times, events before and after. Like remembering Reggie tonight, like this. That was an after. I remember going back into the house and Wei Li saying he was leaving, he couldn't stay, he said, after I had shamed him in front of a *gweilo*—shamed him by accepting what he was to me. I was surrounded by people who wanted to keep everything secret. He was speaking English in a parody of my voice, a sort of comic aristo nasal that made me want to laugh when I was so far from laughter.

"Of course he didn't leave, not that time or any of the other times. He would stay away longer and longer, but he always came back. It wasn't the money or the comfort, not entirely. He had made me mother and father by then.

"The years pass in fragments. I can see now the balance we had at first, and we did have it for a while. Then balance became compromise, and then the hope of compromise, and then salvaging what was left. I see myself now as I was then, finally grateful for his company and for quiet evenings, for things, even for an evening, to be as they had been, and I was twenty-eight, and -nine, and thirty. Wei Li looked after me when I was ill. He always did.

"Was it that summer or another summer? I grew numb with understanding and began to read poetry. He stayed much the same, Wei Li, flashing out of the house in cuff links I had given him, playing the rich, young Chinese.

"Not worth it? You don't weigh it like that. Worth has nothing to do with it. I learned that it isn't whom we love but that we love, and I learned that we must see things through to the end, if there is an end.

"It must have been another summer, later. I see myself in the garden and it has begun to be overgrown. There is a lizard in a flash of sun that has fallen through the trees and warmed a rock. I am on Cheung Chau; one of the new beginnings we went through, there were so many, so many 'this times.' We gave up the house on Kowloon. I had left the government by then and I was fooling myself that I was staying in Hong Kong to study Mandarin. I commuted by ferry to a teacher, an old man who had come from Peking. For a while, anyway. I did that for a while, that and other things, bronzes and ceramics, training my fingertips to tell their age.

"I had, without really deciding, joined the sad group of expatriates who can't bring themselves to leave, who make the excuse of studying—oh, anything—Taoism or Buddhism or acupuncture or ceramics. I even went back to the Peninsula from time to time and played bridge in the evenings, out of homesickness for a home I had never cared for.

"Then I would leave my car in Hong Kong if Wei Li hadn't taken it and take the last ferry back to Cheung Chau and look up from the deck to see if there were lights on the hill, which meant that Wei Li had come home. Sometimes, enough times to keep me in thrall, there were.

"Cheung Chau, the island of longing, the ghost island where every year they placated the hungry ghosts and those who had been murdered. It had been a pirate and smugglers' stronghold for centuries. Some of the houses were older than any on Hong Kong. Although the authorities said all that was past, I watched the single sampans moor in the late evening from my balcony, fishing in the silver twilight, and when night came I would hear the quiet plash of oars as they landed their human contraband. We were in the estuary of the Pearl River, surrounded by islands belonging to the People's Republic. The human cargo floated downriver in the night, and waited all day to land.

"I know. It was 1962, because I remember thinking the lizard had survived Wanda, the worst typhoon in years. The garden we had planted together had been swept flat; there were still broken windows on the upstairs veranda. We had been on the island, let's see, four years?

"Wei Li had thought—how did he say it?—he had thought that if we moved out of what he called the temptations of the city he would be happier. Poor boy.

"We took a beautiful Portuguese house on a hill looking out toward Hong Kong island over the South China Sea. Down below we could see the roof of a temple to the sea goddess, Tin Hau, with its carved dolphins on the roofbeam and its platform, where at the outdoor altar they tried to placate the sea or the ghosts that haunted the island or the wind that blew across it bringing good fishing or storms. When the windows groaned or the shutters sighed, they said the wind was the ghosts or that the ghosts were the wind.

"I remember we walked through the rooms the day we found it as if we had just discovered ourselves along with it. 'I feel at home,' he said, surprised, who had never felt at home for more than a little while, and then, I suspect, any place that let him in, for he was a refugee all the way to his soul.

"It had a two-story veranda with stone arches and columns across the front, and one of the floors was paved with *azulejo* tiles from Portugal. It was very very old, but no one admitted it. It had been built when the pirates owned the island and the people hated to talk about them because they were afraid of the ghosts. Those were ancestors they had to honor in silence.

"We chose furniture together. I sent for photographs of the chinoiserie bed in the V and A and had it copied by a Chinese cabinetmaker. Ever since I first went there with Nanny I had loved it and thought it would be fine to die in. We found a wonderful gold horse the size of a carousel horse, and dragon columns of carved wood that someone had managed to smuggle down the Pearl River.

"There were jokes, as there had been at the beginning. He didn't even seem ashamed anymore. I can still hear him laugh when we bought pillows in the open market that were called Double Happiness pillows. We wandered among the stalls with their piles of thousand-year-old eggs and birds' nests and snake oil, and carried home freshly roasted, russet-colored piglets.

"The whole center of the village of Cheung Chau is an open market where you can find charms and fans and gold and jade and fish swimming against the glass walls of their tanks and crabs the color of blue and red jewels. He would tell me then, This is China. Not the city with its *gweilo* buildings or the People's Republic with its slogans. This. He would point to the shrines on street corners, in front of houses and temples, where the joss sticks always burned and there were always warm ashes from paper sacrifices, and sometimes he would laugh at it all and say, Backward people, peasants, in his fine new voice, speaking English loudly so the old women could recognize the contempt but not the words. He never said such things in Chinese, though, because of the ghosts, emancipated as he thought he was, poor child.

"There he was, poised between three worlds of choice and belonging to none, and so I was more patient with him than I might have been. He was neither Communist nor old Chinese nor English. Like Hong Kong itself, he glowed with a precarious and urgent pride, always poised on the edge of things.

"He tried. He even gardened, at first. On that tropical island you could make a garden in a few weeks. He placed stones and piled a hillock to make a dragon below the veranda. He said it would protect the house from bad ghosts. We grew red lilies, and the lantana tumbled down the hill along the stone walk to the beach.

"Then he tired of it and left it to me. He went more often to Hong Kong. He said he needed freedom; he wanted to improve himself. He talked of trying to take examinations for the university, not knowing that by then he was already too old, and that he had no background for it. He was swimming at the glass like one of the bright fish in the market. I had to let him go. He still said he loved me.

"I think he meant it, but he lied, too, easy lies to uncover. Sometimes I thought he might have gotten himself into something, maybe political, maybe vicious, maybe it was entirely innocent and mundane. I never did know. He became furious if I asked. He said I didn't trust him.

"Later he was gone most of the time, except at the weekends, when half of Hong Kong came to swim at the beaches and I barricaded myself in the house. I could hear the faint yells of boys swimming far away below the temple. Wei Li loved the weekends, and his pride in the house was touching. I could always depend on him being home if the weather was good. He stayed on the beach all day, letting his lovely lithe body grow a dark gold, and at night he gambled. The Chinese love to gamble. You could hear the loud rush of mah-jongg tiles being shuffled all the way up from the beachside restaurant where he liked to play all night.

"Then, one afternoon sometime, it was in summer, in the dry season, I wandered down the stone path in the shade under the heavy trees. I remember thinking, It's cool. That's all. Nothing else. No warning. Then I heard it, a snake or an animal moving in the fallen leaves. I stopped. I am afraid of snakes. It wasn't. It was the animal with two backs tumbling and sucking life from each other, lovely bronze bodies. I couldn't stop watching. You see, they were beautiful, the color of ancient bronze from the sun that dappled their backs through the trees. I had stepped back, though, thank God, so that when Wei Li and the boy, he couldn't have been more than sixteen, when they got up after that mutual sigh that became part of the wind, they didn't see me. They brushed each other off, and helped each other into their swimming trunks and ran back to the beach.

"Wei Li and the boy made tea in the kitchen, playing and jostling each other. Wei Li said he was his cousin, and at the door I saw him give the boy money. That, you see, was what was important about the day. Wei Li had got older, too, and was paying.

"But the last part is not fragmented. I remember it by the year, the day, the hour, where I was. It was the time of the Star Ferry Riots three years ago. I begged Wei Li to stay on the island, but of course he wouldn't. He was still clinging to being young and he didn't want to miss anything. He didn't come back that night.

"I knew something was wrong, even though I had watched the night ferries for years by then, as the sun burned its last over China and the star pattern of lights came on in the village below me and I could follow the ferry lights in the last glow, and then in the hopeless night, and time how long it would take for Wei Li to climb the hill to home from the last ferry before I came in from the veranda and went to bed. It wasn't always that way, just sometimes, when I was nervy and had been too long alone.

"That night was different. I couldn't sleep. I told myself it was the riots. It wasn't just that. It was something more. I was working in the garden when I saw him dragging up the hill at a time of the morning when he never came home. His fine suit was dirty, his usually meticulous linen was drab and stained. His face was brutal with something beyond shame. He wouldn't look at me. He went into his room and stayed there the rest of the day. In the evening he came out. He said, 'I have to leave. I want you to tell me what is mine and what I can take. I don't want to be accused of being a thief.' You see, he had retreated that far from me. I told him not to be a fool and to sit down.

"I finally got out of him what had happened. He had been

picked up at the Cheung Chau ferry by the police. One of them, a well-known womanizer on the take, had decided that since a couple of members of the Reform Club, which was a fairly innocuous political club, were actors, the riots were being fomented by homosexual liberals. It's the same kind of political vulgarity that equates liberals. Jews, artists, homosexuals, sex maniacs, atheists, and Communists. The man was trying, of course, to defuse the rumors that were all over Hong Kong about his own corruption. At any rate, all the Chinese boy-friends, house boys, secretaries, any connections with the names the police kept in what rumor called the Black Book, were picked up and questioned about the connections of their liberal European friends with the riots. Oh, I know to tell it now, it sounds not only vicious but ludicrous, but it wasn't ludicrous then.

"Wei Li had been kept in jail all night among boys who were fish-stall whores and servants, he said. Then he said, 'I—who am going to the university and who speak perfect English.' Those were his two pathetic prides. 'You see why I cannot stay here any longer. You can see that.' He was trying to pull the torn illusion of himself back around him, but the police taunts and bullying had tattered it. He seemed smaller, shrunken, sitting there at the kitchen table getting older.

"After that he did come back, of course, as he always had, sometimes after a week, sometimes a month. I don't know what he lived on. He would accept nothing. I got so that I wandered the island, all its paths and its steep streets, up to the hilltops, where among the dragon rocks I could stand and watch Hong Kong shining in the sun. Sometimes it was a city growing whiter and whiter as the English merchant colony began to be destroyed and the high-rise buildings took the place of its monuments. Sometimes it was a ghost city in the mist, and sometimes it was blotted out by rain.

"I think now that my own illusion of study saved me. Wei Li, in one of his protective explanations in the village, had said that I was a great English professor of Mandarin, no less. He knew it would impress the Chinese, who have an awe of learning, which of course is why so many professors were killed in the Cultural Revolution. The young were trying to destroy their own awe.

"By the time the Cultural Revolution had spilled over into Hong Kong and the '67 riots started, Wei Li was used to coming home again, but he never was the same, not after the night in jail. He never let me touch him again, as if the police were watching within the house, from the walls, through the high windows. Once he cried. I begged him again to stay away from the city, but something still urged him there. He had fallen among the triad boys by then, the Sun Ye On, to show his manliness. He boxed with them and practiced kung fu, all to prove he wasn't what he was. I think that night his triad had told him to go. They knew he could use my car, which we kept parked at the Hong Kong end of the ferry, because there were none allowed on Cheung Chau. Rumor had it that some old scores were being settled by the triads as the crowds raged and rampaged around the city. They burned abandoned cars and buses, and any foreigner caught in the street was beaten. The *gweilos* always come first when there is trouble, the first score to be settled when the lid blows off.

"I stayed on Cheung Chau, and the people at the Peninsula pulled the steel typhoon shutters down and played bridge while the homemade bombs went off and the fires raged outside along Salisbury and Nathan Roads. It was the Year of the Ram. Bute Street went up, and Pitt Street and all those places with English names, and I could see the fires reflected against the clouds over Kowloon.

"The triads did seem to control the crowds. Soldiers had started coming on R and R from Vietnam, and the rumor was that the triads kept the riots out of Wanchai because of the whorehouses and the bars. The Chinese, even in the wild passion of rioting, are nothing if not pragmatic. My God, darling, everybody is gone and the dirty, pearly dawn is clawing at the window. I'm so sorry. You must be exhausted." Noel watched Teresa's face in the dawn. She had cried sometime in the story, but the tears were dry streaks.

Someone had pulled the velvet curtains. Outside, the rain drifted down. The lights had turned pale in the room, and the crystal and the wallpaper looked brackish in the first light, as if they were never meant for day. One person was asleep in a soft chair by the window, and the ice had long since melted around the empty bottle. They tiptoed past the sleeping porter and out into the dawn that had been washed by the rain.

Noel put his arm around Teresa to keep her warm, and pulled the hood of the djelabah over her hair. "There, darling," he told her. "I'm not cold and I don't sleep. Not to worry. I must get you home." He looked up and down the High Street as if the gesture would bring a cab.

"You know I have to ask what happened to Wei Li," she told his back.

He went on looking up and down the street. "I never saw him again. The car was found turned over and burned. I never found a clue. The police weren't interested. They didn't keep a careful record of the Chinese who were killed. They said they did. They didn't. Let's walk toward Baker Street." He took her arm.

"What did you do?" After all the words, she had to make him speak.

"I waited. There was nothing else to do. I was like a queer English Madama Butterfly waiting for a Chinese Pinkerton. I would be there still if I hadn't been forced to leave. One morning I found graffiti, the Chinese characters for Dead White Devil and Running Dog, Yellow Pig, Leave or Die, painted on the stone steps. On another morning I found my cat hanging outside my bedroom window when I woke up. It had a sign

around its neck saying FOREIGN GHOST, and the Chinese characters for bugger.

"I don't think even that would have frightened me away,
except that hope was eroding. I had faced a hundred fates for
Wei Li. He was dead. He had betrayed me to the triad, or for
years he had had a Chinese wife and family. Both of those
accounted for the fact that when I finally looked through his
things there wasn't a jewel left, no jade cuff links, no gold
chains, nothing. He hadn't touched anything of mine, though,
only the presents I had given him through the years.

"Then one day I walked down to the market, and there, sitting on a bench in the sun, I saw myself, a thin old man, sitting
against the wall with a paper parcel beside him, in a waste of
patience, staring dead-eyed out to sea, not even looking for
anything anymore, just waiting to be waiting. Well, it wasn't
me. I? Which do you say? I never know. Here comes a cab."
He walked into the street and held up his arm.

In the cab she said, "Who was it?"

"Who was who, darling? Let it alone." He was watching the
dawn-wet park go by.

"The man staring out to sea."

"Oh, an old English opium addict who called himself a poet.
I went to his house once. It was a hovel, one room, with the
sonnet of Gerard Manley Hopkins, O the mind, mind has
mountains, translated into Mandarin in huge Chinese characters, painted all over one wall. He had been beaten and cut
up by the triad because they said he made passes at boys, but
he recovered from that and they forgot him.

"One of my friends went to see my house this year. No one
will live in it yet. They say it is haunted by Wei Li's ghost, who
keeps trying to get in the door, and by the Englishman, who
is dead, and whom they see up among the dragon rocks in the
twilight. They burn offerings in the little shrine by our steps to
placate us. So you see, darling, I am dead and my Styx is to live
without knowing what happened, whether he is dead or alive,

a story without an end. My God!" he said when the cab had stopped and he was helping Teresa out, "Butcher's Blenheim. You do find odd places to live."

"It is a bit tradesman's Tudor," Teresa played.

Abdul Selim called from his window, high above them, "Rhyming snobbery. Hello, Noel." He disappeared from the window. They could hear him running down the stairs while Teresa searched for her key. Abdul opened the door.

"Hello, Abdul. I didn't know you lived here, too." Noel was going to say something more, but Abdul interrupted him: "Must run. I'm late at the hospital. Whose cab is that?"

"Mine. I'll drop you as soon as I've made my manners, and it isn't rhyming, it's alliterative snobbery. Good night and good morning, darling. I'll ring you, but not too soon." She didn't know what he meant.

"Don't look so surprised. She does, you know. Always has, since she was six. Abdul is my doctor. We were up at Balliol together. Don't you know yet that London is the biggest small town in the world? No escape. The cab is pulsing. Come on." He stopped at the cab door and came back to her, and hugged her close to him. "I'm going to take some getting used to, Teresa," he said, who had almost never said her name. "You give me time. Please."

She still had her head down, fumbling for her key, when she heard the taxi drive away.

The voices below had waked Ewen. He heard the cab pull away and the slow steps of Teresa as she trudged up the stairs. By the time her key was in the flat door, he was fully awake and ready to quarrel, but when she wandered into the bedroom bedraggled and crying, he only got up and helped the djelabah over her head. She fell on the bed, face down.

"What's the matter?" He stroked her back. "What did that man do to you?" When she didn't answer he went on stroking her back and her hair. "You won't have to see him again."

She turned over and looked up at Ewen as if he were a

stranger. "I will, too," the small girl said. "He's my oldest friend. I love Noel."

"Why? He's a draidful man to make you cry like that."

She thought, looking at the ceiling. "Why? I think he has had an awful time." The tears began again to roll down into her hair. "And he makes the truth funny." She went to sleep in her clothes.

But she knew, in what her grandmother called the cold light of day—when the candle glow was gone, and the wine was a hangover, and Ewen had gone off to the BM and left a note: "I didn't want to wake you," and she had waked up still in her clothes, not in an exotic gold house with soft carpets but looking out from her bed into a mundanity of rocks and maps— that she was going to have to get on without the black monk's voice of Noel.

Noel, by needing her so, if only for one night, had killed her Noel simply by being alive and troubled. Compared to the certainty and safety of dreams, even bad ones, reality was a tremulous, changing, undependable thing. She could sense her child worship of him re-forming, reshaping. She felt the added weight of compassion and—she had to face that, too—pity.

She saw him now, not arrogant and beautiful on the sand on Long Island, but standing by a rock that was shaped like a dragon, gazing lost at an alien sea. She wanted to tell him, No, you've taken something away from me, oh, not by being gay. You've done it by being real.

All afternoon she wandered around the zoo. She stopped in front of the tiger's glassed-in square of forest glade, and thought, I ought to learn something from that, but there was nothing to learn, no metaphor she could hide behind to help her "understand." The tiger was asleep in a patch of sun, under a fake jungle tree.

Noel and Pius together had taken her black monk away from her, simply by being there, touchable and real, and she resented the loss. She knew she had wasted her heart on the dead and the remembered, and now she was learning to love the living, and it hurt.

She strolled along the Mappin Terraces, where the bears posed on concrete crags, and thought, Is there ever a time you know how to love? Are you always having to learn? Well, there's nothing I can do about it. Yes, there is. I can do nothing. That, too, was a new and painful idea.

IV

THE MOON

Mr. Evans-Thomas had been right about Mr. Pizz. Sometime around the first week in June the gloomy furtive affair had ended with a last pat on the back of the woman whose face Teresa never saw. It was always covered with her hair and her coat collar.

Penny informed her that it was poor Tommy Malcolm, christened Thomasina because of an inheritance, and that she had known her for simply years. She said she was married to someone very rich and much much older and that it was all so tragic, but Mr. Evans-Thomas said that was sentimental nonsense, as they all stood by the front door and watched Mr. Pizz's bits and pieces being brought down by the movers. There hadn't been much.

"I mean"—Penny giggled—"you don't need much when all you use the flat for is . . ."

"Don't use that word," Mr. Evans-Thomas said. "I'm having a ghastly enough time surviving in 1969."

Had he but known, the real shocks were to come. No London

flat is given up, as Teresa found out when she tried to get the place for Zephyr. It had already been passed on. Mr. Pizz had rented it from his uncle, who had bought it as a hidey-hole when the house was converted, in case he ever left his wife, who had the money. He had been letting it ever since, finding the income sweeter than the freedom. Now it had been passed on again within the family.

At four o'clock on the afternoon of Saturday the twenty-first of June, Artemesia Ambler had stomped up the stairs in boots from Italy, followed by four boys in various states of costume who were struggling up the stairs behind her, carrying objets d'art. One was a marble penis three feet long that Penny, watching with Teresa and Ewen from their doorway, said was marvy. One was an open sardine can about the size of a pram, cast in bronze. It took all four boys to carry it up two flights of stairs. There was a large photograph of prison bars, which Artemesia told them in passing was really human hairs laid side by side. She was carrying that and a Stubbs, which she told Teresa later she had inherited and meant to flog if she ever needed money.

In another century or in another place Artemesia would have been an abbess, a bluestocking, a dowager empress, a suffragette, a nurse at Scutari. As it was, in 1969, having got a first in Greats three years before, she plunged, all six feet of her, into the world she found, and high-booted, miniskirted, Afro'ed, and beaded, with enough money to do what she liked, she became the editor, publisher, and principal distributor of a magazine called *Fuck*, which her boys took around to the newsagents in a mini-moke three steps ahead of the police.

She had been asked to vacate her last digs, a garden flat on the Regent's Park Canal that had belonged to her late mother, because the smell of marijuana from her editorial meetings in the garden made the baby in the first floor back sick. At least the baby's mother, whom Artemesia referred to as its little mother, as if she ought to be wearing a babushka, said so.

It had provided the kind of excitement that made Artemesia feel most alive—the danger of persecution, the singling out for the martydom of being "busted." Her loins were girded for that sacrifice, her soul prepared, until her cousin, who was concerned with getting rid of the Battestin Crescent flat without losing two weeks' rent (he considered that heartbreak was bloody enough), pointed out that the fine would cost a packet and that they would probably shut the magazine down.

Artemesia saw that her crusade was in danger. She preached the panacea of sex and practiced what she preached. She couldn't see her whole allowance down the drain, or worse, herself in Holloway, as she called loudly to Ewen and Teresa after introducing herself and shouting the whole story from the top of the stairs. "Sans boys. Sans grass. Sans fuck. Sans everything."

Ewen was certain that, in the light from the stained glass behind Artemesia, he saw the shadow of Signor Battestini standing very still, but he decided to say nothing about it.

On Monday the twenty-third, after Zephyr had heard about Artemesia Ambler, Fazih Bey appeared at Claridge's with Zephyr and fifteen suitcases to mount a lightning strike on London. Zephyr was now twenty-one, but she still looked eighteen, and as delicate as when Teresa had first seen her, with her lovely small body encased in Dior, her delicate hands and feet, and the face, Fazih said, of a houri. "But we must pronounce that very carefully in English. You see, I thought..."

My family is growing, Teresa dreamed. She looked across the snow-white cloth and the candelabrum and the crystal. It was at dinner. She thought, All rich gentility is crystal and beige and soundless, too dull to thud, and wanted to giggle, but didn't in Claridge's dining room.

"I would be a terrible chaperone." She smiled through the soft light at Zephyr.

"No no no. I am not a fool. You mistake me. I want to leave her near a friend. That is all. She is enrolling in the art school, the Polytechnic, I think you said?" He looked the question at Zephyr.

"I wish to find myself in art," Zephyr informed him.

Fazih Bey grinned. "Codswallop," he said.

Zephyr, after a hug that sent a secret message of joy at her release from Brussels, had said very little, but had looked, somewhere within her quietness, like an imp about to jump on the table.

"So you see, when Zephyr told me that there was, alas, no place in your house, the appalling Artemesia having scoffed the only flat, I decided to bring her to London myself and negotiate. I have not much time."

Teresa thought that since the English use time lag like a weapon to defeat the strongest, there was little chance for him. She was wrong about that.

The next day she showed them her own flat, and explained about Signore Battestini. They were standing in Ewen's workroom, looking out the side window at the house next door that had been Angelina's. Fazih Bey stood there resplendent in his Savile Row suit, a faint pinstripe on charcoal, and said, "Yes, that will do."

When he saw the maps he pointed straight up at the ceiling and said, "There it is. Home. Only a dot upon a map. I have used these maps many many times."

"Please, can you mark it?" Teresa asked him. "I've tried to find it and I can't."

"Well now, let us see . . ." Fazih Bey looked around at Ewen's worktable. "We will use this red marker and you will please find me a broom and a bit of string. Maybe there is some here. God knows, there is everything else in the world." It was a mess. They had bought it at a junk shop in Camden Town and the only time the top had been clear was when they brought it home. "Ah. Here. You see." With Zephyr and Teresa to help him concentrate, he touched the marker to the ceiling and it was there, a small red dot for her. She could trace the road through the mountains, and hear, for a second, the sound of water.

After that they got down to Fazih Bey's business, which was to buy the flat on the ground floor of the house next door, because he had decided that Zephyr should be near her friend Teresa, and also because whoever owned the ground floor owned the land behind it and he thought it unseemly, he said so, to buy property without any ground.

Teresa thought that nothing could happen that fast in London.

At what Zephyr complained was dawn the next morning—it was nine o'clock—they went with one of London's grandest house agents to the house next door. When the house agent stepped out of the limousine north of Regent's Park, he acted as if he were stepping in dung.

It was the lightning strike. Mr. and Mrs. Dibley-Palmer, who owned what had been Angelina's ground floor and the shaven, clipped, precise garden, had been caught in their dressing gowns. They were both wool, both brown with tan braid.

"Shouldn't we warn them?" Fazih Bey had asked.

"No," the agent had said from the jump seat. "Surprise is imperative. I think I should warn you, though, artists and writers and television people live up here. It does little for property values."

"Well, I don't know." Mrs. Dibley-Palmer was looking around as if she'd never seen the place before. She had excused herself and dressed in her brown tweed skirt, the good one, with the fawn-colored jumper she had knitted. "Quite complicated, axshally," she informed Zephyr, who complimented her.

When a price was mentioned, Mr. and Mrs. Dibley-Palmer, after a long, breathless silence, reacted in their separate ways.

"Well, I don't know. Where would we go?" Mrs. Dibley-Palmer looked, as she had for so many years, at her husband for guidance, and as usual, finding none, fell to picking her cuticles.

Mr. Dibley-Palmer knew he was being railroaded and it made him grumpy. "Whole damn place being taken over by Arabs," he muttered. He had refused to change out of his dressing gown.

"We are not Arabs. We are devil worshippers," Fazih Bey informed him.

Zephyr giggled and stopped herself.

"Well, I don't know . . ." Mrs. Dibley-Palmer told her thumbnail. "I've always fancied the Cotswolds. We've talked about it. London has got so . . ."

"Full of Arabs. I couldn't agree more." Fazih Bey knew it was time for speed, precision, and eloquence. All three in their raw form would have stampeded Mr. and Mrs. Dibley-Palmer into saying no out of sheer panic masked as stubbornness. So his speed, his precision, and his eloquence came out as an English upper-class killing kindness. A snow job, Zephyr called it later when she told this to Teresa in her kitchen.

"The princess," he said, "really likes your charming flat. I think"—he turned to the house agent—"there would be no problem about the Cotswolds."

"Not at all." The agent, at last, picked up his cue. "I can take you there tomorrow. We will, of course, put you up for the night. I will have the orders to view . . ."

"Well, I don't know," Mrs. Dibley-Palmer looked panicked, anyway. "It's so soon."

"Oh, knock it off, Penelope," Mr. Dibley-Palmer finally pronounced. "Let's go. I loathe this bloody place."

"You take my Rolls," Fazih Bey said. "It's the least I can do."

"Always have," Mr. Dibley-Palmer went on grumbling.

"It's awfully dark," Zephyr complained when they were sitting in the kitchen with Teresa and Ewen, who, having seen the red dot, fired question after question at Fazih Bey about the Taurus Mountains.

"Never mind, my dear. We'll knock out part of the wall," he told her over his shoulder, and went on explaining the size of the boulders along the high pass that Teresa remembered, where Cüchük Mehmet had hidden the gas.

"And the color. Give me some idea of the color."

"He was so grumpy, but I liked him," Zephyr told Teresa. "He thought we were Arabs. He's trying to protect London from foreigners."

"*Bana inek satmak ister. Fakat almani istemez,*" Fazih Bey interrupted. He and Zephyr laughed.

When they were inspecting the garden, while Mrs. Dibley-Palmer watched through the French windows, Teresa asked Zephyr what he had said.

"Oh, it is a Turkish way of saying it takes two to tango," Zephyr told her, and smiled at Mrs. Dibley-Palmer, who disappeared.

"Oh, God, how marvelous," Mr. Evans-Thomas said when he met Zephyr. "Now I can do something about that constipated little garden."

"But you will be surrounded by foreigners," Zephyr teased him.

"Thank God for that." He was already gazing beyond her head at the garden, planning. "If you were all English I wouldn't know a soul."

"Money," said Fazih Bey later, as if he had made it up, "talks."

It did. It talked to a firm of Jamaican contractors who were used to building theatrical sets, having got past the union problem by hiring an Englishman for each of them. They could afford it. They charged a lot. It talked to Harrods and Peter Jones, and Fazih Bey's favorite antique shop in the Brompton Road.

Two weeks later, in the first week of July, Zephyr moved in from Claridge's to her flat. A huge window looked out on Mr. Evans-Thomas's border between the houses. Zephyr had insisted on white walls. She had already bought two large canvases to inspire her new career, one a bas-relief in papier-mâché of two large pink breasts, the other an Eno's Fruit Salts bottle seven feet high, so meticulously painted that she could read the label from across the room. It wasn't the real label. It started at bowel movement and disintegrated from there.

" 'Analgesic effervescent, sexual stimulus is pleasant,' " she sang around the nearly empty room. She had insisted on that, too—the floor covered with large bright pillows and uncut sheepskins, one long low sofa, white, a coffee table large enough for an electric train, and when Ewen said so, she got one and put it up.

The only antique she would let Fazih Bey buy was a large Italian table inlaid with marble nymphs and flowers. It reflected the stained glass in the windows that had somehow missed being destroyed when the house was made into flats. In the morning, before Zephyr was up, they cast a prism of fragmented colors across the white wall and the sofa. The stained glass was a mark of Signor Battestini's taste. Mr. Evans-Thomas said he had built the house for Angelina, who he feared would never marry.

Zephyr let the table stay after her two first friends, two homosexual boys from what they called the Buildings, had pronounced it a bit of all right.

"Ah mean, it's an accent, init? We might be bent but our tastes are straight. Brings out the stark reality of the rest, know wha ah mean?" Ron was conferring with Reg.

That was when Reg, twisting his shoulder-length curls, pronounced it a bit of aw right.

They were Zephyr's first guests after Teresa and Ewen.

She had put what she called her Fazih clothes in one of the walk-in cupboards built by the Jamaicans, and the other was full of her London clothes, torn patched jeans, leather trousers, six-inch-wide belts, ruffled shirts, six velvet suits in fruit colors, twelve minidresses, four wigs, white stockings, black stockings, green stockings, gold stockings. She pointed them all out. The whole cupboard smelled of new clothes. "Aren't they marvy?"

she said to Teresa. She had been in London three weeks then, including the time at Claridge's, registered at the Poly, or said she did, and was, she confided, terribly lonely, which meant she didn't yet have a lover. "Englishmen don't turn me on," she confided.

It was the blue time of night after the long twilight of summer, and at last the dinner, the discussions, the washing up had ended and Paddy Ryan was giving a final wipe of the countertop, the stove, and the big deal table after everyone but Pius had left the kitchen.

For five floors above them there was a stillness palpable with humans in their separate rooms. That was shocked away by a far tape recorder playing African music as an upstairs door opened, and then it was cut off when the door shut. The rhythm stayed in both their heads.

Paddy looked up. "Jebra is homesick again. We've still got an hour before the pub shuts. We must ask him to go with us." He kept on gazing at the ceiling, worried, as if the music were still calling him. "He dances, in there by himself."

In the two months that Pius had been at Ogilvie House, their friendship had fallen into night, when duties were done and their tenants or charges had gone off to their separate cells, or troubles, or pleasures, and the darkness had fallen at last in the summer so far north.

Paddy went on wielding a large sponge over the whitened table. He lifted Pius's coffee cup, wiped under it for the second time, forgetting, and set it down again. "You know what the trouble is, don't you?" He was aware of chatting; he had been trying to get Pius to answer, but Pius went on staring at the dark window into the areaway.

Paddy tried again. "Volunteers. We suffer from volunteers. When good church people want to help, what can we do?" He sat down, the sponge still in his hand. "Look at the mess!"

Pius grinned at last. "Do you mean the one on the ground floor or the one you got us into?"

"Well, it's sort of the same, isn't it? Who would have known that a simple gesture would grow like something left in the back of the fridge?"

A noise in the basement hallway stopped them both. Some-body was getting something from the big refrigerator in the larder. They stayed as quiet as if they had been caught through the slow sound of liquid being poured into a glass, the slow shutting of the refrigerator door, the slow footsteps receding up the basement steps.

"It isn't as if I even like the thing. Another mountain. Another muddy-looking mountain. There were hundreds of them." Paddy was getting exercised, which he had done on an average of once a day for the last two months. "When you think that it's worth enough to keep every student who has ever come through here, broke and half starved and ambitious and naïve from Africa, for all the time they need to be here without their having to take any menial job they can to survive, and being called names when some of them are brighter than most they come into contact with and any one of them can end up as a British-hating prime minister as a result." There were tears in Paddy's voice, and he hit the table with the sponge, but like his complaint, it didn't make a sound that would be heard by anyone.

Somewhere in the back parlor, lost under the mountain of neglect, the past, and disorganization, still wrapped in news-paper, lay the small Cézanne. Paddy was convinced, from what he had been able to find out, that it was worth half a million pounds. That was in the morning. By the time night came, and the worry had mounted through the day, the potato had gotten hotter and hotter and Paddy was sure it was worth a million.

He had asked Pius, who was no help, and said things like "That's the way this world is," which made Paddy want to hit him. He had asked the air in front of his face, expecting no answer from anyone, what it might fetch at Sotheby's. He watched *The Times* for news about auctioned paintings as if he were planning to flog it.

He had even gone out to Collindale, having bullied the date of the theft out of Desmond, but from that day on there had never been a story in any London paper about its loss.

There had, however, been an ominous lettter to *The Times* signed by a well-known member of the Board of Directors of the National Gallery. It called for more stringent laws to protect National Treasures, capitalized, and demanded Mandatory Sentences of at least twenty-five years for anyone involved in any way with such Desecration.

That did it. Paddy had, after all, spent the first sixteen years of his life in a part of London where the police were the enemy.

The problem had begun the morning after Paddy had brought the parcel in and set it in the corner behind the desk, along with the matchstick Virgin, a huge out-of-date public-transport map that had once hung in the hall, several posters, including thirty or so calling for people to come to Trafalgar Square for an antiwar demonstration to march on the American Embassy, which Paddy had said he would distribute and then forgotten. There was a really dreadful, according to Paddy, painting of the Holy Family, which he said looked like a banner from the freak show at a fun fair at Blackpool. It had so offended the artist when Paddy refused to hang it that he moved out of Ogilvie House. He said he had been inspired by the Holy Ghost and that ought to be enough, and that Paddy had refused to hang it because he had made the Holy Family black. Aesthetics had degenerated into some noisy theological argument in the entrance hall before he moved.

There the Cézanne had been until the next morning, when Paddy, still deeply hung over after six o'clock Mass from Pius's present of brandy, and stealing a little kip in his bed, was awakened by ominous noises from the ground floor.

He was too late. Knobby Green and a pickup volunteer crew

of Irish Catholic bully boys had attacked the downstairs office. By the time Paddy got to them, all the furniture, files, and garbage, not only of Ogilvie House for Catholic Students, but of Ogilvie House for Catholic members of HM Forces, which it had been before Paddy took it over, were piled high in the back sitting room, leaving only a path to the telly and a sofa to watch it from. Under all of it, somewhere near the floor, lay the Cézanne.

"There are twenty-four bloody tins of bloody saltpeter," Knobby said. "I never knew they really used it in the forces. I know your lot don't, not them black fellows." He grinned.

Paddy suddenly realized, just as he was about to start yelling, that he dared not say a word. Like a terrible vista, a possible future opened before him that could be avoided only by silence and guile. It was, he was sure, the way the past is supposed to flash before the dying, but it was the future instead, total anxiety, contingent disaster, Doomsday foreboding, what if?

He saw himself, with the Cézanne still wrapped in newspaper under his arm, walking up the great steps of the National Gallery simply to give it back. He thought he looked, in the vision, a little like Goofy as a Jesuit priest. He could see Scotland Yard plainclothesmen, in mackintoshes with belts, slowly closing in across the marble foyer. He could hear the questioning begin.

His collar might be some protection, not like it once was, but the questions would lead right to Ogilvie House and to Mr. Mburu, the art historian who worked at the V and A. The fact that he was probably listed as a Communist by MI5, having slipped over the border of Uganda in the first place, meant that his return home if he were deported would amount to a rather nasty death sentence.

All through the vision Knobby was bragging, which would have sounded, to a stranger, like righteous indignation.

"I took it orf your bleedin 'ands, Father. I said when I heard about the lolly Father Deng scoffed orf the jock you wouldn't spend a bloody penny on this place, which is a bleedin disgrace, so I got some bleedin white paint and all and got in 'ere while you were still drunk, and you needn't deny it, weavin around at Mass this morning and smellin like a bleedin brewery, a fine thing, so we come in and we done it for you. You owe me for the paint and all."

"Don't say bloody. It's blasphemy. It means by Our Lady," Paddy said by habit to the pile of junk that reached to the ceiling.

"That's a lot of cock, Father; it means bloody like it bleedin says. We didn't throw away a bleedin thing. I told them, I said, you never know what's holy and what ain't, do you now?"

The volunteers who had chosen and put up the striped wall-paper in 1951 had not thrown away any of Father Shannon's past as shepherd of the forces on leave for fear of what might be holy, too. It was the second not generally known short-coming suffered by the priesthood, that some of the laity thought everything down to their dirty socks had the imprima-tur, as Paddy pointed out to Pius, who was still staring at the dark areaway. Far above them in the street they could hear the echo of night footsteps, slower than the day.

"I've thought of another plan." Paddy went back to the subject that had obsessed him for two months. "It's getting urgent now. We've almost reached the bottom."

By this he meant the bottom of the junk pile. Since he and Pius had forbidden anyone else to touch it, they had, at what-ever time they could, and whenever they found a place to put it in a house neglected by not throwing anything away for years, been going through it at last, throwing away, getting depressed by the detritus of old indecision. There hadn't been too much urgency about it, since Knobby's volunteers worked when they wanted to. In an aura of very slow piety they had taken two months to repaint one room, having made it uninhabitable in just over half an hour.

At last it was drawing to a close, the room nearly finished, the junk nearly sorted, after some discussion about who could use the saltpeter; they didn't want to throw anything useful away. They still hadn't uncovered the Cézanne. When Paddy, in one moment of panic or another, had mentioned moving the furniture back, Knobby said there wasn't no use doing it if you didn't do it right. There was more than a hint of revenge against the years of Paddy's high-and-mighty priestly bullying. He seemed pleased. He knew it and Paddy knew it and each knew the other knew it.

"What about this? I go to Farm Street and tell them under the seal of confession that I have the painting and where I got it. The priests at Farm Street know all the nobs. Somebody will know what to do."

Pius was finally listening to him. He smiled. "Why not have Abou Baba Moosa take it? He's convenient, anyway."

There and not there under the green shade over the table in the dark kitchen, and in the hot sun and day of the mission, they were back in Africa, where Abou Baba Moosa had been born, if he was born there or some other place some other time. His immortality was untraceable. Abou Baba Moosa, stern father, little Papa Moses may have once been an Arab a little kinder than the rest, or several Arabs and one Jew, with a pack of wonderful things that shone or didn't shine. He was beyond good and beyond evil, always mischievous, sometimes miraculous.

If a cup was broken when the mission students washed up, Abou Baba Moosa had done it. If a present was left at the gate of the mission, Abou Baba Moosa had left it. The villagers and the farmers at the edge of the jungle often did this anonymously, since they longed for some of the mission magic without betraying their ancestors or their neighbors.

They yearned for the jeep and the tractor, the Land Rover that belonged to the Christian God, and the Christian God ran a good clinic, but it was Abou Baba Moosa who was heard up among the branches of the trees calling from the jungle. Some of the boys swore they had seen him, and he had a face like a big yellow melon that swayed in the air between the trees in the heat haze. They scared the smaller children by saying that Abou Baba Moosa would get them or forget them, since he gaveth and tooketh away, just like the priest's book said.

Some of the older boys swore that they had the power to call him to them whenever they wanted to and they would disappear into the forbidden jungle paths behind the mission, where the younger children were afraid to go, partly because of the priests and partly because of Abou Baba Moosa. They could hear the older boys, the brave ones, the magic ones, deep beyond sight, laughing and calling, Moosa! Moosa!

That he had been ominous sometime was evident in his first name, Abou, a slaver who pounced on the innocent on the jungle paths, that he bore the name Baba was a mark of affectionate kindness, a papa, a daddy, an uncle, a present-giver, but the Moosa was the most mysterious of all. It sounded like the Arab name of Moses, but it had become not a word but a sound, a chant, a whisper, wind in the trees, thieves at the window, breathing in the night, the swish of an aba, a panga, a warning or a softing sigh like a lullaby, moosa, moosa, moosa, hush . . .

He seemed then to be in the kitchen at Ogilvie House, in the dark shadows beyond the hanging light. Paddy, who hadn't thought of him for so long, could almost hear him, could almost see the aba, the *bui bui*, the great leaves he sometimes used to cover himself, could hear the whisper of the footsteps in the street above them, or of Abou Baba Moosa just beyond the jungle clearing.

"Of course," he said. "That's perfect. It wouldn't naturally be under the seal of confession but a solution which I could present at Farm Street. It would be, after all, only something to say if the police wanted a scapegoat. Let them look for Abou Baba Moosa." Paddy was pleased with that for a minute.

"Well, that's done, then. Keep to it. Don't change your mind again." Paddy had thrown away solution after solution already. Pius got up at last. He had seemed frozen there at the table in front of his forgotten coffee. "Let's knock on Jebra's door."

Paddy found a worry he hadn't faced yet as he followed Pius up the stairs, not daring to voice it. The painting could have been stolen. It could have been. After all, how could they be sure one of the bully boys hadn't recognized it, or simply taken a fancy to it, thinking nobody would miss it, left in a corner like that, a nice bit of color for his lounge. "Oh, God," Paddy said silently, part prayer, part sigh. "Let it be safe."

Pius had been dragging and lagging all evening long. He hadn't wanted the day to begin, and he was heartily glad it was ending. He could feel the weight of it in his muscles as if he had been swimming and losing pace all day against a current.

He had overslept, for a beginning. Paddy had run up to wake him. He had spent so much time dressing, brushing and pressing his best trousers from Khartoum, spit-polishing his shoes, losing and then finding his dog collar, worrying a spot off his jacket, misplacing his missal, finding it again, being a nuisance, that Paddy had finally to remind him that it wasn't a wedding but a funeral.

"It's my armor," Pius informed him, slightly offended. "When a black man goes into the street among you people, he must wear his dignity on his back."

"Oh, what cock," Paddy called up the stairs. "Get on with it."

Pius had managed to go past his stop on the tube and end up in Finsbury Park before he came out of whatever dream he was having, which he promptly forgot as soon as he stopped dreaming. Only a sense of heavy loss was left, so he knew it hadn't been good or even a retreat from what Paddy called reality.

"I have the ability to see myself," he told Paddy's back as they climbed the basement stairs, and he found himself able to see and speak of the day at last.

"What I see is this: I see a very tall, dignified black man. There I am, studying the Underground map very seriously with my mind on East Acton. The number of times I have done that, to miss the change and then miss my stop this morning! But then, I hated going there. I hated it and I am ashamed of that, but Joseph Jesus Ngoro, whoever he was, was such a whining, feeble man at the last. All that remained alive seemed to be habits and hatreds, until it was too late for him. Now I see that my compassion for him was being, well, chipped at, if you like . . ."

Paddy knocked on Jebra's door, and the thump of his dancing and the music stopped. He opened the door in his white Marks & Spencer boxer shorts. "Exercising, Father." He still panted. "Keep in trim, don't you know."

"Put some clothes on. We're off to the pub."

"Oh, I would like that. You just wait one minute." Jebra shut the door.

Paddy leaned against the wall. Pius sat down on the top step. Where he was in his memory turned to words again. "I found out that it dishonors a man to make too much of him. It is too great a burden and an imposition, I think."

"Who are you talking about?" Paddy tried teasing.

"Maybe I am talking about Joseph Ngoro, God rest his soul, and maybe I am talking about myself." He smiled. "Do you know what I did? I missed my stop again, well, didn't miss it, but jumped off ahead of time at White City. There I was for one minute in what I will call a white study, and there I saw White City on the tile wall. Why do the Underground stations look like elegant loos? Jumped off the tube in a panic, as if I were late for some appointment I hadn't made. I don't know what got into me. There I was, a black man lost in a White City. At the stadium you could hear them going to the dogs. All those buildings nobody ever liked or cared for, the sullen wind, and a street of women not wanting to do the shopping."

"Just a jiffy," Jebra called from behind the door.

"I don't know what got into me," Pius said, but he did know, and Paddy, honoring that, lit a cigarette and waited.

But Pius was walking along Du Cane Road again, slower and slower, in the pale mist the sun was trying and failing to break through. Even though he was late he couldn't help lagging before he got to the houses and the school. Floating in mist almost as far as he was used to seeing, the green river valley scrubland spread to the horizon, wonderfully flat to the distant tiny hints of houses and ghostly lines of trees.

He ignored the white posts of the playing fields and the dim towers of the prison, named, to him, for gall and wormwood. Instead, as he had done before in the same place, he let himself rest in being a small boy out there with nothing between his eyes and the edge of things under the huge sky. There were only the goats, the sound of their small, searching, maunching mouths, sky silence pierced by bird calls, and a different wind, not capricious and personal as English wind, but a steady stream as the earth turned.

He translated the movement of the boys in their striped jerseys playing in the distance to animal movement, and was, for the moment, at peace, letting himself be homesick for something he had not seen since he was sixteen until the long wandering with Ewen brought it back.

Between leaving and returning, there had been the jungle of the green Congo, then the jungles of cities closing in, Washington in America, and London in the East End, and then the green jungle of the Congo again for so many years.

There had been times, when he was at the hill mission, or in Wales, or at Manresa House, and could look out over the distance of Richmond Park, miraculous in such a small country, when he found moments of return to being alone and spacious that were like food or prayer. He had learned to find his spaces, as Paddy called them, where he could rest his eyes and his soul. He had found the great meadow in the middle of Hyde Park, and now that Ewen had gone to live there, he had found the crest of Primrose Hill, where he could, on a good day, see all the way to the dome of St. Paul's.

Now, for several weeks there had been the distances of Wormwood Scrubs that stretched beyond the hospital and the prison. He remembered the little Balese boy he had let ride with him in the Land Rover once, and who had seen the high plains beyond the jungle for the first time. His eyes, homesick for the close green safety, were afraid of the space and refused to see it. He saw the animals in the distance as tiny until Pius explained carefully about perspective, teaching by habit, using the English word to tell how they were not small but far away. But when they got back to the mission he heard him tell the others, awed and unbelieving, that he had seen cattle and antelope called perspecatifs the size of mice, and when they laughed he ran into the jungle.

Pius leaned against the wall and promised himself a walk when what he had to do was done. That was to bury little gray Jesus Ngoro, a.k.a. Jacob, a.k.a. Joe, who had been a big man but who had shrunk until he was as gnarled as a cyprus, all knees and elbows at the last, when he had finally starved himself into the country behind his eyes.

He had explained it all to Pius over and over, from the time three weeks before, when the RC chaplain had begged Pius to come after a day and a night when Jesus had cried without stopping in English and a few words of Swahili left over from a blank forgetfulness for a black priest.

He said that what he had to confess he couldn't confess to a whitely man. All whitely men were the man he had hit over the head with an iron bar because he had had enough. He couldn't even tell Father Ryan, he explained, although for a whitely man he was better than the rest, and he had given him a table of his own making long ago, but he did want to know if Father Ryan still used the table.

He had served five years of his life sentence at HM Prison Wormwood Scrubs and seemed, the RC chaplain said, reasonably—it was a favorite word—reconciled, very interested in wood carving, as Father Deng was aware, and beginning to take up painting and was really quite good, when he attacked another white man with a tray, and after that, after being in solitary, he decided that he had had enough of the Scrubs, too, and that he had better go ahead and die. He was thirty-four years old.

When Pius told him he should not refuse to eat, he said, "No. I've had enough."

"There is no arguing with him," Father O'Malley told Pius as he unlocked door after door, peeled back the way as they walked, layer by layer, deeper into the prison. The castellated prison so familiar to the outside world against the sky seemed another place within the gray walls, for no one there looked up. They passed blank men, except for a few whose faces were animated by conversion or fury. Once Pius glimpsed men exercising around and around like animals in a corral in a pen made of high gray walls below the parody of a castle with the Rapunzel towers.

There had not been a day when he went there that it had not seemed a dirty, alien land he was invading, one that did not let in the sun. Its inmated people seemed convicted to serve together, and to have more in common with one another than any one with him, even Jesus Ngoro. To the screws, the two nuns, the priest, the convicts, all of them in there, he knew himself a stranger by the simple act of being able to leave.

He was examined each time by an officer with a metal detector that clicked and prattled over his body, up and down his legs, across his arms, and as high as the little Englishman could reach, so, taking pity on the job, Pius bowed his head as if he were praying. He rose above a covey of small wives and girlfriends who tried, self-consciously, to make jokes to bring a smile to the inspector, and keep their own spirits up. It was the wrong place for humans to find themselves in by force of circumstance. He remembered thinking, the first time he went there, that circumstances are what surrounds where you stand, in this case a true heart of darkness. He passed small, neglected men who seemed to him not to reach to the limits of their physical bodies.

They were not so much stunted as poor in spirit, so simply served with not enough of anything, health or mind or strength, that he did not wonder that out of a terrible pity Christ had blessed them with a kingdom at least of heaven. He knew then what poor soul meant, the giving up, the drift. If there was crime there and there was, that was the essence of it.

Nothing was what it was called, as if that changed it. The cells were not cells but rooms, the guards not guards but officers, the towers not prison but castle; it was an antiseptic denial of prison. The iron doors had been taken off the nineteenth-century cells to make hospital rooms. No one, Father O'Malley explained in a whisper, was allowed to die there, for death upset the men. He pointed to the great steel nets between the floors above them, and said that of course they could not control the suicides. Although they took precautions, like the nets, they could not prevent men setting their cells on fire.

All the men in the hospital were the same, retreated, small, and quiet. All but Jesus Ngoro; he lay in his prison room containing a fury that was burning his body into the dry sticks and hide of an old, old man.

He grabbed Pius's hand and began where his mind was, in the middle of things, not waiting for Pius to speak. "What they do not understand"—he spoke a careful English—"is where I am. They have the same country behind their eyes as the one they see every day, these whitely men. That is my name for them, whitely men. I made it up. Now, you and I, we have a different country behind our eyes. A great space. That is where I am living now, today."

His voice was as thin and dry as his bones, and his fingers had no flesh. They bit deep into Pius's hand. When he gave him the Host, that was all he would swallow; even then he was so painfully slow that Pius found himself as impatiently patient as a waiting mother with a spoon in hand too long.

)221(

Was it that first time or another time? There were so many. He lingered. He told Pius, "They keep me away from my Africa. Oh, they think so, do they? I will show them. I think I will kill some enemies. I think a white woman; they cause all the trouble. They think we want to fuck them, when they are the color of death." He turned on his pillow away from Pius and said, "Okay, Father. Fuck off," and passed into a place where he couldn't be called back.

"He does that," Father O'Malley said. He went on watching the back of Jesus's head as if just watching would help him understand.

Sister Ursula was eighty years old and she had spent fifty of them in the prison. She said that if they would only let her talk to Jesus, she would straighten him out in no time. "He dangerous?" She sniffed. "He is as weak as a stick." When she was kept away she swished her skirts with a gesture of angry piety and said, "Men!"

"He was born in Bradford," Father O'Malley said, still watching Jesus, "never been in Africa in his life. It was his father who came from Tanzania. He is living his father's life. Not so strange. We haven't been to heaven and we pretend to everybody that we know it. It's our job." Then he looked at Pius: "No, Father, don't try. Their lies are important to them. They persuade themselves that they are innocent, or someone is waiting for them, when they are guilty as sin and there isn't a soul in the world who wants them when they've been here too long. You can't take their lies away and expose them. It's what they have, you see. I caused a suicide once, when I first came to this job, by forcing a man to see the way things were. Never again."

"Who is he really, then?" Pius watched, too, over the sleeping or feigning man.

Father O'Malley led him away. "His record says he is Joe Gore and for a while he was Jacob Gordon, and then he was baptized Jesus Ngoro, which was the place where his father was born."

Then one day, a cold summer day when the wind blew over the Scrubs and seemed to seek him out, Pius got to the prison to find a note that Jesus had been moved to Hammersmith Hospital. That, as the fine stone gates and the towers were a castellated substitute for prison, was a substitute way of saying the case was hopeless and that, so as not to upset the others, Jesus had been moved out of the Scrubs to die.

Pius had walked into the crowded waiting room of the hospital with his little case, and only the few Catholics knew what it contained. The curtains were drawn around Jesus's bed. A guard sat on one side of the bed, Sister Ursula on the other. Jesus held her hand. All the time Pius was whispering the last rites he could hear the bedpans clatter and someone laughing at the other end of the ward. Behind that, far away, there was the faint sound of a singing commercial on the television.

The soles of Jesus's feet turned gray and he died. Somebody switched off the television, but it had nothing to do with the dying. The guard who had been sitting beside Jesus got up and went to find the ward supervisor. "We never let the men die alone," Father O'Malley had said.

There Pius was again, knowing better, but the fool that he had been since morning, going down Du Cane Road to the great gates of the prison instead of to St. Mary's Cemetery, where they were waiting for him to conduct the funeral. It had been one of many last wishes of Jesus Ngoro.

He could see the twin fawn gate towers with their fine etchings of white stone and Italian crowns of delicate columns, Verona in wormwood. The white welcoming bas-relief busts in their high niches could have been anybody, it didn't matter, the Queen, Lord Somebody, whoever was prison governor in the nineteenth century when the reform prison was built to remind the neighborhood of a little corner of imperial architecture. The sky had cleared for the moment and was pale blue, the pillar box red, not a green leaf in sight. There was a van parked on the street, painted like a psychedelic dream.

Pius was turning to go back toward the cemetery when a pencil-thin girl in a bright yellow minidress threw herself against his side.

Somebody called, "Darling, that's it. That's marvelous. *Jetez! Jetez!* That's divino! Hold it. Now reach. Reach up him. Higher! Higher! What a marvelous *nègre*, darling, turn him around. Oh, God, that divine black against the white trim of the gate. I can't bear it." A small imp in jeans was bouncing, kneeling, jumping, clicking a camera attached to one eye. "It's the most beautiful gate in London that hasn't been used"—click—"Stand *up*, for Christ's sake, you're slouching like an old woman, and used and used, you'll do yourself an injury."

Pius had stood stock-still, too surprised to do anything but support the slim, almost emaciated boy/girl who leaned against him as lightly as if she had been blown there. It was only a minute before one of the guards at the gate house called out, "Move along there."

"Don't be silly, darling." The imp was clicking away, ignoring a cab that had stopped to keep from running over him while the driver held his hand on the horn. "Do stop that bloody noise. Public property. Public right of way. Oi've as mooch rite to be 'ere as the loikes of yew"—sassy mixture of Cockney, North Country, and Haut Chelsea.

"Oh, my God, it's a priest, darling," he said when he had stopped clicking and had straightened up and the cab had passed, and the boy/girl waif in her yellow dress and her red and yellow stockings was starting to chew gum. "Thank you, Father. I *did* need an accent of black. Too kind; run along, darling, and stop that goddamn chewing. Sorry, Father. Come on."

They had both leaped into the small van, the girl in the back, the photographer at the wheel. The last thing Pius heard him call was "No, you nit! The purple. The purple! We've done the bloody blue. We've got to rush. The fog is coming down again . . ."

It came back so quickly that the open land beyond the hospital and the school was already veiled in mist by the time Pius had walked there.

He wondered why fog was called thick, heavy. It made the air float in a purgatory of black trees that rose above a ground that he could no longer see. He walked past shadows along the road toward Kensal Green. It was a long walk, past the vague, high bank of the train tracks, by rows of houses the color of twilight on dirty winter days, but all of them with some little act of anarchy against the drabness. A rose bloomed through the mist, a red geranium pierced it. A bright hedge floated toward him and away. A drab anarchy. England was that to Pius at noon as he heard a clock strike in the distance, that, too, muted by mist. He thought he might be too late for the funeral; he found himself hoping that, and was ashamed of his thought. He hadn't liked Jesus much, all bones and demands and lies to the last, and the small pale bragging he thought was confession.

Pius went to the wrong gate at Kensal Green Cemetery. It was that kind of day. The young man at the cemetery office was overhelpful. His face was swollen with baby fat, as if he ate too much too quickly to keep from identifying with the dead in Dead City. "You just follow along the right-hand road, Father. It leads to St. Mary's. Just go right along. You can't miss it. Brutal day, isn't it? *Good* morning."

A brutal day. No. Something else. Pius, sitting on the stairs at Ogilvie House, was conscious suddenly of where he was and who his friends were. "You don't do that often," he said aloud to that thought. "I must tell you what happened, Paddy. I must try to tell you."

Paddy had finished his cigarette and he lit another from it and then doofered it, a habit from boyhood, a do-for-tomorrow. His pockets had to be emptied of doofers from time to time, and aired. He went on leaning against the wall. He hoped that Jebra wouldn't come out yet and send Pius back into what Paddy thought of as one of his stillnesses, as if he was listening for something and couldn't or wouldn't say what it was. There were places he went to alone, like rooms with locked doors.

He wanted to, but he didn't smile when Pius began to speak, protecting himself with abstractions, as if Paddy were several people.

"There is much experiential truth," Pius said, "in the concept of the interior voice. All cultures recognize it. Some even worship it." He smiled back, hearing himself. "Oh, we do retreat into abstractions when we are afraid of what we have to say.

"No. To explain. It is this way. I am, for the moment, since it still lives in me and I can go there when I wish or need to, four or five or six years old. I am standing in a great space with my bare right foot resting on the inner side of my left knee, just standing stork, swaying a little in the wind that blows from the edge of the world. I am herding my father's goats. It is a great responsibility. I hear the voice of my grandfather, who says to me, Majok, there is a female hyena coming from the east where the sun has risen, and she is hungry. She is an old enemy of mine, a woman I treated badly. Be careful. I take this voice for granted, and why not? I have heard it as clearly as you hear the wind across the grass.

"I expect to hear it that way. It is, you see, no surprise, for even though my grandfather has been dead for three years, he lives in me. I know this. I carry his name and his voice. So I unwind my foot from my other leg, a little grumpily, since I have been having a nice wind-borne dream with birds in it, and I walk to the east between the flock of goats and the sun, and of course there is the female hyena that has been skulking closer, hidden from my eyes by the sun rays, and I chase her away and put my foot against my leg and stand stork again and go back to my dream.

"Now the thing you must remember is that I take all this for granted. So do you, but you don't know it. You could worry what I have told you like a dog, bullyragging, nice phrase, and you would come up with many explanations. I have glimpsed the female hyena under consciousness. It is precognition. It is a trained wariness, a conscience if you like. After all, I know at six years old that I must be alert at all times, since I have been entrusted with part of my father's wealth, and if a hyena carries off one of the flock I will be punished and shamed. But *experientially* I have heard my grandfather's warning and I have found the hyena that he told me was there.

"Something like that, only so much more, happened to me today. As you know, we Africans are taught to fear the dead, the physical dead. That teaching is so early that no matter what comes after it, what logic, what faith, what knowledge, it is still in us as a gene, a history. So when I walked along the cemetery road between the tombs at Kensal Green, I was a man, a priest, but the small boy I carry within me felt some dead spirit chill along his back. I told him not to be afraid. I told him. But you see, it was more than that.

"My father was with me for the first time in nearly four months, since I went to my village and found it destroyed by the soldiers. You know, I lay all day long beside the burned church where they had been killed, my mother and God knows how many others of my family. I had not seen them in twenty years. Ewen and I had to travel on then; we survived to Malakal, where we were carried farther and farther away from that small heap of the ashes of sticks and leaves and dung and my people that the wind and the animals had left.

"I met my father today in Kensal Green. I did not question this meeting any more than I questioned my grandfather's warning when I was six. I accepted him, as it was my duty, after all, and for the first time since that day in the sun I was able to mourn. I leaned against a tree in the fog, a big black man against the black trunk, and I cried all the tears down that had been banking up inside me since that day.

"I was in a strange country with my father, and I saw where I was with his eyes, not my own, which have seen all the places I have seen, but for a little while, because it was my duty to him, I did not stop him seeing. He was loath to be in a city of the dead. He did not attempt to understand it. He found it unclean.

"He said, Majok, why have you brought me here? He spoke no language, not English, not Dinka, that I was aware of, although in this life he spoke both. It was instead a language of images, a speech from his soul to mine, my heart's core, the heart of my heart, to be precise. I was, in my own language, bearing, or rather standing, my father's head.

"He looked, or tried to look, through the gray mist risen up around us that made the tree branches into shadows, like the stick spirits, but it was hard for him to see. He had never seen mist before. But *I*, this *I* could see, all the white stone sepulchers, the little temples, one there with caryatids, one floating in the mist with Doric columns, in the half distance under a tree branch, a hint of a tilted angel, and one fallen angel on the ground I knew was green with grass that the mist had turned as brackish as winter. There was a white marble Our Lady of Mount Carmel blessing a Mrs. Paolozzi, her marble so rusted and damp that she was crying dirty tears through her never-changing smile. I saw the ghost of a cathedral of stone lace the size of a double bed, and betokening the ruin of time a broken column that should have been two thousand years old but was set there in 1956. As far as I could see, there were the names and monuments of forgotten people.

"But what my father saw was a city of white houses full of the haunted dead, who had been kept from going to their long home in the earth that made them. They could not be eaten by fire, as he had been, or by hyenas or lions or birds, or *aci boot*, eaten by the ants and the termites.

"He thought this a curse on them, a *jak* to punish them all, and so their spirits had to linger there, their *ka*. We have beliefs that can be traced to ancient Egypt. We were, you see, the Kingdom of Kush, of which you may have heard. What have they done, my father said, and he repeated, Why have you brought me here, Majok? Take me home. And where was that? Here in this hall, or at the cattle byre, or on a heap of ashes that had been a poor pathetic little mission, a church made of sticks and cattle dung that had cost them their lives? In my father's innocence he thought still that home was a place.

"He did not flog his conscience and have religious Anglo-Saxon agonies. His agonies and fears and hopes were real and simple. He was a tall, stern man who put on the Christian God like a cloak over his old recognitions, and asked this God for water and grass and loyalty, not much more. The rest wasn't important to him.

"He didn't care who said they ruled him; he knew no one did. He had no sense of the state. He never saw or touched such a thing and therefore it did not exist. He had learned for four hundred years to be wary of strangers; it was not fear. He had no fear. You call it historic memory. My father would have said he contained his ancestors. He could recite his genealogy for fifteen generations. He still called all strangers Turks. Slave traders. He called the English who came Turks as well; they were all the same to him, even though he was a friend of the District Commissioner. By the way, I can recite my genealogy for sixteen generations. It is our catechism. I will do it for you sometime.

"So there I was, a tall black man with Africa within me, walking with my father through a strange white man's, a Turk's graveyard, not a priest, not anything I have become since. I walked straight by Sister Catherine, who was standing at the chapel door watching for me. She said later that she tried to speak to me, but when I didn't hear her, she respected my silence and let me go. Those were her words, like yours sometimes, 'respected my silence.'

"We walked the length of the long path, almost to the high wall overshadowed by a skyscape of dirty factories that looked deserted, and a huge silver gas or water tank. Just beyond the wall, the bedroom windows of a row of drab brick houses overlooked the dead. We could hear the traffic in Scrubs Lane. It was there we found Ours, the Jesuit plot for those of us who die in London. It is guarded by Luigi and Rosa Genutti, who lie under their photographs, resting in the Lord and far from home, too. And I made myself say to my father, as Our Lord once said, although I knew it was disrespectful to him, These are my brothers and these are my sisters, and in spite of his ridicule I hoped it was true.

"The last thing I heard him say, he was jeering. You are trusting the white men, you are a fool and no son of mine. I was aware that he was saying this in English. Then he left me.

"I stood there as alone as I have ever been in my life. I was deserted. Everything beyond my own bones and flesh was for me, and at that time, you understand, a sham. A constructed life. No more honest than Jesus Joseph Jacob Gore Gordon Ngoro. I was in layer after layer of motley, new name, new words, wise, intelligent, and cold, and in that hour of grief, the remembered smell of dust and ashes was realer than anything for so long before or since. There in that pale cool place made subtle by the mist I felt as far from my own deep home as I have ever been. I saw myself, seeing not as my father now but as myself, as a fake. There was, for me then, no honest smell about me, no sense of death before a resurrection, but it was all dressed and protected from reality by stone and words like the stained marble around me, as rusted and obscene.

"I knew what we meant when we talked about loss of faith and, suddenly, a miracle. I was amused. I was treating this faith like a parcel I had left on the Underground, or something to lay down and pick up. It blew the trouble from my head, and I saw myself again, but this time a six-foot-nine blue-black *adheng* dressed in black, with my carefully creased Western trousers and my tribal scars and my white clerical collar, and I thought that in the mist the disembodied collar, floating near the Jesuit tomb, was all a white man would see, perhaps one of the Irish gravediggers, and I would scare the bejasus out of him. At that, my laughter rang and bounced back and forth among the black trees and the little stone bone houses. I could hear it echoing as I walked back.

"That Sister Catherine, that beautiful pale lady waiting for me at the chapel, was my sister and that Father O'Malley was my brother was a pig-bladder farce to me. Then I saw her standing in the road in front of St. Mary's Chapel, that dear cheap sandstone gaudy rising up out of the mist like a Gothic garden folly. She was standing beside a nice white marble man dressed in a swallowtail coat, and she smiled when she saw me, and I walked out of that despair as if it had been a place and not a sin and I had been released from it into the comfort of her smile.

"You live," he said to Paddy and to Jebra, who had long since come out of his door and was listening, "in moments of recognition, and in between there are only circumstances. I apologized for being late and she said not to mind, they had to wait anyway, and Sister Ursula said promptness was the politeness of princes. That made Sister Catherine smile again. She has a lovely, wise, witty face. I took her hand and held it, pleased with her. The sun was burning away the mist, and we stood and watched as the cross and the roof began to ride the new blue sky as the clouds ran.

"Inside the chapel the priest had got to 'May the angels lead you into Paradise' in Italian and someone sobbed. Everything was conspiring to make me think of black and white, which, as you know, I seldom do. And hearing the Italian I thought, too, There is another one who has left his body on an alien shore."

"No. Not alien. Distant. A distant shore," Paddy said, but Pius was still at his funeral.

"They came out of the chapel. He was a small man. The English don't waste coffin space, do they? He was followed by a woman drowning in sobs and widow's weeds, held up by a young man who must have been her son.

)231(

"I saw the man, and Jesus Joseph Jacob and myself and so many, but I remembered to pray for the soul of the man passing me outside the sandstone chapel. What else could I do? Then came the worst moment of all. Just when I thought my sorrow was over, I had a vision of us all left there in darkness under the grass and then the snow and the dirt from the factories and the traffic, so alone—as alone as—what? I don't know. Abandoned. We buried Joseph Jesus or Jesus Joseph, whoever he was, and Sister Catherine said they had a fund to buy a stone so he wouldn't be forgotten. Forgotten? He was already forgotten, except by four people at his funeral whose job it was to be there and maybe the man he had hit with a tray. She didn't know what name to put on the stone, so I said, Put them all, he lived all the lives. Now that I have burdened you with this, let's go to the pub."

The story had reminded Jebra of the death of his grandfather, but he told, to be polite, about something else, how he had said to his grandfather that the English wealth was made of paper, not cattle, and how they put the paper in a house called a bank, and he said that was foolish, that paper was worth nothing and it burned. They got to the pub in time for last orders, and they were all laughing. Knobby had to yell across the bar to get their attention and tell them that they were starting on the lounge in the morning.

Just before dawn Paddy and Pius found the Cézanne. By that time Paddy disliked it, so that when they unwrapped it to check it, he said it was not like a mountain at all, but a dung heap, the color of a dung heap. By one o'clock it was in the hands of the Jesuits at Farm Street, and by three o'clock it was hanging back in its place at the National Gallery and the guard had stopped having to tell people it had been removed for cleaning.

So the party really started with Pius, Pius and Paddy. When Pius called and said that they had finally gotten rid of the consignment, Teresa asked what consignment, and he told her to ask Ewen.

"The one Paddy picked up from Liam and Desmond," he said. "Tell him that Abou Baba Moosa finally took it off our hands, I can't tell you any more on this phone. It's in the hall. I don't want the boys to hear me." He was nearly whispering. "You see, the trouble is that now the lounge is buried under redecoration rubble and we can't watch the moon landing. May we come there?"

"Why is Pius being so mysterious?" she asked Ewen.

As they walked down Prince Albert Road on their way to the museum, Ewen told her about the painting and about Pius's Abou Baba Moosa, and by the time they got to Chalk Farm, he seemed to haunt them in the trees. Teresa, when she stopped laughing, said it was the power of myth, and Ewen said, no, not myth, circumstances. He said that Pius had called Abou Baba Moosa the master of circumstances.

Teresa and Ewen watched the blast-off of Apollo 11, huddled close together in front of the television as if it were a fireplace. Even in the early afternoon, the brash intrusive color and cleanliness of NASA in Houston made the old room, so far north, seem dark, drab, and slightly damp.

Teresa made cocoa. It seemed right. They warmed their hands around the mugs and watched the great arrow of fire shoot the tiny capsule of men into black space. Ewen said he was glad they had moved the telly to the northwest corner of the garden room, because they would be able to see the moon rise outside the garden window. Teresa laughed because he was still saying moonrise as if the earth were the center of things, and as they watched the bright arrow go higher and higher, she had one of those glimpses of peace that come so seldom, and she didn't know why.

"Blast-off," she said, "We have a new language. Let's ask everybody. We've got the only color telly. We'll feed everybody, too. Even moon-watchers have to eat."

"It's a new world," Ewen told her.

"That ought to make me afraid, but it doesn't," she told Houston, while they were explaining success, as if you had to.

For four days Ewen watched the telly, as if he were squeezed into the tiny capsule in the black silence with men who had ceased to be strangers to him. "Capsule," he said, several times, "what a draidful thing to call it. A wee thing to be swallowed." By the time they were approaching the moon, four days later, he was calling them by their last names, Aldrin, Armstrong, and Collins, recognizing their electric voices, and he repeated statistics no one understood in his new language.

It was nearly nine o'clock on the evening of July 20. Teresa was debating, all to herself in the kitchen, about when to serve dinner, since at least the diehards, Paddy, Ewen, and Pius, would be there, she was sure, most of the night. They sat in a row on the floor close to the television screen. It was brightening in the twilight. As the silent *Black and White Minstrel Show* made ignored patterns on the screen, they argued about the makeup of the moon. Ewen was sure it was sand.

They had been there on the floor since six-thirty, watching old shots of the earth and the moon in a loss of space. They concentrated as if they were trying to help.

Mr. Evans-Thomas, Abdul, and Penny and Robin, after some fitful watching and some gin, had brought in a card table from Mr. Evans-Thomas's flat, and were playing bridge. Teresa had heard them when she was washing salad, between the on and off of the tap.

"I simply won't play if you two play together." That was Mr. Evans-Thomas.

"Oh darling, you don't know. We have decided." That was Penny. "The solicitor finally let me have Mummy's lolly, which I was going to use to leave Robin, and then when we found out we could, we decided not . . . Besides, I was going to start an affair on Tuesday after dinner, and I found out at the weekend he had a boyfriend."

"After all that fuss." Mr. Evans-Thomas made a performance of sighing.

"We decided"—Robin sounded large and profound—"that anyone else would be just as frightful in time, and we are used to each other."

"It's like a new life," Penny added, "cut for deal."

The English are the least reticent people on earth, Teresa informed the *boeuf bourgignon*, which had been cooking all day and released perfume when she lifted the lid.

The corner of the room brightened in the light from Houston. She went to the door, wiping her hands. They showed a shot of the earth, a child's blue agate marble in the black void. It had been taken on an earlier flight, and she had seen it, but for the first time she saw herself and all of them there on the screen, and London and England as tiny places hidden under the swirl of cloud, as small as the red spot on the ceiling map, a reality and an abstraction. Ewen looked around and saw her in the doorway and called, "They're still out of contact. They're behind the moon."

Pius's deep reverent voice interrupted: "This pendent orb, in bigness as a star of smallest magnitude close by the moon . . ."

"I wonder how he knew." Paddy spoke for the first time in a long time.

"Who?" That was Ewen.

"Milton. *Paradise Lost*. For the most part, as you know, he used the Ptolemaic concept . . ." Pius said.

There was a faraway isolated voice, inhuman through the crackle of static: "Everything is A-OK." A lilt at the end. It seemed to Teresa to contain the cold and black of the void. For a pause she was with them, and didn't want to be, three men crowded into a pill in space. The courage of it made her eyes spurt tears, and she realized that she had not stopped drying her hands.

"God! I wonder how they pee." Robin looked around, awed.

"Robin, you are an ass." Penny began to fuss.

"Well, everybody wonders. I just said it."

"You promised to behave." Mr. Evans-Thomas's voice.

"Groovy," one of Artemesia's editors spoke from where he was lying on the floor, listening to The Grateful Dead on earphones, and once in a while twitching his body.

Artemesia was trying to pick an argument with her other editor about acid.

"I know that," she was saying, "but on the way to madness, he had some marvelous perceptions, like about colors, and angels, and time, and . . ."

"Yeah. And he also, like, bored a hole through his forehead to open his third bloody eye, man. You'd be bonkers in one trip. You were born tripping anyway."

"Was I?" Artemesia was pleased. She unfolded from the floor. "Time to go. We'll be back."

Ewen had told them they couldn't turn on in the flat. He was afraid, he said, that the contact high would make him miss the landing.

"Just leave the door open," Teresa called. It was the third time they had gone, so she knew they would be ravenous soon. She added sherry to the *boeuf*.

"Christ! Why sherry?" Artemesia had paused in her flight. "It isn't, like, classic."

She stomped out, followed by her boys.

"Six clubs." Abdul responded to what he thought of as Mr. Evans-Thomas's spooky club opening bid, which he tended to use when the count was good and he didn't know what else to do.

"God, you play super bridge." Heavy breathing from Penny.

"I learned to play at the Commonwealth Club in Oxford," Abdul said, looking at Mr. Evans-Thomas's dummy hand. He flipped his cards down over it. "It's a laydown," he said, "I give you one heart trick. The first time I went to the Commonwealth Club was with my friend, a prince from Sierra Leone. When we got to the door a limp-wristed Englishman took our names, didn't look at them, just read our color and called out over our heads, Reggie, Africa is your pigeon, India is my pigeon. How to lose an empire."

Pius, who had wandered over while the BBC was filling in time with local comments, and was watching the bridge, said, "Every one of us has a story like that. I call them burns. The time we were burned by stupid men. Yet the paradox is this. We come to here and we go out from here, as a center, a home we don't like very much but trust as we do no place else."

"Your deal, Robin, do wake up." Mr. Evans-Thomas passed the cards. "You chaps don't know how difficult it was. Now, when I was . . ."

"Not Poona!" Penny shrieked her favorite laugh.

"Malaya," Mr. Evans-Thomas told Pius, ignoring Penny. "There was one of me and thousands of you chaps. If I had had any imagination I would have been sick with terror."

"No reason to be." Pius smiled.

"No. No reason. Do you know why?" he asked Robin sternly, and didn't let him speak. "They hardly knew we were there. It was only the rich," he told Abdul, "the ones who could afford Oxford and who could travel to London to seek out insult from our social stupidity, and they were a jolly sight worse to ordinary people than we ever were, let me tell you. While you chaps were whining because you couldn't get into our boring clubs, we were out there on our bloody own administering a bloody empire with little bloody help from the local rich. In Malaya I was two hundred miles from the nearest Englishman and, you know, I quite liked it that way, except for holidays. Oddly enough holidays were bad, Christmas sort of thing. But God! Clubs! No, I'm not bidding. Hold on."

"Pass" from Robin and a wail from Penny.

"Two hearts." Mr. Evans-Thomas glared at Abdul.

"You get all the cards. It's no fun. Pass." Penny sulked.

"Three diamonds." Abdul glared back.

Teresa was aware of Frank Proctor on the sofa watching her

instead of the moon, and she wished he would stop. It made her nervous. She turned back to the kitchen and heard him get up to come after her.

"Let me help." He made an embarrassed S with his body, and she wanted to tell him he didn't need to do that.

"I think"—she drew him into her orbit, she saw it that way, orbital for the first time—"we ought to serve supper at ten . . . Or sooner? It's going to be a long night. What do you think?" She was rattling words at him.

Frank Proctor looked grateful to be asked. He thought. "I think about ten would be right if you think so," he said. His mother had taught him always to give positive answers.

"Oh, by the way . . ." He leaned against the door frame, so elaborately casual that she wanted to giggle, but didn't dare for fear of hurting his feelings. "Pius was just talking about a fellow called Moosa. I used to know somebody named that. Wild guy. Ran guns . . ."

Since she was sure that Pius had only mentioned Abou Baba Moosa on the telephone, Teresa realized at last that Mr. Evans-Thomas was right. It was true about Frank Proctor. The telephone was bugged. She wondered where the bug was in the flat. She wanted to cry, because she was American and shouldn't be treated like that. Then she saw how funny it could be. She saw them as a document among a million others, lost somewhere in a huge bureaucracy, tied in red tape. Ewen, too, had been right about Frank Proctor. "That man was born," he had said, "on the wrong side of a desk."

She said, seriously, trying again not to laugh in his face, "Oh, maybe it is your friend. A tall man with a beard?"

"Yeah. Yeah. I'm sure that's him."

"I wouldn't ask Pius about him, though, if I were you. They had a quarrel. It might embarrass him to talk about it. You know, a priest, quarreling . . ."

"Oh yes, I sure do know. I sure do know about that." Frank was not, he was sure, showing any excitement. He had already started a sleeve on Moosa, and he was almost sure that he was the guy they said was a close advisor of Arafat, a captain. It figured. He had the man but not the connection. Then he decided they must belong to one of those crazy lefty parties like what's-her-name, Vanessa Redgrave, fooling around with Arafat. His boss said they were crazy but still Commies and not to forget that. He had added profoundly, "Don't forget, Frank, they have divisions inside the Commie state, you know, like our Republicans and Democrats. Well, sort of like that, anyway."

Whatever it was, it was hot, hot, hot; he could see himself being rewarded with a Turkish assignment, if he could only find the connection.

When she took a raw carrot from the crudité supply she kept going in the living room and handed him one; he was so deep in his wish that he said, *"Chok teshekur ederim."*

She did giggle then, and answer, *"Affyet olsen."*

That reminded Frank of something else he'd been meaning to check. "Oh, by the way"—leaning against the door again, casual pose mark one—"I ran into an interesting phrase the other day when I was studying Turkish: *Bana inek satmak ister, fakat lanami istemez.* I translated it, He doesn't want to sell his cow, but he wants me to buy it. I don't understand the idiom."

"Neither do I," she told him, thinking of Fazih Bey all neatly taped by the CIA. He would be furious. No. Not furious, amused. He was several generations too civilized for fury. "Some of those sayings don't make sense to anyone but another Turk."

From the living room Ewen shouted, "Teresa, come quick. They're landing!"

The room was full of the bright light of Houston. They heard the scratchy voice from the moon say, "The Eagle has landed." Somebody had repeated it. Teresa heard ". . . on the Sea of Tranquillity," and she was afloat in the Sea of Tranquillity in the middle of a room gone mad.

Abdul knocked his chair over to get to the set. Ewen, Pius,

and Paddy sat like the three monkeys, not moving a muscle. Paddy and Pius were praying. Tears were washing Ewen's face, and he turned his head to look at the real full moon outside the window beginning to shine in the deepening twilight. He looked at the set, and then at the moon again. Teresa could feel tears on her own face, as if he had given them to her. She doubted if any of them knew what they were doing. Robin was still looking at his hand, and then at Penny, whose eyes were closed, and then at his hand again. Mr. Evans-Thomas sat very still. He watched Teresa. When he had made her look at him, he said, "Congratulations."

It seemed only right. Teresa said, "Thank you."

"Dust. Pounded by meteors like a mortar and pestle." Ewen spoke to the moon outside.

She heard a loud sob from the door. It was Zephyr, dressed as a moonbeam in strips of gold cloth. "It's only a rock," she sobbed. "They've ruined the moon."

Night and day became circular as the earth turned, and Teresa was conscious of that, of coming and going, of food, and talk, and light, while they waited for men to step on the moon.

Down below the open French doors Zephyr's party spilled across the grass. Someone had brought sparklers. A dozen figures, all dressed as moonbeams, ran from one moonlit garden to the other, singing all the moon songs they could think of, "Moon over Miami, "It's Only a Paper Moon," "It Must Have Been Moonglow," "Moonlight and Roses," and when they couldn't think of any more or of most of the words, they hummed and sang the same ones again. She heard Zephyr call out, "That's not true, not anymore."

V

AFRICA

T hey heard the faint two rings
of the telephone as they climbed up the stairs from the BM.
Teresa fumbled with groceries while Ewen opened the door.
"It's my parents," she said. "Who else would call us? Damn."
She had dropped a loaf of bread.

It wasn't. It was Noel. "I let it ring," he complained. "I got
tired of dialing. I've given you nearly three months to get used
to the real me, darling, and it's now or never. Anyway, I was
in and out, you know what summer is like. Oh, Lord. I have lots
to tell you, but maybe I won't.

"I had a dreadful time getting your number. You forgot to
give it me, you know, and it's not in your name! Very sneaky.
So I finally went to the Embassy hoping you'd registered and
they put me onto one Mr. Proctor, who wears black socks in the
daytime. What, my dear girl, is the American diplomatic corps
coming to? I know, it's that sweaty Mr. McCarthy who buggered
it all up for the gents. Never mind. I knew I'd have to do something quite special to lure you and your young man into seeing

me again. He didn't like me. Don't make noises, I haven't finished. I've got four tickets to the Bolshoi. They're dancing *Swan Lake* yet again, all those lusty Commie ballerinas, but the new Odette is a joy, I hear, quite like Ulanova. So you come and you bring Ewen and anyone else you like a week from Thursday, and I'll promise to behave. Five o'clock. We will have high tea at my place and go on to the ballet. Now it's your turn. Please, darling." He sounded shy. "I mustn't be shut out. You are one of my oldest friends."

Teresa said, "Yes. Oh yes," knowing she would take Ewen if she had to reach up and hit him in the head, which reminded her of tallness and how Pius had so few treats. "What a lovely idea!" she said, looking at Ewen, who had put the groceries in the kitchen and was leaning in the doorway listening. "What about our friend Father Deng? Pius Deng. He's a Jesuit friend of Ewen's." She knew he wouldn't deny Pius the pleasure.

"Oh, I see." Ewen could hear the phone buzz, and a wide smile appeared on Teresa's face. "He won't refuse on account of his friend. You are wicked. My God, a Scotch Presbyterian and a Jesuit. They'll hate me and disapprove of me and sit on the edge of their chairs and not say a word, but it's all for you. All right. Do you have a pencil?" She waved at Ewen and made pencil strokes. He gave her one from his pocket. "54 Musgrave Square, basement flat. It's off lower Sloane Street, on the edge at least of Belgravia. Wouldn't Mummy be pleased? Come down the areaway stairs."

Ewen heard the phone go dead. Teresa was still looking at herself in the mirror over it, grinning.

"You get as excited as Fama over a phone call. What is it?"

"Well, it is exciting. Now, Ewen . . ." She prepared for battle.

They took the tube and met Pius in Sloane Square, all of them a little shy and hoping they were properly dressed. It was easy for Pius, as he pointed out when they turned the corner past the pub into the King's Road. He just wore his holy clothes.

The whole of the world they had walked into was in some kind of gala, the square, Sloane Street, the queue in front of the Royal Court Theatre. Boys passed them in the boots and wide belts and the long, thonged hair of the month, and inside the pub a girl sat in a green wig with a boy in red velvet with a tangle of curls, a raunchy Little Lord Fauntleroy, with his hand on her thigh at her miniskirt hemline.

Teresa felt old and staid in her best faculty suit. "I'm only thirty and I have a lover, dammit," she wanted to shout, really yell. At least, she thought, my hair is long and shiny, even if I am wearing a cashmere sweater. As they walked on, she could feel her skirt getting longer and longer, and love and lust and friendship all around her, in the street, in the noise, in the Beatles song that came from the pub.

Ewen hadn't said a word. He just wanted to be at home with rocks and maps and Teresa, and not even Pius there.

Musgrave Square was a huge Georgian rectangle of columned embassy residences around a garden. The columns glowed as white as if no London dirt had been allowed to touch them in a hundred and fifty years of arrogance. The few cars were Rolls-Royces. There was a sense that small, noisy cars had never found their way there. The central garden was as smooth as a groomed putting green, with judicious trees and a mounted statue in the center on a bird-dung-covered horse just beginning to rear. The iron railings were glossy with new black paint. The intricate wrought-iron gates were obviously locked.

"Coo," Pius said, who had learned yet another language in the Isle of Dogs. "Init posh!"

They processed solemnly around the square, looking for No. 54, and Teresa tried not to giggle.

They walked down wrought-iron stairs into an areaway that had been made into a maze. A few feet from the stairs a brick wall had been built across four feet of the space. It left four feet open for them to pass through. In front of the wall, a large stone jardiniere held a tumble of red geraniums. Four feet behind the first wall was a second, with another jardiniere, and an entrance through it at the other end, so that the actual door to Noel's flat was completely hidden. Ewen, the first to go around it, was heard to murmur, "Jesus!" When they caught up with him he was staring into a huge mirror on the house wall.

Noel opened the door. "It's because basements have bad *fung shui*. It's to keep demons away from the flat," he explained. "It seems that they are too stupid to go around corners, and even if they do, they see themselves in the mirror and they are so ugly that it frightens them away. Here we'd call this paranoia, but in the East it's a very serious business. For me it's a folly, a caprice, don't you see? Hello, darling; do come in, Ewen. Father Deng, how kind of you." He shook hands and ushered them into the dark hall and hugged Teresa. "Oh, darling, you're wearing your shy clothes. How sweet. So am I. I'm terrified they won't like me." He walked after the others, who had got to the arch into the front room and were standing there in total silence.

Teresa's first thought in the dark foyer was, in her mother's language, that Noel no longer "had money"; her second, when she turned into the arch to his drawing room, was that his whole past had been gathered into one glowing present, a glow she remembered in the night story she had told herself for so long and thought was lost. A marble chimneypiece with the fat caryatids had been fitted into the fireplace of what had been the mansion's kitchen. Beside her, the Mayfair-yellow velvet sofa with its scrolled wood, long enough to seat ten people, which had been in the drawing room of his house so long ago, reached almost the length of the wall.

Ewen and Pius stood back to back in the center of the room. "It's like Aladdin's cave," Ewen told Noel, as if Noel had never seen it. "Och, it's a most beautiful place."

Pius hadn't spoken. He was watching a wooden horse covered

with gold leaf, as if he was waiting for it to move. It stood, in a perpetual pause, on a low black marble pedestal, high enough so the horse's head was level with his own. It was poised there, one forefoot raised, forever waiting to paw the air, its nostrils wide, its head thrown high to fly or plunge or charge. Its accoutrements were green and red and old gold, ready to clank and flow. On one flank the wood showed through, as if it had shaken off flakes of gold in some forgotten battle.

Pius said to himself, letting the others hear, "Hast thou given the horse strength? Hast thou clothed his neck with thunder?"

Noel, who had walked up beside him, added, "He saith among the trumpets, Ha ha; and he smelleth the battle afar off . . ."

"And to think a man made that. You know, I learned in Washington in America," Pius told Noel, looking down at him, "that when the Iroquois, an Indian tribe there, wanted to carve a mask or a god, they prayed to a tree until the face of the god or the spirit appeared, and then they released it by carving it out. Your horse. Can't you see it plunging out of the tree when it was released by the carver?"

"You show me a way to look at my room." Noel took his arm. "Read me the rest. What do you see?"

"First, I see two of everything, like the Ark." There were two columns, standing on either side of the fireplace, where the carver had released dragons that curled around the tree trunks. Two *putti* had bounced out of pieces of pear wood, grinning and flirting. On the wall, a plaque of flowers and fruit had grown out to bloom across a painted panel. Along the curved arch to the foyer, two five-foot angels had been hung, released in Italy, to fly out of their trees, be painted, and linger there, poised, with their wings flung across the wall.

"I see a room where all the wood has been touched and made into its spirits. And here is a scroll with some beautiful Chinese characters. Now you tell me."

"You won't laugh? No, of course you won't. I really do study. Here is the Mandarin character for sea, made up of the characters for water and woman. It is a very concrete image in Chinese. Nothing abstract at all. It is not in their minds."

"Like Latin." Pius still looked at the sea. They had forgotten Ewen and Teresa. "What about yin and yang?"

"Sun, moon, sunny side and shady side of a hill. All concrete metaphor. You see, Teresa, I'm not outré, outrageous, froufrou, or limp. This fine man takes me seriously, don't you?" He pulled his nose. "Oh. Oh dear. I'm really not used to it. I'm too used to being treated like a fool." He pinched between his eyes, and when he spoke, his voice had gone thin. "Come. Would you like to see the rest?"

He let them trail after him along a corridor that went deep into the back of the house. "This was once the kitchen and the storerooms. A cousin of mine," he explained over his shoulder, "was doing the place up, didn't want it all. Vastly valuable. He kept the attics, sold me the basement, and sold the rest—the leasehold—as a dormitory or residence or whatever, to the Rumanians or the Hungarians, I keep forgetting which. They look a bit stern and don't say good morning. Maybe they can't. There's always one sitting just inside the door. I think he must be their OGPU or KGB or whatever they call it. Never mind, my barrier keeps them out. Decadence is a great protection."

They were passing a coromandel screen that covered one wall of the corridor. He stopped at the first door, as if he were showing them through a country house. "This is the kitchen, not so interesting. All mod cons." He pointed to a large portrait over the fridge. "That is Grandpapa the manufacturer. He provided the lolly. Most of it is gone. I spent it. Now I have enough treasures for a basement flat, and some nice treats, and I do work. Yes, I do, Teresa. I'm giving lessons in Mandarin to diplomats, all that awful new language. What are the characters for Chairman Mao honors the province of Hunan with a hydroelectric dam, or, The Communism of Chairman Mao is going to set fire to the whole world, as it says in the song? Here's my bedroom." He put on lights that seemed to come from nowhere.

The room was without windows. It had been the butler's pantry, but the shelves and the cupboards that had held the glass and china and silver were gone, and the walls were covered in dark silk. Taking almost the whole of its space was the Chinese Chippendale bed. Its pagoda canopy towered to the ceiling. Its carved and gilded posts caught the reflection of the light. It was covered with a silk throw. Noel caught Teresa looking at the pillows. "Peter Jones," he said sternly. "Come, we had better have our high tea, can't be late for the ballet. With the early curtain time, I've never figured out when to eat.

"Isn't it odd?" he said when they had gathered around the black lacquered table in the window that looked out between the walls of the maze. "All my worldly goods. Quite something, though, isn't it? Milk or lemon? Oh, Teresa, you be mum. I want to ask questions, of course, about me. Father Deng, I've been thinking ever since I knew you were coming that you wouldn't like all this, and you do, don't you?"

"Why wouldn't I?" Pius laughed. "I didn't go blind when I entered the priesthood."

"You don't think it's sinful to keep all this for one person?"

"People always want me to read them their sins, a sort of holy palmist. My grandfather, who was a master of the fishing spear, a title like your grandfather the baron, did it with cow dung."

"Oh dear. I suppose it is a bit like inviting a doctor to tea and then asking him about your bowels. I'm sorry. I didn't know what to talk about."

Teresa held out her hand when Ewen's cup was empty. They had fallen into comfort. Noel suddenly looked at the table as if he had never seen it before.

"Oh, God! Wine! I forgot the wine and we can't sit through all that Tchaikovsky without it." He came back with the wine and glasses and the silver bread warmer. "Here, have some more hot scones. Please, everybody, they won't stay hot."

"Let me see." Pius studied him while he poured the wine. "You are not priapic. At least, I don't think you are." He looked around the room. "You could fall into the aesthetic sin of seeing only the shapes of things and their relationships. The perfect painting. The perfect distance between the pilasters and the fireplace." He laughed.

"They are a bit skew whiff, aren't they? I did this room myself, and the bedroom and the maze, all the bricks, all the moldings, all the painting . . . Oh, my God—sorry, Father—it's time to go. Now remember, you're coming back here for a bit of supper after. Teresa, help me take all this in so we won't come back to a mess."

"Isn't supper too much?" she asked, gathering the teacups.

"I have a way of doing it," Noel called from the kitchen. "I spent a large part of my money but I was determined to have mod cons if I couldn't afford a servant." His voice was muffled for a minute.

When Teresa and Ewen and Pius marched into the kitchen with the tea things, he was setting the timer on the stove. "You see, it's all in the timing, but then, so many things are . . ."

"No, not that one," Noel called to Ewen in the King's Road. "We need one of the large ones with jump seats."

"The last luxuries," he said when they had found a cab he liked. "No. I'm not being fussy. I'm being fidgety. It's not the same. I so want you to like things, and Father Deng has long legs."

"Pius," Pius said from the back seat.

When they got out, Pius said, looking farther and farther up, delighted, "I've never been to Covent Garden. I've passed it and wanted to, but . . ."

Ewen held Teresa's hand. They followed Noel and Pius up the great staircase.

"We're in J." Noel talked them down the center aisle. "The best seats for the ballet and the worst for the opera. All that screeching and jabbering, you do want to be a bit farther away. We'll be surrounded by balletomanes and critics counting the *fouettés* and judging the *jetés*. It's not the opening, so these will be the weeklies. Vicious but thorough. They have more time and earn less money. I hear they're furious with the Bolshoi for changing the ending," he said to Ewen as he ushered him past into the far seat. "Some people hate ballet. How is one to know?"

Ewen hardly heard him. He was looking up, entranced by the golden circle of boxes. "Is that the Royal Box?" He leaned across Teresa when they were all seated and asked Noel.

"Yes. They have rotten seats, poor dears."

Whatever worries Noel might have had were long gone by the time the white swan maidens in their long tutus whirled and swooped around the night-blue forest formed, set free, and formed again by Tchaikovsky's music. Ewen had leaned forward and rested his arms on the back of the empty seat in front of him, which the critic from the *Conservative Transcript* had left empty after the first act. He seemed poised to spring up on the stage and join the long running lines of swan maidens. "Och," he said, "look at the fairies. They're all fairies. Oh, lovely . . . you are lovely," he whispered to the Russian Odette.

Noel wanted to say, "Watch your language in this company," but he didn't know Ewen well enough. Instead, he whispered to Teresa, "Well, they're certainly not going in for Proustian disappointment."

At the end, Pius, on his other side, sat with silent tears pulsing down his face, saying, "Don't die. Oh, please don't die."

Noel whispered, "It's all right, they've changed the ending."

"Thank God," Pius said, wiping away tears.

"On the whole," Noel told Teresa when they were washing up at midnight, having banished Ewen and Pius from the kitchen, "it's been successful, don't you think? I do mind."

"Oh, Noel, take a look in the living room." Teresa was concentrating on a wineglass that couldn't go into the dishwasher.

When he came back, he said, "They're both sitting on the sofa with their legs stretched across the room, looking at the fire. Ewen has a smile left over and Pius some wine, which he keeps turning in his glass. I think they are there and they are some-place else."

"They are sometimes when they're together. I've noticed that."

Noel followed them through the maze, loath to give up con-trol of the evening. "Now, you mustn't walk. You must get a cab where we got the other in the King's Road. It's the best place. You simply can't walk at this time of night. London is a cesspool under all the new paint and the swinging scene." He leaned against the area railing and looked out at the square, where under the trees the statue was an ominous mass under the filtered light from the street lamps. "It's a cesspool," he said again; he seemed to be remembering things he didn't want to tell them. "Oh, not that. Not the obvious. The leather boys and all. The only leather boys I know have needlepoint contests. It's something else. Something ominous glittering just beyond the shadows, as if there had been rats running in a mews just before you got there."

Pius had to answer him. Noel had thrown the night at them and he knew why. They were taking the evening away with them like a bright present and leaving him alone. "You have given me an evening I will never forget. You make me realize that I neglect something. I don't know what it is, but it is a gift, an eye, an ear, and needs to be cared for. Don't be afraid of the night."

Then he turned what he had once told Ewen around. "Evil is not only in London. You have seen it here. That's all. I lived for two years in a part of the Isle of Dogs where the dock rats didn't run away and women sat up nights to protect their babies. Don't bring the rats into this evening, even though you have been a Pied Piper for all of us.

"Good night, Noel, and God bless you," he said when Noel and Teresa had kissed good night and Ewen had found his own way to thank Noel by offering to show him his rock collection any time, absolutely, that he wanted to see it.

"Please come," Ewen said again. He wanted to make sure Teresa had heard him.

In the street, Pius said, "I am going to walk home. It is not far, and my head is full of dancers and wine and better food than I am used to, and I need the walk and the space and the dark."

"Alone." Teresa understood.

"No. Not this time. If you would like . . . All this formality in the streets. Come."

They called good night quietly along the street and then watched until Noel had turned back down into his maze.

"He is, you know, like a Pied Piper."

"Pius, he always has been to me." Teresa walked in the middle and held both their arms and thought, That's because of Noel, too, not being shy of touching people. I didn't learn it from Michael, and Ewen is just learning from me. "He has always been a guide without guiding. He always made things possible, a sort of oh, well, why not, about him."

"The thing is," Ewen was thinking aloud, and slowly trying to say it, what he could see, "he doesn't mind. That's part of it. I never saw anyone who didn't mind so much." He sensed that he still had to be careful of Teresa's feelings. She seemed to balance Noel like an egg she was carrying. Noel reminded him of a cricket that was thin and lively and didn't mind where you put him down, he went on chirping, but he didn't dare make that comparison, not yet.

Even if Noel had long gone into his house, he was still with them, walking under the white cliff of Buckingham Palace and into Bird Cage Walk. All the way down the King's Road they had been either silent, thinking about Noel, or talking about him. Pius had found him as refreshing as cool water, a naïf, an innocent, he said so. It surprised Teresa, and made her argue. "I've always found him the most sophisticated person I ever knew."

Pius was seeing shadows under the trees as they turned into

St. James's Park, past the small pond where there was the story of the girl who had committed suicide. "I think," he tried again to gather the thought of Noel into words, "it's his surprise. He seems to see everything for the first time. Now tonight; he had seen that ballet a dozen times, but when the swan was dying he had tears in his eyes, too." He laughed. "I saw them through mine. And he talked about the rats and his golden horse and the darkness the same way, the first time. A natural? A child? I don't know . . ."

"In the collective unconscious according to Jung, he would be a Hermes, or the fool in the middle of the Tarot pack, whirling in the center of things," Teresa told him.

"A fool. That's it. We would call him a fool of God or an angel." Pius began to laugh. "We are seeing an angel in the form of an intelligent, attractive, slightly nervous, hospitable, generous, homosexual man, and why not?"

He stopped on the bridge over the lake and looked up at the Horse Guards palace roofscape, floodlit against the pink night sky. "Angels come in many forms. Maybe you are one. Maybe I am. All that is needed, I think, is recognition. I come here often at night after everyone has gone to bed and I can't sleep. There is something about London at night, how it receives its spaces back after the crowded days, that calls me out."

He leaned on the rail. Away under the trees at the water's edge, the ducks and the swans slept with their heads under their wings. "You know, when I was teaching in the East End, I used to have to come up west after daughters who'd gone there to be actresses without a hope in the world and ended up in strip joints in Soho, poor little skinny ill-fed things with their dough-white bodies. Big black me would go into places that were brothels on the side. Nobody ever stopped me. Those little ratty Cockneys thought I was their six-foot-nine black pimp." His laughter stirred the night. "It was like that story of what do you give a ten-ton gorilla—anything he wants. I let them think so.

It seemed simpler. Now, how did corruption like that creep into the fairies and music and golden horse of this evening?"

"It was Noel. Why did he do that?" Teresa asked the water.

Nobody spoke. They all leaned on the rail and looked at the water. Pius remembered the girls and their mothers. He had not found corruption interesting, that terrible evocative word, "interesting." He had found it dusty, full of neglect, and vicious, not as vice reigns, but as badly treated dogs bite, and above all, dumb, as mute, animal mute, but hopeless in humans.

He finally said, "Noel probably thinks corruption happens in another part of town in the dark, late at night, and that it has to do with sex. He has always been rich and the rich are like children. You know why?" He didn't wait for either of them to answer. "They can always leave. There is more freedom in the price of a railway ticket than is dreamed of in their philosophy." He stopped, thinking again of the ballet dancers and how they were standing looking at a swan lake.

Teresa wanted to tell Pius that he was wrong, that Noel knew, and knew with his whole soul, in terrible ways, but he had confided in her and she could not speak.

"Anyway, he isn't rich anymore," she said instead. "It's very sad."

Ewen and Pius both laughed. Ewen said, "He's not as rich as an Edinburgh lawyer, but that is not poor. What about your girls in Soho?" Ewen was talking across her. "Don't forget that I was brought up by Fama, and the Wee Frees are very cautious about sex, to say the least."

Pius thought for a long time and hoped no one would say anything. Finally he said, "It isn't sex itself. That's the mistake. The sin is in using people as things, a sin of things." He stood up then and lifted his arms and stretched high toward the trees. "Oof," he said. "Time to go home."

"Can we walk to Victoria Street, Teresa?" Ewen said, not wanting to leave him.

"Oh yes," she said, not wanting the whole thing to be over, either.

"I think," Pius said under the trees, "that tonight has been the most beautiful . . . I have missed the dancing. You know, in southern Sudan there is a town called Juba, that means dancing, and on certain nights when I was young . . ." It wasn't that he didn't finish. He simply stopped, on the way to Juba.

They walked out into the street in front of Westminster Abbey. Pius had finished what he was thinking, and he stopped, dead still. "You may think me an interfering black bastard," he said, "but have you two thought of marriage?"

Neither of them knew what to say in front of the other.

"I was thinking still of Noel," Pius told them, but he was looking at the abbey. "What I think of as a sacrament of symbiosis, with its legal protection against easy loss, is irrevocably closed to him and to men like him. Symbiosis is not a very romantic way to look at marriage, I know, but it is a strong word, as strong as iron. I have it, of course, in the priesthood. That building belongs to us. We built it and you Prots took it away from us," he accused Ewen.

"Yes, I suppose you people do still mind," Ewen said.

"A bit grumpy about it by now, that's all." Pius sounded like Noel, and then Teresa remembered that he was a natural linguist and picked up languages with a magpie ear.

Pius seemed not to want to turn away from them yet, either. He walked with them into Parliament Square. "I wonder," Ewen said. He sounded very tired, and Teresa wanted suddenly to get him home. "I wonder where we were six months ago."

Teresa thought of being in her house and in her daily habits and not yet knowing that her life was about to end and begin again and grow so bright. She was walking in the middle and she took their arms as they passed St. Margaret's Church, where she had once been to a dumb and beautiful wedding.

"I think you were being sick down my back," Pius said across her. They went on talking across her, being someplace else, trusting her to wait, depending on her to be there to keep them from being lost in the past. She felt solid, like a tree which is always present, twining her arms in theirs to hold them there.

"It's far too late for the tube." Ewen looked up at Big Ben, a shining moon face at the end of the dark Walter Scott medieval roofscape of the Houses of Parliament.

All the way home in the taxi, Ewen didn't say a word. He only held her hand and, from time to time, pressed it, to show her he was with her, or to convince himself that she was really there.

By the time they reached Battestin Crescent, the wind had risen and blew from the southeast. They could hear the grumble of the lions in the zoo and the cries of caged night birds.

Ever since Pius had asked his terrible question about marriage, Ewen had known it was hopeless. He lay pulsing with wakefulness. The late night, the question, the excitement had torn away hope and shown the cold reality behind it. He was exhausted and despair came nearer.

"Can I do anything?" he heard her say, quiet in the darkness.

"No." His mind prowled like the animals when the wind was right, restless in the night. He almost hated her for letting a man like him come into her life when she knew so little about him, the fool, the naïve fool. He couldn't say a word, even though he knew she was awake beside him. He sensed her waiting.

They had come again to haunt him for the first time in months —Gordie, Helmut, Derek, and the never-ending grind of the motor. It was night there, too, and they crept like any other beast along the pale ribbon of track in the moonlight. There were circles of low shambas, humped hillocks among the thorn trees and the chimneys of the termite hills, and no light, not even firelight.

Somewhere he heard a clock strike two. He tried to get out

of bed without disturbing her. Moonlight flowed in when he opened the curtains. He raised the window and the wind found the curtains and lifted them around him. They brushed against his face and made him shiver.

He had almost told her so many times, and failed, had changed the subject, drawn back from an abyss that he feared would end the life with her that he had no right to accept.

He glanced behind him. She was half sitting, leaning against the bed head. The brass rails and pinnacles of the bed and her eyes caught the moon and he thought of animals, night animals.

Moonstruck, he turned around from the window, and he thought he said, or wanted to say, or had to say, "You see, you have to know . . ."

He came back to the bed and sat down at the end of it and began to talk, really talk to the recognition of the moon, and to her. He felt that he had been silent all his life and that it hadn't somehow been fair. He interrupted what she hadn't said: "No. I have to tell you something." He saw her face, made so wan by moonlight that she reminded him of a ghost.

"I remember sitting on that balcony in Mombasa where Gordie had told me to go every evening for what he called a sundowner until he got there."

He thought she had dropped asleep and that the time had passed to tell her what no one knew but Pius, but she reached forward then and touched his foot. Her hand was long and white.

"I'm cold," he said. He settled back against the foot of the bed and she covered him with the eiderdown.

She whispered, "Where were you? Mombasa?"

"Oh, that was in Mombasa. I was in Mombasa, waiting for Gordie. I waited for nearly two weeks, but that was Gordie's way. He came in his own time. He always had. Then it was the first of February and still he hadn't come and I was thinking of leaving. The days were hot; the wind from the Indian Ocean that brought the dhows from the east was hot. Sometimes, you know, I felt so peaceful I could sense the earth turning eastward and me riding it, in that wind that bent the trees toward Africa."

He leaned back, pleased for a minute at remembering, conscious that he had found a route, a map that he could follow to tell her at last, but conscious that, if she didn't understand what he didn't understand himself, he couldn't stay any longer. That made him shiver again. England caught his bone marrow.

His voice in the dark: "I walked and walked there in Mombasa, and thought, well, I did, about my future, for the first time since I was a boy. Oh, not jobs and degrees. I had always found them easy. No, I was like a dog turning and turning, with the whole world as its bed . . ." and then, after silence, "My Uncle Gordie was like a tree, and I grew up in his shadow."

Ewen took a deep breath of the cold night air off Primrose Hill, which tasted of damp and green leaves. It made him feel, for a stolen second, safe, and a place turned in his chest and broke and he was afraid he was going to cry. "You see," he told her shadow, "Gordie drank and Gordie whored and Gordie laughed at everything, and Gordie got any woman he wanted. For all my life, God help me, I admired that. Men do. There's a terrible freedom in not giving a damn. You remember tonight when Pius talked about the sin of things? That was Gordie. He saw all the world as things for him to take—a gun, a man, a woman, a piece of fruit, or, as he would call it, a piece of cake, and the people he touched died or went to prison or broke their hearts, but not wee Gordie."

He got up again and shook off the blanket, and went to the window and looked out. "I've told you how I traveled the Great Rift that goes all the way from where you were in the Taurus Mountains, down through Lebanon and Israel and Jordan and through the Sinai and the Red Sea, all the way down through Africa. It's a new place in the world, a great scar where in our human memory the earth has split and sunk and destroyed. I looked down on the Jordan River from the Jordan side, where for all the ages men had fought for that narrow rift valley, and still do.

"And still do. I sat where Moses had looked across the Rift at the Promised Land, cities and the ruins of cities, ancient forts that had become part of the mountains, Masada and Beaufort, and modern gun emplacements, and all for bottom-land, a little bit of bottomland. Oh, it is all there, and I, raised by Fada, that Old Testament prophet, and trained the way I was, could see in both languages, the Bekaa Valley as Arma-geddon, as Fada had taught me, the valleys made mountains, the hills skipping like lambs, and fire and brimstone raining down on the cities of the plain, Sodom and Gomorrah, and the land of Gad. Of course the Red Sea split and drowned the proud Egyptians. It's a new sea, still being born. Did you know that where the Rift goes down the center of it, there are spots where the deep sea floor is boiling hot from volcanic spew?"

He had forgotten her again. He was seeing at last the south shore of the Red Sea, where once there had been water. He could not reach it, but he knew it. In the distance the high black escarpments of the Danakil trembled in the heat. It was his first sight of Africa, where the Rift turned in to the continent. Standing on the hot deck when the wind was to the east, he could smell the fire and brimstone and salt on land that still heaved, as it had a million years ago as time flies by. At sundown the water turned blood red, and he knew then why it was called the Red Sea.

He turned and leaned against the window frame, no longer concerned at where his vision left off, and his voice began and stopped. It was too late for that. "So I went to Mombasa on a ship going to Yemen, and there I caught a dhow to Mombasa. It's easy to travel any place when you have only a backpack. God, it was heavy, though. The last notebook and the last rock and sand samples. So I got to Mombasa with a change of under-wear and a pack of rocks. I sent them off and bought some clothes and my fifth pair of boots. We will go there sometime. I'll take you there.

"Anywhere, that's where I was going to meet Gordie. He had been in Africa for five years then. I didn't ask him what he was doing there and he didn't tell me much. I see now I didn't want to know. I knew he'd been in the Congo with Mad Mike Hoare, but I'd closed my mind to what he'd done since. I have to admit now that I knew all the time. He had hinted at it when he kept in touch. Maybe he did that because, after Fada and Fama died, I was the only one left that was a tie to home. He'd sold the house and its wee bit of land to an Englishman after all his fine talk, so he had no place to go back to, either. So much for Donalbain, the King of Scotland. He found me in Saudi, and once we met in Cairo, but to me he didn't seem to change. You know how it is. You look for what you know. It's a comfort.

"So I swam in the ocean and listened to the wind and ate at the Fontenelle, and in the evening I listened to the muezzin's cry from the minarets, and I strolled along past the shops among the chattering Somali women in their black *bui buis*, which made them look and sound like flocks of dark birds, and every evening in the narrow streets the Indians sat before their shops, smoking in the half dark.

"But every evening at sundown I was where Gordie told me to be. He was specific about that, all that detail in a creased letter three months old that had caught up with me in Aqaba. I knew he would take for granted, if he wasn't dead, that I would get it and be there. I'd never let Gordie down in my life."

His voice stopped, just stopped, and she waited for him to come back.

" 'It must be the time of the full moon, before the rains begin,' Gordie wrote, 'and we will take you on safari to the Olduvai Gorge and up the Rift, for I well know that is what you want to do. Be at the Wells Hotel at sundown until I come.' I noticed for the first time that Gordie's handwriting was like a child's. Who 'we' were he didn't say, but he did tell me to get a hunting license in Mombasa, and clothes. Oh, there was a list—anti-malaria pills, hemoglobin, first-aid kit, all that. He made a mystery of when he would come and who would go with them. Mystery was Gordie's way of controlling people, that and time. Wait, he'd say, he'd say wait, and later, relax, the word diminishing you, winding the world as his own clock.

"I do know now that I knew what he was up to, but it was an adventure, macho muscles, darkest Africa—that insouciance of the body I'd always wanted, and what man you pass in the street wouldn't secretly like to test himself that way?"

He didn't look in her direction when he said that. It was a confession, and he was ashamed in the moonlight. He told it to his own cold hands, which clutched the window frame.

"But I didn't let myself think too much about it"—still watching his hands. "I'd traveled a long way, and was ready to travel again, a last time, until I had the Great Rift in my pocket, or rather in Barclays Bank. I could already see the book in my hands, written by me with Fada at my shoulder. I would sit on the balcony of the Wells Hotel and see it with a blue cover and my name in gold, arrogant with the dream of it. Dreadful nonsense."

He turned from the window and said, "I will, you know," arguing with the shadows and her moon-pale face.

"I'd sat there for a week, every evening at the right time on the scarred balcony outside my room, looking out over the Kilindini Harbor. It was an Indian hotel, terrible, mostly for lascar sailors, it smelled of ghee and curry and rotten garbage. A fine hotel off Mikanjuni Road, Gordie had written; the proprietor is a friend of mine. The proprietor wasn't a friend of anybody on earth. I guessed from the hotel that Gordie was either broke or hiding out, and I really didn't care at that point which it was. I just watched the sun plunge down to meet

Africa, aware of the cracks in the concrete balcony and the unknown continent beyond.

"Then one evening there was a long black cloud that raced toward the ocean out of the west like a band of Somali angels migrating to heaven, and in the middle of that fancy, a dark shadow between me and the angels. I looked up and there was Gordie against the light and he looked as if he had fallen between the cracks of the world. I hadn't seen him for three years and he was only thirty-six years old, but he looked old and dried, tanned skin as if he had been smoked in some fire, and his bones, Oh, Christ, his bones were sharp against the leather of him. He looked sere and there was no flesh on him. As God is my witness, I saw his skull when he grinned, and I knew for a second that something had driven him mad. His eyes were as cold as a leopard's, those agate eyes that Fama had taken such pride in. His auburn hair had been burned blond.

"I knew then that he had been those places and done those things I never wished to see and do in all my life, but when he spoke he was as playful as ever, and he took me with him. He always had. I put that glimpse away as disloyal, and saw him again as he had always been to me, amused at the world, shaming me a little for all my secrets that he seemed to know but didn't, not anymore.

"Then I looked at Helmut. They had sat down on either side of me, and as we drank they talked across me. They talked like tour guides. They sounded false, as if they were trying to impress me. I can hear that now, but I couldn't then. Gordie had picked up a frontier way of speaking. Extremes. Helmut, he told me, was the best white hunter in Kenya, no comparison. Now they both are fading. I can just hear their voices, a dim whine in the evening wind. Helmut is sitting with his head tilted back. He looks like a man who wants to own the world . . . Helmut von Darmstadt, he calls himself, and that sounds false, too. His almost-black aviator glasses reflect the sunset and the angel flight.

"I didn't know until later that he was nearly blind from an eye disease he had picked up from the Nile water. There were a lot of things I didn't know. I didn't know that Gordie and Helmut were the white hyenas of a new Africa, born four hundred years too late. They had the eyes that an Arab slaver would have had, staring across the warehouse roofs at the roiled water of the harbor, all care and caring burned out of them by some sun I didn't know.

"Through the evening and then the night, Gordie didn't tell me, just let fall, as though it didn't matter, what he and Helmut had been up to for those blank years out of Gordie's five years in Africa and Helmut's twenty-four. No wonder they knew, between them, all the high roads and the low roads and the jungle paths, and an insult of languages. They had fought over them for anyone who would pay. Mad Mike Hoare in Zaire, Obote in Uganda. When I took them to the place I'd found for dinner, they ate like men who hadn't smelled decent food for a long time, and Helmut played the bwana."

Ewen's voice faded then. He seemed to be listening, but there was only the night wind that had veered to the north. He was still trying to be sure about why Gordie had taken his passport and his hunting license the next morning. He thought he knew, but there were such silences and dumb mysteries about it.

He was trying, too, to remember them as strangers, to not know them again, so he could tell her the right way, from the beginning, so she might understand. He didn't want her to know them yet as he knew them after the confines of their mutual hate. He tried to hear Helmut before the rasp of his bragging and his orders had been heard, not with his ears, but with his strung nerves. He picked and picked at a dry bubble of old paint on the windowsill. It wouldn't come off. Goddammit, it wouldn't come off.

"Oh shit" was all he said to the cold night.

He was standing by the old Bedford lorry in the first heat of the morning, and there were Africans watching them but not looking at them. Small boys held out their light palms and chanted, Money money dollah dollah—a game, not expecting any attention. The women wore bright-colored prints to fight the leeching sun. That made them look brave, that and the way they stood. The sun—you could hear it and feel the burden of it. It beat, as Helmut beat and beat on the sandblasted side of the lorry and kicked the tires, both the worn man and the worn machine part of the leftover litter of white Africa.

That morning he saw more Africans than he would ever see again, hundreds of them walking toward Mombasa from their shambas and their villages, dressed in all the castoffs left behind, too-old army coats and ragged shorts, but here and there young men and women especially, their black proud heads above statements the colors of African flowers.

But what he was hearing was the clang of the lorry as Helmut punished it. Kick. Kick. Best safari truck in Africa, everything best or worse, a habit.

Helmut was lecturing, refusing to stop, as if it were a history of himself, his demand for an epitaph. See here. I invent. For viscosity. Mud. He shook the long thick slabs of wood that made a second bed in the lorry. There. You see. I nail rubber tire pieces across for purchase. You lay under the front wheels so and take this pipe so, you understand. A lever. The principle of the lever. It never fails; in cotton mud it never fails. That is extraordinary, you understand?

He was walking around the lorry, touching things. Then the racks for extra petrol tins. I put in five. So? Two spare wheels. Pump. He kept on touching and hitting the metal. The lorry side rang in the heavy air. Jack. Shovels. Pangas. Food boxes. Mosquito netting. Bedrolls. Two-way Marconi radio. He announced them all as he touched them. Water.

You can go many weeks with this, my Bedford lorry with the steel-screened sides. Any place, you understand. The steel net protects from lions. Only a rhino or an elephant can knock it over. He grinned, offering Ewen the same cheap thrill he might have given to tourists sometime in his career, or his careen across Africa.

Then you do this, he said, enjoying himself. He grabbed a panga, the knife tool of Africa, and beat it against the lorry side, and yelled, Olla! Olla! Olla! The Africans were still laughing when Gordie drew up in an old taxi at the tin shack of a petrol station where they had left the lorry all night. He strolled up to them, Helmut checks everything. Helmut is *sehr* efficient. Ewen remembered that he knew then they didn't like each other.

He can't see a bloody thing. Gordie grinned. He has to feel all the equipment. He put a package behind the driver's seat and climbed up behind the wheel. But when Helmut got in beside him, he nodded as if something had been settled. Helmut just sat there behind those black glasses and said nothing, not bothering to move out of the sun. You ride in the back. You'll see more. Welcome.

A white man, a boy, had been leaning against the bright pink tin side of the station, watching. He vaulted up over the tailgate and shook hands, some politeness left over from somewhere else. He had been left there all night to guard the lorry. Ewen never found out where they had picked Derek up. Derek never said. He was a twenty-two-year-old blond boy, not yet smoked by Africa. He had gotten his ticket from the air force, an RT operator. That much he did say. He still spoke the language of the air force; that, and hippie slang, and a few words of Swahili he seemed to take pride in. When he took off his sunglasses to wipe the sweat from his face, he had the eyes of an addict, but in the morning he was still in contact with the world.

For a second, all Ewen could recall were their eyes, the eyes of an addict, the blind eyes of a killer, Gordie's agate leopard stare. And he still saw their eyes when nothing else was left.

Gordie drove, with Helmut beside him and Derek opposite

Ewen across a truckbed full of gear. The truck broke down twice, and Helmut was furious, as if it were a live thing. Gordie wouldn't let anybody help him. They sat there with the heat weighing on them. Then Ewen remembered what pride he took in being able to fix anything.

The black road stretched in the distance beside the railroad, mile after mile, uphill and down through the volcanic upthrust and the thorn desert. Now in England, the veering wind blew the curtains around him and brought the grumble and chuff of a lion or a train into the dark room. But then it was all the same, the thorn, the hills, the rise of the road toward the great central plains and mountains. When they turned off the black-top road at Voi, they drove along an endless dirt track through red dust and deep, dry ruts, and there was only the sound of the engine and the sound of heat, the buzz of it and its weight through midday and into the afternoon.

His first rain in Africa came out of the west, a huge black thunderhead. He could hear it miles away, beating on the continent. Then it was on them, an attack of rain, blinding, roaring rain, slamming down on the canvas roof, pouring through the steel mesh, and in the cab, the voices of Helmut and Gordie, furious and tiny under the huge noise, accusing each other of starting too soon, too late, and still the rain was a dark sheet around them, and as sudden as the stopping of breath it was gone and the sun glistened on the mud and the dripping thorn trees, and ran in rivulets down the ruts of the track.

Was it then, or was it another time, slithering sideways, end-ways, sledding down the river of a track into night, without headlights, creeping along at five miles an hour in a gear so low the engine roared like an animal?

That first day Ewen stared and pointed at the elephants, the elands, the Grant's gazelles. There was a flash of something in a baobab tree that could have been a leopard or a cheetah. They drove through miles of wait-a-bit thorn trees, and in the distance there were anthills, and here and there basalt kopjes from before the Flood. But Derek was asleep. There was no one to share it with. They were driving through the Tsavo, and he thought the elephants were red and then realized they had rolled in the red dust.

That day he still judged the topsoil, the sediment, the metamorphic rock thrust up from earth fire, reading age and movement in the dust. As far away as mirage or clouds, the blue hint of the mountains marked the eastern wall of the Great Rift. He watched a giraffe nibble delicately at the top of an acacia and thought of the way royalty ought to move. They stopped at a crossing on the track for a herd of elephants, which took the right of way and ignored them as the Africans had done.

Gordie called back, No use camping here. Better places farther on. It's too late, anyway. We have to make up time. They talked too much about time. Time is against us. Time is on our side. And always the indifferent back of Gordie's head, driving across Africa.

Oh, Christ, I've got to tell her in all fairness and I'm not doing it, he said in himself to the night of—what had she called it?—gray comforting London. He was still unaware of what he had said, what he had avoided, and what he had only seen for himself, without words, in his mind's eye, scanning a continent as he had done for so long when he was alone—the hot sun, the drought of thin topsoil, red with iron, and after the rain, the drum-hard ground, its spaces, its colors, its uncompromising beauty. Not like England, that gray-green compromise, no, it was the other, the brute, that changed your life, once you had seen it, like one lover, maybe not even the most important one, but the most piercing—for him it had been a Norwegian girl on a ferry when he was seventeen and she was fifteen, maybe even younger, and all the way across to Mull he sat and plaited and unplaited her hair. They did not speak the same language.

Time. All those small phrases about time in that timeless place. They lurched along then, south along the dirt track pounded hard by animals and tunneled with dried-out ruts that only hours before had been rain rivers, bone-shaking, and they said nothing, only drove as if the rain and the dust were after them, never looking left or right where the vast space stretched out and the impala pronged straight up on springs above the head-high grass, or seemed to fly through the air without wings, and the land in the sunset was the color of wheat ready for harvest. Toward evening they drove through the center of Masai villages, where the tall Masai in their rusty robes were bringing in the cattle that surrounded the lorry, ignoring Gordie, caught there cursing and blowing the horn. More than ignored; they seemed not to bother to make that choice. They simply didn't see them.

There seemed to be no dusk, no gentle leaning of the earth toward the night. The lowering sun made the sky and the continent red, glowed, etched the black rainclouds adrift in the vast sky with bright gold.

Derek had made the safari, if it could be called that, before. There was a sweetness about him that Gordie never saw. He had some care left in him that hadn't been burned out by his exile. When the dark came, he began to talk about his mother. He said he wrote to her religiously—he used the word—every week, so she wouldn't worry, and then, in deeper darkness, he laughed and said he never wrote to her at all, he just wanted to.

Dark or rainclouds, then dark with stars, and then the white rise of the full moon constructing hard black shadows, and over the sound of the engine, the roar and scream of the awakened night, more alive, more wary than the day.

Helmut had said almost nothing for a long time, and when he did, it seemed to be an order, spoken quietly under all the night noise. He was sitting straight, officer watch in his taut shoulders, in some army that no longer existed, making a parody of *blitzkrieg* across nowhere where no one cared or saw him in his broken-down lorry, which he treated like a tank, making hand signals that Gordie ignored.

It was nine o'clock when they stopped under a moon so bright that Ewen could read his watch. The moon flooded the land with silver light. That was important, wasn't it? That was why they had kept him waiting before they came down from Lamu town.

The figures of black men in uniform leaned toward the windows of the lorry, casting long moon shadows. Someone laughed softly. It was Helmut who spoke to them in Swahili and showed them some papers. Ewen thought then that they were at the entrance to one of the game parks, but they weren't. It was the Tanzanian border.

They crossed, and Gordie threw Ewen's passport back to him. It had taken him so long to realize what Gordie had done, and there, at the London window, he said aloud, "My God, you arrogant bastard, you were taking for granted that Africans think all whites look alike. You were passing as me. Of course you got by with it, you always did. What was it you said later? *Persona non grata* in half the countries of Africa, except Tanzania. They hadn't caught up with you yet."

He was still again, staring at the night. He heard a roar in the distance that seemed to shake the air, the night air full of the noises of the prowlers, the hunters, the hunted, and it was cold, Christ, it was cold, and he thought then, We'll stop and build a fire, now that we're across, but no, Gordie drove on under that vast night, slower and slower, downshifting for ruts that seemed made of iron.

Gordie was, of course, driving without lights. That was why the full moon was important. They were creeping across the night continent like the predators around them. He and Helmut had known where they were going, like an animal in its territory, a huge baobab tree; an ancient monolith, a living rock. They drew off the trail and parked under it. The engine died and was replaced by night sound. By Ewen's puny watch, for he had not yet stopped marking time in hours, it was eleven o'clock. They had been driving for seventeen hours.

They opened a tin of sardines and ate them on biscuits around their fire, so small a protection against the space. Helmut and Derek leaned then against the baobab and smoked. The sweet smell of hashish mixed with the wood scent of the fire that Gordie kept feeding. They smoked in the black shadow of the tree etched by the huge white moon as if the world weren't vast enough for them. Gordie said it was Ewen's turn to feed the fire. He rolled into his sleeping bag and went to sleep at once, as a trained soldier does, catching sleep when he can.

Helmut and Derek were mounds of shadow against the tree. Helmut had lit a candle. Ewen could see the glitter of his eyes as he stared at it. He spread his sleeping bag on the ground beside the fire, and he lay on it, not wanting to sleep, only to lie there in a place he had wanted for so long to be, a place none of the others seemed to know, that he had waited for like the end of a journey, and after the end a blue leather book with gold letters that captured one of the scars of the world. But he knew, too, that he had been seduced by Gordie, who knew his longing, and that a safari to the Great Rift had no part in his plans, whatever they were.

It was ice cold after the crouched heat of the day. They had climbed five thousand feet from the coast toward the savannah that was the center of the continent, near the mountains that were huge black shadows to the west under the moon. The cold was like the beginning of the world. Derek was crying in his sleep; the sound mixed with the night wind that sighed over the savannah, the giggle of hyenas in the distance, the cough and scream of a leopard, and he could hear, marking his feral territory as they were doing, the earth-shaking rumble of a lion, answered by another, and then another, and near him, moving and munching, the hooves and teeth of the herbivores in the moon-silver grass.

It was a timeless time when his dream of Africa met the reality. The animals, the wind like a sea wind, and across the moon, the black forms of giraffes seemed to sail in the distance, their shadows troubling the grass. Helmut was still awake, murmuring something in the night, a rhythm, an incantation.

Ewen spoke again to the London night, "Gordie scared me, creeping close like that when I thought he was asleep, and he whispered in my ear so Helmut wouldn't hear, 'For God's sake, don't cross him. He can do terrible things. I've seen it with my own eyes,' and his voice trembled like a child's in the dark. 'You see that candle,' he said. 'It's black. Black magic. He worships the devil, and I've seen the devil, Fada's devil'—that was the way he said it—'seen it with my own eyes. You should have stayed away.' It was the only confession Gordie ever made to me from the beginning to the end. 'He does it to cure his eyes,' he said.

"I started to say something and he put his hand across my mouth, and whispered again, 'Listen, I'm sorry. The plans have changed. We have to go on. He's got a plan. Best to follow it for all our sakes. We'll camp in the Rift tomorrow night. You can get a look at it.' I tried to move his hand away. 'No. Listen. Ewen, there's forty thousand Israeli dollars in it for us. I need it.' He was frantic. 'I'm not broke. But I can't go into a bank until I get to Khartoum.'

"There was brag in his voice. Money from Libya, money from Uganda, money from Rhodesia. 'I have a lot of money when I can get to it. Don't let me down.'

"He knew I wouldn't. I never had. He could tell. He let go my mouth and lay down beside me so he could speak close to my ear. He was planning again, boy kingdoms, Peter Pan outwitting Captain Hook, great dreams under a great moon he didn't notice, planning how to gull the world. There was no truth in what he said about plans changing. He'd known all the time, of course, what they were on about.

" 'When we get through to the Sudan, I can get money in

Khartoum,' he kept saying. 'Helmut and I can't go into Uganda, but we know the way through the eastern Congo. Nobody can catch us there. We have friends.' Did they have friends any place? 'I can fly out of Khartoum. There'll be money, a lot of money.' Like a child, a terrible little boy, he said, 'Now that you're here, everything will be all right. If anything happens I've left a letter for you in Khartoum, at Lloyds Bank,' as if he were the only person anything could happen to. Then, still like a child, he turned over and went to sleep on the bare ground.

"And faded away, thank God, and I was again in my Africa. The moon passed over us and I could sense the mountains rise and the earth split and heal and scar, and the seawater come and go, and the Red Sea part, and I lay on layer on layer of earth, and all around me there was the crunch and munching of the herds of zebra and wildebeest, and the little incantation of Helmut, a paper devil, was puny under the vast night.

"I lay there awake until the birds began and the dawn stained the sky. Then, over a mountain or a cloud, the sun etched a wild bright line that was like lightning but absolutely still for a long time. The sun threw orange and pink and purple light into the black rainclouds and one was not a cloud, it was the mountain, Kilimanjaro, reaching up into Fada's heaven as if it had waked up and thrown off its cover of mist. The earth and the river down below us that I had heard in the night and thought was the wind too was bright orange.

"The others began to stir, and in a few minutes it seemed they had brought mundanity back into the world, shitting and grumbling and making coffee and eating, and not one of them looked up at the mountain.

"No one told me not to go into the river; they just didn't notice or bother. I'd been in the interior for twenty-four hours. What could I know? Gordie saw me go. He saw me and didn't say anything.

"God, it was lovely. I watched the animals go down to water, zebra and some kind of antelope, dark brown with great horns.

Across the river a giraffe spread the high triangle of its legs and lowered its head to the water; then it looked up with eyes as brown and gentle as a Jersey heifer's. Oh, it was a lovely morning in a world before the Flood. Monkeys swore in the trees. A family of elephants played in the water. That ponderous playing, all for my sake, I felt then.

"I forgot them all, up there under the baobab tree. At least I had sense enough not to follow the animals down that muddy bank. But farther upstream I found a path through a bamboo grove. Way up above me the wind chattered in the bamboo. It was as high as a grove of trees. I could hear something else moving in it and hoped it wasn't snakes. Then I came again to that deceptive water, with a little sandy beach, and so clear that the fool's gold on the bottom gleamed in the new sun and the bright fish were prisms.

"Under the river trees and the underbrush, oh, an astonishment of violets like the ones Fama raised at the kitchen window, and lilies, vulva-pink lilies in the half darkness. Nothing moved except the fish, just for a minute. Everything was listening. No bird sang. No monkeys called. A blessed stillness.

"I bathed, and even shaved. Gordie was always on at me about that. Excessive neatness, he called it that morning when I got back.

"They were all in the lorry waiting for me. Helmut looked straight ahead through those terrible mirror glasses. He didn't turn his head when I clambered over the tailgate.

"We were only an hour from the main paved road. That morning we raced along it, anonymous, passing a few lorries, a bus. After the more crowded road from Mombasa to Voi, the road to Arusha seemed almost deserted. In Arusha we finally found petrol to refill the tank and the emergency tins. We didn't need much yet, we had enough, Helmut kept saying, to get across Africa, but every time there was a chance he insisted on topping up the tanks. We had to pay the tourist price in Arusha and he was furious.

"An hour beyond Arusha we left the paved road and climbed into the Rift highlands. The rain had kept the fields rich and green. Masai children raced the lorry and waved. Then we were in an endless cross valley of the Rift, corrugated with deep gullies carved by rain, too desolate for grass or many animals, a desert of thorn trees and scrub.

"At least Gordie had to drive slowly enough so I could read the rock calendars and the evidence of old seas, old volcanism, and the dried record of a rushing river that had carved the cliffs into shapes as stark as hatchets.

"And then at last, oh, God, what I had longed for. There we were, poised on the edge of the highlands, looking down two thousand feet into the Great Rift. The road switched back and forth with curves so sharp that Gordie had to back and turn the big lorry so that half of it seemed to tip into the sky, but I hardly noticed.

"I was watching Mount Lengai, the sacred mountain, grow larger in my sight. The year before, the side of it had blown out and spewed lava into the valley. It was the newest eruption in the whole of the eastern Rift. Damped by the rain, white soda streaked its scar, and down below, like a calm after a storm, a quiet river was finding its way again, cutting the rock spew into a channel.

"After we had made camp, I walked along the river until it was long dark, and the only light I could see in the distance was the tiny campfire they had built and, once in a while, a shadow crossing it. The deserted place wasn't empty and it wasn't isolated. I was, for a little while, free in the world and living in its rhythm. The moon cast high escarpment shadows. Before dawn I was out again, where I had been going to all the time, right in the heart of my hope, and I made the last rock collection I could. Some of the rocks were smoothed by the water, and some were so jagged that I would not have been surprised to find them still warm, down in that valley where the earth is forming and growing and re-forming itself.

"The others called it a dead valley; a valley of bones, Helmut said, kicking a rock, but to me it was new and alive as the earth is alive, and I could sense its pulse there under the green debris of grass and trees that had already started to come back after the eruption."

Ewen went on watching, but not the London night street, and it was all the same as it had been, the light and the space and the heat as they went west.

He was crossing a sea of grass, days of grass. Under an umbrella acacia there was a black-maned lion asleep. The trees were wind-carved and the kopjes stripped to bone by the rains. The lorry floated like a ship in the heat mirage. They didn't stop once they had lied their way into the Serengeti park. They just went on, slower and slower across the grass, gold and showing green at the wrong time of the year because the rains would not obey Helmut. As far as the horizon, there were animals in their own Eden, millions of wildebeest, zebras who galloped away at the sound of the lorry so that the vehicle seemed to be parting a wave through them. They drove as fast as the dirt road would allow, past the watchful giraffes, all the skittering gazelles, and the stupid, brutal dignity of the Cape buffalo.

Helmut never seemed to sleep. Late at night, before the incantations began, he talked about the rain, and then his soul, and then the rain. Every afternoon the clouds were winged and then they banked up, huge black cliffs of clouds coming at them from the west, and the rain beat on the continent like a drum. Only the grass withheld surrender to it, that and the animals that kept on feeding slowly through the veils of water.

Helmut kept saying what everybody knew. He said the grass and the tsetse were the great protectors of the animals. He wished all the humans were dead so that the land could go back to the animals, as if there were some hierarchy of time, a procession, and then an intrusion of man, and then he fell back into jabbering about the rain. It was, to him, like a woman, he said, a dishonest lover. The rain is crazy this year, he would say, a voice in the black night. *Verdammt*. Crazy. Finally one night, Derek, who said so little, said, "Belt up, Helmut, you're a fucking bore." Helmut took it from him and shut up at last. He needed Derek to work the radio.

He heard the bed creak and knew she was still awake, still waiting. "I won't be long," he said. "You see, there is something you have to know about me if I am to stay . . ." But he still didn't know where to begin again.

He stood there in his Africa, his deep primordial land, and he knew that what he had seen there only overlay the Africa within him, like the real woman on the bed; he thought of Teresa then as nameless, overlay an image of a woman that had been so long in his soul, or memory, remembered before she was ever seen, and thought he was the first person in the world to see love that way. He knew the Africa that melded in his vision and his training was a young basalt land, but he thought then of age and fear and darkness and the brute sun and the earth-thudding beat of the rain, a place where he had felt more alien and more at home than ever in his life, a fearsome vision of the power and beauty and indifference of God.

Teresa had told him she didn't like to be fooled, but he had been fooled himself, and he didn't know what to do about that; telling about being fooled was part of it. He had to remember when the fooling was taken for granted as an adventure, an episode, a proof of manhood. He had to confess the vulgarity of that first. A holiday? No, holiday meant holy day, and it was not that; that came later. He wanted to go back where it had changed, the moment, and think clearly. That was imperative. Be specific, one fact after another as one mile after another, one foot in front of the other. Helmut had told him that, or something like it, speaking of the kind of courage he said he respected.

Was it on the night ferry across Lake Victoria? No, not yet then, or at least he hadn't yet admitted it. There was, though, a hint of change, a military parody, even a change of language

in Helmut then. He set two-hour watches over his precious
lorry. Ewen leaned on the boat railing once in the day when
the waves danced in the sun, and once at night before the
moon came up and the sky was blacker than he had ever seen
it, black down to the water. The stars were deep and he stared
at the Southern Cross, not thinking yet, relieved of the others,
alone. He could hear a soft murmur of voices from the open
deck, and someone laughed, an African laugh, different, easier,
unmocking, and the waves soughed against the dark hull.

No. It was at Malimba that Helmut took command. He
seemed to take on more urgency every mile of that ten-day
slog through the mountains. At last they turned north on a
good dirt road. Helmut had changed his English bwana hat
for a beret pulled tight over his tight scalp. He and Gordie both
sported—yes, sported, that was it—sidearms, and they took to
lounging easily for the first time, their legs in that genital
spread of soldiers in bad movies.

They both enjoyed it, the fast clip along the road, driving
into their own picture of themselves, with the unnoticed Mountains of the Moon to the east and the unnoticed jungle on the
west, a wall of green as high as a cliff. Every night Gordie said
it was as cold as charity, expecting soldiers' complaining of
himself.

When they thundered through villages, the Africans disappeared. Once, they stopped at a village to buy food and it
was deserted like the others, but not for long. Helmut shot his
revolver into the air and yelled in French. One man came out
from his duka. He sold them biltong. That was all he had. Ewen
could feel and glimpse eyes watching them from behind the
doors.

At night Gordie and Helmut lay by the fire and reminisced.
They sounded like the *Boy's Own Paper*, all those heroics grown
up into a pornography of violence. They were their own admira-
tions under the moon.

At last there was something he could tell her. "You remember

Derek? Derek and I were the quiet ones. I got to liking him more and more. He had in him a gentleness that surprised me, and in the day, before he had turned on and retreated from us, he confessed that when he got home he was going to spend his share to train as a horticulturist. His ambition was to work at Kew Gardens. He would sit on the forest side of the road and scan the wall of trees, hour after hour, while I watched the mountains and Gordie drove on and on, and looked at nothing but the endless ribbon of the road. On the second night Derek sat up the transmitter/receiver. Helmut took over and spoke in German and I could hear a voice crackling, answering him."

He was thrust into silence again, forgetting her.

It was the third day when Gordie turned the lorry up a rocky trail into the hills. No one said a word. There was just that winding trail, not a shamba, not an African, not even an animal. They climbed higher and higher through the cloud forest, and then the clouds parted and they looked down on the endless hills and forest below, with the mountains thrusting up beyond them that were the escarpment of the Mountains of the Moon on the western spur of the Great Rift, but he had no time to think of Rift or book or anything by then, caught in that ludicrous ride across Africa. Besides, although Gordie hadn't said a word about it, only smiled when he caught his eye and remembered he was there, he kept fighting a sense of threat or dread somehow, and trying to save his sense by seeing the humor of it. By then he believed nothing, anyway. When Gordie said they had crossed into Zaire, he didn't even believe that. They could have been any place along the Rift wall.

They climbed out of the forest into what had once been the neat lawns of a small hotel. It still had a faded sign, L'HÔTEL BAUDOUIN, and around it, among the wild mountain flowers, were carefully tended roses, a touch of Europe. Down the slope beyond it they could see a blue lake, and in the meadow a troop of baboons played in the evening sun.

When the man came out on the broken veranda, all he said

was, You are a day late. Major Jean Dupont; they saluted him as if the rank he still used were true. They were a tiny parody of an army, five men. Major Jean insisted by his presence that Ewen and Derek stand and salute wherever they were in that ridiculous time, even in the bar, with its faded graffiti, ONE MORE LOOTING DAY UNTIL CHRISTMAS and AFFREUX NOEL, which he hadn't bothered to clean away.

There were bullet holes sprayed across the bar and along the walls. The place had half fallen down, and Ewen, seeing it again, remembered thinking, Stone ruins have honor but ruined stained plaster is somehow pathetic, a failure.

Five Belgian women and their fourteen children had been shot in that room by the Simba, and when Major Jean had got there, they had been dead a month. One of the women and three of the children had been Major Jean's family.

They found, too, a great cache of Veuve Clicquot and Rémy Martin and Cuban cigars. They had cleaned the place of the bodies and stripped them of what jewelry was left, and carefully listed what names they could; they were careful, Major Jean said, about that and he never forgot that point. He told the story almost every evening.

We threw them in the lake, he said, and I said a prayer, for up until the Simba rising I had been a Catholic. Then we got drunk.

After the uprising he had come back; drawn back, he said. He had brought supplies and tried to start the hotel again. He even had the deed for it registered in Brussels. But no one came, and the Africans wouldn't work for him because they were afraid to come to where so many dead bodies had lain uncared for by humans or animals. Then the Tutsi arrived, a refugee like he was. His family had been murdered by the Hutu in Rwanda.

You are still there, you two, Ewen told the now slick rooftops across Prince Albert Road, for it had started to rain again, a mild rain. I see you checking the lorry loads, and sitting together, drinking in the evening and watching the baboons, you and the seven-foot-tall Tutsi, and waiting for visitors some sweet day like you remembered when you went there as a child and played with the others in the lake, while the Belgian mothers sat on the lawn and talked about escaping the heat of Stanleyville.

Every night they got drunk on champagne, and the Tutsi cooked Belgian food for them the way that Major Jean had taught him, and they slept in beds. Every morning Major Jean tended his roses. Helmut waited for the dark of the moon. He spoke as if he ordered the moon to be dark, and no one explained. They seemed to be pulled across Africa like a tide by the waxing and waning of the moon.

They were a "commando" force, Helmut said. There were only two other ranks in the commando, Ewen and Derek, but they thought in battalions, Colonel von Darmstadt, Major Dupont, Captain McLeod. So they trained Derek and him while they waited.

They would tell him nothing. Gordie only said, You have to wait and obey orders from Helmut, and seeing the look he gave him then, he answered it before Ewen could say a word: For me, Ewen, for God's sake, and he glanced around to where Helmut was sitting in a broken deck chair with the rising sun making his glasses pink.

Christ, don't you understand yet? Gordie was still looking at him, almost whispering, even if he was too far away to hear; he used the old mercenary cliché: There are no Queen's Regulations here, you know. And then a plea: No bloody law, nothing. We're out in what Fada called beyond the pale. He'd kill us in a minute and no one would ever know. He left a friend of mine who was dealing drugs on a hill in Morocco and no one found him until all that was left was his teeth and they identified him by his dental records on the National Health.

Then, aloud again, he was letting her into what he had to tell, another fragment from someplace in Africa.

"I wanted to believe Gordie was as afraid as he sounded, but I didn't. For all I knew it was he who had left his friend on the hill in Morocco. All caring except survival had long since been burned out of him. So there we were, in sight of the Mountains of the Moon, acting like right fools.

"Gordie said that training would start after breakfast that morning and I said, What training? Commando training, he called it, and it was then that I laughed. It had been pending, that laughter, and I couldn't stop. They were both so ludicrous with their little bloody game, a couple of hyenas and a man made mad with fury, tending his roses and waiting for something that was never going to happen. The laughter was my mistake." He came back to the bed, got in beside her, and held her hand, explaining carefully. "You see, don't you, that the laughter was my mistake? Without it I might have escaped somehow, but then I saw Gordie's face and he said, Don't ever laugh at me again, while it was still echoing down the slope and making the baboons scream back. Helmut had got up and was striding down toward us, beating on his pants leg with a swagger stick. I kept myself from laughing again. He touched my face to find it, and then he slapped me almost off my feet, and Gordie jumped me and held me down on the ground.

"Next time I will kill you, Helmut said. Derek called out, Brekkers, from the door. He was always cheerful in the morning."

He stopped again, and stared at the reflection of the gas streetlights, which made an eerie cobweb on the ceiling.

But he wasn't seeing the lights. He was training, waiting for the dark of the moon. Two of them, he and Derek, under the orders of Helmut, who stood there, drilling his army, swishing the swagger stick. He hadn't square-bashed since his National Service, but it was odd, how it came back, like riding a bicycle. The strange thing was they were both enjoying it.

Even though his mind hated it, he fell into trying to do it well. So did Derek. They ran, they fell, got up, clambered up trees and down ropes on an obstacle course that Helmut had had Gordie set up, while the baboons watched and laughed and the sun burned off the mist of the lake. It was foolish, a game.

Inside the hotel lounge, Major Jean and Gordie pored over a map, like real soldiers. But when he tried to look at the map, Major Jean rolled it up and marched out with it. He didn't bother to look at Ewen. He was a parody of another rank, the training a parody of training.

Even the wire was a parody. They couldn't find any at first. They spent the whole morning searching. They finally took down a large picture, its glass long broken, a picture of a lake, he supposed, in Belgium, and used the picture wire.

Gordie had to teach them about the Use of the Wire. Helmut couldn't see them well enough. He took them out at night, Derek sweating and trembling. He wasn't allowed to turn on until it was over. They learned to slither through the grass on their bellies like snakes in the dark, while Gordie sat, feigning sleep, on watch over nothing, his head outlined against the fainter black of the sky, blotting out a small patch of stars. When he finally let them catch him and slip the wire around his neck and touch him with the sticks they used for knives, he let them graduate to Helmut.

Helmut, for reasons of his own, let Ewen slip up, make the touch with the wire and the stick, and even praised him, although the praise came out like ridicule.

"My God, I was actually pleased!" he said aloud. "I was actually pleased to have done so well. That's how far I had gone in the game, to be pleased when the devil drove.

"The next night he threw Derek and broke his left arm. He was smiling. That will teach you to call me a bore, he told Derek. Major Jean set it and tied it on a splint while Derek screamed and some animal screamed back. All the rest of the night he cried in his bed, and I had reached the stage where I just wanted him to shut up and let me sleep.

"The next morning we had a briefing. They called it that, of course, contour map and all. The route was north by north-west off the main road through the forest. They had marked out paths like red veins running through the jungle, blue crosses where there were Zairean patrols, orange crosses that Major Jean explained were Simba guerrillas, still hiding after five years. But after he had left the room, Gordie and Helmut, who sat with his eyes five inches above it, went on marking the map.

"Then they took us out to the lorry and made the Tutsi and me unload it. Derek sat under a tree, sulking, and holding his arm like a baby. We stripped the lorry of gear down to boards under the boards Helmut had used with such pride to get us out of the mud. They had worked, too, I'll say that for Helmut. Then Helmut raised what I had thought was the lorry floor.

"I should have known, and I think now that I did, all the time. We were running three hundred Israeli Uzis, wrapped in gun cloths and packed as carefully as eggs. Gordie patted them, and knowing me, he used my language to use me. We're running these through to the Sudanese Freedom Fighters. You're working for the right side, Ewen; not to worry your conscience. Helmut laughed, and he thought he was explaining, too. The Israelis are backing them. Who would have thought that I, a German Graf, would work for the Jews?

"You are no more a Graf than I am the King of Scotland, Gordie said. A Nazi Kraut from Düsseldorf. It was a joke between them.

"All day long Gordie and I shot at empty champagne bottles in the lake until the Uzi was an extension of my eye. He knew how much I loved to shoot. He counted on that; he'd taught me. For part of that day we almost forgot where we were, and things were like they had been. At the end, Gordie turned the Uzi and shot a baboon that had got used to the noise and crept out of the bush to watch us. He blew it in half. It screamed like a woman. I still wish I had shot Gordie then. I still wish it.

"In the late afternoon we started out, the army of four, one half blind, one with his left arm in a sling—Helmut had been careful about that, he didn't want to put Derek out of action altogether—one, myself, sickened with what I had seen, and Gordie driving. He wanted to get down the mountain path to the main road by nightfall. Gordie had me ride what he called shotgun beside him. He put a Uzi in my lap and said, If a patrol tries to stop us, you have to use it. You're not among the living. Remember that. God, where had he picked up that cheap thoughtless cliché? You are now one of the *Affreux*. If they catch you, they will cut you up slowly until you die. It was melodrama, and we were a joke, but the melodrama, I thought then, was real, and the joke deadly. Remember, I was full of all their stories in the night." He turned to look at her dear face; she was watching him.

"Now, this is important," he told her, carefully. "Twenty-five thousand years ago, there where we were, the earth shook and split. The cataclysm killed everything. There were only the lava and the dust and the new volcanoes. They vomited fire and brimstone containing iron, olivine, peridot, gold, and garnets and rubies and shards of obsidian to use for knives from deep within the world's gut. The hot up-welling basalt was fiery red. The rivers were flung out of their courses in an indifferent wilderness of water, leaving the dead, animal and human. The living who escaped carried the memory of it in their genes. So you see, it is easy to teach us hell when we are children because we remember, and we are afraid in the night to trail our hands over the bedside into the primordial ooze."

It had not been what he had meant to tell her, not that at all. He wanted to tell her about Gordie's voice, but instead went on listening to it again, saying nothing. It was as persuasive as a breeze. He sat beside him in the cab again while Derek walked in front of them, a torch tucked into his splint. He watched the disembodied legs and the thin bobbing shaft of light that guided the lorry while Gordie drove at a walking pace, guided, too, by the walls of jungle on both sides of the trail that slapped against the metal panels of the lorry, and he never stopped talking. Ewen couldn't shut out that incessant voice and the *whish-whish* of the panga as Derek slashed at the bush ahead.

He went back to the bedside. He wanted to touch her hair, but he knew he had no right. Instead, he spoke again, softly in the darkness. "We were in the lorry and Gordie wouldn't shut up. He seemed to think that the fact that I was with him was a kind of proof to his conscience that things were all right. He talked about Scotland and Fama and Fada, playing the homesick Scot, a luxury he could afford when the plans were going his way. He said that when all this was over he was going back, as if he could, and finally, I think, he took my silence for peace, because he had no choice and it was late, and there was some of that—peace, I mean—or at least being lulled for a while in the blackness behind the thin line of Derek's torch. A kind of hypnotized substitute for peace.

"We had got to one of those surprising small open places on a hill by a stream. I could hear it, and I could hear some kind of rhythmic thud away in the thick trees that might have been an animal or an engine. I didn't know how far sound carried there. It filled the silence when Gordie stopped the lorry.

"I think half an hour passed before anyone said a word. We were listening to the traffic moan of live things in their familiar dangerous night. Derek had gone to sleep in the back, and Helmut had climbed in the cab beside us. It was pitch-black at first, and then I began to see faint faint forms of trees and underbrush and the path ahead. We were a thousand miles from anything I'd ever known, but that's no excuse. There isn't one. I am on the other side of any excuse ever made.

"Gordie told me what I had to do, as softly as if he were telling a story, you know, making it unreal and romantic in the bedtime way people talk. It was my turn, he said. Up ahead by the river, he told me this, there was a Congolese guard on duty where the forest had been cleared for a patrol post. There would be one man on guard, asleep. They always were. The others, three or four sometimes, would be huddled together in the post hut. They wouldn't come out unless the guard warned them. They would be, he said, Balese guards, and they were afraid of the forest at night. But if the alarm was sounded, they would kill us and take the cargo."

He couldn't stand there beside her, not when it was so near, what had happened, and he knew it was going to be as alive to him again awake as it had been in his dreams or glimpses. He wanted to, in the way of men, stand and take it alone. He smiled in the dark at that. He went back to the window, where there was space, unconfined, and he was untrapped by love.

When I had killed the guard, he told himself, they could inch the lorry past. Why didn't I question? Was I as afraid as the Balese? Oh well, in that place and in that time I did not. That's all. It seemed somehow part of it all. You see, he explained without speaking to the night lamp across the road, the sound of the engine would blend with the night sounds and the water flow, and they would think it was an animal or a ghost or the river if they didn't hear a signal from the guard. Now, don't you see how logical all that was, I mean there, and then, in that place? Let me tell you, *where* you say a thing is as important as *what* you say.

Gordie said the path was hidden from them by the trees. Oh, we know it well, he said, we've done this often. All in a night's work. He actually said that. Just get through the way I've taught you. It's your turn tonight and it will be my turn tomorrow. What was that echo? I still can't remember. It's your turn now and it will be my turn tomorrow? Then Helmut had to whisper that damned stupid true phrase. No Queen's Regulations here, you know. If you don't obey orders we leave you here.

The bedtime story was over. Gordie wasn't persuasive anymore. He simply told me what I had to do. Well, I did it.

Ewen did not know that he was crying at long last. He was

listening to Gordie telling the scared child in him what he had to do, calling up the hold he'd always had over him. The lamp in the distant room wavered and drowned.

He was crawling on his belly through the jungle blackness. The underbrush was trying to hold him back. Slow, slow as a snake, and he felt how fearful it was to be a snake with all the world against you and only surprise and venom to protect you. He slithered forward like the snake that became the devil in the mind. Then he saw the figure, as they said, sitting on the edge of a clearing near the water where, out of the trees, there was more light. His head had fallen forward in his sleep. He still jerked the wire around the neck and felt him shiver, once, and finished him off with his knife. He still drove it into his side and felt the wet heat, and let him down to the ground as gently as if he were putting him to sleep again, and he was pleased with himself, pleased that he had done it so well. But it was not a man. It was a woman, an old woman with wrinkled dugs. He couldn't see her, but he could feel her with his hands, and he got up and ran with the leaves like the woman's hands trying to hold him back.

Gordie shone the torch on him, and he heard him laugh. Get in, he said, you've done it. One of us now. Get in the back. Then Gordie and Helmut went to sleep in the cab. All the rest of the night he listened to their breathing and the night. At the first hint of dawn Gordie drove past the shadow of a shamba, only a tiny clearing, and no one stirred.

Morning comes slowly in the jungle, the black turning pale, then an opaque brightness, and the sun never comes. He knew it was there. He caught glimpses of it, but for the rest, it was twilight and would have been so peaceful except that the blood had dried on his shirt. He jerked it off and threw it away, and Gordie stopped the lorry and made him pick it up again and called him a goddamned fool. Derek was still asleep. There was his incessant maddening whimper from time to time, like a dog dreaming.

That memory of whimpering made him hear his own crying, and he stopped, surprised at himself, hoping she hadn't heard.

Around noon, the sun directly overhead, they drove into a clearing the size of a small village, big enough so that it was alive with the sun that made the pretty little Belgian house and the garden around it shine, as peaceful in that place as a blessing. There had been a chapel of some kind, but there were only the mud walls left with creepers over them. At the edge of the forest an old rusted donkey engine, half sunk into the ground, was festooned with wild creeping flowers, left over like an ancient monument to some long-gone Belgian mining operation. It lay beside a cave mouth, obscured, too, by the flowers.

An African man and woman the color of dark bronze were working a vegetable garden, but when they saw the lorry they put down their hoes and he saw them coming toward the cab to welcome them. He could still hear their soft voices, *Bon jour, bon jour*, and *Bon jour, bwana*, and he was glad he had taken off his shirt.

Helmut spoke to them in a language he didn't know. They seemed glad to see visitors. They explained something by their gestures, and offered them food. Ewen could wash at last in their little creek. Helmut patted their child on the head and said something that made them laugh. They sounded proud.

They ate together, a picnic under the trees at the edge of the clearing. The man said grace in French, and the woman was silent and beautiful. She had gone into the neat Belgian house and dressed herself for the meal to honor the visitors. She wore several gold necklaces, one with a wedding ring suspended from it that kept catching the sun.

When it was time to leave they gave them biltong and plantain and lettuce, and Helmut gave the man tobacco and the woman tea. *Merci, adieu, bwana*, they called after the lorry, and then *adieu*, over and over. Ewen could hear their voices still in the London night, lonely bronze people, glad they have come, *adieu* as they disappeared into the jungle again.

Helmut signaled for Gordie to stop. Ewen heard him say, You saw the nigger woman and the mine entry. It's the place. That was all he heard. Now that he was blooded, they paid no more attention to him than to Derek. Get some sleep. You'll need it was all Gordie said. You'll be guiding tonight. They walked away together down the path.

It was easy to rest in that hot jungle twilight. Quiet. A bird called and there was a flash of bright red in the branches. Derek walked in an enchantment. Look, he called out. He roused a swarm of butterflies like blue snow dancing and then falling. Ewen, nearly asleep, heard him climb back into the lorry.

It was late afternoon. He had slept without dreams, and Gordie and Helmut were in the cab again. *Verdammt*, Helmut said. He was holding up a gold necklace with a wedding ring on it. He let it tumble into his lap. Nothing. I was sure it was the place. There was the old mine. There was the cave.

I have always thought it was only a rumor, Gordie told him. There are always stories of treasures. The Belgian jewelry. The buried gold at Watsa. Always stories. Shit. Out of our way for nothing.

No. Not nothing. There is always Mambeli. What they said about Mambeli.

Oh, belt up, Helmut. Gordie turned his back to him, and in a little while they were both asleep. Dead asleep. The twilight had changed, too much light behind them and in the wrong place. It flickered and then began to fade.

Now closer, the memory too close for retreat, he wiped his tear-wet face, hardly aware he was doing it; he wanted to clear his eyes so he could see the little lamp across the street in the night. He wanted to explain something so unexplainable it still stunned him beyond tears. He saw what had happened through a gray limbo, a burial of hope.

Derek touched me and motioned me out of the lorry. We had the sense to keep quiet. In the clearing around the little Belgian house it was late day. The sky was the color of a rose. There was the smell of burning everywhere. The roof had collapsed and the walls of the house were still smoldering. The man was dead, half burned, lying in the garden patch. What you notice . . . he lay in a bed of Cos lettuce. The woman was dead. She lay on the path that had been edged with small white stones; not one had been disturbed. Only her face had not been assaulted, and I was glad of that. Vultures rose from both of them; their heavy wings creaked like leather. In the distance they didn't move. They were covering something that must have been the child. Two leopards who ignored us strolled among the ruins, and one lay down in the sun and stretched and purred like the rasp of a saw.

Derek was crying or retching or both. I was trying to pray, but all I could remember was Our Father. Our Father. I kept on saying it until Derek stopped me and cried out, Shut up, I can't stand it.

On the way back to the lorry he babbled about the perfect ecosystem of the jungle. Two hundred feet above us the trees warred for a place in the sun. Crazy monkeys escorted us, laughing in the branches. Derek's voice went on and on, high and piercing. Latin words for plants, one after another; right or wrong, he named them all.

Gordie and Helmut were still asleep. We didn't say a word. It is quiet in hell; all the words have been said. At darkness it was time to move again, that slow crawl through the jungle. Derek babbled on about the ecosystem. I could hear his monkey voice behind me as I guided the lorry along the path until we found another clearing and I heard the lorry stop. I walked through the branches like the dead men they say the witches raise from their graves.

Gordie and I made a fire. We ate the food the couple had given us, a dreadful wee parody of our picnics on the brae when Fama packed us a lunch. It was like a nightmare where everything is very simple and familiar, but in hell. Helmut lit his candle and started his chanting. I saw the tiny light of

Derek's hash pipe behind us. Gordie called out softly, You shouldn't smoke so much. It's bad for you. Derek laughed and answered, Are you fucking hearing what he is fucking saying?

Gordie knew he had won. He talked on and on easily, trusting the power of what he had made of me, about his monstrous plans. He knew I was as exiled from the human race as he was. If he were in Glasgow or Edinburgh he would be by now a cheap street crook calling himself a fine revolutionary like we saw at Noel's house that night, but there, beside the jungle fire, he was seeing himself a king of Africa, a pathetic little king by a pathetic little fire.

Then he turned sentimental. That was harder to bear than his bragging. He said, I have a feeling, the second sight. I have it. You don't because you are half-Irish. I'm not going to make it out of here, he said. His eyes glistened with self-pitying tears in the firelight that flickered over his skeletal face. He didn't say we. He never did. It was I, always I. Then he crawled away into the lorry and came back in a little while with a note he had written and, of all things, his passport. He had teased me about wearing a waterproof belt to hold my passport and traveler's checks. I had been wearing it all the way down the Rift because I was afraid my sweat would ruin my papers. He begged me to put the passport in my belt, and I did it to shut him up, thinking him a fool, but maybe he did have the second sight, after all. Now read the note, he insisted.

This will introduce my nephew, Ewen Stuart McLeod. He has my power of attorney. Signed, yours sincerely, Gordon Edward David McLeod, a huge pretentious flowing signature. At the end of it he had added, D.S.O. He watched me fold it and put it in my belt. I had sense enough not to smile.

We did not hear Derek until he had crawled up right beside us. You see, he whispered. I did it right. I could have killed you, Gordie, but I didn't, he said, pleased with himself. He won't say I don't do it right now, will he? He sat up by the fire. You see, you and Helmut shouldn't have done what you did to those people. You really shouldn't have done that. You broke, he paused, finding the words carefully, the laws of hospitality. Now I will explain, still carefully, I am Hassan the Assassin and I am letting you live, Gordie, so you can drive us out of here, and after that you will be executed by the Grand High Mucky-Muck, and he started to giggle.

Gordie looked at him and then back to where the soft chanting had stopped and the candle was out. Helmut was not asleep. He was dead, with Derek's wire so tight about his neck that it had nearly severed his head.

We sat there, Derek and I, Derek smiling at something in himself. I watched Gordie stamp out the fire. All night we went through the jungle while I held the torch and Derek sat beside Gordie. I could hear him imitating Helmut giving orders. Gordie without Helmut was lost. He drove in a daze, not caring what noise he made crashing along the path through the underbrush until we came to an old clearing at the edge of the jungle where someone had abandoned a shamba and the ground was taken over by new scrub. He stopped the lorry long enough for me to climb into the back. In the distance we could see the glow of the volcanoes where the Mountains of the Moon rose, and we went on toward volcanic light until it faded in the sunrise.

Along the forest edge, there was a better dirt road, and Gordie drove along it like a madman, not toward anything, but away from the darkness, trying to pull free of Helmut's body, and all he said for miles was one remark, not to me, and not to Derek, who slept beside him, smiling like the boy he once was. He said, The animals have found him, and I saw the leopard again, stretching in the sunlight, and heard it purr. But at last, when he had got to the main dirt road going north, even Gordie had to pull off under a tree and fall asleep.

Ewen thought the brush of light in the distance might be dawn, but it wasn't. It was only the faint pink dome of light that never disappeared over the sleeping city. He could see the twin beams of a single late car on Prince Albert Road. Nothing else moved. The wind had died. He yearned for sleep. Now that he had relived it, handed his confession to her, he felt empty. He waited for her to say something. He didn't know how long it had been since he had said a word.

Sometime he had pulled a chair up to the window, the chair he used to fold his clothes on. He knew that Africa had not finished with him yet, and never would, no matter how much he confessed.

He went over to watch her, asleep in the dark room. She had turned away from the window and had thrown all of her pillows but one onto the floor. She had nuzzled her head in it. It was covered with the tangle of her hair.

He had to test her sleep for its depth. He needed her to listen. He said, "Teresa?" very quietly, and then, hoping, "Teresa?" a little louder.

She turned back toward him and opened her eyes and told him she hadn't been asleep and they both knew she had been and neither of them cared.

"It's so cold," he said. She heard him go into his workroom and the hiss of the gas fire as he lit it. He left the double doors open so that they could see it and got into bed and leaned against the pillows she had propped up. Four each. She insisted on that. Big, jelly-bean-colored pillows from Habitat. She picked up her own, which she had tossed onto the floor, and sat up against them, and for a while they watched the blue fire turn its white mantels that looked like toffee sticks red, and hiss and breathe and flick shadows on the maps on the ceiling and the shelves of rocks, and their faces. He was suddenly so at peace, so without weight, that he almost forgot why he had waked her, and then remembered, and his laughter was a relief.

"Oh, my God, you should have seen him then, looming up there."

"Who?"

"Pius! Your living breathing black monk. Elegant Pius."

"Where?" She took his hand. "Where are you now?"

"There. Oh, I'm sorry. We were on the road to Faradje. Congo. In the Congo. I told you. I woke up first in that late, hell-hot afternoon, and he was standing there beside the lorry as still as a tree. There was a tree, too. We'd parked under it, one of those huge trees that had been left when the forest receded, refusing to die.

"He didn't look the way he looks now, I tell you. He was wearing sandals made out of old tires and a pair of ragged khaki shorts, and around his neck a gold cross against that wonderful pure-black skin, and that was all. You know his smile. He didn't smile then. I didn't see him smile until later, much later. Make me tell you. Make me remember all about Pius." But Ewen didn't wait for any answer. He watched the fire on the ceiling but he saw Pius.

"He simply stood there, and then he said, Good afternoon, may I ride with you? Gordie started awake at that bass-drum voice and stared at him. You see, he explained, my donkey was killed last night by a leopard. I am on my way to Faradje to the mission station. I am a priest.

"Gordie didn't seem to be able to speak. But Derek had waked up, too, and he said, Get in. He was already taking Helmut's place. He had Helmut's revolver in his lap. Pius picked up a large bundle wrapped in white cloth and slung it into the back of the lorry and climbed in after it. He called out thank you, and then he closed his eyes. Gordie got out the map. I don't know where we are, he told Derek. From the back, Pius said, You are perhaps a hundred and fifty kilometers from Watsa. From there it is another sixty kilometers to Faradje. There is a good road all the way.

"We stopped at a petrol station, a tin hut surrounded by silent Africans. At first the African who ran it said they had no petrol, but then I saw Pius nod to him and he said in French to Gordie something about finding some.

"They knew Pius. They gathered around the lorry so close

that Gordie couldn't start it. Two policemen seemed to be arguing with Pius. They were in worn green fatigues and their feet showed through the holes in their old sneakers. Finally Pius seemed to win whatever the argument was and they slapped hands. Pius slapped hand after hand thrust up at him, his big black hand, their dark bronze ones. Did you know there are as many different colors of skin in Africa as there are here? I see them—lepers' hands, old hands, children held up, and over and over the words *muzungu* and Faradje. No one looked at us. We might as well not have existed.

"We drove again toward night, until the volcanoes began to glow and the stars were so heavy in the black sky they could swoop down on us, and Gordie wouldn't stop. We passed the wrecks of lorries and, from time to time, one pulled off the road with the black driver asleep, picked out by our headlights.

"Is he asleep? Gordie said once. I thought he meant poor Derek, who hadn't said a word since the petrol station, only smiled from time to time at someone in his own mind. We followed our own lights down the endless road. Pius spoke from the darkness. I think it is dangerous for you to drive at night. There is a rest house about five miles from here. Gordie didn't seem to hear him.

"The rumble of the lorry was putting me to sleep. Gordie said again later, Is he asleep? The nigger? Pius's eyes were closed and his head was dark against the stars that followed us. I don't trust him, Gordie said, and nothing else.

"We had to stop at a river where the ferrymen slept in a hut, bundled side by side. Gordie blew his horn. No one stirred. I know I slept, but he never did. When the dawn came his eyes were sunk in his head. I have never seen a man more quietly terrified.

"Pius had disappeared. Then I saw him. He was saying his prayers; that and the fact that we had survived Gordie's wild driving in the night were a comfort to me. When he had finished, he walked back to the lorry, that long stride along the bank under the trees, where grass sloped down to the water. It was a blue-green cool dawn. The fire he had made was turning white. He had put a kettle on it, and when he came up to the cab window to see if we were awake, he said to me, I have made tea. Will you join me? He didn't speak to Gordie or to Derek, only to me.

"You can wash here. Upstream there is a little pool. No crocodiles. The water is safe. He pointed the way. The river was eighty feet wide and shallow. I found the pool and lay in it under some trees that grew out over the water and made a canopy, and the small fish nudged and nibbled, and I remember laughing, forgetting for a pause where I was and what had happened. I had a sense that the dawn was new; I laughed at a young colobus monkey, with a white fringe of hair like an old bearded man, who was swinging through the branches above me, playing and fussing. It was strange to find those moments of peace and delicacy in the middle of the vastness and the fear. I felt light-headed. I know now that it was the first sign of my temperature rising.

"When I came back, clean from the river, Pius handed me tea with lime and sugar in it. When we had finished, he filled the two tin cups we had used and motioned to the lorry. I had a sense that he didn't trust himself to speak to them.

"I want Derek up here with me, Gordie said. He was trying to take command again, but Derek was already in the cab. Pius had packed his kettle and cups back into his bundle. Gordie watched him and told me, I don't like the way he looks. You watch the nigger.

"He didn't seem to care if Pius heard him, Pius whose English, what little he had said so far, was better than his own. These are Balese, he told me when we were standing by the river. They have the reputation of being sorcerors. Pius and I were watching the ferrymen get the ferry ready to take us across. He had been talking to them, and they glanced at us, only that. I heard the word again—*muzungu*—and asked him what it meant. Oh, only white man, he said, and looked away across the river.

"And you know, I still cross that river on the pontoon ferry while the Balese chant and pull the ferry to their chant. I can still hear them. Pius helped them. He was oiled with sweat along the great muscles of his back. He was as different from the others as a different species, but when I said that to Gordie, he only said, They're all niggers, just down out of the trees. The tea and the daylight had cheered him. A group of young girls played and swam along beside the lorry. A gaiety of black girls.

"Gordie seemed to have left the bodies and the forest behind. When we were back on the road he kept up that running nostalgia of talk that seemed to comfort him, thrown back over his shoulder at me. Do you remember and remember, and it had a pattern of mischief remembered in it, as if what he had lured me into doing back there in the night had been no more than mischief, those acts that made my life change utterly. The abyss of what he and Helmut had done had ridden beside me ever since I had seen the burned house, and I sat in a hell I was part of and I knew that it was myself who did it, and if that act had not already existed in me to be called out, no one, not Gordie, not Helmut, not death could have made me do it. You see, there is no innocence, none in the world, except among the saints that Pius talked about. So I knew that, whatever I thought about what they had done, I had lost the right to judge them. So I rode on, jostled around in the back of an old lorry, feeling nothing, not even anger or disgust or grief. Nothing."

That confession to himself and to her drove him into silence again. He was listening to Gordie's incessant remembrances about when he had poured the sugar in the Sassenach's tank. Then he could feel the wrinkled dugs under his fingertips and the damp, but it was only his own sweat, and he could smell his sweat and the blood of the woman in the sun. He had to make Gordie stop the lorry, and he had the first attack of

diarrhea behind a tree, and when he came back he was shivering. Everything seemed small, like looking into the wrong end
of a telescope. He remembered thinking that he had achieved
a kind of withdrawal from them all, some kind of peace, anyway. When he looked down, his arms were blue and all goose-
flesh. Under the canvas roof, where the sun beat down, it must
have been well over a hundred degrees and he was as cold as
charity. Pius reached over and felt his head.

When we get to Faradje I think you had better see the
doctor, he said from so far away that it made Ewen smile.

Have you chloroquine? I heard him ask Gordie.

A kit, Ewen thought he said a kit. There was something, a
box, in Pius's hands.

There's nothing in it. Only the bottles.

I told you to check it, somebody to somebody. Amusing.
Far away. Ewen was sunk in cold. Somebody had put a blanket
around his shoulders and it smelled of blood and he thought
he was crying. Everything smelled of blood and there was a
noise of rushing water so loud that he could only hear Derek's
polite voice away in the distance saying, Oh, I sold it in
Mombasa. Helmut refused to pay me until the run was over.
That was very selfish of him, and he played with something in
his hand, a gold ring.

Ewen's head was in Pius's lap. The trees slid along the sky,
and Pius's voice above him was saying, Listen to my voice and
don't go to sleep. We are taking you to the mission hospital.
Mission hospital. I think you must stay awake. Your temperature is very high. You will have fever dreams and you will not
like them if you sleep.

He told Ewen later that he didn't want him to tell anything
in his delirium that would make Gordie think he had to kill
them.

Did he say a temperature as high as the trees?

But there were no trees. They were climbing; Ewen felt
climbing and no trees and Pius was still talking. He told him

he was a Jesuit priest, a Dinka from the southern Sudan. It was a long story to keep him awake. He heard Gordie's voice, and Pius said, Yes, southern Sudan, and the lorry groaned on and Pius's voice, and when Ewen fell toward sleep, he said, Listen. Listen to me, and shook him. He thought of the baboon, not the woman and not the child, the baboon, and remembered trying to tell Pius about the baboon, and he put his hand over Ewen's mouth.

No, Pius called out. You've missed the road. Go back.

No bloody fear. Ewen thought it was Gordie. I know what you're up to. I saw you with the police. You are going to take us across the Sudanese border. Nobody will stop a priest.

The attack was beginning to pass. Ewen was warmer and he could hear them clearly.

No, Pius seemed to be begging. Maybe he hadn't heard it clearly. Let me take you to Faradje. You are in great danger and this man is very ill. You are safe only if you let me take you to Faradje. They won't let you get to Sudan.

But the lorry didn't hear. Ewen remembered thinking, How can he make a lorry hear? They drove on toward night. In that high savannah the road was iron hard and the stars were heavy again. Finally the moon was beginning to rise, a new moon.

They crossed on more ferries. Ewen remembered them vaguely. Gordie seemed to be on a more familiar road, and he remembered that Gordie had made this run in '64. Pius had made him sit up, but he let him lean against his shoulder.

Down a long slope ahead, there was a ghost of a bridge in the new moonlight, one the Simba or the mercenaries had not knocked out, a stone and wooden bridge left over from the Belgians. Gordie stopped the lorry, and he and Derek walked across to inspect the Sudanese side of the river for patrols. They came back, satisfied.

Pius had taken his bundle and was trying to help Ewen out of the back of the lorry when Gordie saw him. Get in; he was quiet. He had a gun in his hand. Ewen could still see it. He could still see the gun.

Pius held him at the edge of the tailgate. Do what I say, he whispered, but no more, because suddenly, as if the water had stopped flowing and the night birds and insects had paused to listen, they were in the center of the bridge in a well of black silence.

Pius yelled, "Jump!" and pushed him out of the moving lorry and over the bridge side and, my God, he was still falling toward the black water and there was a flash so white that it was day in a white hell and the blast and his body crashed at the same time against the water. From under the water he saw flashes and thuds of bright light, and when he surfaced something brushed past him, a fish or a body. It was Gordie's dead face in the light of the flares, and he grabbed for him but he was gone, and someone had taken Ewen's arm. Ewen had thrown off the coverlet and gotten up. He was pacing back and forth in the firelight.

Pius whispered under all the noise, the tracers, red, yellow fireworks against the stars. Swim. Fragments of bright light fell into the water, and hissed, dying. Pius pushed his bundle ahead of him. They swam side by side downriver and toward the bank, and over them they could see the steady flames now around the skeleton of the burning lorry and hear yelling from the bank, and there was a splash of bullets in the water and Pius pulled him under.

It lasted a few minutes and a lifetime, and they were lying in the dark of the riverbank, exhausted. The darkness had come back and there were only the nightjars and the *hee hee* of animals and their panting.

He went into his workroom and sat by the fire and said nothing. There was only the hiss of the gas.

Away across the river the Congo border guards had lit a fire, and shadowed figures stood around it. Someone laughed. It carried across the still, black water.

Come, Pius whispered. We must be gone from here before the dawn.

In the first attacks of the malaria, he didn't remember in time. It was like remembering dreams, or when he was a wee child. Pictures. Fragments. A voice. A face bending over him. The fever dreams were real and what was real was like fever dreams. The first thing he remembered in his life. Two, three years old? He didn't know. It was Fama hanging out clothes in the wind, and he thought, She's hanging out the birds to dry.

It was like that much of the time. Then sometimes his mind was clear. He was lying by a fire under a shelter of leaves. He was naked. There was a cover of something soft. A white djelabah. Pius was busy, domestic, making tea; everywhere the sun touched the ground he had put out things to dry. Ewen's clothes. His shorts, his money belt, all in the morning sun. A panga. Two books. He remembered a breeze fluttering the pages. There was a little stock of tea and some kind of flour, a frying pan, the kettle, the tin cups. There was a round net on the grass weighted down with little stones.

For the first time Ewen was warm. He watched Pius, naked except for the chain and the gold cross, his long black legs, the muscles of his back moving in the sun as he picked up the net and loped down through the grass to the water and stood in it, a crane. He threw the net. Ewen saw it land; a perfect circle lingered on the water and the little stones pulled it under. Patient still body. Pius waited, sun and shadow from the palm trees rippling across his back. He lifted the net and came back with three fish. He saw Ewen then and smiled, that sweet smile he seemed to save. Then his face was solemn, drawn so that the scars on his forehead seemed to stand out.

He said, in a matter-of-fact voice, Oh, you didn't die. Good. And he started to clean the fish.

Where are we? I don't remember . . . Then Ewen did. The darkness, the blasts of light. Nothing else.

We are in Sudan. It was the same matter-of-fact voice, but

Pius didn't look at him. He was busy with cooking. It reminded Ewen of Fama somehow. We have been here three days. The smell of fish cooking.

God, I'm hungry. Ewen could hear his own weak voice again in the silence and darkness pierced by the gas fire, and he remembered Pius's hand giving him tea. He had even rescued and dried sugar. Robinson Crusoe. Fama's voice, then Pius's. Ewen must have said it. Am I your Man Friday? Pius's grin. I didn't mean that, Ewen told his back.

He remembered lying there as useless and limp as yesterday's paper while Pius cooked, and he remembered hearing his own voice whining. He was ashamed of being so weak, so sick, sick of the fancies and, worse, reality. You knew all the time. Christ, why didn't you let me die, too?

I did not let anybody die. Pius sounded almost angry. I begged Gordie to stop at the mission station, but he wouldn't. I think he knew I was going to turn him in. But not you. That's why I followed you and found you on the road. I was a witness.

He brought Ewen the frying pan with the fish and set it on the grass. He had put his own on a broad leaf.

Do you remember when we stopped to buy the petrol? They would have killed you then, but I said no, you must be turned over to the police at Faradje. He still wouldn't look at Ewen. I told them you were innocent.

I wasn't. He thought he said it then.

I didn't know then what you had done. Come, eat. The fish smell sickened Ewen.

Would you please eat that? Pius was stern. I cannot carry you to Khartoum.

Then, while Ewen was eating the first breakfast he remembered in Sudan, Pius talked to him, in that calm voice, whether it was horror or daily bread or prayer, the same. He told him first that sometimes he gave up on white men, so many fools, natural predators. He called them that, and then: But some good men, too. You thought you were alone. He smiled at that.

We had been watching you as you watched the lions or the leopards, or the habits of the elephants, ever since you came to the Congo. You see, we knew Gordie and Helmut.

Masoudi's older son saw the lorry parked in the path by the shamba and saw you eating with Masoudi and Safini, his mother. He ran back to the mission two miles away. Helmut and Gordie had been recognized, for there are long memories there of *les Affreux* at the time of the Simba.

Do you know what the white man is to them, what *muzungu* is? White is the color of death. They say you have mockery eyes—too mockery, too cheaty, too thefty. If it were not for a few of the priests . . . I knew two good Europeans when I was a boy, a Verona father and a District Commissioner. He gave me that book. He pointed to one of the books in the grass. It is Conrad's *Heart of Darkness* and *The Shadow Line*. I like that better, that man alone. I learned to read English in that book, and a gift is sacred, you see, a part of the person who gives it, so I carry it. Africa is not dark. It is full of light.

He seemed to be avoiding what he had seen. Then he said, You see, Father Steadman, an old priest, a Walloon, lived in that house. He is greatly loved. When he said the Mass, he used to pour a drop of wine on the ground for their mother, and with him it was not blasphemy because he served Africans and he had been there so long that he understood like an African that everything is alive, even when it changes to earth. He had been taken to the mission hospital. Masoudi and Safini looked after him. She was very proud of her wedding ring. Father Steadman had brought it to her from Belgium. I buried them and their other son. You are not eating. We had run back together through the woods. But we were too late. We could see the fire in the swirl of air ahead. By the time we got there it was nearly burned down. I stood and watched you and Derek, and I heard you trying to pray. I thought then, There is something decent left in this man.

He made Ewen eat the fish.

You know, he told him later, after he had stamped out the fire and was making the bundle again and wrapping it in the djelabah. He held up the panga. I had this. I knew Gordie wouldn't give a big nigger a ride if he saw it, so I put it in my shorts. He smiled, but not sweetly at all. A big black man standing on the roadside with a panga. No. There wasn't any donkey. I was going to ride to Faradje in our Land Rover. I was on my way to England, but I had permission to go by way of Khartoum, because I had not seen my father and mother for over twenty years. I asked them to let me out just beyond where you were asleep, so I could go as a witness for you and Derek. I didn't know then that you had killed, too, or what had happened to the man you called Helmut.

Are you going to turn me in? Ewen was ashamed of asking.

Who would I turn you in to? Now get up and put on your clothes.

He was so weak that he got as far as his hands and knees. Pius watched him, a dog in the grass.

He said, Wash yourself in the river. Come, man. He dragged Ewen to his feet, hoisted him up, and half carried him to the water and threw him in. He stood on the bank and watched.

You have a peculiarly virulent form of malaria.

Ewen laughed aloud in the night. Teresa called out, "What is funny?"

"I just remembered Pius standing stark naked on the riverbank, saying peculiarly virulent. We were by a river in the morning, and he had thrown me in the water because I was filthy. I began to giggle then, but he was so solemn. He said, You will have twenty-four hours before the next attack. That is the nature of the disease. You get a day off, and on that day you must walk. Come, that's enough.

"He let me flounder into my clothes. Then he hoisted the bundle to his shoulder and started out, still stark naked, on a game path that went through the grass beside the river. He was headed northeast along the river flow, and I remember thinking, This must flow into the Nile. The rivers we had crossed after we left the Hôtel Baudouin had flowed west.

"I managed to walk behind that silent figure for an hour before my legs gave out, and I sat down on the grass and to my shame I started to cry, and I heard myself say in a little peepee voice, You don't like me." He was telling it all to the fire, and letting her hear.

"Pius turned around, and I have never heard such a whoop of laughter. He pulled me to my feet. He said, I carry you for a night and a day thirty miles over my shoulder, and I carry the bundle, too, because we could not survive without it, and all the time you dribble shit down my back so I have to wash us over and over. Thanks be to God, the rains are early this year. And when you are not in a fever dream and talking crazy you dribble memories in my ear. Oh, he knew Fama and Fada and my mother and Gordie and sand. Dear heaven, I had told him all about sand over and over, and he knew about that poor old woman who was sitting there in the night with a clapper to scare away the animals from her poor little patch of corn, and I had confessed all of it over and over to him, and then he said, You say I don't like you! I like you. Now, come on, we must make time while we are in the shade of the river forest.

"To keep me going he pointed out the birds and the monkeys and once a tiny little deer, no bigger than a rabbit, a duiker. He kept talking, looking back over his shoulder, and when I flagged he said, Listen to me. Sometimes he sang until I was staggering along to the rhythm of his voice and I sang with him. Oh, God, I can hear us under the vast sky on the savannahs where there was no direction, only the lion-colored grass, and down under the river trees and along the game paths, singing to make our feet keep going. When I stopped, he would say, Sing!

"We sang 'Gloria in excelsis Deo,' and I taught him 'A Mighty Fortress' when we were tired of the 'Gloria.' We sang to the dry slither of snakes in the bamboo groves, and the cries of birds and monkeys. We sang all day, except once when Pius stopped me, and we slipped past a poor village in the distance, and he whispered, Zande, some of them are Nyam Nyam—cannibals. They are short of protein, this as matter-of-fact as all the rest. He said it as if one thing balanced another.

"That night by the light of the fire and the animals' eyes and the moon, he told me about himself." Ewen called to her from the workroom, "Are you awake?" and when she said yes, "You know the strange thing is that sometimes I remember not what he said but as if I had seen him. Pictures. He is ten years old and he is walking along the road to the mission school four days away. He is naked and he carries his school uniform wrapped up on his shoulder to keep it clean and a little dried corn to eat. He refuses rides because he is proud of going to school on his own. He sleeps at Dinka villages along the way. His father is a Christian and says he must be educated, but he would rather stay with the boys of his own age group and grow up to go to the cattle camp, or net fish. I see his bullock and his pride in it. It is the best color, black and white. It goes with him like a dog. But he has to leave it behind, and there he is, ten years old, walking for four days across the vast savannah, lonesome and proud and refusing any help from anybody. He can already recite his ancestors for fifteen generations, and he has been herding goats alone in this space since he was four, so he is not afraid.

"When he comes home he and his brother, who has been to the mission school, too, and who is already a man with scars, who goes to the cattle camp, play a game for the villagers. They sit in a circle. Little Pius is escorted out of the circle far away so he can't hear. His brother asks for a word. Somebody says *koor*, lion, and they argue, and finally his brother says *koor* and makes scratches on the ground with a stick, and they call Pius and he comes and looks at the scratches and says *koor*. They all laugh and make him go and hide again. They play the game all day. Pius has learned to read.

Then he is sixteen and no longer milks, and he is standing while his father and his teacher, Father Sessa, and the District Commissioner sit and discuss him as if he were not there. Father Sessa says he has taught him all he can. Pius has been helping teach at the mission for three years. He has read all of the District Commissioner's books. The District Commissioner and Father Sessa are the only white men he knows. So he has learned Italian and English and Latin. They say he is a natural linguist, and he remembers the word as linguish, a natural linguish.

"They tell his father he ought to go to the Congo to the Jesuit secondary school, because he is bright and should have a chance. His father is sorry about it. He knows that what they say is true, but he insists that Pius become a man before he goes. I see old men wrapped in cotton cloaks with runneled faces, discussing the matter of Pius as I saw them later in the Dinka villages, sitting in that fly-covered patience waiting for things to change, and nodding at each other because the world was spoiled.

"Later, and I see it at night because he told me at night, but I know that is wrong, he lies on the ground. His head is over a hole, and gashes are cut deep in his forehead; that will make him look wise, and even slightly surprised. They are winged upward like raised eyebrows. His blood pulses into the hole and the ground drinks it, and so do the dogs. He passes out, but he has not made a sound through all the dancing and music and feasting, because he is now a man.

"He told me then that he went through several months of recovery and of being spoiled with the other new men, so that when he finally started out he was as fat and glossy as a bullock. This time he walks four hundred miles along the paths that we are following the other way. He hitches rides when he comes to the roads, four hundred miles. He knows no French. He has nothing but a note from Father Sessa, and the book that the District Commissioner has given him.

"I see him at the border. He speaks no language that they

understand, those dark bronze—what did he call them?—Arab-colored men. They turn him back with guns and laughter. He simply goes upriver several miles and swims across. I see him swimming, that white bundle pushed ahead of him, or is that when we are in the dark river?

"We stopped that day and rested under a tree by the water while I had an attack, not so bad as it had been before, and I went to sleep. It was later, toward evening, that he shook me awake.

"The Lord is with us, come. I have found a camp and they have medicine there, thanks be to God.

"It was a guerrilla camp. Anya Nya. Some of them were Zande, some Nuer, and Dinka, too. Some of them had been at war with the north for fifteen years. There was an Israeli doctor with them. He gave me chloroquine. We stayed there, oh, I never did know how long we stayed, several days. Part of the time I was someplace else, fever dreams. There were men in the ragged castoffs of Second World War uniforms, some in skins, one in an old formal dress coat, a motley of men."

He went someplace in his mind where Teresa couldn't go. She waited for him to speak, thinking of the times in her life that men had talked in the night, hidden from exposing light, letting the truth loose in the darkness.

She glanced at the little clock beside the bed. It was three o'clock. Five minutes later she heard a clock strike three. She kept her own time five minutes ahead of the rest of the world; anyway, that's the way Ewen said it.

When he began again he was on a high savannah and it was deep twilight, when the green was greener and the blossoms of the tree they camped under bright yellow in the last light, and the fire was still blue. She heard him speak so softly that she leaned forward and wrapped her arms around her knees, listening hard to the dark shadow before the fire. He was talking again about Pius, but she had no idea where they were.

"Pius said his Nunc Dimittis. We watched the stars appear.

By that time we had learned that we could trust each other. Had it been that day?—no, earlier. It was earlier that we found the burned remains of a mission and the Dinka village around it. Pius had apologized for stopping to see his family. He said he had not seen them for twenty years.

"The church and all the houses had been burned by government troops, Muslims from the north. Only a few trinkets were left to show that the people had been praying in the church. Nothing else. Africa cleans itself—the leopards, the lions, the vultures, the hyenas, the ants. Even the bones were gone. I saw Pius pick up something in the ashes and hold it for a long time against his face.

"We didn't move that day. Pius lay on the ground, his face buried in his arms. I left him alone. There was not a word said between us. The sun was white, the heat so heavy it seemed to crush us against the ground, and still Pius didn't move. Toward evening he got up, and whatever he had gone through was over.

"He said, Being with you is like being alone, and I knew it was one of the best things anyone had ever said to me.

"No, that was the evening we were sitting on the savannah just before dark, listening to the space around us become more nervous, more alert, noisier as the night came on and the hunter's moon began to light the east. Yes, I know it was that evening, because I was aware that he was trying to connect things that were random and terrible in both our minds.

"We were just sitting on a high bank of a river watching the moon come up, hearing the cries of things and animals drinking and grazing and the silences that came even in the noisy night, when we heard the wild dogs. A pack of them. Their shadows chased an eland across the moon and we watched it slow down and speed up again, and I could feel its terrified despair when Pius said, as if he had read my mind, No. He said that just as the eland fell out of sight in the grass, only a horn appearing and disappearing as the dogs tore at its head. Pius went on, Dr. Livingstone said that, when the lion mauled him, he felt nothing but a strange peace, a lassitude, as if God had provided for that. When he stopped struggling . . .

"After the dogs the vultures, after the vultures the hyenas, and after that the bones we passed in the dawn were already dry in the grass, and clean, like the bones of the mission church. Pius wore two crosses then around his neck. One was half broken. He stood and stared at the white bones of the eland and then he kicked a bit of fawn-colored hair. He said, Sometimes I think we are asked to understand too much.

"After that he talked all morning. I think he was reminding himself of how far he had come in a circle. He told me about being sent to Catholic University in Washington, and how he had resolved quite coldly to be a Jesuit priest because it was the best educational training he could have to go back to Sudan and begin to teach his own people when the civil war was over."

In the dark of the workroom, before the fire, he was listening to Pius. "I remember him saying that it was one thing they didn't have in the south. He said, The British kept us ignorant. They were romantic about us. Unspoiled. That's what they called it. You know, oogie boogie doogie boogie. Frightfully interesting! And then that laugh. Pius said that when independence came they turned the country over to the better-educated Muslims in the north, who had enslaved the southern tribes for four hundred years.

"And they thought we could survive, he told me. There have been half a million people killed, a genocide, and no one outside knows this. The fire lit Pius's cheek as he turned his head away and stared out into the darkness. Then he said, So we have four hundred years of slave raids and eighty years of white men to shift from our souls. It will take time to burn the hatred out. But four hundred and eighty years is no time in Africa.

"I thought then of the Great Rift and the three-million-year-old hominids. We had both seen time as we had been taught to see it, either the flick of days or the slow movement of eons.

"Pius was quiet for a long time. We could hear the wail of a hyena in the distance, and a herd somewhere feeding on the grass. A lion roar shook the ground. Then I saw God, he said in that selfsame matter-of-fact voice, standing in front of Selfridges waiting to cross the street, and suddenly the whole of Oxford Street was full of joy and light that came from Him, and it was gone and He was gone. At that minute I became what I was pretending to be—a priest.

"I didn't know what to say. It was embarrassing. God is. At least talking about God. But I must have said something, because Pius said, My Jesuit director had some difficulty with that, too.

"We walked the savannah. We walked down roads marked by mango trees where the old slave routes had been, roads for men and ivory, both commodities. We walked for days, not miles. There are no miles; just the earth turning, day and night and space. We walked through clouds of butterflies and golden-yellow grass, and we saw the sun through veils of rain. We walked through desolations of brush and desert. That was every other day. The days I didn't have an attack. The nights before attack days we stopped where we were. If we were in a village we stayed all day. There I would be shivering beside a smoking cow-dung fire, and if we were out in the space, we made a lean-to near water for the next day, or found a baobab to protect us from the sun.

"We were in Dinka country then." Ewen was suddenly so alone that he thought he had lost her, and he turned back toward the bedroom. She was still sitting up, hugging her knees, and her eyes and the four great knobs of the brass bed caught and held the dim firelight and made it brighter, as if the fire were there surrounding her.

"You stayed awake," he said, surprised, and sat down beside her. "You don't mind?" He took her hand.

She didn't know what she was supposed not to mind. She shook her head no and said, "'Go on, tell me," as he had asked her to.

"You know"—he turned her hand over and ran his fingers along her palm—"oh, you know when you are small and you have the comfort of grown-up voices as you go to sleep?" He saw her nod, and felt her hand move in his. "That's how it was in the villages, in the dark huts smelling of grass and dung and bodies—clean, the Dinka are clean—and there were bats rustling in the thatch and you could hear the cattle lowing and moving in the dark, and someone would be telling a bedtime story, a fairy tale. I couldn't understand, but I drifted toward sleep in the lull of the voices and the closeness of people and animals.

"Pius said that there were always stories in the night about people being turned into lions and snakes and about ancestors. That's when he told me first about Abou Baba Moosa, to help me forget how cold it was. I remembered that when Pius had found the Anya Nya camp he said that Abou Baba Moosa led him there, and laughed, and said he would tell me about him sometime. After he had told me, when anything went wrong, we had Abou Baba Moosa to blame.

"I would lie there listening to the bedtime stories in the dark, not understanding a word but seeing in my mind's eye the frog prince, the werewolf, the vampire, and the Billy Goats Gruff and the trolls, and I knew then that somewhere in the depths of night we all had the same visions, only we used images of our own familiar longings and fears.

"Just outside of Wau, Pius put on the djelabah. I remember that he sounded sad. You know, he told me several times, we Jesuits study Arabic and Islam, but they don't bother to study Christianity at all. It's more politics than religion with them. It is a dangerous shame.

"Then he stood beside the road and flagged a government lorry that took us all the way to Malakal. I don't know how he explained me. By that time I looked like a beggar, all rags and bones, about as heavy as one of those dust devils that skitter across the desert in the wind. Even my beard was thin.

"He talked us onto a boat going down the Nile to Khartoum by telling them that he was on a *hadj*, a holy pilgrimage, and let them think it was Mecca he meant, but he explained to me that it was not a lie, because all life is a pilgrimage, and I laughed and said he was being Jesuitical, and he said there was nothing wrong with that under the circumstances and I ought to kneel down and thank God for it and laughed at me. He prayed five times a day on the hot deck with all the rest of them. When I asked him how he could do that, he said, What difference does it make with whom I pray? That formal turn of speech I had learned to love.

"Do you have any idea of the luxury of a bare hotel room with the ceiling fan creaking you to sleep and the mosquito net moving in its breeze, after a lukewarm bath? I lay there for three days in that Khartoum hotel room while Pius disappeared and reappeared and disappeared again. Then he came in, in a new black clerical suit with his white collar. He told me he had borrowed money from a Coptic priest and had gone to an Indian tailor. He looked religious and regal at the same time.

"Now we are ready to go to Lloyds Bank, he told himself, looking in the mirror and obviously pleased with what he saw. When he saw me watching him he said, I think I am a bit of a dandy. It may be sinful, but it will be useful at the bank.

"I never was so glad in my life to see Lloyds Bank and cash money to get myself some clothes and for Pius to pay back the Coptic priest and for both of us to get back to England. With Pius with me, all dressed up like that, and with mine and Gordie's passports, it was easy to prove to the bank who I was. He made me present Gordie's wrinkled, dirty, almost illegible power of attorney. They gave me Gordie's letter.

"Gordie had made me his heir. I still am, heir to more than I want of him. He had even paid into a burial fund to have us both sent back to Scotland, wherever we died in the world. That strange mixture of sentiment and icy brutality. What I did with the money was this. I have kept the sum that was in the bank in Inverness, for that was from the sale of Fada and Fama's croft. What was in Africa I signed over that morning to Pius for Ogilvie House. My power of attorney was accepted, so they didn't need to wait eight years to prove death. It seemed the right thing to do with ten thousand pounds of African blood money.

"My God," he said, "six months. Only six months ago." She felt him touch her shoulder and then comb her hair through his fingers. "Now that you know about the woman . . ."

When she didn't speak he stopped stroking her hair and sat with his back to her, waiting and watching the dawn.

There hadn't been any woman in the fragmented story he had told her. There had been long silences, and there had been someone called Helmut, and his Uncle Gordie, and a Derek, and Pius, and Abou Baba Moosa, and all the other spirits, and terrible times, but no woman, no woman at all. But he didn't know that, and she knew she never would tell him, for fear of making him live again all that pain of trying to tell. It had been some woman he had loved, or hurt, but that was past. It was the telling, the trusting her, that was important, not what she had heard or hadn't heard.

"I don't ever want you to leave me," she told him. He turned to look at her, and the cold light behind him made his face dark. He said nothing. She knew then that he wanted only to stay. Only that, nothing more. It was as if Pius had never asked the question at all.

Beyond the bedroom wall in the white dawn, two feet from Teresa's head, Frank Proctor lay staring at the ceiling. He was not aware of her for once, her breathing, her turning, the times he had had to get up and go into his living room in the last two months when they had finally been able to make love.

He hadn't know what the sound was at first. They were tender with each other. No sweaty moans and groans and yelps, just the sounds of tenderness. When he had realized at last what it was, he had almost cried for them. Almost. He was aware of listening to the sound of love, not lust. He had gone in to his boss with the news, still trying to protect them, the bastards, but his boss only said, "Those mothers will do anything to keep from blowing their cover. It's disgusting."

But now he didn't even follow the ceiling pattern through to her. He had thought of that as a kind of tragic poetry, but not anymore. He was too excited, and, Boy, he told the ceiling, he wasn't going to tell his boss or anyone else yet, not that there was anyone else to tell.

Ambition soared in him. He was on his way to Turkey or any other damn place he chose, and to hell with the GS14s. No limit. He did the isometric exercises he had been told to do for his back after sitting too long at a desk in Saigon, his great lumbar muscles tense with fear, but stopped when he realized that he was making the bed squeak and they were right there, well, practically in bed with him, and he didn't want them to think he was . . . you know.

His mind rioted with sleeplessness and success. The connection! He had finally made the connection!

He went once again through all the steps to be sure, to be absolutely sure, even though he had done it a thousand times, waiting for morning and for action. Oh boy, hot shit, action at last, everything paying off in spades, hearts, and no-fucking-trumps.

Jesus, he thought, and then apologized to his mother in his mind for thinking blasphemy; it was hard not to in his profession. "What a connection!"

He hadn't been mistaken. The first clue had been right on the telephone tape. Boy, had his boss been right about the Jays. That bit about Abou Baba Moosa, Abou Baba Moosa, hell, Captain Moosa, PLO; he was sure about that at last, after listening in the night, my God, you couldn't help hearing it, could you, all that talk and then the silences when he had nearly dropped asleep and nearly, Jesus, missed it.

It was suddenly so obvious. He decided to call in sick and work at home to firm it up and recap. He didn't want his boss to read the excitement in his face and take all the credit. Even before he knew what the delivery was, he knew that Captain Moosa had smuggled something all the way to Ogilvie House. He had that on tape.

How the hell he had gotten it through Heathrow Frank knew he would have to find out. In his opinion it was no problem. Heathrow security was notoriously lax. They had spoken to their opposite numbers at MI5 about it and had been well and truly snubbed, no less, and those guys didn't even have decent offices. What did they care? Down the drain, anyway.

He had checked on Father Ryan's movements. Whatever it was, it must have been some kind of directions, flat anyway, wrapped in newspaper, as if they thought that could fool anybody. His man who was watching out a window in the Connaught Hotel said that was all it was, anyway. He put in for exorbitant expenses for lunch.

They had thought they were clever, delivering it in broad daylight to Farm Street, of all places. It was where all the top Catholics went. You couldn't trust anybody anymore.

It had been taken from there to somewhere else, but the man was so busy filling his damned face he'd missed that. Ewen was so familiar with the delivery that he didn't bother even to mention it when he was talking about Moosa in the night. Confession, hell. He called *that* a confession? Poor dumb Teresa.

Identifying Moosa had been a coup, but only half a coup. Now he had it all, and he had it right there on tape, cuddled beside him in the bed. He had been so excited that he couldn't trust the floor, too far away for him to watch closely. You couldn't trust mechanical stuff without having it right there under your eye, not when it was so important.

God, no wonder the Third World thought the CIA was a magic power behind everything. There was little he couldn't uncover now, at least lying there in the bed in Battestin Crescent. Then he remembered with a sinking feeling the stupidity of his boss. But the feeling didn't last. Oh no. Not now. Not with what he knew to blow that asshole right out of the water. He could see the light at the end of the tunnel that President Nixon talked about, shining there.

He almost dared not think about it, it was such a keg of dynamite. Jesus, he thought again, this time not apologizing to his mother, remembering how it had leaped out at him. First there was the mountain hotel camp where Ewen had found the Uzis; Frank didn't believe for a minute all that crap about not knowing what they were smuggling. Of course he knew. He was just telling her that innocent stuff so she wouldn't know what a real bastard she had in her bed.

Then the contact with Pius Deng. He had to admire how that was dealt with. Then Pius going with Captain Moosa to the Anya Nya camp, the Commies in the south of Sudan, and there they were—what was it he said—for several days, you betcha ass several days, with Pius Deng and Ewen and Moosa in the rebel camp, where they made contact with the Israeli doctor, who was certainly Israeli intelligence; they all were, weren't they? I mean, you know, they had that natural sneakiness from being in business so long, didn't they? And right there it was, a secret connection *through the Jesuits between Captain Moosa from the goddamn PLO and Dr. Izzie Whatsit from Israeli intelligence to smuggle Israeli Uzis through Sudan to the PLO! Jesus! Jesus! Jesus!*

VI

CELEBRATION

"My God, doesn't she know any nice people?" Frank fumed at his kitchen table. Annoyance had replaced excitement. It was only nine o'clock, but he was already exhausted. "God," he said to Mr. Evans-Thomas's ass in the garden below, and he was tired of that, too, "doesn't she know any nice people? PLO gunrunners, street-fighting priests, and a faggot, probably a Commie like Burgess, a lot of them are, they get blackmailed, you know."

He even lived at the Monrovian Embassy residence, how dumb could you get? Monrovia was a buzz word for all the satellite countries. It was really the Hungarian, no, the Rumanian, oh, hell—he poured his coffee—Monrovia would have to do until he checked it out. Then, of course, what else, the Russian Ballet; boy, he *would* take them to that.

Frank didn't know what to do about her. Maybe if her parents knew what she was up to, but her old man had retired and moved to some snob county in Virginia. He would. He'd be easy to find, though; those guys always hung around the department, getting in the way. Anyway, he knew better than to mix business with—it wasn't pleasure, but it was responsibility, a nice American girl like that. God knows, he thought, stirring in saccharin, it wasn't personal anymore, like love and stuff. Not after what they had been up to, even if he did still like them, and he had to admit that. He got up after his coffee and threw away all but two pairs of black socks. He kept two for what his boss called black tie, but he still thought of as his tux.

Her mother's letter came in mid-October. "Don't you know any nice people? Really, Teresa, I know it's what everybody seems to be doing, but do you have to? And in Primrose Hill? Your father is very upset with you, just when he was beginning to settle down. He still goes in to the State Department from Upperville. They find his advice very valuable . . ." which Teresa interpreted as her poor father, dimmed by years of diplomacy, hanging around the State Department restaurant. He had taken her there when he was on one of his Stateside assignments. She remembered a long queue of polite men, some of whom had been in the department for so long they had shrunk in their clothes like ex-cons.

The letter shook in her hand. Ewen, across the breakfast table, had learned not to say anything when he was shut out by a letter from America. He wanted to comfort her, but at those times she wouldn't let him near her.

She went on reading: "Your father has picked up gossip that *appalls* me"—underlined. She was an underliner, and later, the inevitable "Why on earth," as her writing grew larger with fury. Teresa put down the letter and walked out of the kitchen.

In a little while he followed her into the bedroom with only one glance of longing at his maps. He found her sitting on the bed, staring into the bathroom.

"I love you," he said, and sat beside her, and she put her head in the hollow of his shoulder and began to cry.

"I don't know what to do," he said later, seeking Noel's advice after what had become a ritual of weekly dinner. He walked with him along the street to Chalk Farm, along the wall where he always remembered laburnum, although it was now late fall and the trees were bare.

Noel was huddled in his greatcoat with the collar around his ears, complaining about the weather.

"Sometimes Teresa isn't happy, especially when she hears from her family. Maybe she misses them. I can't think of anything else . . ." he said loudly into Noel's covered ear.

"No. No. It's not that. She has one of those frightful American mums, a sort of American copy of mine, who was a copy of Daisy Fellows, like Mrs. Simpson. All a sort of *Vogue* history of the Western world. I think sometimes that Teresa needs a really bucolic marriage. You notice how she goes a bit bucolic when she feels happy and safe. But there, you're getting advice on marriage from a friend who is as gay as a wren, and who only knows about it from Mum and Dad, not a good example to follow, or from Swann and Odette, and God knows that's nothing to go on. Oh, God, it's cold. I'll never get used to it. Never," he moaned as they got to the station. Since Ewen knew neither Noel's parents nor his friend Swann, he put what Noel had said out of his mind and walked sadly and slowly back through the dark streets to Battestin Crescent. Now that the trees were bare, he could see Teresa moving about the kitchen, high up above the street, and he stood there in the raw November cold and watched her for a while and wondered how to make her happy again.

He had thought, or hoped, after his confession to her, that all was well, as well as it could be. For a while she had seemed happy, almost expectant. But the sense of expectation had faded, and she had become, in the last few weeks, too quick to answer, as if he was getting on her nerves. He was afraid it was what he had told her, that she had finally realized with her whole heart what he had done, but when he tried to ask her, she said, "Don't be a fool, Ewen, I don't care what you've done. It's what people haven't done that usually matters in the long run."

But she said it in a surly way, and when he said it bothered him, she said, "Don't dictate the tone of my voice to me. I'm not a whore who has to chat you up." That was one of Noel's favorite phrases.

It was when he saw Mr. Evans-Thomas raking leaves for mulch in what had become a large double garden behind both houses that he thought, He's had three mistresses and I've only had one—well, two—really. He thought of a nice girl in Saudi who flew in with British Airways whom he hadn't thought of in a long time, but that was different.

He had to do something. He felt selfish at the thought, but when something bothered her, it kept him from working all day, although he hid in his room and puttered.

"Things are not right," he said as he walked past Signor Battestini on the stairs. He was so used to him, and the cold breeze he always stood in, that he hardly noticed. He was too preoccupied with trouble he couldn't understand. He walked out into the garden and said, as if he were angry about something, "Would you have a drink with me at the pub? I want to talk to you."

Mr. Evans-Thomas unbent slowly and held his back, too curious to think of refusing.

"This evening. It can't wait," Ewen told him.

"Well, let me see. I have to go to a banquet tonight. That's at eight. What about seven o'clock? Will that be time—half an hour?" He was calculating how long it would take him to get to Westminster.

) 324 (

"Could you make it six?" Ewen's despair came out as sternness.

"Oh dear." Mr. Evans-Thomas knew better than to ask, but he did anyway. "Six o'clock, then. I'll see you both at the Athlone." He was conscious of prying.

"I'll be alone." Ewen turned and stalked out, right through the precious pile of leaves Mr. Evans-Thomas had raked together.

Mr. Evans-Thomas was late. It was already six-fifteen and Ewen was ready to leave. He had been so taciturn with Teresa that she had obviously been relieved when he said he was going for a walk.

"Yes, for God's sake, Ewen, go walk it off, whatever it is," she had said, slamming the door behind him.

So he sat in the Duchess of Athlone, all brass and red velvet and etched glass, and waited, and waited, and for the first time in as long as he could remember, he wanted to be in a well-lighted Presbyterian pub where people drank wee nips of Glen Grant and got drunk and fought like decent men, instead of the cat's piss they drank in the south by the bloody pint, hating the English, who were always late, and ashamed of himself for his mood, a civilized man who ought to have put all that prejudice away.

It was all Teresa's fault.

Mr. Evans-Thomas stood in the doorway, looking around. He wore dark curls down to a lace collar that reached beyond his shoulders, a yellow satin wide-awake hat with an ostrich plume that swooped across the back of his yellow satin coat. A sword in a scabbard hung from a wide red sash. The froth of lace at his wrist fell back as he raised his hand and motioned to Ewen when he saw him. He walked through the fashionable gloom, manipulating his sword around the tables, striding as best he could in the narrow space, in jackboots with wide tops stuffed with what looked like yards of lace.

Ewen, who had never learned not to, said the first thing that came to his mind: "You look wonderful!"

"Do you like it? Do you really like it?" Mr. Evans-Thomas's face, under the great mass of curls, was small and shy. He turned around so that Ewen could see the back. He managed to put the sword where no one would trip over it and sat down beside Ewen on the red velvet banquette. He stared back at all the people who were staring at him.

"I won't tell them." He turned to Ewen. "It's none of their damned business. You see, I am a member of the Society for the Restoration of the Stuart Monarchy. Two Glen Grants and two glasses of water, please," he said to the waitress, a student at RADA, who had breathed, "Bloody marvy, sir, what'll it be?"

"Thank you," he told her back. "We have three celebrations, and we dress in our Stuart clothes. One is when we march on the Houses of Parliament to demand the restoration of the Stuart monarchy. Of course, nobody pays any attention, but we like to dress up."

He passed his whiskey over the water glass, and Ewen did the same, polite and grinning. "Fada used to do that," he said. "My grandfather in Ross and Cromarty."

"Then there is tonight, the nineteenth of November, the birthday of Charles the Martyr, and then there is the thirtieth of January." He seemed to take for granted that Ewen would know that date.

"Now." Mr. Evans-Thomas took off his wide-awake and put it down, a great bouquet of yellow satin on the red velvet banquette. He leaned his curls against the mirrored wall. "You sounded so urgent. Plumbing? Electricity? No. Teresa? I thought so. I've been thinking about it all day, and I'll say it for you, because you are probably too dumb with confusion to put it into words.

"After all, so far as I know and the way you behave, it's obviously your first," he said, as if they were talking about being fathers, not lovers. He took a sip of his whiskey. "It is a classic progression. At least I have always found it so. You see, most women, I don't care how emancipated they are, want, sooner or later, to marry. I was damned lucky to find three who didn't, but believe me, there were several in my long life who did. You know, they start out quite unconscious of it, the poor dears, fooling themselves and one." He took another long sip of his drink and slammed the glass down on the table, which brought the waitress running. It was a gesture he never would have made in the clothes of his everyday self.

"Symptoms. Is she touchier than usual? Don't tell me. It's none of my business, just check for yourself. Do you find her crying before her period? Excuse me, but that is important. Stop staring, you little bit of nasty," he said to a boy in jeans who had just come in. He was looking as much like Donovan as he could. "You ought to see yourself. Where was I? Is she seeming, *seeming*, mind you, to be more independent, sort of talk about it a lot. Fooling herself, of course. Sort of intellectual don't-touch-me-you-beast. Let me tell you, she may be a free woman, but she has several thousand years of nesting genes behind her, and very few can live that down. All that can be got over, but if she's started to clean in corners it's really a danger signal, better to cut loose, my boy. Another?" He waved a lace cuff at the waitress, who had subsided at the end of the bar.

"You are bloody fucking marvelous!" a voice boomed from the door.

"Oh, God, the Amazons have arrived."

It was Artemesia. She clumped over.

"Bring another," Mr. Evans-Thomas sighed to the waitress.

"You're *gorgeous*. The only thing I've seen today that could cheer me up." Artemesia turned a chair around and straddled it. "I won't ask what you're up to in that drag. I don't want to know. Jesus, what a day. I've got NSU for the second time. Non-specific urethritis, in case you're too out of touch to know.

I caught it fucking my assistant editor. He promised me he was clean." She moaned, and upped her glass and drained it. "I'm not even supposed to drink. I'm firing him tomorrow."

"Why don't you ask for your two guineas back?" Mr. Evans-Thomas muttered. He was an admirer of Boswell. "Now don't forget what I told you. Cut clean," he told Ewen, who was getting up. He stopped by the waitress and paid for the drinks, a farewell gesture, because he would probably never see any of them again.

He seemed to himself not to know what he was going to do until he did it. He stopped at the off-license and bought a bottle of Glen Grant at what Fama, who had somehow come to sit in the middle of his evening, would have called—or did, he could almost hear her—a draidful price. Fada, whom he could hear, too, in the November night wind off Primrose Hill, was saying his chorus: . . . feed a family of four. It made him laugh, out there by himself. When he had been a boy, Gordie had egged him on to ask, For how long, sir? and he had received, not an answer, but a whipping and a prayer for his insolence, which Gordie knew would happen. He thought of Fama and Fada and the croft, run for anybody to come and stay, by the alien English.

He was being blown up the windy street. On Primrose Hill he could hear the trees swaying and creaking like a country wood. He couldn't think. He couldn't plan. He could only hurry home, clutching his bottle. He burst into the flat as if he were still being blown by the wind.

He could hear Teresa running the vacuum cleaner in the living room. He walked in, furious with her. She was cleaning in the corner behind the telly with a special wee nozzle for the bloody thing that she had bought to do corners. She complained she never could get them quite clean. It was seven o'clock in the bloody evening and she was still at it.

"Shut that goddamn thing off." He had to yell over the noise.

She even had a scarf tied around her head like a bloody skivvy. It was a paisley scarf he had given her for a present, silk, all different colors. For some reason he had liked it, and had bought it and brought it to her, not for a birthday, not anything, and there she was using it to do corners.

"I have been drinking with Mr. Evans-Thomas," he told her, "and I have brought some home. Now we are going to drink together." He went into the kitchen for glasses, and when he came back she was sitting in the most upright chair with her hands in her lap, like a little girl who'd been invited. Everything she did was making him furious. "You bloody come and sit here." He folded onto the sofa and slapped the place beside him.

"We're going to Scotland. Don't argue," he said so sternly that Teresa began to laugh, really laugh for the first time since her mother's letter and her shame at its effect on her after three years of therapy and a whole new life.

"I'm not arguing," she said.

He planned it as carefully as he could. He reserved places on the night train from Euston that drew into Inverness early in the morning, and he wanted to show Inverness to her first, or her to Inverness, because it was his city, the first he had ever seen, and all other cities compared with it somehow. When they got to Euston, she found that he had bought second-class sleepers for them in separate compartments, which amused her and touched her too. He was taking her home to a family that didn't exist and he wanted it all to be respectable.

Early in the morning, she looked out at the dawn moors below Inverness and the tears ran down and she knew why Ewen had been in Saudi, and Africa, and would go with her where she went. It was a beautiful gray-green moorland of granite outcrops and dark streams in folds of the moor, and lovely deceptive green hills, but it was without topsoil, without a place to plow and, she thought of the word without knowing what it meant, "harrow."

She didn't know he had come into the compartment and was standing behind her until she heard his soft voice: "We are near Culloden moor. Do you know that all Highlanders know exactly where their clan stood at the battle, or massacre more like. We fought stark naked, you know, because we were so poor that we didn't want to ruin our tartans, and the soldiers of the Duke of Cumberland mowed us down like the wheat that will not grow in this poor soil. But, then, we Scots hug our defeats to our bosoms."

Teresa dressed and wondered if Ewen had gotten them separate rooms at The Croft, now in capitals. They had been sent a brochure, with a picture of the "ancient" stone house on it, and the Great Hall, as they called the room of his childhood by the fire in the stone fireplace. It was all in color, with tartans covering everything that could be covered, and thrown every place they would stick. It cost twenty guineas a night and was authentic, the brochure said. Ewen laughed more than he had in so long that it gave Teresa hope—she hadn't known what was the matter with him—and he said that all it lacked was a tartan horse.

He had booked separate rooms at The Croft, and she said nothing about that. She knew that if they quarreled there, and if they left separately, it was all over.

Ewen was careful not to make a joke of the scones, or the kippers, or the black tea, or the terrible haggis, or the tartan slipcovers and cushions on the same old chairs with the shape of Fama and Fada still in them. He didn't mention the antlers over the fireplace, but he did tell Teresa when they were alone that Fada would turn over in his grave. He told her, "Fada used to stand up on the brae and wave his arms, with his beard blowing in the wind, to save the deer from the Sassenachs, not caring if he got shot. He said that was God's will. He didn't

approve of hunting the poor wee wild things." Ewen's accent
had grown stronger. "Fama used to go out and call to him, You
old fool, come down from there. Who do ye think ye are?"

Mrs. Green, who did the work of six ablebodied men, lived
up to her name. She was small, as thin as a twig, and she dressed
in green tweeds. "We don't wear tartan. Foreigners." She made
her little joke several times. When Ewen told her, to get it over
with, that he had been brought up at The Croft, she said, "Dear
heavens, you must be . . . Gordie?"

"No, Ewen."

"Of course, I should have known that," she rattled, as if she
hadn't talked for too long. "I didn't quite register the name.
Ewen McLeod, of course." She giggled, and then said, "Oh
dear. Well, I certainly have heard all about your grandparents,
oh my, I really have. This is still the McLeod place, the old
McLeod place, and it always will be, no matter how much we
pour into it."

She insisted on showing Ewen every change, and apologizing,
a little twitter, for all of them. "The central heating, we must
have it, for the Americans, you see," and then jumped round
to Teresa and said, "Oh, I *am* sorry," as if she had been insulting,
and went on pointing and apologizing in all ten rooms, including
the kitchen, with its large new shiny Aga cooker. "But it is still
the old table," she said, running her hand over its silk-smooth
surface. "I'm sure you recognize that."

She flung open the door to Fada's study. "This is the new
dining room. We've enlarged it, so you see, there is something
new . . ."

"We were never allowed there except to be punished or told
some vague approximation of the facts of life," Ewen told
Teresa when they had escaped out onto the moors. "No," he said
before she asked, "I'm not even disappointed. It's too far from
anything I remember. Just the walls are left, and sometimes
the smell of the wood when they light the fire in the evening.
I won't say I shouldn't have brought you, even if it is fucking

awful and I know that, but it is something I had to do and I can't tell you why, because I don't know myself. I am not," he made himself clear, "being sentimental." But he held her more often when they were walking, and when, in the evening of the second day, they were sitting by the fire, he found a way to sit on the floor in front of her and lean against her legs and stare into the flames.

They walked the stream where he and Gordie had poached salmon. They walked the brae where Gordie had called out his ancient battle cries at the Englishman. It was the third day and they were walking along a low old road sunk between high banks where Ewen said he wanted to show her some ruins from the highland enclosures. The air was so soft it didn't seem cold, but she knew it was. She could see the ghost of her breath.

As they walked, he talked, faster and more than usual, as if he was talking about one thing and thinking something else. He told her how terrible the enclosures had been for the Highlands, worse than even the genocide by the Duke of Cumberland after Culloden, and how the bailiffs came in and tore down their houses and herded them out into the roads to wander as if they were the sheep that were going to replace them. They wandered to the ports, where ships took them far away from home, if they had managed to save enough for their fares; they were pushed out to America and Canada and New Zealand and Australia. Then he stopped in the road and said, "You know that we never stopped being Scots. I told you that my Uncle Gordie paid into a burial fund for my body to be shipped back to Scotland wherever in the world I died."

He didn't want any answer. He took her hand and led her up the steep bank, and they walked across a field to where a few gnarled old apple trees still grew in a rubble of stones that had been a tenant's croft. "My great-grandfather was given the freehold of the croft as a reward for doing this. He was a bailiff. He had bad blood. His mother was a Campbell," he told the stones.

She wanted to laugh or cry at how her love was standing there, stripped down to atavism, as if all the training, all the travel, all that had happened to him, even meeting her, had been like the tartans and the antlers, alien to the basic stone of him, and easily removed and forgotten. She had to get away from him for fear of crying, but when he realized that she was plunging through the deep rain ruts back across the field to the road, he caught up with her and said, "What is it? Tell me what it is."

"I wanted to get free of those stones. They were holding on to me." She pulled free of his hands and jumped down into the road. "It's like—oh, what is it like?" She was fighting to say anything except what she meant. "Oh"—relieved—"like I used to feel when I was teaching. Caught; all those faculty meetings and all that talk."

"You make me bloody sick," he yelled from the top of the bank, standing up in the wind like Fada stopping the hunters. "Always complaining about how hard it is to bloody teach. You'll never realize how bloody lucky you are. Cushy bloody job where you can think and you can travel and . . ." He paused. "You don't have sand in your bloody mouth all the time. One day you bastards will have to work for a living."

Always, and never, they threw the basic words of argument back and forth in the wind.

"I thought you liked the taste of sand," she yelled back. "You're always talking about it. You never shut up. Sand. Sand. Sand. I'm going home." She trudged down one side of the road and he trudged down the other. It was difficult to pretend they weren't together, since the road was only six feet wide. One kept dropping back, or the other.

By the time they reached the croft they both knew they were going to get married, but neither of them could ever recall who had said so first. They were sure they didn't tell Mrs. Green, who was waving an elaborate yoo-hoo at them from the door. Teatime. Teatime. She sounded as if she were calling chickens in to be fed. It was understood between them that Pius, who had said it aloud first, and who had been embarrassed at their silence ever since, should be the first to be told.

All the way back to London in her second-class sleeping compartment, Teresa lay awake and worried about whether Ewen would carry what she saw in her own defense as an atavistic charade, now that they were going to marry, as far as sleeping in his workroom until Noel came back from Hammamet after his winter break. Teresa had insisted on that one thing. "He's the only brother I have," she said.

But when they got into their flat, pink-nosed with cold, and he put the bags down in their bedroom and fell onto the bed in his coat and said, "Thank God," she knew it was all right.

It was Noel's idea. He had appointed himself auntie. On the thirtieth of January, at five-thirty in the afternoon, he was standing on a kitchen chair in Teresa and Ewen's living room over the garden that glittered in the light from the windows. The mist had frozen and made a pattern of ice branches on the shrubbery.

Mr. Evans-Thomas had asked them not to close the curtains. They could hear him down below beating the ice off with a cane.

Noel turned around on the chair to Pius, who was standing, looking judicious, across the room. "Yes," he said. "It is absolutely straight now." It was a large scroll on heavy white silk which Noel had ordered from Hong Kong when he heard about the wedding. He was hanging it over the fireplace. The characters, two feet high, were painted red.

"It looks like a modern abstract, doesn't it?" He didn't wait for Pius to agree. "You see," he said, still standing on the chair, "they say *hun li*. The two characters for wedding. I had the day looked up. Tomorrow, I mean, and it is an especially auspicious day for a wedding. All over Hong Kong today, it's tomorrow there, or yesterday, I never can remember, there will be weddings, because the fortune-tellers have said it is a lucky day." He jumped down from the chair and stood beside Pius. "I told you that Mandarin is very concrete. The pictures, that's what they are, pile image on image for a new image. See there. Family plus daughter, and you have felicity. I once had a good-luck charm of jade, and it read, May you open a shop, on one side, and May you have four sons to run it, on the other.

"Let's have a wee drink, as Ewen says. There's so much to do. No!" he shouted. "Not to come in!"

Ewen's very tentative voice drifted through the closed door. "We're just going. We'll be back at eight." They heard the outer door shut.

As in weddings for hundreds of years, this one had been taken over, the bride and groom no longer names but titles. Plans, at least for the night before the wedding, had been hidden from them. Noel had insisted that they go to the pub or the flicks, he didn't care which. "But go," he ordered.

"I feel like one of those brides in the Turkish mountains," Teresa said, struggling into her coat. Ewen was treating her as if she were breakable. He wrapped his wool scarf around her throat.

"It's freezing out," he said.

"At least I'm not being locked up."

"In Turkey," she told him as they went down the stairs, "for the family and the neighbors, marriage and death are something alike, the beginning and the end. For a month, when the girl is married, all the work is done by others. They fill the house to serve the bride. Then come years of hard work. Then, when she is widowed, they come again and do the same, recognizing love and grief as two forms of madness." They had reached the front walk, and when she giggled, her breath was white in the air. "God, it's cold. But something more than cold is making me shiver. Someone is walking over my grave, as my grandmother would have said." They walked toward Chalk Farm.

"It's affecting everybody," she said. "They've gone conservative on us, well, not on us, but on the wedding." She remembered her vision of Ewen stripped down to some ancient and essential self behind all his learning and his love. She herself, even more herself, she had to admit without saying, had fallen into reactions she wouldn't have known in her dreams. At least she didn't think or hope so. She had been unable to eat, and had actually cried, ashamed of herself for it, at her mother's approving letter, with all her sweet coo words, she usually called them, as conventional for the occasion as if she had copied it from a book of protocol. Conventional. Convenient. Convention, that was it, to meet with, the ceremonies of innocence not dead, but amusing, no, more than that, affectionate, going back to some source they couldn't recognize or name, no matter how they tried.

Her mother's letter, as they always had, in any crisis in Teresa's adult life, started with an apology for their not being able to come. "Your father is far from well." Never sick, never that word, but far from some norm. "I am taking him to Florida, though he *hates* it. *So*, you are marrying such a dear boy, I hear," as if she were at last marrying the boy her mother would have chosen for a daughter who never existed. She could see Noel's handiwork in what followed. He did admit he had dropped a tiny note explaining what a "thane" was, feeling quite safe, since to his knowledge the title had not been used in some centuries, and hinting that Ewen was, after all, a McLeod (he had actually said Ewen was the McLeod of McLeod, fallen on times which demanded that he work for a living). When Teresa told him she saw his hand in her mother's letter, he just said he had known what to say to fit the occasion.

As they walked to the tube station, the ice-crystal-laden laburnum made Adelaide Road look as if it had been decked for their wedding.

Inside the garden room, Pius and Noel sat side by side on

the sofa, taking a little rest before they got to work on the evening, and sipping Ewen's whiskey.

"We're the fairy godmothers," Noel said. "Now what could be more benign than a nice black Jesuit and a queen of England?" He was staring at the Mandarin characters still. "Don't laugh," he said, "but I'm writing a monograph on the character you saw in my living room; I will call it that. I don't draw in it. I live in it. The one for existing; the character, I mean. Being. Is-ness. Don't tell. I don't want to ruin my reputation for a wasted life; it would be too disappointing for the friends who have cast me in the role of the one who was *so* brilliant at Oxford, and then never amounted, as the Americans say, to a hill of beans. I call it the Branwell complex. All those droopy sisters, coughing and writing. Nobody ever asked Branwell how *he* felt, did they? Anyway, that's what I'm doing. Concrete. The character is the same as 'to see.' If you can't see it and touch it, it doesn't exist. Something like that awful man Wittgenstein at Cambridge, who had such bad manners."

"It can, of course, be conceptual without being abstract. You have to define the difference." Pius, familiar with the busy peace before a sacrament, and at home in it, sighed and sipped his whiskey. 'I mean as in *haecceitas* of Duns Scotus, or in Kant's *Ding an sich*. That's why I love Latin, though. You can touch it. Take the Latin *exsistere*—to be—which I believe can be traced to the same source as the entrails used for divination . . ."

There was a thunderous knock at the house door. Mr. Evans-Thomas called up from the garden, "Harrods van!"

"Thank God, they've arrived." Noel jumped up and ran out through the hall to the flat door and flung it open. "Up here," Pius heard him call. Artemesia called from upstairs, "Down in a minute, darling," and Zephyr from the lower hall, "Am I late?"

Mr. Evans-Thomas sounded harried: "I'll be back in an hour, sorry," to the Harrods men, Pius supposed, and then: "Why the white roses? For the wedding? I'll take them." That was Zephyr again.

"No, these are to throw into the Thames over Westminster Bridge. I have others. Bring them up later. Must run." The outer door slammed.

"He's gone loony!" Zephyr's voice echoed through the caverns of the hall.

Pius set his empty glass down. His wedding was gathering around him, and he said, before the others came back, his thanks to God, in Latin.

Ewen and Teresa came up the stairs, frozen from the night. The house was completely silent, as if everybody had gone, and Teresa thought they had been deserted until Ewen opened the door and ushered her in, which was odd and special in itself, for the special night. She usually had her key out first. When she was tired, the speed of her movements paused just before hysteria.

She heard first, as she was hanging up her coat, a scurrying that sounded like small animals, and then a giggle that could only be Zephyr, and the *shhh!* and then total silence again. Her first instinct was to run, her second was to wait for Ewen to hang up his coat so they could walk, quite formally, down the hall and open the door as if they were opening a present together.

The pause as short as a catch of breath seemed to last a long time. At least she remembered it that way. The room was new and old, white and gold and red. Along the wall beside the door, opposite the balcony, four card tables had been put up to form a long banquet table. She could just see their legs. They were covered with a snow-white cloth of lace and linen. At the back there were white chrysanthemums and white roses, and along the front stretched flat silver, damask napkins, champagne glasses, bottles in a huge silver tub that caught the light of the fire. Candles. There were white candles. Behind the table a dragon, coming out of a cloud, sprawled across the wall, in a five-foot-high cartoon. At the far end of the table, a stranger, a waiter in snow white and anthracite black without a face; she never could remember it, anyway.

Over the fireplace there were huge red Chinese characters on a white silk banner, and beside the fire Mr. Evans-Thomas had put his old brass coal scuttle he took such pride in because it had belonged to Signor Battestini, in place of their own, which they had bought at the ironmonger's when it got cold.

Someone had turned the television around and put it on the floor; she thought it was so it couldn't see them and felt laughter rising, but was careful, it might be tears.

Then she saw the golden horse. It stood, on its plinth of black marble, in front of Noel's Thai silk curtains, ready to rear, or neigh, its foreleg curved to step, its mouth opened to whinny. Its gold wood muscles strained against its trappings.

She remembered the room like that, in that second, glowing and empty, but of course it hadn't been. It had been full. They were all standing there, holding champagne glasses; either they stood like that then or it was later for the picture. There was Zephyr, as demure as was possible in white leather from jockey cap to boots, which Artemesia said later made her look like she was by Mondrian out of Courrèges. Abdul was beside her, in a perfectly cut dinner jacket; then Pius and Paddy, looking formal in their holy clothes. Penny and Robin were wearing their old sweaters; they hadn't realized it was going to be so grand, Penny shrieked later.

Noel beamed in his dinner jacket, with a bright red tie and a frilled shirt. Artemesia, in a zeal to do what was right, had dressed in the only skirt Teresa ever saw her in, which made her look like she was applying for a job in a bank. Frank Proctor was in a dinner jacket, too, with a careful, thin black tie he had tied himself.

But at the end, Mr. Evans-Thomas stood in full regalia, the

yellow satin wide-awake, the ostrich plume, the yellow satin jerkin, the ruffles, the boots, the sword, which later got in everybody's way. His little wrinkled face looked out from behind a hedge of lovelocks and kiss curls. He wore a white mourning ribbon on his arm. He looked like a burgher in a municipal painting of a provincial Dutch town in the seventeenth century.

Noel raised his glass and called, "To the bride and groom," as if they didn't have names. It was everybody's idea of what a wedding party ought to be. Artemesia explained that she had had the linen and silver sent from—not Chatsworth—she couldn't have said that. No, "Chadfield," she said, demanding familiarity with it. "After all . . ." she said, and didn't finish.

Noel, who was drinking a lot of champagne and darting from soul to soul, as he called them, explained several times about the characters and the five-toed dragon and the white chrysanthemums, all of which brought good luck, and then he led Teresa over to the horse. He said, "Horse is yours, darling, keep him well. I want you to have him for your wedding present. I won't have a wedding, ever, and you are my dearest."

She was afraid to speak. She went on looking at the raised foreleg, and the silk curtain behind it.

Later, he confessed, "As a matter of fact, darling, if it weren't you, it would be banished to the country, and I couldn't bear that, and you simply cannot live a day longer with those ghastly green curtains, and well, you see, I have a confession to make. I've found someone, oh, not like Wei Li, not that, but . . . well, he's awfully nice and he is the last abstract painter left in the world, I'm sure. He has totally cleared the living room and painted foot-wide stripes, all different colors, around the walls. He calls it an environment and we sit on the floor. His name is Ron, I'm afraid. I seem drawn to that. We met in Hammamet and we knew at once that it would be all right to live together.

"So most of the Chinese things have gone to the country. I've bought a house I call the Villa Detritus, where things will go when life changes, as it does, God knows. I can't wait to have you there as my first guests. I refused to turf the Chippendale bed out, though. Love me, love my bed. I absolutely insisted on that. It is, after all, two of a kind, and I *do* plan to die in it. But wait until you see the living-room ceiling. We've hung a marvelous blue Moroccan tent, just like sheiks and Elinor Glyn, from the center of the ceiling out to the walls. Oh, Christ, darling, you might as well know before you see it. It's like living in a lampshade, but Ron likes it, and what the hell! At least I didn't have to move. I just struck the set."

That was before she and Ewen were ushered in front of his worktable, also covered in white linen, and trundled in from the front to stand beside the kitchen door. Everybody gathered close for them to open their presents. Behind them the two waiters lingered and waited. There seemed to be two of them, one in her kitchen who, in her state of shock, quick warmth after the cold of the night, and glass after glass of champagne, she hadn't noticed.

There was a large library globe from Pius, so old that it showed the Middle East in the green of the Ottoman Empire, and Tanzania as German East Africa, which he said he would explain later. Artemesia, true to the conservatism she had dredged up from a long-neglected part of herself for the wedding, had brought a blue leather desk set from Asprey's, which she explained she had found when she went there for her Christmas presents, little blue leather notebooks with *My Trip* in gold, for all of her friends who dropped acid.

"You simply haven't heard Mozart until you've dropped some acid and then watched blood pour out of the gramophone with the music," she explained to Abdul, who said he preferred his Mozart without blood, thank you.

Mr. Evans-Thomas had found a silver frame in his collection of rescued Battestini treasures. "To remember Battestin Crescent," he said, hiding behind his curls. Penny and Robin had gotten things slightly wrong, too, about their present. They had brought a large poster of the Rolling Stones' heads on naked bodies, which Noel explained there wasn't room for and, mercifully, rolled up. Abdul had, on Noel's advice, given them a silver bread warmer with TCM etched in convoluted initials, which Noel told him everybody simply must have, and Paddy had brought two Crown Derby teacups and saucers, which he had nicked off his brother.

Sometime in the evening, when everybody had wandered away from the table, Frank Proctor lifted a large copper jug and put it in Teresa's hands. "It's Turkish. I want you and Ewen to have it," he said. "I bought it for my mother, but now that I'm being sent out there, I can get her another one." He had drunk a lot of champagne by then.

"You know something?" He sounded confused. "What I can't understand is that I was bucking to go there, learned the language and all, and my boss acts like it's some kind of punishment, a kick downstairs. He called me"—here he leaned close and whispered—"an asshole. He told me I had put my foot in a big pile of—excuse me—shit. I didn't even make GS12. You know something"—he had backed Teresa up against the new curtains—"the government is being run by a lot of dummies, just because they have security clearances. They don't speak anything, and you know, they all wear black socks in the daytime. It is a crying shame."

Zephyr hadn't put her present on the table. She came up to Teresa after supper, while they were waiting for the out-of-season strawberries, the pastries, the cheese, the coffee, to be cleared away so that Noel, who had announced it was going to happen, could have his speeches. "I've brought you this," she whispered. "Think of it from Baba." She put an old leather box in Teresa's hands. In it was the gold and jasper necklace that Zephyr had worn the first time she had ever seen her. "You liked it," Zephyr whispered. "Baba said it belonged to Semiramis. That was his *masal* about it." Oh, he would be *chok memnun* to see you so happy"—she smiled through both their

tears—"on his Primrose Hill. Maybe"—she looked around—
"there are angels . . ."

Frank, who had taken to lingering nearer and nearer Teresa,
said, "That means very happy," pleased with himself.

"Well, sort of, you Mister CIA, you've just got it a little—
English, English . . ." Zephyr snapped her fingers. "Oh, bitchied
up!" she finished in some triumph.

Teresa was sitting very close to Ewen on the sofa. His worktable had been taken back to his room, and the sofa had been
pushed nearly against the wall, so that there was only room
enough to squeeze past to the loo. Noel, who, as he told everybody over and over, had appointed himself auntie, was standing
in front of the fireplace.

"I am, as we all are," he began, "slightly drunk with champagne and joy. Now, you may wonder why we have chosen this
night before the wedding for our celebration." Nobody did.
They had taken the time for granted. "I chose the thirty-first
for the wedding day and they agreed, just to please me, I know.
It is the most auspicious day of this year for a marriage, and
God knows, children, you need all the luck you can get—oh
dear, I'm going to say it, so I must be drunk—before you
embark in the frail craft of love on the unknown sea of matri-
mony. Isn't that *awful?*"

"Yes," Abdul called, "do be quiet." He had taken to holding
Zephyr's hand.

"So here is to the happy couple." Noel held up his glass yet
again, ignoring Abdul.

"The happy couple" echoed over their heads. Teresa couldn't
look at anybody, so she watched the firelight play on Horse's
lifted golden hoof.

"Now there is another occasion tonight that we are here to
honor. I am persuaded that they have to do with each other,
but I don't quite know why. Mr. Evans-Thomas, it's your go.
Oof!" Noel sat down.

Mr. Evans-Thomas had removed his wide-awake, and seemed

to have learned through the evening to wear his curls with some small hint of dash. He stood up in front of the fire, and then moved a little away, explaining that the satin was getting too hot.

"Um," he began. "Well. You see, tonight is the anniversary of the death of Charles the Martyr of blessed memory. That is why I am dressed like this." He had told everybody this, too, but not, as he said, formally. "The white roses are a symbol of Blessed Charles the Martyr, and every thirtieth of January we throw them in the Thames. Tonight, when I took mine down, there were white roses as far as I could see, floating on pieces of ice down the black river. So you see, Zephyr, I am *not* loony. Oh, I heard you. So why do we combine the memory of his death with the celebration of the wedding? Well, I will tell you. Oh dear, I've forgot the connection. Noel, you do it."

"At least say your little poem, dear, and then I'll explain," Noel said from deep in his chair.

"Oh. Oh yes, of course. Sorry." Mr. Evans-Thomas stood very straight. "This is by the Puritan poet Andrew Marvell. On the death of Charles the First," and then mumbled, "of blessed memory. Um. He nothing common did or mean / Upon that memorable scene . . . But bowed his comely head, / Down, as upon a bed."

The firelight fragmented into prisms in Teresa's eyes.

"That's all," Mr. Evans-Thomas said, and again leaned against the wall. He didn't like to sit down in his satin.

Noel jumped up again. "Now, don't you see? That's the reason." He seemed to be pleading. "I know you all." He looked around him. "Almost everyone here has crossed what Teresa calls the river Styx in one way or another." To Artemesia and Penny, who were standing together, looking blank and polite, he explained, "You see, something has to happen you can't retreat from, the knowledge of death in Teresa's case—a person whom she loved who would be happy for her tonight, and her own death, which she has faced so recently. Pius here, who has committed himself to a priesthood on an alien shore . . ."

"A distant shore. Nobody ever gets that right," Paddy called.

"Ewen's eyes carry a secret that tells me he has crossed, too. And I have. I have to live without knowing, like those people who have ones they love missing forever in action. He may be here, too, watching. I simply do not know. So what are we left with? All that we know is that we must love, hard as it is, and we, not other people this time, but we, lovely us, must die. All we can do for one another finally is to do both of those things gracefully, and with as little fuss as possible, so as—how is it said in wartime—not to frighten the others unduly. And so to Charles the Martyr. He wasn't a very clever man, a bit dull, I'm sure. The Royals tend to be. Stop fidgeting, Beverly. But he did do two things for us, and he did them gracefully.

"It was a day as cold as today when he walked from St. James's Palace down to Whitehall, and the little river that is now the lake was frozen solid. He dressed himself in several layers of heavy underwear so that nobody should see him shiver with cold and think that he was afraid of death and, I'm sure he thought this, be afraid themselves.

"Then, as he stepped out of the banquet hall window at Whitehall Palace onto the scaffold, he looked at the sky, and then he looked over the huge crowd; maybe he was trying to find someone who had the courage to look back at him, and then—he spat. Stop fidgeting, Beverly. There has been argument ever since about why King Charles spat. Was it contempt? Was it arrogance? No. The crowd he faced had seen many executions and faced their own deaths in a brutal time, and they all knew that if you are afraid your mouth goes dry. He spat to show them they need not be afraid. It was a lovely act. And then, as Andrew Marvell says, he bowed his comely head. To Charles the Martyr."

. . .

There had been more toasts afterwards, but that was the moment she remembered when she woke up in the silent room. It was late—three o'clock? She couldn't know. Her watch had stopped and Ewen had taken his downstairs, where he was staying the night in Mr. Evans-Thomas's flat. Noel had insisted on that, too. He said it was bad luck to see the bride before the wedding. It was dark, and she was cold and lonely without him, and something—she suspected it was too much champagne —had waked her in the night.

She made herself get up and put on her woolly robe and go into the bathroom to find Veganin, and then remembered she had put it in the kitchen and said, "Damn" to the ceiling. "I don't want to be hung over for my wedding; everybody's wedding, whatever . . . I've got to know the time so I'll be on time, ready . . . Oh hell."

She wandered down the hall to the back living room with its ghost party. Most of it had been cleaned away. She remembered hearing voices as she went to sleep when she had been sent to bed at midnight. Noel had said she had be out of Ewen's sight by then, as if she were going to change into four—or was it six—rats and a pumpkin. "At least," she grumbled aloud, "they aren't making me henna my hands."

A few embers were left glowing in the fireplace, which the golden horse caught, faintly. She went carefully around Horse and drew the curtains. The garden below was covered with a sprinkling of snow that cast a false white dawn into the room.

She saw Pius's globe in its light, and she heard him again, in that wonderful cathedral-organ voice of his, saying, "I found it in the Portobello Road, and this is why . . ." What was it he said? Why? Then there was his voice again. "We live within our outer walls," he had said, looking around the room, riotous and a little bedraggled by then, as parties are at the end if they have been good ones.

"You see, like this globe, this room contains a world, a globe you can't see. It was in this room that we stepped on the moon and saw ourselves blue in space, a little pendant orb, and here tonight we celebrate a wedding of each other, a wedding of the soulscapes that in this room make up that world. I knew a man once who called it the country behind his eyes. You and Zepyhr have in your soulscape the mountain where Noah landed." She remembered that he was whirling the globe as he talked, and then he laughed and drew a long line with his finger. "Here you see Ewen going down the Great Rift to Africa, across the Serengeti, and here am I in the jungle and we are both going across Sudan and down the Nile to Khartoum and then to Cairo, and then we come to Victoria Air Terminal. A miracle!"

He whirled the globe again, playing with it and with her. "Here comes Teresa from New York State in America, and here am I in Washington, and here"—he whirled the globe again— "is Noel come all the way with Hong Kong in the inscape of his soul. Father Hopkins called it an inscape, but I call it a soulscape, where the soul lives. Here comes Mr. Evans-Thomas from Malaya, and Mr. Abdul from India, and here we are back again, the whole mind globe, here in this room, as Mr. Eliot, the poet, said, Now and in England. So I have given you the world and where we have all been and can go again any time we are silent."

Given her? Then what had he given them both? She tried to remember in the dark, but she was nearly asleep again, oh yes, his blessing, he had given them his blessing. If she didn't turn around but went on looking at the white garden, she could still see him standing there, her tall, tall, beautiful black monk, real and in front of the fire. He was blessing her at last and seemed still to be blessing her, back there in the dark, so long as she didn't turn around.

. . .

Even on the coldest night yet in the winter, Pius wanted to walk, and Paddy, respecting that as he always did, left him at the entrance gate of Primrose Hill and went on toward Chalk Farm tube station. For some reason that he didn't question, Pius stood under the frozen trees and watched him until his footsteps no longer crackled on the icy street and he was out of sight and hearing.

All Paddy had said was "Keep your scarf on. It's so cold."

It was one of the joys of going to Ewen and Teresa's, one that was all his own, to be able to walk across the hill at night when there was no one else, except once in a while another late walker and, from time to time, police patrolling in pairs. Once, he had been stopped and questioned. They had seen that he was black, but when he told them who he was, one of them said, "Father, you want to be careful up here at night," but that was in the early autumn and the nights were still warm enough for Noel's rats to be out.

He walked up the familiar path toward the waning moon, past the winter skeletons of chestnut trees that he could smell in memory. Now there was only the dark and spacious night, the white dust of new snow, and as he moved into the grass as far away from the line of streetlights as he could, his night eyes showed him, gradually, ghosts and then realities of trees. There was only the crunch of his own footsteps, only a branch falling, overladen with ice crystals, only the grumble in the distance of a late car climbing Primrose Hill Road.

He was cold and at peace and entirely happy. He was seeing Ewen and Teresa married, or almost, it was inevitable, but he added *inchallah*.

He was climbing under the faint globe of city light, past the shadows of the old wartime allotments, etched by snow, toward groves misted by cold and the moon. His breath trailed him. He stopped at the top of the hill, where in the daytime people sat on the benches and gazed out over the city to where the river curved southeast. On clear days there was the dome of

St. Paul's, and faintly, if you imagined it as well as looked for a long time, the Tower of London, Londinium, and that always pleased him, to think of it that way.

Even on such a night the Post Office Tower was like a beacon to him, and he stopped and watched the city grow from Londinium, and wax and wane again in the night, and the Post Office Tower rise and fall again. Standing up there in the wind, with the moon reflecting the snow, all this was possible. There was no time. As he did sometimes in the new barbarian city, slightly drunk from the champagne, he had to admit, though the cold and wind were blowing that away, he saw himself from outside, standing there, a tall man of Kush, a warrior in the darkness, and he let himself go down into a country where he was at home below the surface of changeable ground and place and time.

A lonely lion roared and chuffed like a train shunting in the zoo below him in the park, and another answered it, and the wind brought its rumble, which seemed to slash the silence, but it comforted him in the country where he was, contained in his own body, rising there over the hilltop, all Kush and Ethiopia, the ancient land.

He thought of the new, short-lived empire that had spread out and then drawn back in less than four hundred years to the island of the Britons and of its center, the city he stood, not in but over, a watchman in the night. He thought of the language it had left on all the distant shores, and of its laws, and of the District Commissioner.

He thought of the booty of empire still lodged in the city, the granite Assyrian judge, the little primitive king from Kadesh with his great eyes, before whom the world had once bent its knees. He sat down on the bench and looked out, veil behind veil, mist behind mist, over the city as it was in that one night where all but a few watchers like himself were asleep.

When you have walked four hundred miles alone, he told the city, you know who you are and what you carry. When you lived in the trees with your tails painted blue, I was a kingdom. Did you live at the river Gihon that God made to flow around the lands of Ethiopia at the genetic beginning? Did you take the name of your country from Cush, the son of Ham, the father of Nimrod, a mighty hunter before the Lord? Have you survived the invasion of Assurbanipal the Assyrian, and your cities laid waste? I come from a land shadowing with wings, a swift messenger from as far over the edge of the world as the shepherd prophets dream in dreams or see in visions, like a naked man from beyond the rivers, bearing gold.

Is an ancient name of your tribe written on the obelisk of Thutmose from Karnak, which you have brought to stand for such a little while on the bank of your Thames and call by the name of a Greek queen? Did your gods rise from the volcanoes of Punt in Ewen's Great Rift?

He was tired and the night stretched within him and he could feel the spaces of fatigue, slips of time when he was nearly asleep, and then his head fell forward and jerked him awake again. He had been dreaming a little, he was sure, he did sometimes, of Punt and Tarku and Pathros and Cush and Tandamane fled to Kipkip in Nubia, of Hadad, who reigned in Damascus, and himself a shadow with wings.

He could if he let himself, and it was one of the reasons he loved the hill at night, sense the land under the layers of the city and the turning of the globe toward morning. There was no light yet, but a smell of dawn and the cry of a bird in the zoo to herald it, and the roared breathing of the lions, and once the scream of some other great cat he couldn't name. He thought he heard the snuffling of an animal and the pawing of a hard hoof on the frozen hill, and put it away as dreaming, but the hint of sound had waked him and he knew for a second a cold flash of panic and was ashamed of himself.

It was time for prayer after the indulgences of feasting and happiness and dreams and pride all the way back to Hammurabi; he was amused at himself for that. It wasn't often he let himself indulge in the past. He remembered studying it all at Catholic University in Washington, not yet aware that he had a past beyond the sixteen generations, not like that, all the way back to one of the rivers of Eden.

He heard the sound again. It was nearer, and it raised the hackles at the nape of his neck, and he turned his head so quickly that the scarf fell loose. An animal escaped from the zoo? A lost dog? He looked around and there was nothing there but space and silence; but he fell into a heard rhythm, as if the night itself had whispered, You packy, nignog, nignog, nignog, and dismissed it as his own shameful fear that had formed the evil words out of the whispering wind.

He got out his rosary and promised himself a special prayer for the wedding, his wedding he had worked for and prayed for, because he wanted to see Ewen safe within the protecting sacrament. After that he saw and heard nothing but the prayers, and felt nothing but the prayer beads moving through his hands.

All they could see was the big shadow looming up there against that bleedin cold and perishing black sky that was so brutal in the night when you've been kicked out of your digs to come back when it's all over, whatever it is they don't want you to see, as if you didn't bleedin know and hadn't since you was old enough to toddle, but there's money after it, there's always money, only you wish you didn't have to get out on such a perishing cold bleedin night, even if your pals come wif you and make it a challenge and you have to prove to them you are a man.

It was one fing to shave your head and get into a bit of bovver at the football games and wear them bleedin bovver boots, but that wasn't enough for them, oh no, you had to bleedin prove yourself all the bleedin time or they said you couldn't join the Knights Commandos of the British Empire and wear the skeleton badge, like what they done, and it was, as they pointed out, a perishing privilege and you only fourteen and still in school. It was the bleedin law. So there you was on the bleedin cold cold ground, but they said if you was a sodjer you would have to do that all the time, that's wot sodjers done.

All he could see was the perishing great shadow up there against the sky, the only one they could find to pick, the old fool, didn't he bleedin know better, some old fool that didn't have a home to go to, either, something left over outside when everybody else had gone to their beds. And there he was taking up their bleedin space and their vigil, that's what they called it, their vigil, got it from the telly, in the night.

Well, only him really called it a vigil. The other two didn't have no telly, they didn't have a bleedin thing, them two, but they was brave and older than wot he was, that was all, and he ought to be proud of himself to be picked out like that for a job they done, or were going to, after a lot of practice scurrying around the back alleys, they ought to have been ready for something to happen at last after all that. No, they didn't call it nuffink, it was just wot you done. There wasn't no chance of good pickings on such a cold night, but it was practice anyway, and they done it for the empire, the Knights Commandos of the British Empire, because them perishing nignog bleeders was taking over England, his mum's friend said so.

One of them touched his arm and pointed to the scarf on the ground and made his thumb and forefinger into a circle, a yes, like they seen at the flicks. They slithered forward, a little nearer, and when the old fool turned his head they went still like they practiced.

There wasn't a bleedin thing in the pockets, a pound note, a few coins, something that glittered in the cold moon, a little book.

One of them whispered, "Go on, wot's in 'is 'ands? Go on, find out, you bloody git." He had to, because he was the youngest and they let him come. The old fool was only knocked out there on the ground, anyway. He had been asleep when they threw the scarf around his neck, he hadn't felt a thing. He thought, I'll give him a kick and wake him up just before we go so he'll have sense enough to get up off the ground and out of the perishing cold, the bleedin git.

When he got near enough he saw the open eyes on that black face. He touched the hands and what was in them, the beads, and he jumped up and ran. He was crying like a bleedin baby he was. His granny had done her perishing best to train him, even taken him to Mass when she could catch him and beat him into going, and he knew what he had touched.

He was being sick all over the snow, the beer, the chips, the yellow bile, so sick he had to kneel on the ground. "Oh, Jesus," he kept saying, and then, " 'E died in a state of fucking grace."

Paddy said, "You have to. You just have to, that's all. There's no question." He was crying over the phone. "It was his dearest wish," and then, primly: "He was quite concerned about you."

Later the wedding and the funeral crossed in Teresa's memory. She couldn't remember whether the reredos she stared at was in St. Dunstan's or at Farm Street. What she did remember was that the color was in the funeral, as if it were a wedding or a coronation for Pius, not a funeral.

The priest at St. Dunstan's had seen them only once. He was too young and too pink and he hadn't married many people. They had to wait in the cold while he unlocked the church. He was nervous. He mumbled and lost his place, and sprinkled too much holy water on the ring, so that it splashed on the new dress she had bought at Liberty's, blue to avert the Evil Eye.

There were only nine of them in the big, ugly church, where the space was empty instead of spacious, and somehow a little mean, as if some burghers had been trying to cut corners in 1890. St. Dunstan's was brick, but its pinnacles and towers were imitations of the shape of some ancient stone church. It was very cold, and the day was dark, and Zephyr couldn't stop crying.

Teresa remembered that there, or was it at the funeral, Ewen held her hand so tightly that it hurt, as if she could keep him from flying off the turning world. When he murmured, "I thee wed," he reached forward and touched her cheek and kept his hand there while he said the words. It was strange to remember his hands that day and the next, but not his face, not the way he looked at all. She could see him reach out from the pew at Farm Street Church and lay his palm flat against one of the dark granite columns, as if that, too, were an anchor.

At the Farm Street Church, at the funeral Mass for Pius's soul, the whole Jesuit community was there, at least fifty of them lined up in the pews on either side of Pius. All the men from Ogilvie House sat together, as if they could draw strength only from one another. The church was filled with strangers. Teresa was embarrassed because she didn't know when to stand up and when to sit down and when to kneel, and she was surprised at so many in the church at the funeral. There was a beautiful nun, Sister Catherine, who came up to her and held her hand, and said that Pius had spoken of them. It made the tears sting.

Ewen and Noel stood on either side of her, as they had at the wedding when Noel gave her away, and Ewen whispered when he saw all the people, "What you realize is that you have touched only a part of a friend's life. He had a whole life we couldn't know about." He sounded as if he felt left out of something.

Candles glistened against the gold of the altar and in her tear-laden eyes, so that the color seemed to dance. The gold thread of the Father Provincial's chasuble mingled, for her, with the dance of light.

Pius's long coffin lay in the aisle between the ranks of priests, a regiment of Jesuits in their white chasubles with great stripes of gold for Pius's wedding. And he, and not he, but someone lay under the cross, with a chalice set on his coffin lid as if it were a table.

She could hardly follow the Mass; she kept getting its words mixed with the wedding service, the fine poetry, the resounding chant of fifty voices in the con-celebration of Pius's release from what her grandmother called the perils of this wicked world, and then, hearing her grandmother's voice, she did sob, and Ewen put his arm around her. But he went on letting the fingers of his other hand examine the granite column, connecting her to the earth, not knowing. Noel, on her other side, touched her shoulder, and went on making responses.

She told herself in the midst of it all, as she had when she saw St. Francis standing around in the painting so long ago, Pius is out of place in all this, my black monk. For God's sake, let him go.

It was no longer Pius, no longer anyone being carried up the long aisle, and his brothers followed in their white ranks and sang *"In paradisum deducant angeli,"* and they sounded so full of joy that the singing filled the great vault of the church. She heard the word "Lazarus," and began to sob again, not knowing why, and Noel leaned close and whispered, "They are singing, with Lazarus, who once was poor, May you have everlasting rest, *requiem.*" Then it was Pius. It was, and he was gone.

They were standing beside the path through the gray snow at the Jesuit plot at St. Mary's, Kensal Green. It had gotten warmer and the whole world was smothered by mist and dirty patches of snow, and the trees were black. Beyond the still-open grave, how grave it was under the dark sky, with its fake grass covering its reality of piled dirt, the black men from Ogilvie House stood in line to sprinkle holy water on Pius's coffin as if the vial were filled with tears.

Paddy had shed his wedding/funeral garments and was in black again. They seemed to be mourning at last in the black of their skin and Paddy's clothes. The only color was the gold-laden chasuble of the Father Provincial who buried Pius.

The trees dripped melting snow. Beyond them there was only the stained wall of the cemetery, and behind it a row of drab houses, a dirty silver water tower, an abandoned factory, and the sound of traffic passing in Scrubs Lane. Somebody opened the window of a bedroom in one of the row houses, looked out, and slammed it down again.

They passed the marble mourners and the city-streaked tilted angels, the temples, the cathedrals the size of beds, all the houses of the dead, forgotten there on the dark day. Noel said, "Do you think they will ever find out who did it?"

Ewen said, "What does it matter?" and there was no more to say. He wouldn't have heard, anyway. He was crying and he walked like a blind man.

But Pius had always said that you lived within other people, in what he called their soulscapes. If that was immortality, then he was immortal. Teresa knew that it was true for her. Pius lived on in her with Michael and the Derebey and the Sheika and her grandmother, and Ewen when he was in another room, and Noel across London. It was all the same. In the middle of the dark walk on the dark cold day, she felt full of light and constructed by the love she had been given, and held within her.